Rachel Rosing

A Novel

by

Howard Spring

A Memories publication

2000

Published by:
Memories
222 Kings Road
Stretford
Manchester
M16 0JW

Also published by
Memories:
Shabby Tiger
by Howard Spring

ISBN: 1 899181 93 8

This edition organised by

Originally published in
1935 by Collins Clear-type Press.

Printed and bound by:
M.F.P. Design and Print
Longford Trading Estate
Thomas Street Stretford
Manchester M32 0JT

Rachel Rosing

For my Mother
ORIGINAL DEDICATION

*All the characters in this book
are as near to living persons as the author
could make them.*

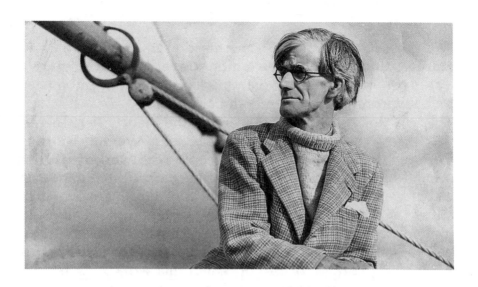

HOWARD SPRING

Born in Cardiff in 1889, Howard Spring joined the
newspaper industry as soon as he was able to leave school. He
started work on the South Wales Daily News, and his
command of words soon led to a junior reporter's post. He
moved up to reporter on the Yorkshire Observer in Bradford in
the early years of the century. It was while working on this
paper that he developed his writing skills and became known
for his easy to read reports.

In the spring of 1915, with war clouds hanging over the
country, he joined the Manchester Guardian, lodging with a
Mrs Matilda Kruger on Clarence Road, Withington. Howard
was torn between joining up and carrying on with a reserved
job, and ultimately his conscience told him that his country
needed him. He subsequently spent three and a half years with
the Service Corps.

After the war he rejoined the Manchester Guardian, and
during a spell in the London office met and fell in love with

Marion, a secretary there. They married in Bradford on a wet Saturday and spent the evening travelling to lodgings in Heaton Moor. That weekend was their honeymoon, and Monday morning saw them both back at work.

He worked for eleven years on the Manchester Guardian settling in a tall, thin house in Hesketh Avenue, Didsbury, where his two sons were born. People who worked with him spoke of his easy-going nature and he gained a reputation as a descriptive reporter, whose command of the English language and use of adjectives made his work a pleasure to read. Fellow reporters remember his lovely speaking voice that was always clear and a pleasure to listen to when taking his dictation from the far-flung corners of Britain where his work took him. His articles on the contemporary political scene were considered to be masterpieces.

In 1931 he was tempted away from Didsbury by the offer of a job on one of the nationals in London. He went as book reviewer and gained a reputation second to none for fairness and fine reviews. He wrote a book for children called 'Darkie and Co.' in 1932 and followed this in 1934 with his first novel 'Shabby Tiger' which was an instant success.

Until March 1939 he continued to split his life between reviews, newspaper articles and full length novels, but then, with the clouds of war gathering once more, he decided to move to Cornwall and make writing novels his full-time job.

Success came almost immediately as 'My Son, My Son' and 'Fame is the Spur' followed each other from his typewriter. Hollywood turned its attention to 'My Son, My Son', but the outcome did not please him; neither did the English film version of 'Fame is the Spur'.

Howard Spring died aged 76, on May 3rd 1965 at his home in Cornwall. His ashes lie in the village churchyard at St. Mylor.

Quotes from Howard Spring:

"I came to know and love Manchester as I have known and loved no other city."

"I am often referred to as a Manchester novelist. I am not, but wish I had known the place sooner."

"Manchester entered more deeply into my blood and bones than any other place I have lived."

"It was to Manchester I took my young wife. It was in Manchester my sons were born and in Manchester I found happiness."

"It was not until I started to write novels and took Manchester as their settings that I realised how deeply the city had bitten into my consciousness."

Shabby Tiger

HOWARD SPRING

Chapter One

I

IN the wine lodge the air was thick and blue with
smoke. You could have cut it with a knife or
knitted it into a muffler. The counter was a vast horse-
shoe, and Mike Hartigan stood at one end of it. He
leaned his elbows in the beer-rings, craned his head
forward, and sent a glance raking down the length
of the bar. Not a soul he knew, and he felt damned
lonely. He banged his tankard on the mahogany and
ordered more beer and a beef sandwich. He pushed
his black felt hat back from his eyes, back till it barely
kept a hold on his head, and he scratched vigorously
in the black, curly mat of his hair.

He could just make out the reflection of his own face
in the glass behind the tempting bottles : blue and
red and amber bottles on varnished shelves, and below
them tubby barrels of beer and pipes of port. What
with the bottles and the eddying smoke between him
and them, it was not easy to see his reflection, and he
moved this way and that, piecing together an impression of a stout, humorous face, with a nose much
too big, eyebrows black and bushy, handsome teeth,
and a ridiculous growth of hair—a small black oblong
—alongside each ear.

Mike fingered the side-whiskers in doubt. Every

9

Dago on the films was wearing them. You wanted to be thin and slinky and have hair like black glue. Then that sort of side-whiskers was all right. For himself, he wasn't sure.

And then Mike was looking past himself in the mirror, down into a murky deep where a woman's face swam dimly. His hand paused irresolute in its stroking of the side-whisker. The woman was looking at him, smiling enigmatically. She seemed as though under water, smiling up at him. It gave her an illusion of mystery, remoteness. But she was only smiling at his folly, his too evident childish vanity, smiling through the choking fume of the wine lodge.

He stuffed the last of his sandwich into his mouth, took his tankard in hand, and slung himself round on the tall stool. The woman was sitting against the wall at a small table, alone. In two strides Mike was alongside her.

" Would you have them off? " he said. " Or shall we give 'em another chance ? "

She levelled at him a long, considering glance. Then she carefully removed from a chair her gloves and a handbag. Mike accepted the invitation and sat down.

" Have them off," she advised.

" Give me ten minutes," Mike said. He stood up, threw the remains of his beer down his throat, and slipped a watch off his wrist. " Time me," he said, slapped the watch on the table, and was gone.

Rachel Rosing twirled delicately the stem of her port-wine glass, watching the light smoulder in the ruby rinsings. She looked at the watch lying on the table. It was a good watch. She could see that. She was in the habit of noticing such things. She had noticed that Mike Hartigan's clothes, though thrown on without care, were good and well cut.

She opened her bag and made up her face. She took pains over it. There was something solid about that man. He was different from most of those gathered round the great bar. She had taken them all in long ago—it was her way—Lancashire operatives and their wives, mostly, with here and there a clerk or a shop-keeper. For some time before he noticed her, she had been watching Hartigan. He had paid for his beer and sandwich with a pound note. That too, was the sort of thing that Rachel noticed.

She forgot the clack of the crowd, the shrill pleasantries of the barmaids, the smoke and smell wedged between the sawdust floor and the blackened ceiling. She might have been in a dressing-room. She crimsoned her lips and with a delicate finger worked the colour to her satisfaction. She smoothed down her cheeks, whose skin was like ivory on her high cheek-bones, and noted that her eyebrows, mere pencillings that slanted upward, could hardly be improved. She buffed her red pointed nails and patted into position the thick masses of her blue-black hair. She felt well and vigorous. She had been at Blackpool for a month, in the air every day, and she was radiant with health. She needn't tell this mad, strange man, who had slapped down his watch and departed, that a Manchester bookmaker was paying for her keep there. Or should she?

She snipped-to the fastening of her bag and looked up. Mike Hartigan, shorn of side-whiskers, was almost leaping across the room. A grin showed up his big white teeth. His black felt hat was shapelessly crushed in one hand. The other raked through his hair, but failed to derange the close coils of his curls. A red gash alongside one ear still oozed a little blood. He snatched up the watch. " Done it, begod ! " he cried. " With fifteen seconds to spare ! "

He fanned his face with his hat. " 'Tis like hell itself in this place," he said. " Come on out. There's nothing between Blackpool and America."

" Except Ireland," said Rachel.

" Ireland doesn't count," he said, " since Mike Hartigan left home."

" And you are Mike Hartigan ? "

" From County Cork."

" My name is Rosing—Rachel Rosing—from Manchester."

They walked down a side-street to the front. The tide was nearly full, and there was a wind behind it. The waves piled up, and the wind caught the white foam of the crests and hurled it across the promenade. They stood facing the weather. Rachel held her hat and felt the wind shaping her clothes to her body. She could hear the hem of her skirt clacking like a blown banner. It was not the sort of weather she liked. She would have preferred to be indoors with a fire burning and the wind on the other side of the rattling panes. But life was a very insecure business for her just now. This good-humoured creature with the thick black hair, which he kept bared to the wind, represented some shred of stability. She mustn't let him go till his possibilities had been sounded. So she stood there with him, facing towards the water, depressed by its dark welter stretching away towards the dusky streaky crimson of the horizon. She hoped he would soon suggest something snug and sensible : the cinema or the dancing floor at the Tower.

But such schemes were far from Mike Hartigan's thoughts. " Grand, isn't it ? " he shouted above the shouting of the wind, and he stretched out his arms as though to embrace the weather. " The lights'll be going up in half an hour. I'm going out there to see 'em. Will you come ? "

The mere thought of it made Rachel shudder. Nothing, she said to herself, nothing would induce her to venture out on to those dark, rolling waves, with the night coming down and the wind snapping cold teeth. But the idea of leaving Hartigan was unpleasant too.

" I've never been on the sea in my life," she said. " Not so much as in a boat on a summer day."

" Then, begod, there's a grand experience in front of you," he said, jammed on his hat, and took her arm in a masterful fashion. " Just leave the details to me, and come on," he said.

III

And to her own amazement there she was, roaring across the water. The engine was boxed in, amidships, and on the thwart by it Mike Hartigan sat, one hand on the steering lever. Sitting in the stern, feeling grotesque in a great creaking oilskin coat, she could see him blocked darkly against the sky in which, by now, only the last thin washings of light remained.

He turned his head, his teeth gripping a metal-lidded pipe whose reek blew back to her. " Warm ? " he shouted.

" Yes, thank you." She eased her back against the cushions he had provided, and was surprised to find that she was enjoying herself. Now that they were beyond the rollers there was not much of a sea. Hartigan kept the boat's nose pointed at the waves ; and once Rachel had accustomed herself to the switchback progress, she loosed her clutch on the gunwale and abandoned her belief that death was a matter of moments. The wind lashed her face ; now and then the bows divided a sea that pattered like hail sharply upon her oilskins. Her face glowed ; her body tingled ; she felt better than she had done at any time since leaving Manchester a few weeks before. Then she had felt at death's door.

The boat roared forward, and there was nothing to be seen but the black, tumbled water and a star or two winking itself awake. No other craft was visible. It seemed as though all the world was theirs alone. Then suddenly the water all about them and before

them blushed with light, and Mike Hartigan shouted :
" They've switched on ! Hold tight ! " The boat
took a great right-handed swerve, and as she came
broadside on to a travelling wave Rachel bit her lip
so that she should not cry out with terror. They rocked
nearly gunwale under, and then they were round, with
the following sea lifting their stern and pushing them
towards what looked like a town in flames.

" Come up here ! " Mike shouted. " What d'you
think of it ? "

Very cautiously Rachel stepped over a thwart,
hampered by the oilskins that made her feel as though
she were dressed in buckram. She sat down alongside
Hartigan whose face glowed in the great light that
beat out from the town. " Grand—isn't it ? " he
shouted.

" Wonderful," said Rachel.

She had never seen anything like it. From the water's
edge to the topmost pinnacle of the Tower light rose
in tier upon tier ; and the length of the miracle was
greater even than its height. From the Pleasure Park
on the South Shore the light seemed to stretch northward for miles : red light and blue, green, yellow, white
and orange. Aeroplanes of light soared in the sky ;
garlands and bouquets of light, festoons and fountains
of light, flamed and danced ; and, small at that
distance, the tramcars, super-charged with radiance,
crawled like salamanders, themselves aglow, in a festal
inferno. There seemed in that fiery façade no pin-
point where so much as another candle might be lit ;
and all its brazen and disproportionate opulence fell
upon the breakers that might almost have been heard
to hiss as they fretfully beleaguered the town aflame.

Mike stopped the engine and kept his hand on the lever, holding the boat's nose steadily towards the shore. The waves lifted her up and down, drifted her slowly nearer to the beach. Rachel held her breath at the wonder of the spectacle. It was the sort of thing she understood, and liked, and desired. It moved her, as the sight of an expensive motor-car moved her, or furs, or orchids, or the people whom she had seen leaving the theatres during a visit to London. It was showy, luxurious, as magnificent as it was meaningless.

Suddenly she was overcome with revulsion from the fate that lay before her. More than ever she desired to find in Mike Hartigan a means of escape. Acquisitive, selfish and unimaginative as she was, she yet had romance enough to find in their roaring dash to sea something symbolic. " Oh, God ! " she prayed ; " to get out of this mess ! To get straight again ! To have another chance ! "

They were almost level with the Central Pier when Mike started the engine again. " Get back and make yourself comfortable," he said. " We're going to have a real run this time."

She climbed back to the seat in the stern, and snugged herself down into the cushions. Hartigan took a great woollen muffler out of his overcoat pocket and threw it to her. " Put that on," he shouted over the chatter of the engine. She did, tucked it between her neck and the cutting edge of the oilskin, and felt the better for it. Then Mike let the engine go. They swept round in a half-circle and headed for the sea again. The wind roared in Rachel's ears, and the spray soused aboard in bucketfuls. She kept her knees up and the oilskin pulled down tight to her very feet. Hartigan sang an exultant song as the boat leapt from wave to wave, and the sky now was full of stars with their eyes wide open.

Fear came back to Rachel. She realised that on their first run Hartigan had not taken out of the boat anything like its best performance. Now, crouched on the thwart amidships, he was like a jockey gone insane at Aintree, urging his mount to incredible feats. Rachel began to people the dark water with snares and gins : hidden spars which would trip them to their doom ; even rocks and reefs were not outside the scope of her imagining. A creature completely of the town, she knew not what to expect, and expected everything disastrous.

When she could stand it no longer she crept forward, clutching the gunwale. She touched Hartigan on the arm and he stopped singing and slewed round with a start as though he had forgotten her presence. " Go back," she shouted. " Slower."

" Are you afraid ? " he roared.

" Yes."

" Good for you," he said. " You're honest anyway."

She remained at his side as he slowed the engine and put about. The transfigured town had disappeared. Nothing showed but a pulsation of light, like aurora borealis, miles to the east. And high above it, serenely contemptuous, was a full moon that had climbed out of the flat hinterland of Blackpool.

" That's a rum 'un," said Hartigan. " The old moon's as dead as a door nail, but it's got ten million candle-power licked to a frazzle."

Rachel did not answer.

17

"Are you not interested in philosophical ideas?" Hartigan demanded.

"No," she said.

"You're honest, anyway," he repeated, and they said no more as Blackpool, bit by bit, heaved its incandescence out of the ocean.

IV

The boat had been returned whence they had hired it. They stamped their feet on the concrete of the promenade, easing the cramp out of their legs. Like Shadrach, Meshach and Abednego, they walked, unscathed, in the burning fiery furnace.

"Have you had your dinner?" asked Hartigan practically.

"I'm staying in the cheapest boarding-house in Blackpool," said Rachel. "We have dinner at one o'clock."

"It's time you had another. Come on," he said.

They sat at a little table in the Metropole, with a shaded light between them. Coming as they did from the excessive glare without, it was like being in a friendly cave after too much sunshine. Rachel drew off her gloves and sat back in her chair with a happy sigh. She had enjoyed that mad trip in the motor-boat; it had done her good; it had shaken her out of the lethargy that had begun to fall upon her. But this was better than that. To be luxuriously indoors was always better for Rachel than any conceivable condition of affairs outside. She left the ordering of the meal to Hartigan, coolly weighing him up, wondering what

18

this chance encounter might bring, hoping that he would soon become loquacious about himself. Most men did, pretty soon. The food and drink would help him. She was glad that he ordered champagne. Not that she wanted it herself, and she thought it flashy of him ; but it was a hopeful sign of expansiveness that might be profitably developed.

"Well," said Hartigan, when the waiter was gone, "that surprises me—what you were saying about the cheap boarding-house. You don't look cheap."

Rachel shrugged her shoulders and achieved with her hands a beautiful deprecating gesture.

"Begod," said Hartigan, "you've said everything without opening your mouth. Did no one ever tell you you're a great actress ? "

"I should think," she said, with her slow provoking smile, "that in my time I've been told everything that men could lay their tongues to."

"Do you wonder at it ? " said Hartigan. "That's the sort of woman you are. Look at me now. I could no more help speaking to you to-night than a monkey can help hunting fleas. You didn't mind ? "

"If I had minded, I should have said so. I only wondered *why* you spoke to me."

"Begod, then, and why does a man speak to a pretty woman ? Isn't it optimists we all are ? We take the plunge and hope for the best."

He gave her a good-humoured, impudent look, but could not trick her into a responsive smile. Her face was enigmatic. She did not help him at all. For a year life had been hurting her very badly. She was not going to be hurt again. She took a dusky chrysanthemum from the vase between them, snapped it from

19

its stalk, and her long, red-tipped fingers shredded it slowly to pieces. The performance moved Hartigan deeply. It took on a significance that seemed absurd but that he could not put from his mind. There was the circle of lamplight on the table and in the light her long pale hands. He saw nothing but the hands, slowly and dispassionately shredding the flower to pieces, as though it were a bird being stripped of its living feathers, and the finger-tips were a vivid red.

Presently she dropped the mangled flower and brushed her finger-ends fastidiously together.

The waiter brought the soup, but somehow Hartigan's gaiety had received a shock from which it did not recover. The evening went flat. Rachel too, was disappointed. The champagne was wasted. Hartigan got nowhere, and when he had hurried through the meal he apologised and said he must be off. He made no suggestion that they should meet again.

Chapter Two

I

RACHEL ROSING had nothing to do at Blackpool. A few months before, in Manchester, she
had made a superb bid for fortune. It was a gamble,
and she had lost. A few weeks hence she would be
taking up meagre and precarious employment with a
man she mistrusted and disliked. In the meantime
there was nothing to do—nothing.

So it was her habit to stay in bed till nearly noon,
fending off the wrath of her landlady by making her
own bed when she had left it, and contenting herself
with a cup of tea in place of breakfast. Then she would
spend an hour making herself a picture, dressing as
though for goodness knows what stylish occasion. And
when she was ready to go out, she felt that the trouble
had been worth while. She was a good judge of such
matters, and she was right.

In the afternoon she would saunter about, up and
down the promenade, taking it easy, from the South
Shore to Uncle Tom's Cabin in the north. She didn't
allow herself to get tired. There were innumerable
seats and shelters all the way, and trams if she decided
that she didn't want to walk at all. She looked with
irony, tinged with a little contempt, at the robustious
young women tomboying about on the sand. Her

own foot had not once been off the concrete. She would sit for a while watching their antics, then rise and walk slowly on, her long slender legs, supported on high heels, taking her forward with an attractive feline elegance.

When the evening came, a sense of expectation wakened in her. The lights went up. Her walk became slower and more provocative ; her dark Muscovite eye, betraying nothing, was yet aware of every glance cast in her direction. She kept away from the pleasure beach, where the night was raucous with mechanical music, and the rushing of switchback cars, the clang of bullets on iron in the shooting booths, the shrieks of the young men with their girls in the magnetised motor-cars that charged and swerved and collided under a ceiling of blue hissing sparks. She had once drawn near to that most animated acre of Britain and seen the swinging-boats rocking up to the stars and heard the braying of the roundabouts organ, and she had gone swiftly away, murmuring " My God ! My God ! " The clinging and bumping and jostling of body to body shocked her sense of how she wanted to arrange things.

Girls shrieking ! Shrieking ! My God ! She stole away dignified as an affronted cat.

Sometimes a man would speak to her. She always stopped if he seemed the sort of man who might be of use. She had eaten with two or three of them, but nothing had come of it. They wanted to take her to bed. That was all. It was monotonous. If you wanted to go to bed with a man it was easy enough to arrange. Anything else seemed difficult.

But it was a lazy life, just the life she ought to be

leading after the dreadful summer she had been through. Her face, which had been drawn and haggard when she came to Blackpool, took on again its smooth oval beauty. The dull ivory sheen came back to her skin. Her body, which had suffered the pangs of abortion, filled out into slender healthy lines. There had been at first a panic period of despair, a time when she told herself that all was over. She thought of the brief, simple pattern of her life : the slum to which she had been born ; the innate elegance which had combined with her loathing of the slum to lift her suddenly and completely clear ; the incredible months when, engaged to marry Sir George Faunt, she had daily walked with the luxury that her soul cried out for as an infant cries for milk ; and then the swift blow that had laid her flat in the gutter. She might, indeed, have been pardoned for thinking then that all was lost ; but now, with this body that was her weapon daily taking on again its power and beauty, reinforced, as she felt, by the dark background of knowledge and suffering which it now possessed, she looked to the future with growing distaste for the arrangements which had been made when she was under the harrow. She knew that Piggy White and his pub would never see her now, but she did not know what other course was in store for her. Some premonition stirred in her when she met Michael Hartigan. She could not understand his sudden fizzling out. She went back, disappointed, to her cheap lodgings, yet feeling that the matter was not ended.

II

You may have noticed that here, there and every-where elegant shops have been springing up in England. There is a fascia painted sage-green, and on it in an attractive shade of red is the one word—" Bannerman's." In the window are sweets, priced a little more expensively than in other shops ; and behind the shop you see a tea-room where everything is a little more expensive than in other tea-rooms. You don't mind that, because of the quiet—Bannerman's abhors bands and would sack a waitress who shouted—and because of the carpets, and the thinness of the china, and the excellence of the tea and cakes. And you are not offended by being asked not to tip the waitresses. " Tip ! Of course let 'em tip," said Maurice Banner-man, when he was working out his idea. " It makes 'em feel superior."

So one by one the shops came into being, each exactly like all the others : bow windows divided up in old-fashioned style into many little panes ; no Neon lights—" My God ! No ! " Maurice Bannerman shouted, nearly apoplectic, when some one suggested it—waitresses looking rather milkmaidy ; and, above all, quiet. " Do you know the biggest blessing in life ? " Maurice Bannerman shouted at the top of his voice. " Quiet. People have got to be able to turn out of the noisiest street in Birmingham or Newcastle or Manchester or London and feel as though they'd stepped into St. Paul's or the British Museum. Every one of these shops has got to be a rest cure—see ? "

24

And so the carpets were thick, and the very light was the quietest light imaginable, diffused from some source that was not apparent. In a Bannerman shop one instinctively spoke in whispers. And everything was of an almost fantastic cleanliness. The prices were printed—beautifully printed too—on little folded-back slips of pasteboard ; and if Mike Hartigan, inspecting here and there, up and down the country through which the Bannerman shops were scattered, found so much as the smallest tea-stain on one of them, there were ructions ; if, improbably, one had been fly-blown, there would have been hell to pay. Such were Maurice Bannerman's orders. A waitress in Wolverhampton had been ruthlessly thrown out for biting the nails of a hand that was to come into contact with Bannerman's cakes, and a manageress in Bristol lost her job over a brass ash-tray that had gone two days without being polished.

" To hell with it ! " Mike often exclaimed. " It's a woman's job." And in manly recoil from the finicking functions which Bannerman's imposed on him he would, at the day's end, seek a pub or wine lodge where a swipe of the dish-cloth across a counter was called a clean-up and a glass was held to achieve purgation by baptism in a zinc bowl full of unseemly rinsings.

And now, on the morning after his meeting with Rachel Rosing, Mike set out to meet the great Maurice himself. He did not feel happy about worrying Maurice. Maurice was a busy man. Bannerman's was hardly more than a side-line to him—a side-line that Hartigan was supposed to have mastered. He had been sent to Blackpool to decide whether it was the sort of place in which a Bannerman shop should be opened, and if it was, it was his business to find a site. "And be damned if I can make up me mind," said Mike, crushing his black felt hat in one hand, scratching his curls with the other.

He had never been stuck like this before. He knew he had been good value to Bannerman's. He had chosen most of the sites, engaged the staff, and never made a mistake. But Blackpool had him beat. "Begod, now, 'twould be like St. Francis preaching to the birds in competition with the bookies at Epsom on Derby Day," he said. " 'Twould be incongruous."

And, indeed, as he walked along the front and listened to the babel of Blackpool, as he looked at its shine and glitter, there seemed good reason for doubt. "The noisier the place the more they'll want to turn in for half an hour's quiet," Maurice would shout. But Mike doubted it. Blackpool seemed the one place where people *liked* a noise, to which they came to make a noise ; and a demure little Bannerman façade would have as much chance as honeysuckle grown in the miles and miles and miles of Blackpool's concrete roads and escarpments and cliffs. And so, as Maurice was in Manchester on some other affair, Mike had asked him to come over and see the place for himself. Maurice was snappy. "Very well. Metropole Hotel at eleven," he said, and smacked on the receiver.

III

All night long Rachel Rosing had tossed and turned in her bed. The bedroom nauseated her. It was just such a bedroom as she had been brought up in, just

26

such a bedroom as she had fled from, determined that never again would she endure the ignominy and ugliness of poverty. She loathed poverty as a saint loathes sin. It was to her the foul and inexcusable thing ; and to be back again in such a room as this, after the bright brief miracle of her escape, was a wound in the very heart of her self-esteem.

She kept on the light, glaring down from under its crude glass shade, and looked morbidly at the things that hurt her—the sagging wallpaper, the cracked linoleum on the floor, the yellow-varnished dressing-table whose mirror hung on a faulty swivel, so that she had had to stuff a wad of paper in to keep it from swinging over, glass downwards.

She thought of Mike Hartigan, who seemed to her a good-hearted simpleton, and when, now and then, she dropped into a light doze, she would feel again the unaccustomed motion of the boat and would start awake, feeling dizzy. She wondered if she would see him again, and she longed passionately that she might do so, that she might find through him the loophole for which she was now frantically seeking.

But however frantic might be the swirl in the back of Rachel's mind, no one would ever be aware of it. She was completely the mistress of her outward bearing. She awoke after the most wretched night she had spent in Blackpool, a night of fits and starts and unrefreshing snatches at sleep that never fully came. And because the night had been so bad, she gave to her appearance more than her customary care. She surprised her landlady by appearing at breakfast with her fellow-lodgers. She surprised her fellow-lodgers, a honeymoon couple from Accrington, by the very fact of being.

The young man, who served groceries in a Co-operative store, could not keep his eyes off her. This was the sort of thing one was accustomed to at the cinema, not in one's own boarding-house at Blackpool. The young woman, who was clean and wholesome but nothing more, seemed painfully conscious of her clean wholesomeness and did not know what to do to make them effective in such a situation as this. What, indeed, *could* she do against this woman with the red nails flickering like little flames on the long tapers of her fingers, with the slanting provocative eyebrows and the hard, mocking eyes over which, now and then, lids of astonishing transparency were lowered? The biting seaside air that made most cheeks shine with candid health had imparted to Rachel's a luminescence that seemed to come from within, and the scarlet line of her lips had the perfection of long-practised art.

The young couple from Accrington remained in the stuffy dining-room long after Rachel had left it. Their appetites could not, like hers, be satisfied with a few thin strips of toast, a little marmalade, and a cup of tea. They crowded the window to watch when she went out, gaped at the long lace gloves, the small round hat that held somehow to the side of her head, the veil that slanted alluringly across one eye.

" Ah doan't reckon yon woman's mooch good, if you ask me," said the young man, with a cheerful relish that caused his bride to turn from the window and bounce petulantly into a chair.

Blackpool's glory is all façade. The street down which Rachel made her stately way was cheap, blowsy and nasty. But she did not much notice it, nor did she notice that there was a tender blue sky above the black

28

jagged teeth of the chimney-pots and that the air was like iced wine. The morning was very still, and when she came to the front the sea was far away and an immensity of tawny sand lay where, last night, she had been blown and buffeted in the motor-boat.

The tranquillity of the day meant nothing to her except that she might walk in peace. She disliked the wind disarranging her clothes, causing her to clutch her hat. A day like this was a perfect stage on which she could choose her own gestures. She wondered if she would meet Michael Hartigan, and then she met him. He was outside the Metropole Hotel, and her impact upon him was immediate. He had thought a good deal about her and had decided that there was something cold-blooded and revolting in her. He was a gay, impulsive creature, and a hint of something calculating and ruthless behind her beauty had shrivelled him last night as a gaudy braggart dahlia is shrivelled by a spear of frost.

But this morning, sentimentally responsive to weather as to everything else, Mike was expansive and happy and at peace with every one. He damned himself for a hard-hearted boor as he saw this loveliness, expertly tricked out and presented, bearing majestically down upon him. He advanced to meet her, bursting with goodwill, and was rewarded with a smile that made last night's premonitions seem foolish and ungrounded.

" Good-morning, Miss Rosing," he said. " And a good morning it is—a grand morning, a broth of a morning, a real hell of a morning."

" So it is," she said. " I hadn't noticed. I was thinking."

"Ach, that's a thing a pretty woman should never do," said Mike amiably.

"No? Well, I was thinking how kind you were last night and that I'd never really thanked you properly for a lovely evening. Don't you think a pretty woman ought to think about things like that?"

"Such thoughts are jewels," said Mike. "I wish I could reward them by asking you to step inside and have some coffee. But at this very minute I'm expecting the boss. That's what I'm waiting for."

Rachel continued to smile, and Mike Hartigan continued to think what a glorious smile it was, one eye shining through that damned fool of an attractive little veil, the other bright as a blackberry when the dew is on it, like the ones he had often gathered in County Cork. He did not know that Rachel's mind had clicked instantly round those words "the boss." Behind the smile, they were being turned over and examined. That's the first real thing I've learned about him, she thought. He's an employed man. He's not his own boss. Perhaps, if she could contrive to stay, she might see the boss, deduce something from him. It was fated that this should happen.

The boss, indeed, arrived almost at that moment. Mike Hartigan had been so taken up with Rachel that he did not see the Rolls-Royce till it had slid to a standstill alongside him. Then he shouted "Maurice!" and leapt to open the door. Rachel's brain was as clear and nippy as the frost-tinged air of the morning. She recorded everything with magnificent sharpness. She saw the almost adoring nature of Hartigan's approach. She saw the rich embellishments of the car's interior: the scarlet leather, the silver fittings, the

30

great brown bearskin rug, the perfect roses in a cut-glass holder.

Maurice was his own driver. He threw the rug off his knees, squeezed his bulk through the door, and stood up massively, clad in a belted overcoat of rough camel texture. He looked twice as big as Hartigan. His face was broad, clean-shaven and swarthy, with a huge blue-black promontory of chin. Thick black eyebrows made a continuous bar above eyes that shot from their clear brown depths one appraising glance at Rachel.

" Hold that," Maurice snapped.

He handed his cigar to Hartigan, and Rachel watched with growing excitement as he stripped the hogskin gloves from his stout hands whose backs were almost as silkily hairy as the backs of moles. Across his left wrist was a deep-bitten scar, white and livid.

With no word spoken, Maurice's eye moved from Rachel to Hartigan and asked a question.

" Oh, this is Miss Rosing, Maurice—Rachel Rosing."

Chapter Three

" SEE you at three, Mike. I shall be lunching with
Miss Rosing," Maurice Bannerman said ; and
when that lunch was over and Rachel was gone he
went to the smoke-room, let himself down into a big
leather chair, and lit a cigar.

" Morris Fahnemann." It was a long time since he
had heard that name. What, in God's name, had
possessed him ? There was hardly a soul in the world
who knew the story, and the fewer they were the better
he was pleased. Yet at his first meeting with this girl
he had babbled along like any silly fool who had made
a little money and was anxious to magnify the hardships
of his beginnings. He had told her everything ; and
she, he now realised with a shock, had told him nothing.
She had been born in Cheetham Hill ; that was all
he knew. " So was I ! " He had blurted it out just
like that ; and then had followed it up with that long
narration, she saying nothing, but pulling him on and
on with those amazing eyes.

And now, sitting there puffing at his cigar, he
couldn't get his own story out of his mind. What a
detestable hobbledehoy he must have been ! Going
to and from his father's house in Cheetham Hill to the
Manchester Grammar School. He must have looked
a great lump, wearing a cap with rings of colour round
it. He would need shaving, yet not be shaved.

He could remember how he loathed the squalor of

Cheetham Hill. He and this girl Rosing would be in sympathy over that. He had been haunted by magnificent dreams. The violin would bring them on. He was the best violin they had ever had in the school orchestra. The school plays, too, excited him. He could act, but, more than the acting, the whole feel of the thing stirred him : the lighting, the props, the dressing up. He became a megalomaniac. His own name used to float before his eyes as he wandered through the dismal mirk of Cheetham Hill. MORRIS FAHNEMANN. He would see it flickering in fire on house fronts, and imagine himself bowing before an audience tense with expectation—Morris Fahnemann, master violinist ; Morris Fahnemann, actor of genius ; Morris Fahnemann, great impresario or entrepreneur. And now he could see his name anywhere—just " Bannerman's " on a teashop. My God ! The come-down life was ! For every man who found it bigger, grander, than he had hoped there were ten thousand to whom it was a brief street in the night, and they walking along it with the lamps going out one by one.

There was his father ; he had been a megalomaniac too, old Lazarus Fahnemann, a cotton merchant of sorts, with a bit of a warehouse in a basement. Wealth ! That was the dream of Lazarus. Had not a Rothschild lived in Mosley Street ? Lazarus would take the small Morris by the hand and lead him down that grim thoroughfare, where now nothing could be seen but warehouse blocks that seemed to be carved in ebony ; and he would pause just at the spot where the Rothschild house had stood, and say in a tranced voice : " It was there, son, there on that very spot." It was his Mecca. The thought that Rothschild feet in ancient times had trodden the common mud of Manchester was holy to Lazarus.

Under the shadow of his father's obsession, seeing the thin hand twisted covetously round every shekel, Morris grew up and learned to be diffident about the things that were in his heart. Only once did he mention that he would like to study the violin seriously. Only once . . .

And then, when he was seventeen, a big awkward lout, there came the day when his father was ill, and the money in the house had run out, and he was sent to the bank to cash a cheque. The detail of the cheque was burned into his mind like the detail of a great picture that has stormed the imagination. It was the first cheque Morris had ever been allowed to handle. He could recall the image of his father sitting up in bed, steel-rimmed spectacles low down on his bleak nose, a thin goatish straggle of hair under his chin. He could see the purple veins on the old withered hand as Lazarus handed him the slip of paper : " Pay bearer, five pounds," and in a shaky scrawl, " Lazarus Fahnemann."

" You just sign it on the back, and they give you five pounds—see ? "

It was a day of mid-winter, and he got to the bank just at closing time. He put the five golden sovereigns in his pocket, and dallied about the town, in no hurry to return to the cheerlessness of Cheetham Hill. Nineteen hundred and eleven. Twenty years ago. It was then that he cashed his first cheque, held a golden sovereign in his hand for the first time.

At last, he walked slowly home, chinking the money against his thigh. The sound of it ! And to know that it was sovereigns—not pennies ! A deep racial passion that he had not suspected woke in him. Here and there under a street lamp he would take out the coins, turn them over in his hand. And all old Lazarus's love for money bloomed suddenly in his heart, bloomed alongside his other loves ; and he saw himself fabulously rich, a great patron of the arts, living in a house full of glorious pictures, commanding the services of great violinists, financing the loveliest pieces in the theatre, and himself no mean executor of the things he nurtured in others.

Maurice Bannerman hurled the stump of his cigar into the fire as the vision that had lit the mean streets that drear night reeled again across the screen of his memory. It was amazingly sharp, one of those indelible moments that come to men on their various roads to hell or heaven, to Damascus, to Emmaus, to a Pantheon or to Wall Street.

He caressed the great white scar on his wrist, thinking how swiftly fate had intervened to tumble his exalted moment literally into the gutter. With the coins jingling in his hand, he slipped on the pavement and down he went, money and all, into the mud. Four sovereigns he picked up ; the fifth he saw roll on its edge, topple off the pavement, and disappear down a drainage sink.

In a sweat of agony, the thought of his father's wrath came over him. He could not, dared not, go home with a sovereign missing. The sink was in the light of a street lamp. He went down on his knees, removed his coat, rolled his shirt up above his left elbow, and then heaved up the hinged lid of the sink. It was heavy ; it came up with difficulty, and poised itself precariously. He plunged his left arm down into the sink, bringing up handfuls of malodorous muck and sorting it fearfully on the pavement's edge under the wan eye of the lamp.

Then the sudden toppling of the iron lid, the horrible grinding of bone and sinew. But it had done one thing—that mutilating weight of iron : it had kept him out of the war. Even now a sudden wrench was dangerous to that wrist. He was a fool to drive a car. Yes ; he knew that, and Mike Hartigan didn't let him forget it. But to sit at the wheel of his own Rolls-Royce, to propel with his own hands that opulence made both beautiful and powerful : that was something that Maurice could not resist.

" Why did you leave Cheetham Hill ? "

With just one or two of such questions the woman had led him on.

" We went to America—my father and I."

Sitting in the deserted smoke-room, he thought again of the queer, sudden rush of it all, and how puzzled he had been till years and experience helped him to see it straight. Poor old Lazarus ! There never had been a less likely candidate for the rank of millionaire. What was that joke the fire brigade chief used to pull off ? " My friends, there are several causes of fire : candle-light on the first floor, gas light on the second floor, or electric light on the third floor. But the most dangerous of all is the Israelite in the basement." Lazarus must have bungled it badly, and so they went, helter-skelter, early in 1912. He recalled a long furtive visit to his mother's relations in Cardiff, and then the couple of years in New York. His mother didn't go with them. She was to follow when they

36

had settled down. She died of influenza before their boat reached New York.

It was all too much for Lazarus. The new world didn't suit him. But it suited Morris marvellously. Shorthand and typewriting took him into a financier's office ; a genius for figures made him a secretary whose ear could lean in many a secret place ; and when Lazarus died soon after landing in New York, Morris knew more about the technique that makes Rothschilds than the old man would have learned in a century. A stout and well-fed youth, careful about his clothes and his finger-nails, calling himself Maurice Bannerman, reached England in June of 1914, with £5,000 of capital. Hardly was he landed than the war-drums began to roll, and Maurice knew the primary adage of finance : War means money. In a third-rate London hotel he did some quick thinking. Britain was not yet in the war, but Maurice decided to gamble every penny on her coming in. He packed a bag and hurried to the West Country. He found what he wanted. In a ship-breaker's yard at Falmouth was an ancient iron hulk. In a yard on the Dart was another. They were ready for the knackers, but Maurice got them first. He went back to London, the penniless possessor of two lumps of wreckage, and waited breathlessly for the situation to develop. He walked up and down in front of the House of Commons on the fateful night. The news came, and the crowd cheered that Moloch's jaws were open. Maurice did not cheer. He went home soberly, pondering the raising of money.

Ships they would want, and ships they should have, and he would sell them ships ; but first the ships must

37

be created out of the old tin cans lying in the West Country mud. He raised the money from his Cardiff uncle, and he patched the ships till they would at least float and belch smoke through their funnels and make a shift of moving through the waves.

And when all that was done, he was in no hurry. He could afford to wait. He waited for a year ; then he sold his ships for £100,000. He was twenty-one. It was just four years since he had groped in the drain for a lost sovereign.

Chapter Four

AT three o'clock Mike Hartigan came into the smoke-room and found Maurice Bannerman walking up and down with the heavy velvet tread of a bear. Maurice was chewing the ragged wreck of a cigar. He took it from his mouth and threw it impatiently into the fireplace as Mike approached.

" Sit down ! " he commanded, and himself sank into a leather chair. Mike sat near him, began leisurely to fill his pipe, and considered the man who was both his employer and his friend. As ever, Maurice was perfectly dressed. He could not cure himself of an extravagant taste in overcoats : great garments heavily ornamented with astrackan, or such things as the rough, camel-coloured coat he had just left in the car. But stripped of his overcoat, he had reticence. When he sat, his head habitually sank down into his shoulders. That was why he would never wear a hard collar. So he sat now, the fingers of his stout, well-kept hands joined under his chin. His hair was perfectly black, amply oiled, and it fell in a slant across his forehead.

He glowered at Mike Hartigan with sulky eyes, like a bull that would like to charge but can't be bothered.

" Well," he said, " you want to worry me about a shop front. What d'you think I employ you for ? Haven't I got enough to think about without shop fronts ? That's your job, isn't it ? Or are you handing in your resignation ? "

Mike passed a finger between his neck and his collar and wriggled uneasily. " There's no resignation about it, Maurice," he said. " When you want to sack me you can sack me. But now isn't this the first time ? Forty Bannerman shops I've fixed up and never a word of worry to you about one of the whole damn shoot. But this place is a problem. I can't see a Bannerman shop here. No, begod, I can't. 'Twould be like introducing a bit of Mozart into non-stop variety. There's something you can understand now. I'm talking on your level."

" Then why didn't you say ' No shop in Blackpool,' and have done with it ? "

" Ach, it's hard to do that, Maurice, and you the keen devil you are on the johnny o'goblins."

Maurice's eye smouldered dangerously, but he delayed his reply, and then said with perfectly urbanity, " It is a great comfort to feel so well understood."

" I knew you'd see my point," cried Mike Hartigan affably. " Well, what about it now ? Will you spare the time to come and see the site ? "

" No."

" Then I can call it off ? I can wash the whole thing out ? "

" I've already called it off, Mike," said Maurice lazily. " I sold all the Bannerman shops yesterday. That's what I came to Manchester for."

" Then, begod," cried Mike, leaping from his chair, " why have you been dangling me on a bit of string ? "

" You are so impetuous," said Maurice, lowering his fingers from under his chin, and drumming them on the arms of his chair. " And why should I tell you anything till I want to ? "

He got up and shambled about the room, his great body seeming top-heavy on his small neat feet. " Shops ! " he said, almost under his breath ; and then, turning suddenly upon Mike Hartigan, he spat the word out again loudly and venemously. " Shops ! What do you think I am, eh ? I !—that I should run shops ! I am sick of shops, I tell you ! Money ! You think that is all I care about—eh ? Oh, yes, you do ! " he shouted, as Mike shook his head. " What did you say just now ? A keen devil, am I ? Oh, well. We shall see. We shall see."

Mike half-rose in his chair. " For the love of the dear good God now, Maurice——"

" You sit down, you ! " said Maurice, and with one hand pushed Hartigan back into his seat. " All day long must I sit and do nothing but listen to your insulting tongue ? I—Maurice Bannerman—I have done with shops, I tell you. It is a strange thing, that girl, that she should have come to-day——"

" The dear God preserve us," cried Mike. " Now you haven't let that fancy piece get hold of you, Maurice ? "

" What do you mean, get hold of me ? " He gesticulated blindly.

" Maurice, will you sit down and listen to me ! " Mike took Maurice by the arm and led him back to his chair. He sat him in it and with his own handkerchief wiped his wet brow. Maurice became quieter. " You treat me as if I needed a nursemaid," he grumbled.

" And so you do, sometimes," said Mike, " though it's a grand sensation we'd cause if I wheeled you along the promenade." He looked at Maurice

41

reproachfully. "This is the second time this year, Maurice. Now just calm yourself and tell me what it's all about."

"I am an artist," Maurice began proudly.

"Oh, no, you're not," said Mike. "We've had this all out before. You would like to be an artist. Good. That's another kettle of fish."

"Always," said Maurice, "from the time I was a boy, I have loved music, the theatre, painting, the great books——"

Mike gazed at him earnestly, with his pipe clenched between his teeth. He passed a hand despairingly through his rumpled hair, and shook his head.

"Maurice," he said, "will you not try now to look at the way the good God made the world. He made the great whale and the elephant. He made the gazelle and the money spider. Use your own gifts."

"My gifts——" Maurice burst out.

"Believe me," Mike interjected quickly, "your case is not peculiar. There are thousands of men on the stock exchange who want to write novels. There are regiments of merchants who long to paint pictures ; and there are thousands of poor devils who have spent their lives painting pictures or playing the fiddle or writing books who would give their right hands to know Maurice Bannerman's secret of making money. Why, Maurice," said Mike, warming to this task, "if I had your talents, I'd buy up Wall Street and turn it into a skittle alley."

Maurice rolled his head mournfully. "It is not enough," he said obstinately. "It is a strange thing, this. You will not understand it ; you have no mind. When I was in Manchester I *walked* up to Cheetham

Hill. No car ; no taxi, even. I—I walked." He said it grandly ; and Mike grinned.

"A good thing for your liver, Maurice. You should do more of it."

"It was a good thing for me in here," said Maurice, striking his chest. "I remembered again all the things I had forgotten. I did not want, when I lived in Cheetham Hill, I did not want to be rich. No ; I wanted to be famous. And that is a better thing to want—yes, a better thing."

"'Tis an obstinate devil you are," Mike complained. "Aren't you famous already? Can you open the *Financial Times* any day without seeing your name somewhere? Aren't you director of a dozen companies whose capital would pay the national debt? Be reasonable, Maurice. Fame! If Tussaud's knew their business they'd devote a floor to you and make it pay."

Maurice looked at him pityingly. "Mike," he said, "you are just a great big mouth. You are like the mouth of a dolphin on a fountain. You spout. My God! How you spout!"

Mike Hartigan moved to the fireplace and knocked out his pipe against the heel of his shoe. "Well, I'd better be going, Maurice. I guess you don't want to hear the truth any longer."

"Sit down," said Maurice. "You'd better know where you stand, Mike. You haven't said, 'What about my job?' I like that. But now just listen to this. It's final. Understand? I'm not asking your advice now. I'm telling you something."

Maurice lit himself a new cigar, considered the glowing end for a moment, and said : "I don't know how much money I've got, Mike, but a man who began

43

with a hundred thousand pounds in war-time and his wits about him could hardly be poor to-day. If you said half a million you'd be underestimating it."

"Ach, to hell with half a million," said Mike grandiloquently. "That's no more to you, Maurice, than a spit in the eye."

"Whatever it is," Maurice said firmly, "it's enough. I've finished. I've got enough money, see? I shall turn my mind to other things."

He paused for a moment, puffing meditatively at his cigar. Then he continued : "You don't know Cheetham Hill, Mike. I was walking there last night. Poor and bleak and stony. Not a blade of grass. Miles and miles of miserable streets and dirty shops and soot and smoke and wretchedness. I said to myself : 'Some one's making money out of this.' My God, Mike ! The things we make money out of ! "

"Now don't be sentimental, Maurice," said Mike uneasily. "There are millions of poor people, and the poor must live somewhere."

"Yes, and I've been poor, and I've lived there, and the only thing that made it bearable was a set of lunatic dreams that all came back to me last night. And now I'm not poor any longer. I can realise my dreams. That's what it comes to, Mike. I can realise my dreams."

"You can try to."

"I can do it, I tell you," Maurice shouted. "People shall hear of me—people who never heard of my money—they shall hear of *me* ! "

"Well, good luck to you, Maurice," said Mike dryly. "What line do you propose to excel in ? "

"I shall write—plays, novels. They will be successful.

44

They will make money—much money. So I shall know that I am successful."

" You'll have to give parties—meet the right sort of people. You don't know any literary blokes."

" I shall do all that is necessary."

" Your money will be helpful."

Maurice's eyes flamed with anger. " Do not keep on about money," he said. " I shall not buy what I am after this time."

" You'll buy the leisure to work with a bellyful of good victuals, to begin with," said Mike. " Now, don't get all worked up about it. God knows I'm not grudging it to you. But just tell me—where do I come into the scheme ? "

And then Maurice expounded all that he had had cut and dried since last night. Mike would go back to London at once. Bannerman's was finished, and bit by bit Maurice's connections with many other concerns would finish too. Mike would establish himself in the house in Portman Square. " Your rooms will be ready. They are expecting you. I telephoned this morning. You are going to have an easy life. You will grow fat like a pig. You will look after me. You will see no one disturbs me. You will say ' No, Mr. Bannerman is writing. He cannot see you. He cannot see any one.' You are going to be lucky, Mike." Maurice got up and began ambling about the room. " You are going to see some grand dreams come true."

His big, heavy face was lit by a happy smile. All the raillery and mocking doubt faded out of Mike's mind. Maurice was serious—damnably serious—and Mike did not like it. But like it or lump it, there was nothing he could do about it. He had never yet heard of a

45

financier who had suddenly in middle-age become a great artist. But Maurice was Maurice. Perhaps the miracle was going to be worked this time. He took Maurice's hand. " Begod, you're a rum 'un," he said, half in admiration, half in reproach. " It's anxious I am, Maurice, and I won't deny it. But if any one can do this you can."

" I believe I can, Mike."

" Then I'll be away back to town at once, and I'll point a hundred quills. You'll be following on, Maurice ? "

Maurice looked evasive. " I don't know when I'll be with you," he said. " I'm tired. I must have a little holiday. I've never been in the Lake District, and now that I'm right on the doorstep I'm going to have a look at it."

" Well, mind yourself if you're driving a car about there," Mike warned him. " 'Tis all hairpin bends and hills'll make you feel you're climbing up the side of a house. Just you watch that wrist of yours, Maurice."

" I'll watch it."

" You never told me," said Mike anxiously, " what you meant when you said it was strange meeting that girl."

Maurice scowled heavily. " Never mind what I meant," he said. " You go home and get the inkpots ready."

Chapter Five

I

WHEN Mike Hartigan was gone Maurice got into his car and began to drive slowly back to Manchester. It had become a habit with him to drive slowly. For one thing, he would take no chances with his damaged wrist ; for another, he was not interested in speed. It would have seemed almost sacrilegious to him to urge the Rolls-Royce to an unseemly pace. He liked the feeling of something pompous and processional about the way it rolled along the roads, bearing him, Maurice Bannerman, preciously enclosed with the silver fittings, the gleaming mirrors, the expensive rugs. He had never got over the feeling that it was better to be seen in a Rolls-Royce than to be in a Rolls-Royce.

He had not told Mike Hartigan that the girl had turned down his invitation to take tea with him. And what d'you think of that ? Lunch and tea on the same day. He raked his memory. He could not remember that he had ever made such an offer to a woman before.

He had been too busy : directors' meetings, wanglings and wire-pullings, rushing hither and thither. He had been getting sick of it for a long time. He had said nothing to Mike, but this had been no sudden mania. He had been laying his plans for a year, and now he would just walk out. Time for women ; time for cultivating those gifts that he believed in so profoundly ; time to be alive.

But he knew that, so far as Rachel Rosing was concerned, he was bluffing himself. It was not merely his new leisure that allowed him to be attracted. It was not merely the odd chance that, coming straight from Cheetham Hill with his mind in a ferment of provoked memories, he had met a woman who held those memories in common with him. No ; beyond and above everything else, was the woman herself.

Rachel Rosing was a self-sufficient attraction. Her beautiful proud head with the blue-black hair tight upon it ; the ivory skin that revealed the shapeliness of the bones beneath ; the eyes whose dark slumber concealed their hard watchful spark ; the lips whose lovely lines the girl's artistry knew so well how to enhance : all this had struck Maurice one swift blow that Rachel's soft voice and stately carriage had driven home. She was a woman with the fatality of physical perfection upon her ; and Maurice felt importunate, but not a fool, when, lunch being over, he said : " Would you think me very greedy if I asked you to have tea with me too ? "

Her eyes dropped to her plate, and the scrap of lace, the delicious ridiculous veil that seemed to conceal nothing, was yet enough to hide from Maurice the agitation and delight that troubled her.

" No," she said at last. " I wouldn't think you greedy, because I like you. Do you mind my saying that ? "

Maurice shook his head. " And I like you," he said, " or I wouldn't ask you to tea."

" But I can't come," she said, and gave him a long

48

glance that was forlorn and regretful. " I can't possibly spare any time to-day——"

" To-morrow ? "

". . . Or to-morrow, till the evening."

" Dinner, then. Would you like that ? Dinner, here, to-morrow evening. Eight o'clock ? "

Her smile was radiant now. " Yes. I could manage that."

As he drove through the flats behind Blackpool, heading towards Preston, Maurice did not regret what he had done. He felt quietly happy about it. He had a room reserved in Manchester. He must get back there for the night. He would run over to Blackpool again in the morning.

II

Rachel hurried. For the first time since she had been in Blackpool, she hurried. There was something to hurry for now. The beach was crowded with shouting, sweating hoydens, and she smiled at them secretly as she sped along with lithe eagerness. Shouting, jumping, wrestling with the boys. My God ! she thought. Shouting ! Jumping ! No, No ; that was not the way to do it.

What a temptation that had been—to say Yes when he asked her to tea ! She laughed to herself at her cleverness in pushing the engagement forward to a time when she could take the best advantage of it. Dinner, with new clothes !

She had just enough money to carry through her scheme. In her loathsome lodgings she packed a bag and then hunted out the landlady in her kitchen.

49

"I've got to go to Manchester, but I'll be back to-morrow."

"Oh, you will, will you? And supposing you're not?"

Rachel understood the hint and opened her purse. "That pays for my room till the end of the week."

"That's all right, Miss Rosing."

Rachel smiled till she was down the passage, out of the door. Then she did not smile. A venomous scowl distorted her face. Always people of that sort to deal with. Suspicious, grasping sycophants. Always the problem of money. Always living on the verge, with God knows what horrible drop under your feet if once you slipped. She knew to a penny what money was in her purse. She could just do it : get to Manchester, buy the clothes she wanted, get a cheap lodging for the night, and be back in Blackpool on the morrow. Hurry, now! If you miss that train there'll be no dress shops open in Manchester when you get there.

It was not a very full train. Rachel had a compartment to herself. She put her bag on the rack, rested her feet on the opposite seat, and smoked a cigarette as the train jolted through the weary flatness of the Fylde. She thought of all the things she had never done ; all the gay, expensive things she would like to do. The train drew into Preston. Think of that now ! They were on the main line—the line which, if she were going in the other direction, would take her on and on into something incurably romantic. Lancaster, Penrith, Carlisle, and over the border into Scotland. That was the sort of journey she had never made. She permitted herself a nostalgic thought of lunching in a car that swayed on between the hills, the heather, the streams, into Scotland. Though what the end of the journey would be she could hardly conceive, unless it were the Gleneagles Hotel, and waiters, and baths, and—oh, any sort of luxury. That was how Rachel's dreams all ended.

Proud Preston. She had heard it called that ; but she couldn't see much to be proud of. And Warrington was worse. The day was thickening. There was little light. The tall stalks of chimneys above soap works were spewing a blackness into the sky, and that was all she saw of Warrington, that and the yellow eyes of houses looking blankly into the foggy dark. On they went, over the moss-hags, low unstable ground, seamed with shallow black canals from which the peat had been dug. The peat was piled up, parapets and paradoses of a soggy trench system, stretching away to a grey infinity.

Rachel's eyes looked out on the cheerless prospect and she gave a little shiver. Even so must her life be, she knew—a procession of grey and level days—unless she did something to pull herself swiftly away from the dangerous acquiescence into which she had been falling.

She did not express the thought. She did not so much as form it in her mind ; but she felt an instinctive reaction from the blear, bedevilled landscape they were running through ; she brought her eyes into the warmth and intimacy of the compartment, and gave herself up to a pleasant consideration of all the things she was about to do.

The houses closed in. The train roared between the stony cliffs ; ten thousand reeking chimney-pots ; ten thousand windows blurred with light. It stopped,

51

coughing out its white steam like an exhausted dragon, in the smelly cavern of Manchester Central Station.

And now Rachel was at home. Now she knew her way about. Even in Blackpool, for all its raffish sophistication, she had been uneasy. The restlessness of the sea, its sighing and moaning, and sometimes its frantic howling, disturbed her to the very bowels with its suggestion of untamed, inimical forces. But Manchester was her washpot.

She did not wait even to take tea. She left her bag at the station, and as she came out into the station yard she took a deep breath of the damp familiar air and felt a conqueror.

The tall red trams were grinding round the corner by the Midland Hotel. Their trolley-poles exploded violet stars here and there upon the black velvet of the night. The Town Hall's tower lost its crown in the darkness, but the face of its clock shone reassuringly above the great square seething with the familiar surge and jostle of humanity. Rachel launched herself upon it all as upon a sea whose waves bore her up. This was the sea she knew. This was the sea whose buffeting she liked.

She passed through the Square and along Cross Street, and turned into Market Street. There over a shop window—a window all glass and chromium plate —was the name Arlette et Cie. A wave of sickness seized her for the safety that once in that shop had been hers—the shop that she and Miriam Jacobs had run together. She thought of its dove-coloured carpets, its gilt-legged chairs, its faintly perfumed warmth. Then, resolutely, she walked on. No ! That was done with. Only a fool would cry for what couldn't be mended. But one thing the shop had taught her. She did know what a dress cost. She did know down to what price she could haggle and chaffer. Hugging the thought, she passed up and down the street, and then she saw what she wanted.

It was a black dress—black as ebony, but aëry as a spring cloud. Her mind darted into a little by-way of finance. It wouldn't do alone. It would need a black underdress. Stockings? She had none that would do. They must be black too, but so exquisitely fine that the texture of white skin shining through them would give them a cob-web grey.

She could see it all. Where clothes were concerned she had an unerring pictorial imagination. And she could see the whole thing : the ivory of her complexion that had almost a hint of dull gold in it rising out of that filmy black, the severe coils of her black hair surmounting all. Yes ; but there must be one note a little more emphatic. Her imagination added a scarlet flower—no, she corrected herself, a crimson flower—to the blue-black of her hair, and she knew the picture was complete. She would have liked a new cloak ; and the cloud that darkened her face at the thought that she could not afford one lifted as she asked herself : " What's the betting that I shall have one by this time next week ? " The smile parting her lips lent her a radiance that startled the stout Jewess who stepped forward to meet her. And to meet Waterloo. It was a memorable half-hour that the old Jewess lived through. " It is for no profit at all, it is to give dresses away then that you want me to keep a shop," she was declaring passionately as Rachel moved towards the door.

53

" I would like to leave everything here till morning,"
Rachel said. " You open at nine, I suppose ? "

" What does it matter—tell me—nine, ten, eleven,
if we give dresses away ? "

" Nine, then. I'll call for them all at nine."

She crossed the road and went into the Lyons
Popular State Café. Happy and exhausted, she sank
into a chair. Now she could take tea. There was a
cheerful din. The strings and woodwind of the orchestra were at some honey-throated business through
which the brisk clatter of tea-cups went on unheeding.
Lovely ! It was all lovely. Noise and lights and movement, islanded amid miles and miles of dear familiar
streets. " A roll and butter, please, and a pot of tea."

She opened her flapjack, made herself up, as a
soldier repairs the ravages of battle, and then, when
she had slowly taken her tea, she went to the only
chemist's shop she knew where she could buy real
attar of roses. Once—and her heart shook queerly at
the thought—Sir George Faunt had taken her there
and bought some. She did not know what it had cost,
and now when she inquired the price seemed fantastic.
She wavered, rallied, and decided heroically. She
slipped the precious phial into her handbag and set
off for the station to recover her suitcase. She could
buy bath salts at Blackpool on the morrow.

III

While Rachel sat on the edge of her bed in an obscure
lodging gently massaging her face with a night-cream,
Maurice Bannerman was finishing his dinner in the

54

French restaurant of the Midland Hotel. He was content. No colleagues to meet ; no business acquaintances to worry him about this or that. He was alone, and how, for years, he had longed to be alone ! With his bull-neck sunk into his shoulders and one hairy-backed hand crumbling the bread on his plate, he pondered on the work he was to do. A waiter silently replenished his wine-glass, and suddenly Maurice took it up, emptied it at a swig, and went ponderously out of the room. Now ! What reason for delay ? He had always gone straight to his objectives.

The lift gates clanged behind him, and all the noise of the great hotel and of the city without died away. He could hear his own footsteps shuffling over the deep-piled carpet as he passed along the corridor. In his room the silence was absolute. He had ordered a fire to be lit. He switched on the desk light and rubbed his hands at the cosy look of the place. He took off his shoes and placed them outside the door, put on his dressing-gown and roomy slippers lined with lamb's wool. He laid out paper and pen on the writing-table and then for a moment or two stood with his back to the fire, his hands in his dressing-gown pockets.

This was the moment he had dreamed of so often. This was the moment for beginning those acts of creation which he had promised himself to perform. He pushed a chair across to the table, sat down and took up a pen.

IV

When Rachel Rosing reached Blackpool next morning she ordered a taxi-driver to call at her lodgings at five minutes to eight. She was cutting her resources fine, but this was a grand gamble. The price of a taxi must not stand in her way. And as she went through the unappetising back streets lugging her suitcase, she prayed devoutly, though to no god in particular, that the gamble might be successful, that the time for asking whether she could afford a taxi might soon be ended.

When she had eaten her lunch she went to the bathroom. It was revolting, so revolting that she had used it as infrequently as possible. It was worse than she had remembered. It was no more than a dark, dirty cupboard. A black tide-mark smudged the bath half-way up. The enamel was worn from the bottom ; the iron showed in rusty flakes and blotches. The electric light had never been brought to this room. A crude gas-burner stuck out from the wall. The oil-cloth on the floor was trodden into holes, and on a hook behind the door a soiled towel was hanging.

Rachel leaned her hands suddenly on the edge of the bath, overcome with nausea. This was where she must perform her rites before leaving the house that evening ! She recovered, and remembered her land-lady's habits. Every afternoon she went out between half-past two and four. And so at three o'clock Rachel was busy with a scrubbing-brush and a tin of paint-cleanser, her hands encased in old gloves. The bath looked little better when she had done, but she knew that it was clean. That was something. Then she lay on her bed. She did not believe in being either flustered or tired for her great occasions. Her body was her only weapon. It must be in perfect temper. For some that might be induced by exercise ; not for Rachel.

Hers were the melting graces of the harem, and she was intelligent enough to know it.

A bath at six-thirty seemed to the landlady so preposterous an idea that she could hardly believe Rachel was serious.

" I'm going out to dinner," Rachel explained.

" Didn't you 'ave dinner at one o'clock ? "

" Well, I didn't eat much."

" It was there *for* you to eat, choose 'ow. And remember the doors are locked at eleven. Going out to dinner ! "

" Oh, you barbarian, you beast, you cat, you bitch ! " Rachel raged inwardly ; and with a charming smile she asked : " And the bath ? "

" Very well. I'll do the best I can for yer. It'll be a shillin' extra."

By the grace of God rather than by any care the landlady took, the water was hot. Rachel spread upon the floor half a dozen newspapers that she had gathered for the purpose, and folded her garments upon them, carefully away from the wall. She stretched her long thin legs gratefully in the hot, scented water, whose steam made a nimbus round the gas-burner and obscured the scabrous walls and ceilings. You could almost forget the foul room. She closed her eyes. Like that, you could forget it altogether. She inhaled the steam sensuously and allowed her thoughts to linger about a table spread with a white cloth, laid with silver, lit by a shaded lamp. She did not think at all of food ; only of its luxurious accompaniments, and of Maurice Bannerman, with the blue promontory of chin, the massive shoulders, and the hairy hands.

She stepped out delicately on to the newspapers.

57

There was no bath mat. Nor was there any towel save the small one she had brought from her bedroom. That was already damp ; and suddenly, as she began to use it, she laughed aloud at the difficulties that hindered the arraying of her beauty. They seemed so foolish, so ineffective, because she knew that hers was a beauty that nothing could impede when it was on the march. And in that triumphant mood she ran across the bleak landing to her bedroom, her clothes clutched in one hand, the other holding a bathrobe about her.

With nothing but the blurred and spotty mirror on her dressing-table to help her, she went swiftly to work in the sickly light of the bare electric bulb. She brushed and brushed at her hair till it gleamed like spun glass, then gathered it into a hard knob on her neck. It was parted down the middle of her skull and fitted close as a cap. She slapped and smoothed and massaged her face, attended with particular care to the exquisite line of her lips. Her eyes she did not touch. Her lids were translucent and had a damson bloom that owed nothing to art. The lashes were long and silky and Rachel was wise enough not to stick them together with black sludge.

She turned to her long fine-boned hands, tinting with care the nails that were shaped like almonds, and then, ritually as a priest puts on his vestments, she began to put on her clothes, dropping the bath-robe and standing for a moment naked, tall as a lily and smooth as an ivory tower. She passed her hands once over her body and approved herself, dispassionately as a connoisseur might approve a statuette. And when all was done, and she pulled her cloak about

58

her, she knew, though the misty mirror could show her nothing, that she was as perfect as the given circumstances could make her. She was satisfied. She could think of nothing that she might have done that she had not done. Sniffing delicately the odour of attar of rose that her clothes exhaled, she put away carefully the bottles of lotion, the manicure set, all the impedimenta of her art. She did not leave those things lying about in that foul room. When they were in the trunk, and the key of the trunk was in her purse, she stood for a moment listening, heard the taxi draw up at the door, and slipped out upon the dingy stair like a superb actress who had received her cue.

Chapter Six

I

MAURICE BANNERMAN got up in a bad temper. He had asked to be called at eight and when at that hour a chambermaid came in to draw the curtains and give him his tea, he sat up in bed wondering dully what it was that laid an oppression on his mind.

His eye wandered round the room, came to rest on the waste-paper basket alongside the writing-table, and he remembered. The basket was full of the litter of last night's efforts. Litter : that was what it had all come to.

There was, of course, Maurice told himself as he sipped his tea, every reason why the endeavour should have failed. To come like that—rushing up from dinner. Writing, after all, was not so easy as ringing up your stockbroker. And then, this room. He needed his own surroundings : that lovely study in Portman Square where all the ground-tone was a rich golden brown, picked out here and there with olive-green paint.

There was that woman, too. His mind would go wandering in her direction. He knew nothing about her, and yet there she was, dancing in his imagination like a flame. Just a casual introduction from Mike

Hartigan. Mike had said nothing; probably knew nothing; and the woman had said next door to nothing. Cheetham Hill: poor as a church mouse, he guessed: but she was lovely . . . lovely. He could not get her out of his mind. But he would have to. He would meet her at dinner as he had promised, and that would be that.

He poured a second cup of tea, telling himself that he had reached a wise decision, that this obstacle would soon be set aside, and that then his life would go forward according to plan. But the gnawing in his mind was not stilled when he had thus reasonably set forth his situation. Despite the suddenness of his rush at the work, despite the unfamiliar surroudings, despite the woman, his failure was not accounted for. In his heart he knew that the job itself had beaten him. There were all sorts of easy things that he might have done; but he had not found a way to begin to do the thing that was in his mind.

He thrust his feet into slippers, pulled on a dressing-gown, and padded into the bathroom. He shaved with great care. He was proud of the big, strong lines of his face. When he had bathed, he powdered his face, oiled his hair, and finally went down to breakfast in a better mood than was on him when he got out of bed. A temporary set-back. He would soon find his stride and keep it up, he said, scooping into a grapefruit. He shook open the morning paper and turned instinctively to the financial columns. Then with a smile he crumpled the paper and dropped it alongside his chair. He had done with all that.

It was a foul night. Rachel thanked goodness that she had had the sense to order a taxi. The back streets of the town were full of murk and drizzle, and as the taxi swung out on to the promenade the insane blaze of the illuminations flared beneath the sodden sky and beside the sullen sea. Rachel's was a practical mind, given to concentration on the immediate point ; she had no imagination ; but even to her, sitting in a little twilit coach that hurried over the asphalt shining in the rain, it seemed as though she had shot out of the dark wings on to the sudden stage, magnificently lighted for a play that was about to begin. She would leave it to Maurice Bannerman to speak the first word. Her heart was racing with excitement, but she had never felt more competent to play a part.

Maurice was lounging in the vestibule of the hotel. He had reserved a table for two, but he was not expecting much pleasure. He had reasoned himself into a cold state of mind. This was an engagement, and therefore must be met, but he would get it over as soon as courtesy made possible.

And then he saw her, tall and radiant, an imperative utterance of beauty. With remarkable agility he was at her side, alive, alert, proud to claim her in the sight of those who stood there.

" You shame me, Miss Rosing," he said. " I should have dressed." He looked ruefully at his lounge suit. " I didn't know. . . ."

She gave him a smile that understood and pardoned.

" Of course you didn't know," she said. " We know nothing, do we ? About one another, I mean. That's why it's so good of you to ask me to dinner."

She laid a hand lightly on his arm as they went towards the dining-room, and there was laughter in her eyes at the thought that he had not asked her at all. She had very cleverly asked herself. She wondered if he had realised that.

Their table was near a fireplace. A lamp upon it threw an amber light on some drooping chrysanthemums. Maurice intervened as a waiter was about to take Rachel's cloak. He performed that service himself, laid the cloak across the back of a chair, and waved a hand impatiently towards the flowers. " Take these away," he said : and when they were gone, he said : " I would have ordered some nice flowers if I had known. You are so—so unexpected."

With his big, well-kept hands clenched together on the table before him, he considered her with mingled enchantment and perplexity.

" But you've been expecting me ever since lunchtime yesterday," said Rachel with a laugh.

" I did not expect what I see now," Maurice answered gravely. " Then you were attractive. Now you are beautiful."

" Is there such a great difference ? "

Maurice pondered for a moment, drumming his fingers on the table. " Yes," he answered at last " Do you know anything about music ? Perhaps that might help me to tell you."

" No," she said frankly. " Not a thing."

" Then what do you love doing best ? "

" Once I went to London. It was a day trip from

63

Manchester. We had only a couple of hours to spend before rushing for our train back. I went to Bond Street. I have never loved anything so much as those couple of hours wandering up and down, looking in the shop windows."

" Ha ! Now I can tell you. Supposing I am walking in Bond Street with a lot of money in my pocket, and I see something, and I say, ' Yes, pretty good,' but I don't want it, though I could buy it ten times over. That is an attractive thing. But then I see something—a painting—a little bit of porcelain—and I can't go on. I know if I come to-morrow and it has gone I shall tear my hair and feel that something very important has been missed out of my life. So I go in and buy it because I can't help myself. The thing is stronger than I am. That is a beautiful thing. Beauty is one of the terrible things in the world, because it is stronger than we are."

Rachel looked at him in perplexity. No one had ever talked such nonsense to her before. It was on the point of her tongue to say : " It seems lucky that I'm not a Bond Street window," but the gravity of Maurice's face warned her to be silent. She had never met any one like this before. Well, go carefully. Don't rush about like a fool.

So she said : " Don't worry about the flowers, anyway. It's very kind of you to have thought that those were not good enough," and then the waiter returned and they gave their attention to ordering the dinner.

Maurice considered her covertly as the meal proceeded. The lamplight falling evenly on one cheek, the firelight flickering on the other, seemed to illustrate the stillness and the animation that both belonged to her beauty. He found her a disturbing enigma, and presently he remarked : " When you said just now, Miss Rosing, that we know nothing about one another, I wondered whether we could put that right. How did you meet Mike Hartigan ? "

Rachel produced a most disarming smile. " Well, it's not difficult, is it, to meet a cheerful Irishman ? "

" I see. It was as simple as that."

She gave him a frank, level look. " Mr. Bannerman, it may not be easy for you to believe it, but I talked to Mike Hartigan because I thought it likely that he'd give me a cheerful evening and stand me a dinner. He did. I was glad of it."

Maurice frowned, as though he were reproving himself for some gross discourtesy. " I'm sorry," he said. " You must forgive me. Why are you smiling ? "

" I was thinking that it seems strange to hear you say ' It was as simple as that.' Because you didn't find it difficult, did you ? "

Maurice smiled, too. " What fools we are," he said. " I believe I felt jealous of Mike."

" Please don't," she begged him. " He is just one of the—attractive things."

Maurice took up the wine bottle to replenish her glass. " No—please," she said ; and he put it down and considered her steadily. " I tried to come to a point," he said, " and we slipped right off it again. Whose fault is that—yours or mine ? "

" What was the point ? "

" Well, who or what are you ? I want to know something about you."

" There's very little to know. I kept a dress-shop

in Manchester. It did well for a time, then——"
She shrugged an expressive shoulder. " Finished. It
made me very ill. I came to Blackpool to rest and
think what could be done. And now here I am—
rested enough, but still in a fog. That's all. Fortu-
nately, I'm on my own. I haven't a relative in the
world."

It flashed through her mind that she had said that
to more than one man, but that at last it was true.
Maurice was silent, so she said : " Why do you want
to know about me ? "

" Well, if we are to be friends. . . ."

" But how can we be friends ? Here you are in
Blackpool on business. You will be gone in a day—
two days—I don't know. And I shall still be here."

He leaned back in his chair and swung the wine
round in his glass. With his chin sunk into his chest,
he looked at it with deep concentration. He did not
look at her. " Need you ? " he asked.

Rachel feigned denseness while her heart gave a
quicker beat. " Need I ? " she repeated. " Need I
what ? "

" Stay here." Still he did not look at her.

" But certainly," she said with a little laugh. " Why
should I not ? What else is there for me to do ? I
must be on the spot. I must look around. I have a
living to earn."

He put down his glass and waved away the hovering waiter. " A living to earn," he said. " And how
are you going to earn it ? Once, your shop has sunk,
you say. Have you any capital to start another ? "

She shook her head. " I must borrow some."

" Yes, I know. You go to some one and say ' Once

66

I have started a shop and it is now bankrupt. Will you please lend me some money to start another? I will try not to go bankrupt again.' "

Rachel smiled wanly. " It does not sound too good, does it ? "

" It doesn't sound any good at all," said Maurice. " Now if you came to me, I would say : ' Yes. You are beautiful. I want you to have your shop—to be happy—to be near me, so that we can meet now and then, and be good friends.' What would you say to that ? "

For the first time, he looked her full in the face, and she met his gaze with clear starry eyes. She stretched a hand across the table and laid it on his. " Say? Why I should say you're a darling."

" Very well, then," said Maurice, clouds of doubt and anxiety lifting from his heavy face, " very well, then. Now we can have some coffee."

He snapped his fingers and the waiter came running. He gave Rachel a cigarette and lit a cigar. He leaned back in his chair, feeling such relief as came when a difficult board meeting was ended or when doubtful shareholders had been given honey for another year. " And what are we going to do now ? " he asked.

" I should love to dance," said Rachel. " Take me to the Tower Ballroom."

" Dance ! I've never had time to learn to dance." And then he reflected that that was all done with— that time when he hadn't a moment to do this or that or the other. By God, he would learn to dance, and he would start that night.

" You'll love it," Rachel wheedled. " Now you must come along and try," and to Maurice Bannerman's surprise half an hour later he was ambling upon a waxed floor, jostled by a great democratic throng who moved their limbs to the strains of the Wedding of Mr. Mickey Mouse.

Maurice did not stand up to it for long. " It's not fair, Miss Rosing," he said. " It's not fair on you. Look at all these young fellers—look, they're like laths and as light as feathers. You want to dance with one of them."

He looked at her anxiously, fearing she might take his advice, saw her contemplate one or two of the faces about her : the sleek hair and negligible heads and vacuous mouths. He saw her nose wrinkle faintly in dislike as she turned from them all and took his arm. " Let us go if you are tired," she said.

" My God, she's clever," thought Maurice. " Or does she really like me ? "

He would have given a lot to know.

Outside the Tower he hailed a taxi. " Now I must see you home," he said.

" Please, don't," she pleaded. " It's a horrible place, and I don't want you to know any of the horrible things about me. I hate it, and you're not to see it. You get off at the Metropole and then the taxi can take me home."

" Very well," he said. " I'm going to take a run up to the Lakes to-morrow. Will you come ? "

" I should love it," she said fervently, knowing that all she would love would be the luxury of travelling in a Rolls-Royce.

" Eleven o'clock, then, at the Metropole."

He extracted his huge bulk from the taxi, and stood watching as it turned and rolled away. He saw her

68

face pale as a ghost beneath the red flaming flower. He saw her slender hand wave through the open window, and for long that night he tumbled in his bed with an absurd dance tune singing in his ears, with the feeling of that slender hand upon his arm, and with Rachel Rosing's fatal beauty throbbing before his eyes.

As for Rachel, her only emotion was a profound satisfaction with the night's work. She took off her clothes with care, folded them and put them away as tenderly as a good workman puts away his tools. Then she got into bed, stretching her long limbs beneath the sheet in one sensuous relaxing movement, and within five minutes was sound asleep.

Chapter Seven

I

MAURICE was already seated at the wheel of his car when Rachel arrived at the hotel in the morning. It was a great cream-coloured vehicle, with mudguards enamelled pale green. You do not see many Rolls-Royce cars that are not dark and reticent in colour ; but Maurice liked his car to be distinctive. He liked people to say not merely " That's a Rolls-Royce," but " That's Maurice Bannerman's Rolls-Royce."

A porter opened the door and Rachel got in. " Good-morning," she said. " You look very nice."

Maurice did look very nice. He was dressed in brown from head to foot : a brown lounge suit so light as to be almost fawn, a nigger-brown silk tie, brown socks, and shoes that had the polish of old mahogany. He was hatless, and his great shaggy overcoat was slung into the back seat.

The late autumn day was doing its best to throw back to summer. The promenade, tier upon concrete tier, was alive with people. There was no breath of wind. The tide was out. Tawny sand ran almost out of eye's reach to meet the distant blue smudge of the sea, and over all the sky was a vault of unstained blue.

Maurice drove with his customary restraint. The

horn occasionally gurgled with honeyed politeness.
" Soon," he said, " we shall see trees."

" Trees ? "

" Yes. Have you not noticed that in Blackpool
you can walk from one end of the promenade to the
other—how many miles?—and never see a tree?
Trees are the only things they have not learned to
make from concrete. They will do it soon, no doubt,
and decorate them with canvas leaves."

" I hadn't noticed that. I never missed them."

Never mind, thought Maurice. You are very
beautiful. You look well in tweeds, with that nice
tweed hat.

Soon they came upon trees enough : all the rich
gold of autumn standing upon the sturdy oaks and
streaming down the pendant boughs which the beeches
wore like gorgeous folded wings. They droned through
a country incredibly rich in poultry farms, through
little stony villages whose houses were painted with the
bright orange of lichen and draped with the more
transient loveliness of late roses. The hills began to
show on their right hand. They crawled through
the tortuous streets of Lancaster and shot forward
on to the alluvial flats that edge the wide scallop of
Morecambe Bay. Across the bay the great crests
of the Lake Country lifted into the blue.

Maurice had little to say. He was quietly content.
After the fretful night that he had passed, he was
content that Rachel Rosing was at his side. And he
was content, too, with the loveliness of the day and
the scene. There were deep emotional springs in his
mixed make-up, and natural beauty never failed to
touch them. So, almost idly, he kept the car at its

stately business, and his mind ranged now outward to an apprehension of this district he had never seen before, now inward to an analysis of the strange restfulness which Rachel Rosing's presence gave him, and which, also, was something new in his experience.

And as for Rachel, she, too, was satisfied to be silent. What more, she thought, could she ask than she was now enjoying : this seat on which one sat as on a cloud's softness, this leisurely, inexorable progress in the most luxurious vehicle the mind of man had devised? Her eye was within the car as often as without. It took a deep satisfaction from the gleaming silver, and polished glass, and shining leather. The rug beneath her feet, the solidity of Maurice's hand upon the wheel : it all rejoiced her in the deepest part of her being. She noticed a diamond glittering in a ring on Maurice's hand. The sunlight, striking through the window, fell upon it and danced in fierce little sparkles of red and blue. She drew a deep breath of happiness, sank into the cushions, and slept.

They were passing through ancient Kendal when next she opened her eyes. Maurice had noticed that she slept ; he did not see her waken. He was startled by a sudden question : " Why are you and Mike Hartigan such good friends ? "

Maurice swung the car carefully round a corner and headed for open country. " Well," he said at last, " I've done a bit of good to him, and he's made a lot of money for me. That's a safe enough ground for friendship."

" Do you often do good to people ? "

" No," Maurice answered frankly. " I've mostly been completely wrapped up in myself. Any good

72

I've done has been by giving away money, and I never gave away a penny till I had so much that I wouldn't miss it. Most reputations for generosity are built up like that. You screw all you can out of thousands or millions of people and then give a bit of it back to tens or hundreds. It's an old game, thoroughly well understood by those who play it. There are some cigarettes there in front of you."

Rachel took a cigarette from the tortoiseshell box, lit it at the electric lighter, and held it towards Maurice's mouth. He shook his head. "I never smoke them."

She put it to her own lips, blew the smoke out thoughtfully, and said : "You're very frank about yourself."

"Why not ? I may have been all sorts of things, but I never fooled myself. That's the main point."

"But you say you did some good to Mike Hartigan ? "

"Yes. Towards the end of the war I was making so much money that it frightened me. At least, I wasn't making it. Some fools will tell you it was making itself ; that as I started with so much it couldn't help increasing. Now that's another thing you mustn't believe. Money doesn't make itself. All sorts of Toms, Dicks and Harrys were making it for me—piling it up, heaps of it. I felt I had to do something about it. Then there was all that palaver about the Unknown Soldier. D'you remember ? "

Rachel suppressed a yawn. "I don't remember, but of course I know about it."

"Well, that gave me an idea. All these goings on about an unknown dead man. I'll do something more intelligent than that, I said. I'll find an unknown live man and put him on his feet. I'll give him a blue sky instead of the roof of Westminster Abbey, and if he's got any sense he'll know he's had the best of the bargain. So I found Mike Hartigan."

"Where?"

"In a hospital for neurasthenics. Gibbering idiots, half of them, as far as I could see, and the other half likely to become so if they stayed there much longer. It wasn't easy to pick a man, but I picked Mike because he had a damned impudent eye, knocked out though he was. I made myself responsible for him. I took him home and said : ' Now that the doctors have had a shot at you, have a shot at yourself. What d'you think would cure you ? ' ' Nothing to do,' said Mike, ' and the world to walk in.' ' It's yours,' I said, and so it was. He went where he liked and did what he liked for a year. He went to South Africa and lay in the sun. He went to Australia, and wandered back across the Pacific to America. He went down into Mexico, and I heard nothing from him except what he could say on three postcards in twelve months. Then he came home, and believe me he was worth looking at."

A flock of sheep headed towards the car. Maurice brought it down almost to a crawl, and like a steady prow it divided the sheep into two grey waves that flowed by and met astern.

" Then he told me he wanted a job," said Maurice, pushing the car to a careful twenty, " and that's all there is to it. He's been a good investment."

" I don't like him calling you Maurice."

" Why not ? " Maurice asked with a laugh.

74

" You could buy him up a hundred times over."

" That's just where you're wrong, Miss Rosing. I know Mike. You couldn't buy him—not once."

So that's that, thought Rachel, and she was wise enough to say no more.

They passed through the village of Windermere, and came out on to the road that skirts the lake. Maurice fell silent again, his eye engaged by the loveliness of the trees that made a screen of gold and red and brown between the road and the water. Far away beyond the lake he could see the mountains rising, and on his right the pastures sloped up steeply as though they, too, were eager to be off on the sky-defying feats of Skiddaw or Helvellyn. Green islands on the bosom of the water looked upon their own drowned images, unruffled by the tremor of a single ripple.

Maurice stopped the car at the Salutation Hotel, and before going in for lunch, stamped his feet on the road, stretched his arms, and filled his lungs with the clear vivid air. He smacked his hand on the green mudguard of the car and demanded : " Why do we cage ourselves in these things ? "

" I've loved it," said Rachel with a happy smile.

And suddenly, seeing her standing there with her head held high and the tempered light of the autumn sun falling tenderly on her warmly pallid face, seeing the thankfulness with which she accepted what he was able so cheaply to bestow, Maurice was seized anew with admiration and desire. Trees and lake and mountains and green, climbing pasture : was any of it, he asked, of such moment to him as this woman's beauty ? His legs trembled with a sudden

75

onset of emotion. He took her arm and led her into the hotel.

He found that everything tended to please him more than, in reason, it should. The rum-butter seemed to him an astonishing confection. The window immediately over the great fireplace, which made it possible for you to stand before the blaze and look upon the world without, filled him with fantastic conjectures about where the chimney went to. He was prepared to find everything pleasing, amusing, diverting. By Heaven, he thought, let him get back to London in this mood and fall to work upon his book, and something good would happen!

In this mood—yes! But how maintain the mood? Was it all dependant on Rachel Rosing? He knew it was, knew it in his bones, but what he did not know was what he wanted to do with her.

Women were among the things Maurice had never had time for. But now that he was to have time for everything—what now? Did he want to marry, and, if he did, did he want to marry a penniless girl in whose company he had spent a few hours? All the spontaneous instincts of him, all that part of his being which in childhood had reached out towards lovely unsubstantial things, cried Yes; and all the accretions of caution and reserve that had turned Morris Fahnemann into the enormously successful Maurice Bannerman said No.

He crumbled the bread upon his plate, his big forehead corrugated by a frown. He did not speak. The joy he had felt at everything in the room seemed suddenly trivial and inappropriate. Rachel did not understand the swift change of his mood, but she

76

accepted it. She had always found it a good working rule not to break in on a situation of which she could not be completely master. So she sipped her coffee, and smoked her cigarette, contenting herself by communicating to Maurice her satisfaction with him by unveiling now and then the full radiance of her smile.

" Come ! We must be off ! " said Maurice suddenly, almost gruffly, and she meekly followed him out to the car. When they were seated he added, as if to extenuate his sharpness : " The evenings come on quickly. I want to see a bit more."

They left Ambleside behind them, and Rydal Water with its close battalions of reeds now turning sere and dry, and Grasmere's grey stony huddle with the Rothay singing through it ; and so they came out under the shoulder of Helvellyn and beside the long crescent of Thirlmere. The lake was leaden and sullen and in the dense coppices planted between road and water the little fir trees were almost black. The sun had dived steeply into a bank of cloud that was growing up from the west, and in the twinkling of an eye the landscape had put on a mantle of austerity.

Out of a town, Rachel was never at home. She could tolerate the gayer aspects of the countryside, but this sudden grim indifference, this grey majesty of earth and sky and water, gave her the creeps. To her right, unmortared walls made crazy and haphazard patterns of the fell-sides that climbed and climbed into infinity, clothed with harsh grass, populated by scurrying sheep that looked wild and dirty and unkempt. Before her the road ran on, with never a building or a lamp to make what would have been

77

for her a welcome interruption of its inexorable march. On her left the lake gloomed from grey to black, and a sudden splatter of rain hit the windscreen. She shivered, withdrew her eyes from the world without, and lit a cigarette.

Maurice, whose mind had been occupied with its own problem, turned to her with a swift solicitude. " You're hating it," he said. " We'll go back."

" I think we've had the best of the day," Rachel said tritely, pleased with the possibility that to-night she and Maurice would dance again at the Tower Ballroom.

" We certainly have," he agreed. " I hoped we'd get to Keswick, but there's no sense in going on through this."

A rough lane running at right angles to the road offered a turning-place, and Maurice put the car's bonnet into it. Then he began to back slowly towards the road again.

II

It was all very well to decide after the event that a wise driver would not have turned in such a place. A twist in the road twenty yards from the lane's mouth hid the manœuvre completely from on-coming cars, but the two young men who were also concerned in the accident were too solicitous, at the moment, to stress obvious points.

They were unhurt. So was Rachel, though she was white and felt her legs quaking beneath her as she stood upright. One of the young men put an arm beneath her elbow to steady her. The rain had come on in earnest. The clouds were surging down Helvellyn's flanks and the raindrops were pitting the dark surface of the lake. She felt intensely miserable, standing there with a young man holding her arm while the other opened the door of the Rolls-Royce and asked anxiously : "Are you all right, sir ? "

Maurice was magnificent. There was not a tremor in his voice as he answered : "My leg's hurt, but I think I can stand up. I'm going to have a shot."

He pushed his left leg out and got it to the ground, squeezed his big body through the car door, and then pulled the right leg after it. It would not take any weight, and his helper propped him suddenly as he stumbled.

"It hurts—badly," Maurice conceded with some reluctance.

The young man looked rueful. "Don't worry," said Maurice. "It was my fault. I was a fool to try and turn there. I hope your car is all right."

It was, and so, as it happened, was the Rolls—right enough for driving, though its elegance was somewhat diminished. "I am glad you are not hurt, Rachel," Maurice said. "Please get in out of the wet."

It was a difficult moment. They were all frayed and nervy ; but she did not fail to notice that Maurice had called her Rachel. She got into the Rolls, and came out again with Maurice's shaggy overcoat. "You must put this on," she said, and managed to convey intimate solicitude by her tone.

The three men conferred. "I must have a doctor," Maurice said. "I shall wait till I get to Blackpool if you are going anywhere near there and can take me. I should stay at Grasmere or Windermere, but

79

all my things are at Blackpool. Could one of you drive a Rolls? I couldn't trust myself with it now."

The young men said they were making for Preston, and they would be glad to take Maurice to Blackpool. The one who had held Rachel's arm leapt into the Rolls and tried the engine. "Right as a trivet," he announced cheerfully. "I'll be proud to drive a bus like this, sir."

"If you are there first, Rachel," Maurice shouted, "see that the hotel people have the best surgeon they can find. Tell them it's probably a broken leg."

"We'll be there first all right," Rachel's escort announced. Over the roar of the engine he yelled : "Race you, Charlie!" and while Rachel gathered through the blur of the weather a fragmentary impression of Charlie making Maurice comfortable in the battered Sunbeam the Rolls shot away at a pace that Maurice would have considered indecent.

III

Rachel, glad to be again in comfortable surroundings, leaned back with a bearskin rug over her knees and watched the speedometer needle run up to fifty. She had no sense of anxiety or discomfort. The hands on the ivory-coloured steering-wheel were thin, brown and flexible, very competent. A couple of inches of elegant shirt-cuff, secured by a link of plain gold, extended below the coat sleeve and did not obscure a neat wrist-watch. There was something inescapably well-bred about those hands and their furnishings. The rest of the young man was in keeping. Rachel had noticed the tall, rakish figure, the thin, ruddy face with eyes as blue as forget-me-nots and the small, clipped moustache. He was like a good-looking military subaltern, hard as nails, thin as a lath.

They were almost at Windermere before he spoke in a pleasant voice. " Well, it might have been worse, you know. I might have been carrying a corpse to the morgue instead of a living beauty to Blackpool. I hope your father isn't badly hurt."

" He's not my father."

" Oh—sorry. You both look—er—"

" We both look Jewish. We are Jewish. But we're not related in any way. His name is Maurice Bannerman and my name is Rachel Rosing."

" And my name is Julian."

" Is that enough—on cheques, for example ? "

" Cheques ! My God, Miss Rosing, I don't write cheques ; but if I did I should have to sign 'em Julian Heath."

Julian Heath gurgled the horn, swung round a great bus that was lumbering on ahead, and said : " I say, that's not *the* Maurice Bannerman we've laid out, is it ? "

" There's only one, so far as I know."

" Of course there's only one. By cripes, fancy laying out a Crœsus like that ! In the good old days we'd have gone through his pockets and been made for life ; but now if he prosecutes us for bodily damage we'll be ruined. We haven't got a penny to pay. We'll have the bums in."

The horn was one of those that sing a small tune, and at the thought of having the bums in, Julian Heath now induced this pleasing cadenza. " Never had the

81

bums in," he said. "That's one thing Charlie and I have never done, and we've done most things in our time."

The thought that appeared to afford Julian so much pleasure did not enchant Rachel : she could imagine nothing more loathsome. So she switched the conversation. "I hope we haven't hurt your car very much or taken you out of your way."

"We don't bother about the old bus," said Julian. "So long as she keeps four wheels to the ground, she'll do us. And we were going to Preston anyway. That's near enough to Blackpool. Do you ever read modern novels ? "

" No."

" Oh wise young judge ! How I do honour thee ! Hold tight a moment and watch me make this Bentley hop. It won't matter to Maurice Bannerman if I wreck a Rolls or two. . . . There ! Wasn't that pretty ? Just a coat of varnish to spare, I'd say. . . . Well, if you don't read modern novels, you haven't read *The Pillars of Hercules*. I'm not boasting about it. I'm just explaining myself. I live on advance royalties. Do you know what those are ? "

" I've no idea."

" Well, never mind. That's how I live. Charlie and I have been buzzing round Scotland on the advance royalties of *The Pillars of Hercules*. We decided to switch into the Lake District on our way home. Hence our ramming your stern. To-night we shall be at Preston. To-morrow, heading for London. My card."

He dexterously flicked a card from his waistcoat pocket and held it towards her. " If ever you are in London requiring the assistance of an experienced courier, bell-hop, page or souteneur. . . . What on earth am I talking about ? "

" I haven't the least idea."

" That is as well."

Julian Heath swung up his left wrist with an elegant gesture and consulted his watch. " Charlie's got as much chance with us as M'Ginty's moke would have with Pretty Polly. I can already smell the stout, sweat and oysters of Blackpool's concrete strand."

" You sound as though you don't like Blackpool."

" I don't. Do you ? "

" No. I can't stand the women. They run about and shout and get hot."

" And you prefer to walk, and speak in a level voice and keep cool ? "

" Yes."

" Well, if you'll excuse my saying so, Miss Rosing, it suits you. Stick to it."

" Thank you. I shall."

" Would you by any chance consider a level-voiced, cool conversation over dinner to-night ? I could stay and go on to Preston later."

She turned her head, almost for the first time since they had been in the car together, and considered him dispassionately. He was looking straight ahead, one hand lightly on the wheel, and a faint flush had deepened the ruddiness of his cheeks.

" Why ? " she asked.

It was disconcertingly point-blank, and Julian Heath, who was not unused to issuing invitations of the sort, stammered a little in his reply. " Well—er— you know, Miss Rosing—to speed the jocund hour, and so on, and so forth."

83

" Thank you. I don't think so. I shall have Mr. Bannerman to look after."

" You cut me to the heart. Let me break my leg and put in a first claim on your services."

" Right. If you'll do that—if not, perhaps we shall meet in London."

" That's a promise—you'll look me up ? "

" Yes."

" But when are you coming to London ? That's the catch, I suppose."

" I don't know," Rachel answered, looking thoughtfully ahead. " Soon, I hope. Yes, I believe soon."

Chapter Eight

I

IT was an absurd, a damnable affair, Maurice thought, when the surgeon was gone and he lay in bed with his leg swathed and bound like a section of a mummy. It was a million to one chance that a limb jerked against a hard piece of wood should be broken, but there it was and he must put up with it.

The manager of the hotel attended upon his wealthy client to ask if there was anything he could suggest for his comfort.

" Thank you," said Maurice, " there's one thing I should like you to see to at once. A lady named Miss Rosing is in the lounge. Perhaps you will bring her to see me now. And she will be staying in the hotel. Will you please see that she has everything she requires. Give her a good bedroom, with a bathroom."

II

This is better, Rachel thought. This is something like it. She stood for a moment at the window of her room, looking out upon the promenade. The rain of the afternoon was gone. The illuminations were in full flame. Hundreds of people pushed and pelted along through the pitiless incandescence. To Rachel,

85

they might have been restless souls in hell and she looking on from a temperate paradise. She sighed, more in thankfulness for her lot than in pity for theirs, drew the curtains, and turned towards the warmly-lit room.

There was a knock at the door. " Come in ! " Rachel called and her heart thrilled as she uttered the words. She had a room of her own, and people stood outside. Only when she said " Come in " could they enter. She seated herself in a chintz-covered easy-chair as a small maid staggered in with coal and sticks.

" The gentleman in No. 45 thought you might like a fire, miss."

That was good. A fire was welcome, but better still was the thought that Maurice had ordered it.

When the maid was gone Rachel hung in the wardrobe her few possessions. She took as much care as though she were dresser to a finicky musical comedy queen. The things had all been brought in a taxi from her lodgings. " Do things comfortably," Maurice had said. " To please me, don't worry about a shilling or two." Those were the sort of instructions she liked, and she acted upon them with full enjoyment. She walked back to her drab back-street room, packed everything she possessed into her one small trunk, and then casually told her landlady that she would not be coming back. " I believe I have paid you till the end of the week ? Good. A taxi will be calling for my things."

And now here the things were, and when they were put in place Rachel gave herself up for a while to the enjoyment of her surroundings. Never before had she had such a room as this for her own. The bedroom

86

of Sir George Faunt's house, in which she had once or twice arranged her hair, was even more luxurious ; but that, alas ! had never been anything but a place of passage. Now she was for awhile mistress of privacy and a moderate luxury.

The room was carpeted to the skirting. She strode up and down lithely and silently. She switched off the lights over the dressing-table, switched on the lights over the bed. She was as enchanted as if she had been a stage electrician achieving marvellous effects. She left all the lights on, and went into the bathroom to run her hand over the smoothness of the blue porcelain, and hard shine of the plated taps. She turned on the water said to be hot. It *was* hot. Good. She smelled sensuously the soap, and looked with approval at the row of her own lotions, powders and unguents laid out in pots and bottles on a glass shelf. All in order. Splendid !

It was nearly seven o'clock. Maurice would not be able to dine with her, but that was no reason why she should not dine herself. Perhaps she would ring up Maurice and say how sorry she was that he could not dine with her. He would like it, and it was as well to do what he would like. She took up the house telephone and called his room.

" Well, how are you ? "

" Not so bad. Not so bad. They're just going to bring me a bit of food."

" Thank you—Maurice—for making me so comfortable. I've got a lovely room."

" You deserve a lovely room."

She hesitated with careful calculation ; then breathed : " You darling ! "

87

" What d'you mean ? I look a pretty darling with a leg like a bolt of unbleached calico."

" I'm so sorry, Maurice—so sorry you can't have dinner with me and dance again afterwards."

" Don't be sorry. Enjoy yourself. I've told them to look after you. Good-bye."

She hung up the receiver. Excellent ! She felt she had achieved a good effect. She listened to the silence of the room. It was broken now and then by the rustle of the fire in the grate, a happy, comforting sound that seemed the very voice of privacy and security. To think that so near at hand were moiling crowds sweating on the Pleasure Beach, shouting, struggling, swinging violently in crazy boats, crashing in the artificial catastrophes of crazy diversions. To think that outside her very window was that crude blare of light, like a power station in a strait-jacket, screaming at the top of its voice. And here silence, and such light only as served to frame the picture of discreet luxury.

She locked the door of her room and went again to the bathroom. Even the sound of her heels clicking on the large black and white tiles of the floor seemed intrusive. She turned the taps, went back to the bedroom for her slippers and dressing-gown, and a few minutes later slipped under the warm water. She would be dining alone, but she saw no reason why she should not dine in comfort. It had been a strange, exciting day. She thankfully allowed her body to relax. A delightful languor came over her, and leaning back her head, she lifted her dark, slanted eyes to the scented clouds that rose to the ceiling. As though they clothed Sinai, she prayed with fervour : " Let it last ! Oh, God ! Let it last ! "

But even as the words formed themselves in her mind, she smiled at their futility, knowing that what she could not do for herself would not be done.

III

She turned on all the lights to survey herself in the long glass. Yes ; that was all right. She wore the dress she had worn when she dined with Maurice, and the crimson flower above her left ear. Her blue-black hair was taut about her head, drawn down from a central parting, and fastened in a tight knot on her neck. She gave herself a smile, was pleased at the gleam of small white teeth between the parted red of her lips. " You look better than ever," she said to herself. Dangling a wisp of handkerchief from her fingers, she descended the stairs, holding herself as queens would like to hold themselves.

Julian Heath started up from a chair in the lounge through which she passed.

" My God ! " he said. " You're superb ! What an entrance ! "

His attitude laid himself at her feet. She was surprised, and was not herself aware of the daunting dignity with which she came to a stand and looked down at him. " I didn't expect you," she said.

" If you'll excuse my saying it," Julian faltered, " I didn't expect you—not the marvellous you I see before me."

She let the flattery go. " Well, what are we to do about it ? "

Julian tugged his tie uneasily. " I'd feel better," he said, " if I could meet you on equal ground——"

" Could you ? " she demanded with arrogance.

" By cripes, Miss Rosing," he admitted frankly.
" I don't believe I could. But what I meant was if I
had some jolly old glad rags on. I'm a pretty picture
in tails."

She did not help him out. He looked downcast,
and went on : " You see, I knew Mr. Bannerman
wouldn't be able to dine with you, so I hung on on the
chance. Charlie Roebuck went on to Preston by train
and left the old bus with me. He's a sport. He
understands."

" I don't."

She liked him. She liked the clean cut of him, his
spick-and-spanness, and the fresh way the blood went
rushing to his cheeks. But her wits were working hard,
telling her to look out and watch her step. Maurice
wouldn't like this. He would get to know somehow
or other ; and, anyway, Julian Heath didn't look the
sort of man who would allow his first dinner engagement to be his last. He had been quite frank about
his poverty : living on advance royalties, whatever
that meant. It wouldn't do, whatever way you looked
at it. This world was a weary land—didn't she know
it !—and the present shadow of a great rock was
Maurice Bannerman—Maurice upstairs with a leg like
a bolt of unbleached calico.

So she continued to look coldly on Julian Heath,
and said : " It was understood, wasn't it, that we
could not dine together ? "

" Oh, yes—but you know how it is. Hope springs
eternal and so forth."

She merely shook her head ; then unbending a little
towards his distress, said : " It was most kind of you

to be so helpful this afternoon, but, if you don't mind, I must dine alone. You don't understand."

Julian took up his hat, which he had thrown into a chair. " I think I do," he said.

I wonder ? thought Rachel. He doesn't look a fool.

" Well, so long," Julian said. " Remember that date in London. After seeing you to-night, I shall look forward to it more than ever."

She held out her hand. " Good-bye."

" This is for you," he said. He put a book down on the table beside him, raised his hand in a military salute, and departed.

Rachel went on slowly towards the dining-room, carrying the book, *The Pillars of Hercules*. Maurice's instructions had been explicit. The head waiter himself was already at attention behind her chair. He told her what wine Maurice thought she should drink, what she should eat. She left it all in those expert hands, and idly turned to the dust-cover of the book. " The author," she read, " the younger son of Lord Upavon . . ."

She put the book down thoughtfully, troubled by a doubt. Then she remembered that London was to come. Yes ; she was sure of it. How much easier to leap off upon London from the security that Maurice could give ! No ; there was nothing to worry about. On the whole, it was as well that she had acted like that.

She watched the wine dance and sparkle as a white-gloved hand tilted the bottle.

Chapter Nine

1

"WHO is Lord Upavon?" Rachel asked. For a moment Maurice did not answer. He went on reading the letter—one of a batch that Mike Hartigan had sent on from Portman Square. He was arrogantly attired. A dressing-gown of scarlet silk with a broad black-tasselled sash was over pyjamas whose fabric could only be called cloth of gold. One of his legs terminated in a scarlet slipper. The other was still a bolt of unbleached calico. A couch was drawn up before the fire in the sitting-room of his suite and he reclined upon it, tossing most of the letters to the flames after he had read them. At last he took off his horn-rimmed spectacles and looked at Rachel. "Upavon? Oh, no one in particular. A director of this and that. I've sat on boards with him. A nice old man, but rather a fool. Call him just a name that helps a prospectus to look respectable. Why?"

She handed him the copy of *The Pillars of Hercules*, and pointed to the dust jacket. "This is by one of the young men who ran us down."

Maurice put his spectacles back upon his nose. "H'm. Read it?"

"Yes."

"Any good?"

"I don't know. It didn't interest me much."

"Leave it with me, will you? I'd like to look at it. Now, what about answering these letters?"

He began to dictate, and Rachel, sitting at a little table, to write in a large elaborate hand. The day after the accident, Maurice had wanted to send to London for a secretary, a typewriter, goodness knows what.

"You could hire all that on the spot—if you wanted it," Rachel pointed out reasonably. "But do you? Can't I do all that's necessary?"

"I've no doubt you can," said Maurice; "but why should you?"

"Because it will be something for me to do," Rachel answered. "I understood, when you arranged for me to stay here, that that was the idea : that I should be on the spot to do what I could for you."

Just as well, she thought, to make him face the question, make him decide in his own mind what *was* the idea. They would have to come to it sooner or later. Maurice himself saw that clearly enough, and, rather to shelve the problem than to solve it, he accepted this convention that Miss Rosing was indispensable—as a secretary.

II

So a fortnight passed. Winter arrived with a growl. Visitors hastened out of Blackpool. Even the illuminations ceased to afford their garish titillation. Wind came, and rain, and on the few occasions when Rachel ventured out of doors she shuddered in a harsh world of wet, shining streets, concrete, and grey tattered skies. The sea was at its spectacular trick of pounding on the

93

promenade, spouting up into white hanging veils that the wind caught and sent hissing inshore. It made grand photographs in the newspapers, but Rachel hated it. She began to hate everything to do with Blackpool. There were no longer even sweating hoydens to excite her pity. She wished Maurice would hurry up and get well ; and then, sitting alone at a table in an otherwise empty café, taking a mid-morning cup of coffee, she reproved her own impulsiveness. Hurry up, indeed ! No, that was not how things got done. Patience and perseverance and no stone unturned : that was the way. Even this damnable Blackpool must not depress her or flurry her. She made up her face, paid her bill, pulled on a gleaming white waterproof, and went back to her long task of watching and waiting.

And the next day the weather relented. The wind dropped, the sky became blue and silky. Rachel, in a cheerful mood, went up after breakfast to Maurice's room with his newspapers and letters.

" Now," he cried, " you must take a holiday. Just look at that sky ! I won't have you indoors to-day. Where will you go to ? You must get right away."

She hesitated, and Maurice added : " I shall order a car for you—to take you right away into the country."

" Thank you, Maurice," she said. " I don't want to go into the country. I know what I'll do. I'll go to Manchester."

" My God ! " he cried. " What is the idea of that ? Manchester ! "

" Well, I want to go, anyway. You're sure you can spare me ? "

94

" I must spare you. I've been a regular slave-driver. Go along then. Off with you to your Manchester."

It was a passionate wish to tread city streets again that was stirring in Rachel's heart. She was prepared to wait and wait in Blackpool or anywhere else, so long as she thought the waiting worth the candle ; but now that a holiday was offered her she turned to shops and pavements and the moving bustle of affairs as instinctively as an exile turns his heart homewards.

The glory of the day meant nothing to her. She spent it in her own fashion. She loitered through the great stores ; in and out of lifts, up and down stairs, all over Lewis's, all over Kendal Milne's, round and round in the warm scented caverns of Boot's. She made herself thoroughly tired, thoroughly happy, bought a few negligible odds and ends, and at half-past four went into Parker's in St. Ann Square to take tea.

It was warm and cosy, the band was playing, and life was pretty prosperous, fairly safe again. In a mirror she caught a glimpse of her own face beneath a tight-fitting round hat of astrakhan. Yes, she thought, that girl looks all right. Nothing here to touch her. She took the shining metal lid off her muffins and ate with contentment.

The night was fully come when she went out into St. Ann Square again. The arc lamps were flickering over the rush of people escaped from work. Market Street was seething with its thousands. The trams thudded by with a clamour of bells, and the cross-roads at the Royal Exchange were a dithering maelstrom of motor-cars and trams, cyclists, pedestrians, and news-paper carts pulled at great speed by spanking little ponies. A horn sounded somewhere behind her, and

95

at that signal out they came, with a jingle of harness and a rattle of wheels, scattering this way and that, beautiful and unexpected as a song in prison.

Rachel thought how often she had stood out there on the mid-road island, fighting her way on to a tram bound for Cheetham Hill—bound along the darkest and dreariest of all the ways that centred here at the city's heart. Never again !

And yet, why not ? Why not once more ? She would miss the train she had intended to catch, but there was another. Probably, she thought, I shall never see Cheetham Hill again if I don't see it to-night. Why see it at all ? She did not know what the reason was. It was because she held it in deepest detestation ; because, feeling happy and secure, she wanted to exult like Miriam in the moment of victory.

She clambered to a top deck. The tram was full ; the windows were all shut. Every seat was occupied. In almost every mouth was a pipe or cigarette. The atmosphere was stinking and the windows were opaque with the condensed breath of the travellers. The conductor edged his way through the narrow gangway, treading the garbage of a day's smoking. Everybody seemed all elbows ; there was no room to move, to breathe. To Rachel, after even so short an absence, it seemed odious and brutal. These trams were galleys, bringing slaves to and from their chains.

She could not see through the windows. The lights they passed were dull red eyes that loomed up and receded. Then, when they swung left towards the railway bridge, the sharer of Rachel's seat swabbed the window with a newspaper that sponged up grease and soot. He threw it down and trampled it underfoot.

Rachel peered out across his shoulder and even as the window filmed over again saw the deep valley filled with railway lines, blurred with cloudy jets of steam, pricked with points of red and green light, and the savage glare of a locomotive's open fire. Then they were over the bridge, and the long steep climb of Cheetham Hill began. The tram ground upon its rails, swayed itself onward and upward with sickening lurches. Rachel could stand no more. She made her way precariously down the rocking stairs and alighted at the next stop.

She stood on the corner of Derby Street and took in deep breaths of the damp, raw air. She felt that her clothes would stink for ever. Fastidiously she brushed herself, as though her fingers could dissipate the clinging malodours of that slave galleon. The tram was roaring out of sight, not unimpressive in the distance, " but, my God," she said to herself, " how did you stand that sort of thing day after day for so long ? "

And this Cheetham Hill too, this district that was all about her, this most famous ghetto, how had she ever brought some cleanliness and decency out of it ? She thought of a saying of Nick Faunt, a profane artist she had known. " We've bred some bloody good artists in Manchester, and can you wonder ? I'll bet the pictures of heaven that get painted in hell are better than heaven itself."

Perhaps that was it. It was all an escape, and she had found her method. She went slowly on up the hill. The sky was full of proud stars, but the ground about her crept with too humble an acceptance of its desolate destiny. From the central road with its pinchbeck shops, garnished with scraps of dirty meat or wretched vegetables or soiled depressed-looking clothing, with its grim grey synagogues and houses into whose fabric acid soot had been eating for generations, there ran off street after street, mean, shoddy and decrepit, disreputable ribs of that deplorable spine. In all those streets little houses huddled together, with their shoulders hunched and their heads bent, their eyes veiled save for a slit of grudging light here and there.

Still she walked on, and old men with grey stringy beards went shuffling by her, their eyes on the ground ; and children with the large liquid eyes of gazelles were revealed by the sudden light of a lamp, and young women, cheap and flashy, and old women waddling with the burden of their years.

Rachel knew it, every nook and corner of it ; and she knew that were it daylight instead of dark, there still would be no amelioration in sight ; no tree or shrub or flower, no graceful form of a building, no sudden sight of a bough against the sky ; nothing to catch away the eye from the stony hideousness that sprawled upon the hillside for mile after maddening mile.

She turned to the left when she came to the street where for so long she had lived. It stretched before her in all its dreadful blank inanity. Save for the street lamps that burned here and there, the darkness was almost without relief. Behind a cheap curtain from time to time she saw a dim light burning. For the most part, she knew, the people lived in their kitchens at the back. She thought of the kitchen in which she herself had made shift to live. She walked the entire length of the street with the thought of it in her heart like the memory of a foul disease from which she had incredibly escaped. Then she walked back again and came to a halt outside the familiar door. She looked at it, fascinated, allowing her hatred to consume her.

Not a footstep had fallen in the street since she entered it. It might have been a graveyard, and she the only ghost walking. She gave a last look up and down, and skywards to the indifferent heaven. And, as if embracing God and man for her audience, she cursed the place with black curses. " No more," she swore to herself. " I'll lie and deceive and fornicate first. Anything's fair that beats this. Anything." Then she walked away from Cheetham Hill forever.

She would have taken a taxi-cab to the station, but only by accident do you find a taxi-cab in the Cheetham Hill Road. She knew that the trams going towards town would not have many passengers at that time, so she boarded one and remained in the comparatively clean air of the lower deck. She thought of Maurice, and a fiercer barb than ever began to goad her mind, urging her to use him. It was as though all that she was fleeing from were stretching hands after her, and a new urgency for security came driving to her aid. Gradually, she calmed herself. Excitement would not do. She had told Cheetham Hill what she thought of it ; now it was a question of practical politics. And, as she alighted from the tram, practical politics presented themselves in the shape of great yellow mop-headed chrysanthemums making a glory of a hawker's basket.

Maurice might like some in his room. She had never thought to put flowers in his room. Whether he liked them or not, he might like to think of her having bought them for him. So she took a great armful and made her way to a first-class carriage on the train.

As she laid the flowers on the rack she noticed her face in the mirror beneath it. "My God!" she exclaimed fervently. And as soon as the train started, having the compartment to herself, she pulled up both windows to make a comfortable fug, took off her hat, and gave her face the attention it called for. She took a long time over it. After all, she thought, there was nothing else to do. Could she be better occupied, seeing that she would be meeting Maurice so soon? The job satisfied her. She looked at herself in the mirror from this angle and that. All marks of emotion had been carefully erased. "Yes," she said, "you'll do."

Then she kissed the chrysanthemums. "Be kind to me," she said. "Make him like me more and more."

III

It was an unsatisfactory day for Maurice. Everything went wrong. He tried first of all to get on with his novel. His leg was comfortable enough ; there was nothing to distract him. This was the first time he had seriously sat down to the job since that night in Manchester. And the result was the same. By lunch-time he had flung his writing-pad across the room.

Then he took up Julian Heath's novel. It was based on the ancient belief concerning beautiful undiscovered things that lay beyond the Pillars of Hercules, and it tried to present a modern mind living always on the brink of adventure just outside the confines of common experience. Maurice tired of it and threw it after his writing-pad. He thought the world in which Julian Heath's hero lived was a world of bunk and bluff. Men tried to escape into that world not because the common world was too small for them, but because it was too big. It frightened them. He could not understand how a simple-minded young motoring animal like Julian Heath—so he had summed Julian up—could take such things seriously. But did he? No, Maurice decided. He didn't. That was why the book was a ghastly wash-out. The man didn't believe in his own bunk. It was just young and pretentious. At any rate, the boy could write. He would grow out of this. He would probably do something good. He would be worth knowing.

That was the sort of thing, Maurice reflected, that he could do for Rachel Rosing. If people were worth knowing, he could help her to know them. And then it occurred to him that she knew Julian Heath already. After all, it was she who had given him the book. How did she get hold of it? He had weighed her up well enough to know that she was not likely to buy books. And, so far as he knew, the only time she had spent with Julian Heath was the time necessary to get from that smash in the Lakes to Blackpool. He did not think it likely that even very young authors carried copies of their books in their cars in order that they might present them to chance acquaintances. Why, damn it all, he exclaimed, the man wasn't in his own car. He drove the Rolls. Then he must have seen Rachel since that occasion, and she had said nothing about it.

If Maurice had had two legs to stand on, he would by now have been stamping about the room. As it was, his mind seethed with senseless speculations. He was missing Rachel, missing her badly. This was the first day since the accident that he had been left alone, and it showed him how much her unobtrusive presence had come to mean to him. He was suffering too, from unaccustomed idleness. He had abandoned a full, adventurous career and was chafing at his difficulty in settling to a new one. Altogether, he was in a devil of a state, and it all boiled down to a nagging wish that Rachel might soon be back.

He rang for a time-table and looked up the trains from Manchester. He reckoned she would take the first one after tea-time. That meant that she should be here at any minute. " When Miss Rosing comes in ask her if she would kindly see me," he ordered ; and then he decided that he might as well lean back and calm himself. He did not wish to appear a perfect dithering fool when she came.

He was awakened by a maid asking if he would care to order some dinner. He looked with an exclamation at his watch. " Isn't Miss Rosing in ? "

" I'll inquire, sir."

Miss Rosing was not in. He took up the time-table again. The last train to arrive had got in twenty minutes ago ; she could not have been on that. The next was not due for nearly an hour.

" No," he snapped, " I don't want any dinner. Tell them to send a car to the station to meet Miss Rosing on the next train from Manchester, and if she's not on that, send a car to meet every train till she comes."

" Yes, sir."

" And please let me have that book."

The maid brought *The Pillars of Hercules* from the

corner. Maurice scanned it to see if there were any inscription which he had overlooked. No, nothing. But he continued to scowl. He was not good at deceiving himself. He lived in a real world. He knew that he was approaching the forties, that he was getting fat, that there were plenty who would call him a damned ugly Jew. And then there was that title : "The younger son of Lord Upavon." You never knew what fluff girls would fall for.

"My God—titles ! " he groaned. " Couldn't I have bought one with a week's pocket money ! "

But Maurice had a lot to learn about Rachel Rosing. She would have turned down the throne of Sheba if there were not enough apes, ivories and peacocks attached to it.

She was in a calm and conquering state of mind when the train reached Blackpool. The hotel chauffeur saluted. " Mr. Bannerman is all worked up, miss. Shoutin' to see you."

She did not answer, but dipped into the car, carrying her chrysanthemums like a gold-headed sceptre. She had not calculated on her truancy having this effect. What effect ? Oh, well, she hoped it was that effect, anyway. The hotel manager reinforced the chauffeur's urgency. " Mr. Bannerman is *very* anxious to see you, Miss Rosing. *Very* anxious."

" Thank you," Rachel said, and smiled to herself. But she did not rush straight to Maurice's room. She went to her own, took off her hat and brushed her hair, examining her image with the dispassionate appraisal of a connoisseur.

" Yes," she said, " that's all right." And then she took up her chrysanthemums as briskly as though they

103

were an agenda that she must take to a committee meeting. But once she was in the corridor her body rippled like water ; her arms cradled the flowers ; her eyes were as starry as though they had been permitted to look upon the last enchantments. She knocked, then flowed into Maurice's room without waiting for him to reply.

" Rachel ! " he cried. " You are so late ! I have been anxious—worrying."

She stood a little away from him, holding the flowers and smiling.

" It's been a lovely day," she said ; " but this is the best thing in it—to know that you've missed me. You see "—holding out the flowers—" I thought of you too. Let me find a vase for them."

" No, no. Put them down and come here," Maurice said. " I've been imagining you under buses and in all sorts of terrible troubles."

She stood near his chair, and he took her hand and stroked its long delicate beauty.

" And all the time "—she smiled—" I was visiting Cheetham Hill."

" Cheetham Hill ! My God ! Why Cheetham Hill ? What have you to do with Cheetham Hill ? "

" I was saying good-bye. I had a feeling I would never see it again."

He pulled gently on her wrist—till she sank to her knees alongside his chair. Then he put an arm round her and drew her close to him. " You needn't, Rachel," he said. " You needn't see it again. You needn't see anything harsh and ugly any more. I should love to make life beautiful for you as you are yourself. What d'you say—eh ? "

He held her so close that he could see each eyelash lying against the smooth amber of her cheek, and the dull shine on the damson colour of her lowered lids. Her eyes themselves he could not see. She kept them hidden, lest her exultation should shine through too clearly.

" Well ? " he said, and his embrace tightened.

She did not answer, but with her eyes closed and a great sigh surging from her lips she lifted her face towards his. He switched off the table-lamp, so that there was no light in the room save firelight. It gave to the face that floated below his a strange hieratic beauty, that drew his lips downward as though by enchantment.

Chapter Ten

1

BY the time Maurice was able to get about with the help of a couple of sticks, the Rolls-Royce had been re-conditioned and looked as good as new. " It'll be a long time before I trust myself to drive again," Maurice said.

Looking like a huge crippled bear, he came out of the hotel lift, hobbled slowly across the lounge, with Rachel in attendance, and, outside, took a deep breath. " Good ! That's fine ! " he said, and raised his eyes to the grey-clad chauffeur whose hand had gone in smart military fashion to his cap.

" Good-morning," he said. " You're the feller Mr. Hartigan engaged, are you ? "

" Yes, sir. I was told to report here this morning."

" I hope you're a better driver than I am."

" Never had an accident, sir."

" How long have you been driving ? "

" Since before the war, sir. And during the war I drove a staff car in France."

" H'm. You've been lucky. What's your name ? "

" Oxtoby, sir."

" What ! " Maurice cried sharply.

" Oxtoby." The patient Oxtoby stood with a hand on the handle of the open door, a rug over the other arm.

Maurice recovered from an obvious surprise. He eyed the man closely. " Rather an unusual name," he said.

" It is rather, sir."

"Very well. Take it easy. No speeding. If you jolt this leg, you're fired. Just an hour's quiet run about the country."

Rachel got into the car. With her help from within, and Oxtoby's help from without, Maurice was at last embarked. He leaned back among the deep springy cushions and stretched his leg out before him with a grunt. Oxtoby leapt to his place, and Maurice waited, strung to attention. With hardly a tremor, they were off. " Like velvet," said Maurice. " He'll do." And dismissing Oxtoby from his mind he turned to Rachel. "Well, my dear," he said, patting her hand. " I congratulate you. You look well. You look fine."

Rachel did not need to be told that. She knew it. The close-fitting short jacket of leopard skin, the nigger-brown skirt, the round hat of brown astrakhan : her mirror had already told her all she needed to know about them. She had been for a day to Southport, and was enchanted to find these attractive clothes there. She had money in her pocket. Maurice had said : " This is weeks and weeks now I keep you hanging about here waiting on me. I must pay you your wages." He signed a generous cheque.

Rachel protested, faintly alarmed. She did not want wages. She did not want Maurice to put their relationship on a business footing. Yet she dared not say so. She did not wish him to see what relationship she desired. The desire must be on his part. So she pocketed the money with a smile.

"Yes," said Maurice, "that little hat, it is altogether Russian, and Russian effects go well with you. You would have been a great success at the old Russian court."

Rachel permitted herself a sly smile. "In what capacity?" she asked. "I have heard the Grand Dukes were gallant." And then, with that disconcerting abruptness which she sometimes used, she asked: "Why were you so taken aback when the man said his name was Oxtoby?"

For a moment Maurice did not answer. With his blue, jutting jaw cupped in his hairy hand, he stared straight ahead. At last he said: "Rachel, I have not been fair with you."

They were passing through the flat lands behind Blackpool. A ruined windmill stood like a great up-turned flower-pot against the sad grey of the sky. Rachel kept her eyes fixed upon it, although it did not interest her in the least. She did not look at Maurice, though what he looked like interested her tremendously. There was something in his voice that made her heart give a thump against her ribs. "Now it's coming," she thought, every nerve tense to deal with what might follow. In a level, unexcited voice she answered: "How do you mean, Maurice—not fair? I think you've been splendid. Anyway, I don't understand. I say you seem surprised to hear that this man's name is Oxtoby, and you answer that you haven't been fair."

"Rachel," Maurice said in a voice so strained that she hardly recognised it. "You have been expecting me to ask you to be my wife, haven't you?"

Then she looked at him—a long, lingering look that made him put an arm round her and draw her closer

to him. " Maurice ! " she said. "No—I never dreamed
—I would have done anything for you, I liked you so
much. I would have been your mistress," she whispered
into the shoulder of his shaggy coat. " But your wife—
I never thought you would ask me such a thing."

She disengaged herself timidly from his embrace, and
sat back in the corner of the seat. Maurice's fingers
drummed impatiently on his knee. " I have told you
so little about myself," he said. " You know I was in
America. You know my name was once Fahnemann.
You do not know that when I was in America I
married a girl named Oxtoby."

Rachel's fingers laced themselves together and
gripped hard to prevent her hands from trembling.
" She is alive ? " she whispered.

" So far as I know—yes."

They were both silent for a long time, looking at the
rigid back of Oxtoby, a grey statue, presiding over the
car's leisurely progress through the grey funereal landscape. They came to a little rise of land where the
road took a left-handed turn, and far away Rachel
could see the flat pewter smudge of the sea.

" Was she a nice girl ? " she asked quietly.

" Nice ! Hell ! She was a waitress in a third-rate
restaurant. I told you my father died almost as soon
as I got out there. I was lonely and wretched, and
that's how it was. She got me like that "—he opened
his big hand and closed it again—" and squeezed me
like that." His fist contracted till his knuckle joints
stood out in four livid knobs.

" She didn't—help you ? "

" Help me ! Every time I went home she'd got
another thing on hire purchase. A vacuum cleaner, a

refrigerator, a gramophone. And I was getting fifteen dollars a week! I walked out one day and never walked back. It lasted exactly six months. The moment I left her my luck turned."

He fell silent again, pondering the strange tricks of time, thinking of the uncouth young Jew with his dreams of fortune, his agony in a stale, cheap New York apartment as he saw every dollar, every cent, slipping through a fool's fingers. And then he thought of Maurice Bannerman, and the house in Portman Square, his collection of pictures by the French Impressionists, his estate near Chichester, his cars, his half a million. And the two men, strangers in all else, were still joined together by that stupid little bitch Lucy Oxtoby.

" You see," he said, these thoughts taking voice, " if I married you, for all I know I should be committing bigamy."

Still Rachel did not speak. Her thoughts were in a tumult, charging this way and that, defying her resolute effort to bring them to order. Only one of them was constant in the mad pack. It recurred again and again, and she hated herself because she could not chase it out. But she could not, and slowly it took possession of all her mind and she allowed it to stay. " If he *does* marry me," she thought, " and that girl's alive and I can find her, I've got him—got him like that."

And, not knowing what it meant, Maurice saw her small beautiful hand clench and clutch as his had done when he thought of the hold that Lucy Oxtoby had gained upon him.

They did not mention the matter again during that
drive. That night, for the first time since his accident,
Maurice came down to dinner. There was by now,
the season being well advanced into winter, hardly
another visitor in the hotel. The dining-room was
almost deserted, and when their meal was ended and
coffee had been brought Maurice lit a cigar and began
to talk with no fear of being overheard.

"That woman," he said suddenly and without
preamble, "doesn't know that I've left New York.
She doesn't know that I've changed my name. I've
changed my face too. Look at that. I found it this
afternoon among some papers. It was taken in New
York the week after I arrived. It was to send home to
my mother. We didn't know she was already dead."

Rachel crushed out her cigarette and took the
photograph. She looked from it to Maurice, leaning
back in a chair, his leg propped up on another, a stick
in one hand. She smiled. "You've improved."

"Yes," he agreed simply. "No one would know
me—do you think?"

The picture showed a fat, ungainly youth, with oily,
curly hair. There was something pathetic in the cheap,
gauche, uncouth figure. The clothes were poorly cut
and badly worn, the trousers baggy, the shoes like
sabots. The face was at once distrustful and defiant.
Rachel put the photograph down beside her plate,
and looked again at the massive face, the assured and
easy bearing, the admirable clothes of the man opposite
her. "No, Maurice," she said. "If this was the

young man Miss Oxtoby married, then I'm sure she could walk into this room to-night and not know you."

Maurice held a glass of Cointreau against the light. He sniffed the colourless liquid, sipped it gently, and said : " What sort of marriage was that ? None at all. What sense would there be now in going to all the trouble of finding out whether that woman is alive or dead ? And if she is alive, what sense is there in dragging up things that not a soul knows about ? That is all that would happen if I divorced her or asked her to divorce me. What sense is there in it ? None at all."

He leaned across the table and placed a hand upon Rachel's. " My dear, there is no risk in this. Shall we get married ? "

For a moment she did not answer. She did what she had done that night she dined with Mike Hartigan. She took a flower from the vase, and with cold-blooded abstraction shredded it to pieces, looking past Maurice as though he were not there.

" My darling," he said, perturbed by her silence, " I'm asking a lot——"

" You are offering a lot," she answered. He must not think that she was rushing blindly into his arms. " You are offering me things that I have dreamed of all my life . . ."

" I am offering you my love, Rachel. Did you ever dream of being loved ? "

" No, Maurice. I've never dreamed of anything except being safe and rich." She thought of the misery of that house in Cheetham Hill outside which she had recently stood and cursed. She thought of her desperate efforts in the little Manchester dress shop, with the bank overdraft that was always about to be reduced, but never was. All her life had been lived on a thin edge with the swift irrevocable slide into poverty yawning beneath her feet. " My God, Maurice ! " she suddenly exclaimed in a voice of low, passionate honesty. " If you knew the life I've lived ! If you knew how I've loathed and hated it all ! Love ! I don't know," she said wearily, " whether I shall ever love anybody, but I tell you this, I shall worship any one who takes me out of that pit and makes me safe. Do you think that's horrible ? D'you think it's mean and cowardly to want to be safe ? If so, you'd better not have anything to do with me, because at the moment I think it's the only thing that makes life worth while."

She looked at him defiantly and saw that he was deeply moved. " My dear one," he said. " I know, I know. You have suffered. I am not a child. I understand these things." He looked at her compassionately for a while, and then said : " I think I could make you like me a great deal, Rachel."

" I do, I do," she protested. " I like you immensely, Maurice ; but this love—I don't know."

" You will marry me ? "

" Yes."

He leaned across and squeezed her hand tight. " You make me very proud."

He called a waiter who helped him to his feet. With a stick in each hand, he hobbled towards the lift. " Take a little walk before you turn in," he said to Rachel. " You look tired."

She accompanied him to his room and kissed him, then rushed away.

She walked out under a sky that was thickly sown with stars. She went from the promenade on to the hard firm sand. Down there it was dark, and she strode along soundlessly as a ghost. She came to a great tangle of iron pillars and trellis work supporting a pier, and in the deeper darkness of that retreat, where the air was damp and salty with the hanging flags of seaweed, she could see the dim forms of men and women huddled together, some standing, some prone on the sand.

She shied like a nervous filly, swerved to the right, and walked out to where the sea lapped with hardly a ripple upon the shore. This love ! God, what was it ! A tangle of arms and legs, a straining of breasts and bellies on the earth in the dark !

" Let 'em keep it. Let 'em keep it ! " she cried to herself. " It's not *that* that I want."

She stood there for a moment, the toe of her shoe digging delicately into the sand, looking blindly out into the unplumbed prospect of the sea and the darkness. Then she turned and walked sharply up the beach towards the lights twinkling with the promise of comfort and warmth and security.

Chapter Eleven

I

ABOUT a fortnight later the cream-coloured Rolls-Royce with the pale green mudguards stood under the gloomy shadow of All Saints Church in Manchester. The young ragamuffins of Hulme, the young students entering the art school whose ugliness was so unmitigated that art's first business was to destroy it, looked with a like respect at the sumptuous vehicle.

Impassive as a Roman supreme among barbarians, Oxtoby sat at the ivory wheel, his grey overcoat displaying its rows of silver buttons, his gauntlets, cap and leggings impeccable. His pink face gazed straight ahead, disregarding the low, leaden clouds, the foul soot-poisoned shrubs that desecrated the churchyard, the uproar of Oxford Street that faced him, and the squalor of Hulme that lay behind him. All these things had nothing to do with him. His but to wait until Maurice and Rachel came out of the registry office. " Though why the hell he wants to get married here," Oxtoby pondered, " beats me. And him rolling in it. If it was me . . ."

And if it had been Oxtoby no doubt it would have been a different matter, with peals of bells and roses round the door.

But there it was. The only concession they made to sentimentality was to be married in Manchester. " I don't care where it is," Rachel answered frankly when Maurice asked her about it. So Maurice decided on the All Saints registry office. "After all," he said, "we were both born in Manchester, so let's be married there."

"As you wish," Rachel said. "I hope we don't die there."

And now there they were, coming out of the registry office. Oxtoby was out of the car in a flash, standing deferentially at the open door. He had the ability to look like wood, to efface his personality, as though begging his employer to act just as though he did not exist. But all the same, his eyes missed little. He saw very clearly this amazingly contrasted pair. There was Maurice, still halting, though he could now get along with one stick, a man of burly body and powerful face—"a reg'lar Mussolini," Oxtoby thought—buttoned up in a long black overcoat with an astrakhan collar, and with a soft black felt hat upon his head. He had a gardenia at his buttonhole and wore gloves of dove suède. Rachel was still wearing her leopard skin coat and nigger-brown skirt and round hat of astrakhan. She looked frail beside her burly companion, and Oxtoby commented to himself that Maurice was twenty years older than his wife, if a day. They stood for a moment surveying the grim scene that was so familiar to them both. Maurice's eyes were brown and liquid, Rachel's as black as night and hard as steel.

Then they came down towards the car. Rachel got in, and Maurice bent his head to follow. Oxtoby relaxed his wooden face, and said : "May I wish you both the best of luck, sir ? "

Maurice stood upright again and smiled at the man.

116

"That's very nice of you, Oxtoby," he said. "Thank you." He gave the man his hand. Then Oxtoby helped Maurice in, adjusted the great bearskin rug, and leapt to the wheel. He felt cheered, more human. He had liked Maurice's face when he smiled. "A decent old cove, shouldn't wonder," he reflected. "But her——?"

For Rachel had not said "Thank you, Oxtoby." She had not smiled. She sat there, staring straight ahead, beautiful, cold, implacable. It was only when Maurice said : "Oxtoby wishes us luck, my dear," that she turned her head with a start, and said :

"Oh, thank you, thank you ! "

II

Oxtoby was in no position to understand the tumult that was in her heart. And now she blamed herself because Maurice had had to remind her of a necessary courtesy. But he understood her mood and permitted her to be quiet. She had expected to feel nothing but a sense of liberation and release, nothing but gladness at the thought that this visit to Manchester would probably be the last she would ever make. But as Oxtoby sounded the horn, swung the car into Oxford Street, and headed south, she discovered that to say good-bye even to something you hate has a bitter finality that is not easy to bear.

Almost before she had had time to settle in her seat the car's majestic velvet progress was rushing her past the church of the Holy Name. She craned her neck to look down that street where mad Nick Faunt had lived, he who had brought her life so near to disaster ;

and a moment later they were sliding past the level green of Platt Fields, with the house of Nick's father, Sir George Faunt, upon their left. She caught a glimpse of a " To Let " board at the front gate, and wondered how far her own brief commerce with Sir George had been the reason for the disarrangement of life which the board betokened.

It was all dead and done with, dead as the child Nick Faunt had given her, the child that had never been born. There were so many things that Maurice did not know about, must not know about ; and she ought to be feeling a great uplifting of spirits because all these things were being put behind her. But the gnawing tug of use and custom was persistent, refusing an easy anodyne.

They came to the White Lion Hotel where the road forks, and she was glad when they did not follow the fork's right arm. That would have led near to the lodgings she had occupied in those summer days of her great and disastrous adventure. She didn't want to see that district any more. A white sign-post pointing down the road's other branch said : " Cheadle and the South."

The South ! The South ! Then, at that first concrete pointer to their destination, she felt her melancholy begin to fall away. The country began to open up into flat, uninspiring fields. The car swept across the humped back of the Mersey's stone bridge, and Maurice said : " You know, the Mersey is Manchester's boundary hereabouts."

So they were out of it ! She put Manchester resolutely from her mind. " Maurice," she said, " I've never seen Portman Square. Tell me something about it."

This was it. She stood at the window and looked out. The sky was full of a violet pulsation of light. In the big garden round which the houses were built tall plane trees stood up in winter nudity. The street lamps poured their light upon the blotched, peeling trunks. There was incessant movement in the square. Cars and taxi-cabs slid along the black, planished surface of the road, and beyond the square itself she could hear the throbbing undertone of the town. But all the noise seemed curiously muted. There was a deep peacefulness about her.

Maurice's house was on that side of the square which ran parallel with Baker Street. Straight before her, through the tangled branches of the trees in the garden, Rachel could see the bright lights of shops ; on either hand, running at right angles down towards those lights, were houses like her own.

With her left hand stretched above her head, holding back the tall curtains of heavy crimson velvet, she rested her forehead on the cold glass and allowed it all to flow over her in a rich, satisfying tide ; the trees with their stark branches and little dangling rounded fruits, the steady lights of the shops and the sliding lights of the cars ; the big red buses, so different from Manchester's nippy single-deckers ; a walker glimpsed in the light of a lamp with an opera-hat on his head and a white scarf round his neck. Now that was a thing you never saw in Manchester—an opera hat ; and as though the small, absurd experience of seeing that hat were the culmination of the moment, she dropped the curtain and turned to the room.

" This is *your* room," Maurice had said, leaving her there. " Have a good rest now. Dinner will not be for another hour." He kissed her shyly and hobbled away.

Only a tall standard-lamp was burning. She walked across to the switches clustered near the door and pressed them all down. Dripping from the elaborately moulded plaster that made the centre of the ceiling were hundreds of drops, icy but radiant, flashing with diamond brightness as the cut edges caught the light that was snared in their crystal net. Above the fireplace light glowed behind sconces of rosy silk, and between the sconces leapt into view a canvas whose rich colour drew her with a few swift strides across the room. She put her face close up to it and was puzzled. The picture seemed to vanish and nothing remain but streaks of paint so emphatic that she could see it standing in thick ridges. Then she stood away and became aware of white sails and blue water, green turf and red roofs.

She went up close again, and read in the corner " Claude Monet " ; and she remained to run her fingers over the smooth cupids and garlands of the Adam fireplace. A fire purred and tinkled in the grate behind a screen of brass mesh.

There was not a whisper anywhere. She might have been the only person in the house, the only person in London. Her feet made no sound as she strode to the middle of the great crimson carpet to look all round her at this room which was her own. There was no picture but the Monet. The walls were panelled and cream-painted and affixed to them here and there were more rosy sconces like the ones over the fireplace. On either side of the fireplace was a recess, fitted with book-filled shelves to the height of a yard and above that with shelves housing a jolly jumble of pottery and porcelain. A huge settee covered with a gay cretonne stood in front of the fire, and before the window was a writing-desk. There was nothing else save a small table or two of mahogany so highly polished that the surfaces mirrored the tulips and daffodils and mimosa that stood on them in vases of Waterford glass.

But to Rachel, back at the switches, and dimming the room again of all save the light of the fire and the standard-lamp—to Rachel most of this meant nothing. She did not know that the glass was Waterford, that the little mahogany tables were gems, that the fireplace was Adam and the writing-table a masterpiece. She did not know that the books upon which she gazed, relaxed now upon the settee, were rare and lovely things, chosen with discrimination and acquired at great price, or that the porcelain above them represented Maurice's conviction that the genius of Henning and Malinowski, flowering at Copenhagen in our own day, had touched a point rarely excelled in the long story of the potter.

She knew nothing of all that ; but she knew that this first hour, quiet in the house of her husband, had troubled her with a strange feeling of awe. She felt with a swift and certain intuition, the something more than money that life meant to Maurice. She felt herself to be in the presence of things that she did not understand, but something racially subtle and instinctive told her that they were precious and important. And, without understanding them, she liked them. Out of her feeling of awe there emerged slowly a feeling of comfort. The things about her had the power to soothe and compose her spirit ; and giving herself up to the peace dwelling in that spacious, seemly room, she felt suddenly that she would not be out of her depth. And then she realised how great had been her fear that she might be. It had been in the back of her mind all day. But now, she said, she need not fear. After all, she, Rachel Rosing, was lovelier than anything here before her—lovelier than the marble cupids and the glowing canvas ; the rich embossed morocco or the weeping fauns and nymphs and satyrs whose postures in porcelain were fixed for ever. Instinctively she stood up and looked about her for a mirror, that she might be reassured concerning the beauty whose present vitality was her guarantee against the power of all these things that were lovely but inanimate.

There was no mirror in the room. She crossed to the door that led to her bedroom. That too, had been a surprise. " This is mine," said Maurice, " just through this door." And besides that door to Maurice's bedroom, there was yet another which led to a bathroom. There was access to it from Maurice's bedroom too.

And now, when Rachel entered her bedroom, she found the light up and a girl putting away her few clothes which had come in a trunk strapped to the back of the car. The girl rose to her feet and looked incredibly submissive. " I am your maid, madam," she said.

Rachel had met Mrs. Bright, the housekeeper, and her husband, who was Maurice's butler. " Oh," she said, " I suppose Mrs. Bright engaged you ? "

"Yes, madam."

Rachel thought, without betraying the thought by the flutter of an eyelid, of the few and miserable clothes that she possessed. She could see some of them lying here and there, looking alien and inadequate in that splendid room. The one fine dress she possessed —the one she had bought in Manchester for her dinner with Maurice—was laid out on the bed. "I thought you would want this for dinner to-night, madam," said the girl.

"Yes, I shall. What is your name?"

"Rose Chamberlain."

"Very well, Chamberlain. I hope you'll be happy here. Will you get my bath ready now?"

And she gave Chamberlain a smile because she had nothing else at the moment to give; and it was such a smile as Rachel could make a reward in itself. Chamberlain went into the bathroom, impressed by her mistress's dark, golden beauty; and Rachel went back to her sitting-room feeling that she had not come badly out of a difficult encounter.

There was a ball of tawny fluff on the settee. Rachel's noiseless approach caused it to stir. She stood looking down as a head disengaged itself from the coil and a mouth yawned with contempt. The head, magnificently ruffed, was like the head of a small lion in shape and colour. The cat blinked at Rachel, unafraid and unimpressed.

"Well, cat," she said, "whose cat are you?" She put down her hand to stroke the cat, and he leapt to the ground, turned his back upon her, and walked away, his great brush of a tail switching to and fro with annoyance. "Come on, there's room for us

123

both," said Rachel. She picked him up, her hands
sinking into the rich depths of his coat, and sat down
on the settee with him beside her. He at once jumped
down again, walked to the middle of the carpet, and
washed himself carefully where he had been handled.
Then, giving himself a vigorous shake all over, that
seemed to loosen his skin from head to foot, he retired
to the door and sat there as though resolved to exercise
any amount of patience provided it would at last
permit him to be free from company he did not desire.

" Well," said Rachel, looking at him with distaste,
" if you want to go, go—damn you." She opened the
door, and the cat, not looking at her, not hurrying,
but with complete resolution, walked into the corridor.
His up-raised and wide-spread tail gave one contemptuous flick as he disappeared.

" No cheers from the cat," said Rachel, and went
to the bathroom.

IV

She had never before been helped to dress. She was
not sure whether Chamberlain was a help or a nuisance;
on the whole, she thought, a nuisance. But she was
pleased with the girl's obvious homage. Rose Chamberlain had had but one place before this, and that was
as maid to a gross old woman who had difficulty in
seeing her own toes. To attire Rachel's lissom loveliness
was a great change and a great delight. When all was
done and Rachel stood there with her splendid dress
looking none the worse for its journey, and the red
flower in her black hair, and all the weariness of the

124

day soaked and massaged from her limbs, she could not help saying : " And how d'you think I'll do, Chamberlain ? "

And the girl, all a-flutter, and not knowing whether it would be received for a compliment or insult, answered timidly : " You'd look grand on the stage, madam." For Rose Chamberlain's secret, romantic desire was to be dresser to some great lady of the theatre.

Rachel did not answer, but in her heart she thought that Portman Square was theatre enough to be going on with, and she did not think that she would let down her part.

Maurice came through from his bedroom. She had not before seen him in evening clothes. He wore them elegantly. His black tie was efflorescent, a good deal bigger and looser than was customary, but he could carry off a small extravagance.

" You have not seen my room," he said. " Come now."

They went downstairs together, and Rachel savoured to its finest essence that first descent of the stairs in a house of which she was mistress. In the flurry and rush of their arrival she had noticed little. Now, rested in body and collected in mind, she observed the light and elegant mahogany rail, supported by uprights of white-painted iron, twisting down to a newel from which a tall lamp rose to light the squares of black and white marble that paved the wide hall. She looked with pleasure at the hall's great fireplace, in which a cage of wrought iron contained the flaming coals. Above the fireplace was a large dark canvas in a frame of tarnished gilt. Slender, vivid, young, she paused and considered the gnarled old face, sad and disillusioned, of the woman in the picture. It was a face she had seen many times, on many old women in Cheetham Hill. She plucked Maurice's sleeve. " Who is it ? " she asked.

" Oh, just some old Jewess. But she was painted by Rembrandt."

He spoke lightly, but Rachel shuddered. " Just some old Jewess." It was the terror that had always been before her mind, it was the fate from which, for years, she had been passionately fleeing. " I don't like it," she said.

The old woman looked as wise as she was sad. In the corners of her eyes were sparks of red like the haws in the eyes of an old bloodhound bitch. She gazed serenely down with irony and compassion, a drab shawl cowled about her head, skinny fingers gathering it together at her breast. Rachel turned away. " Let us see your room," she besought him.

" I hope you will like it better," said Maurice, drawing her hand through his arm, and patting her fingers.

She did like it better. It was a lovely simple room, opening off the dining-room. It was not so large as Rachel's room, and she thought it cosier. The fireplace was plain and painted olive green. Olive green were the bookshelves which went right round the room to almost half its height, and above the bookshelves on the buff walls were more bright pictures like the one in Rachel's room. They were gay and cheering. The one over the fireplace showed girls in gossamer ballet skirts, insubstantial as thistledown.

" Oh, I like this better, much better," Rachel cried. " These girls are cheerier than that old woman."

"Degas," Maurice explained. "Yes, it is nice, that picture. These others—Monet, Manet, Sisley, Vlaminck. Yes, they are all right. They are good."

There was nothing else in the room except a writing-table and chair, and two big chairs upholstered in green leather by the fireplace. Rachel threw herself down into one of them, and again she noticed the extraordinary quiet. Fires burning everywhere, but she saw no one tending them. Spotlessness and smooth-running, but she neither saw nor heard the signs of work being done. Maurice, stiff in the leg, began to lower himself into the chair opposite hers. She leapt up and helped him. When he was seated she knelt at his feet and rested her head against his breast. "Thank you, Maurice," she whispered. "Thank you for all these lovely things."

He fondled her hair, bent down and kissed the nape of her neck. "It was always a nice house," he said, "but now it is perfect, Rachel. If you will be happy. Will you be happy?"

She looked up, and with her two slender hands stroked his face. "I was so afraid," she said, "I should become like the old woman in the hall. Yes, I think I shall be very happy now."

Chapter Twelve

I

LEAVING aside that brief holiday in Blackpool, when her mind, tormented by anxiety, could find no rest, Rachel had never, in all her life before, had nothing to do. There had been the dress shop in Manchester, and before that there had been the cellar of a Jewish sweater, and before that there had been the weary life of a little general maid, clattering buckets up and down stairs, wringing out greasy dishcloths, plunging her hands into filthy water, and dusting, sweeping, scrubbing and running errands, all in the grim streets and under the grey skies of Cheetham Hill. And before that there was school, and evenings spent in helping a mother she could already but dimly remember. Always something to be done. And now, nothing. Days and weeks and months of doing nothing but what she wanted to do.

She lay in bed and allowed her mind to loiter ahead of her down those long avenues of freedom. She was glad that Maurice had been so considerate last night. He came to her bedroom and kissed her, and said : " Now sleep well, my darling. You are tired. You must get used to me—eh ?—and this house, and all these strange people. Don't let things hurry you." Then he gave her a hug and another kiss and went away.

She thought she was going to like Maurice very much. She had heard him speak so brusquely to Mike Hartigan, but with her he was wonderfully gentle.

And now Chamberlain came and drew her curtains, announced that it was a lovely day, and said that breakfast was coming up. She propped Rachel up in bed as though she were a sick child, and swivelled a little table across the bed to take the tray. With the tray came one perfect rose, as creamy as butter and sparkling with water-drops. A note on the tray was from Maurice. " Good-morning, darling. Do not get up in a hurry. Take it easy. We shall go out at eleven."

There was a boiled egg, and toast, and marmalade, and coffee, and fruit. There was also *The Times*. Rachel gave it one scared look and threw it to the floor. " There are no letters, madam," said Chamberlain.

No ; there wouldn't be. She had not thought of that before. There was not a soul in all the world to rejoice with her, to wish her luck. She felt a fierce pride at that. She had fought a lone hand, and she had won.

She was nibbling alternately at a piece of toast and a peach when the sudden jangle of a bell startled her. She had not noticed that there was a telephone alongside her bed. " See who it is," she commanded.

She admired the girl's pert self-possession. " Yes," said Chamberlain. " Mrs. Bannerman is at home. I don't know whether it will be convenient for her to speak to you at the moment. I'll inquire."

" It's a Mr. Julian Heath," she explained to Rachel.

Rachel considered. " I'll speak to him," she said at last, and wondered that her heart gave a sudden tremor. Chamberlain handed her the receiver. Rachel took it, and stared at the girl fixedly. She flushed suddenly, murmured, " I beg your pardon, madam," and disappeared.

" Well ?" said Rachel languidly into the receiver.

" Oh, good-morning. *The Times* gave me an awful shock this morning."

" It did me, too. I don't think I've ever seen it before. Isn't it forbidding ? "

" Oh, rather. Give me the *Daily Mirror*. But I didn't mean that. I mean the Births, Marriages and Deaths. You know—Bannerman-Rosing."

" I didn't know Maurice had put it in."

" Oh, it's in all right. Well, congratulations—that's what I rang up for—congratulations, best of luck, long life and many of 'em. Old Thingummybob, too, you know, old Whatsisname, joins in same."

" You mean the man who was with you in the car ? "

" No other. He's here at this moment picking over a bloater. Hence my averted gaze, could you but see me. Well, anent customary gift. What d'you fancy ? Be imaginative, but keep within five bob."

" Really "—Rachel laughed—" do you think a present is called for ? "

" I do in very troth. And I've got just the thing for you."

" That's very kind of you."

" Wait till you see it. You'll be surprised."

" I'm sure I shall be delighted. Would you care to give me a hint ? "

" It's a greyhound in plus-fours."

" A what ? "

" Oh, well, be prosaic. An Afghan hound."

" That will be lovely."

"You've still got my card?"

"Yes."

"Well, remember we're two lonely likeable lads here. And expect delivery of hound on even date. Akbar, the name is—the hound's name. My respects to Mr. Bannerman. Good-bye."

Rachel put down the receiver slowly. So, after all, there *was* just one person to wish her luck. She had never had a pet in her life. She disliked animals ; but she lay back wondering what sort of creature an Afghan hound could be. Akbar. She must remember that. Akbar.

II

She went out with Maurice at eleven. To please him she wore the cream rose that he had sent her. Old Bright was fussing all over the hall ; hat, coat, stick. A big stick with a wad of rubber on the end. "You're sure you ought to walk, sir?"

"Oh, I'll walk all right," Maurice declared, but Bright helped him down the front steps on to level ground.

It was a grand day. A man went by carrying a basket piled with daffodils and jonquils, tulips and narcissi, lilac of mauve and white. The sky was blue, and with all London before her Rachel wanted to run and hold her arms out to the morning. But she had not made a few paces from the house, with her arm in Maurice's, before she realised that there would be no running that day. Maurice went slowly, resting heavily on his stick, but declaring gamely his intention to see it through.

"Wouldn't dream of a car," he said. "Your first day in London. I want to show it to you myself. Can't see London from a car. We'll get into Oxford Street and cross over into Bond Street. We'll see all the shops there and come out in Piccadilly. I'll manage. I'll manage."

And suddenly Rachel felt depressed. She had been seeing everything so vividly ; the tall houses, and the green grass, and the tree trunks scaling into patches of green and yellow ; and now a film shot across it all. It seemed not exciting but merely strange. She felt shackled. This was to have been such a busy, exploring morning ; and now it would be a hobble.

"You're sure you ought not to have the car ? " she asked.

"Oh, no. I'll manage. I'll manage," Maurice repeated. " Unless you'd like it, my dear."

"No, no," she said dutifully. "Let's walk."

And then she saw Julian Heath bounding across the road. Akbar was with him, on a lead of scarlet leather. Rachel stopped and clapped her hands with delight. She had never seen such a creature before. Pets she might abominate, but this, she saw at once, was something different ; this was an enhancement of her own personality ; and she had in one sharp moment a perfect perception of the picture it would make—her own tall beauty towed along by this fantastically lovely thing with the richly feathered tail and pendant ears, the golden colour, the almost heraldic originality of outline.

"Oh, Maurice," she cried. "Look ! I forgot to tell you. Mr. Heath rang up this morning to say that he was bringing us a dog for a wedding present. He read about the wedding in *The Times*. Isn't it an adorable creature ! "

Maurice stopped, leaning on his stick. " Yes, it is nice," he said stolidly. " It is good of Mr. Heath to think of us."

Julian was now upon them, a remarkable contrast to Maurice muffled in his great overcoat and heavy on his legs. He was without overcoat or hat. A blue jersey with a rolled collar did duty for a waistcoat, and from the close-growing golden curls of his head down to the brown suède shoes on his feet, he looked as lithe and taut and vivid as the creature that pulled at the lead. His brown hand caressed his small military moustache and his blue eyes twinkled as he saluted Maurice and Rachel. He gripped their hands in turn. " Congratulations ! " he cried. " Old How-d'you-do and I had no idea when we rammed you that we were precipitating a romance. I rang up Mrs. Bannerman this morning, sir, to see if she'd accept this." He flicked Akbar's dangling silken ears and the creature swayed its lovely tail and looked up at him with adoring eyes.

" It's very kind of you," said Maurice formally.

" I didn't know whether you'd be at home," Julian went on. " I thought you might have barged off on a honeymoon."

" My wife has never lived in London," Maurice explained patiently. " It is a great pleasure for her to see it. Perhaps later on we will take a little trip somewhere."

" Well," said Julian, " I hope you'll give the hound a good home. Shall I hand him through your hospitable portals ? "

"Oh, no, please," Rachel cried. "Let me take him now. D'you mind, Maurice?"

"Well, perhaps, in these rather crowded streets——" Maurice began, but seeing her look darken he added: "Still, we will try. We will see how we get on."

Rachel took the scarlet lead, and Maurice bent and clumsily caressed the dog's ears. Akbar looked from one to the other, his liquid eyes overflowing with indiscriminate affection. Julian raised his hand in salute. "Good-bye, then. Hold him tight, Mrs. Bannerman. He may try to follow me."

He walked away, and the dog strained after him on the lead. Rachel held tight, wondering at the creature's wiry strength. Once Julian was round the corner Akbar did not struggle so much. He turned soon to Rachel, asking with his eyes what was to be done next.

"Come," said Maurice. "Let us go now."

But it was awkward going. The dog was as full of the eager morning as Rachel had been when she left the house. He hauled impetuously on the lead, making Rachel progress by a series of little runs, so that she had to unclasp her hand from Maurice's arm, leaving him now a few yards behind her, now struggling abreast again.

They turned into Oxford Street, and there the situation ceased to be the joke which till now Rachel had made it. She waited, after one of Akbar's energetic bursts, for Maurice to come up with her, and said: "You were right, darling. We must take him home. We'd better have a taxi."

Maurice considered this for a moment. "No," he said. "This is your first morning in London. I must not spoil it for you, and I'm afraid that's what I am

134

doing. This old leg is no good, after all. I am being a nuisance."

He looked humble and crestfallen, and Rachel's heart was shot by a remorseful pang. She took his arm. " Let us both go back," she said. " Then we can get out the car and have a quiet look round."

" No," said Maurice. " I will not be a nuisance." He smote the rubber cap of his stick soundlessly upon the pavement. " You must have a happy morning. Explore everything by yourself." He waved his hand abroad, giving her the city. " If you are lost, just get into a taxi. It is simple."

And so he would have it. He called a cab and Rachel helped him in. She thought he looked lonely and forlorn, but he managed a smile and a wave of the hand, and a moment later, under that silky sky of earliest spring, amidst the jostling crowds of the Oxford Street pavement, she found herself alone. She was conscious of an instantaneous release of spirits. The film cleared from before her sight. The buses and the cabs, the hurrying crowds, the flags fluttering from the tops of buildings, the mechanical toys that ran and turned somersaults on the pavements, the baskets of the flower hawkers, bursting with colour : all this broke with a sudden fresh significance upon her vision ; and in her ears was a satisfying thunder of wheels and scream of brakes as the waves of traffic ebbed and flowed about the guiding lights.

So this was it. This was London, and she abroad in it. She kept the dog upon a short lead and moved slowly on with her swaying provocative gait. She thought of Manchester. " And what is this, after all," she asked herself, " but a bigger Market Street ? "

She was not afraid of it. She would manage this all right. She calmly appraised the women. "Dear God," she said to herself, "as ugly as anywhere else, but more of them." And she caught the wandering glances of the men, and knew that here, as elsewhere, she could conquer. And so she took London affably to her heart because its first impact had done nothing to daunt her. It had strengthened her confidence in her own sufficiency.

III

Mike Hartigan stood on the black and white chequer of the hall pavement, warming his seat at the cheerful fire. But Mike was not cheerful. He scowled at everything in that beautiful antechamber of Maurice's house—at the flowers which Mrs. Bright was arranging on a table, at the slender grace of a boy in bronze by Gilbert, at the affable and harmless Mrs. Bright herself. He had strode straight in, thrown his bag on a chair, and strutted across to the fireplace. There he stood, his shapeless black felt hat crushed in one hand, the other trying vainly to disarrange the black clusters of his wiry curls.

"Well, Mrs. Bright," he said at last. "I suppose he had a good deal to say about my not being here last night?"

"Why, no, Mr. Hartigan," Mrs. Bright answered in her soft voice. With a sharp knife she slit the stem of a mauve tulip before putting it into a vase. "I hardly think he noticed you were not here. At all events, he said nothing."

Mike seemed none too pleased at that. His scowl thickened. " Too taken up with her, I suppose," he said. " What do *you* think of her, Mrs. Bright ? "

The old lady, whose face was wrinkled and apple-bright, gave him a look of mingled amusement and reproof. Mike was so obviously itching to hear something disparaging. " Well, Mr. Hartigan," she said gently, " I wish I were as young and as beautiful. Then I shouldn't care what any old woman thought about me."

" Ach," said Mike with disgust, " you talk as soft as an old dove cooing round a rickyard. Young and beautiful ! Is Maurice young and beautiful ? "

This time Mrs. Bright's eyes were all reproof. She swept together the snippings of flower stalks, threw them into the fire, and, with no further word, departed.

" There you are ! " said Mike, crashing his hat to the floor and with a lifting kick placing it neatly in a chair, " the blundering Hibernian once more crushed and humiliated by the soft-spoken Saxon." Then through the hall window he saw a taxi draw up without, and a glance showed him that it was occupied by Maurice alone. He dashed through the front door and down the two shallow steps, and in a bound was across the pavement.

" Well, Maurice, Maurice," he shouted, wrenching open the door, " it's good to see you again. Come on in."

Maurice's face lit up with pleasure. " Help me out, Mike," he said. " Don't forget, since you last saw me I've found a wife and lost the use of a leg."

" To the devil with that," Mike cried. " Before you know where you are we'll have you and Mrs. Bannerman playing hopscotch all over Portman Square. Come on. Let's see you toddle."

Maurice toddled well enough. He shed his coat and stick and hat in the hall, and went through to his study.

"Now sit down," he said. Mike subsided into the green leather chair opposite his employer's. "What happened to you last night? A damn' good welcome you gave me and Rachel, didn't you?"

Mike Hartigan blushed and shuffled his feet on the carpet. "Well, you see, Maurice, there was an urgent matter——"

"And thanks for the wedding present," Maurice cut in.

"Oh, that's all right. You haven't got me that time." And Mike produced from his pocket and handed over with pride a silver cigar-case with Maurice's initials upon it.

"Thank you," said Maurice, opening the case and snapping it shut again. "That's for both of us, is it?"

Mike's hands, hanging down between his knees, knotted themselves uneasily.

"Well, as you like, Mike," said Maurice. "You cleared out because you're jealous of Rachel. You acted like a damn' great child. You are a damn' great child, and I like you. But whether you like my wife or dislike her, you're bloody well going to act as though you *did* like her. Is that understood?"

Mike nodded his head without speaking.

"Very well. That suits me. Now, look here, I'm going to talk to you about this novel of mine."

Maurice began to talk. Mike filled a pipe, leaned back, and listened attentively. They were happy together—all three of them. Omar, the cat, had come into the room, leapt upon Mike's shoulders, and, curled there like a sumptuous boa, seemed to listen with unwinking attention to what Maurice had to say.

IV

Rachel had not walked far beyond Selfridge's in the direction of Oxford Circus when Akbar's tugs on his scarlet lead became embarrassingly emphatic. Clearly, he had made up his mind that there was somewhere to go, and he intended to be a nuisance if he were not allowed to go there.

Seeing that all London was before her and that it mattered little to her where she went, Rachel allowed him his head and followed after. He crossed the road, ran forward for a few hundred yards, and then turned abruptly to the right.

This was disappointing. Rachel had decided very soon that there was nothing much to Oxford Street. But still, it was a street of shops, and that in itself had some appeal ; but now Akbar was leading her into the shoddy hinterland of poverty, dirt and decrepitude that crouches behind the flashy façades of most cities.

She was disappointed, and rather shocked. She felt out of place. Whatever London might be, it shouldn't be this ; it shouldn't be these massy cliffs of dirty brick, pierced by a thousand windows, like a huge decomposing honeycomb. She saw unkempt children playing in dreary asphalt quadrangles, and all about her was the grey and inescapable evidence of that profound hopeless poverty that had hung over her own youth.

She had no philosophical reaction ; she felt no sudden violent flame of anger that Portman Square should be on one side of Oxford Street and this on the other. She felt simply that she hated it, that those who wanted to put up with it could put up with it ; but for herself, she was going back to the gay uproar of the street.

Akbar thought differently. She pulled him round, but he would not budge. He dug his forepaws into the pavement, and she could make no headway save by hauling him as though he were a dead thing. She stopped, perplexed. As soon as the pressure on him was relaxed. Akbar sprang to life, lifted his front paws up to her breast, slavered out six inches of red frothy tongue, and mingled smiles with pantings. Then he dropped down and started off again in the way he wanted to go.

She followed. He zigzagged in and out of short streets and back ways. His tempo accelerated. His feathered tail began to wave furiously and he dragged her along at a brisk trot. Presently he swerved to the left. She noticed affixed to a wall the name Duck Yard ; and half-way along Duck Yard Akbar stopped, thumped his sides with his tail, and barked joyously. A window opened and Julian Heath's head appeared. "Well, I'm blessed !" he shouted. "Blessed is indeed the word." And then he began singing lustily " Hold the fort, for I am coming " as he turned from the window. She heard his agile legs clattering down a wooden stair. The door opened, and with a final hurricane of emotion Akbar tore the lead from Rachel's hand, leapt upon Julian, and slavered his face.

" Welcome to Duck Yard," Julian cried. " Look

about you and see the lordly estate in which we live."

Duck Yard was a mews. On one side were the high unsightly walls of tall buildings that turned their backs disdainfully on the yard. Nothing but that; save that in one place a plane tree grew, an old doddering plane tree, cut back so often that at those spots whence again and again it had sent its branches aspiring to the sky there was nothing to be seen in those early branchless days but a series of hideous spotted wens that looked as though they would never again try to send up leaves to the light.

On the other side were the old stables, garages now, and there were a few handsome cars drawn up outside the garages, and chauffeurs were washing and polishing them. All the old doors had been painted in bright colours, and so had the window frames of the small flats above them; so that, if you forgot the one blank, eyeless side of Duck Yard, the place took on a toy-like gaiety that was helped by the bright red of a telephone kiosk closing the view.

Julian had left open the small green door alongside the big double doors of the garage. Akbar had leapt up the stairs and now appeared with his front feet on the window-sill and his mouth pantingly open as though he were about to announce some good news to the world. Julian said nothing, but moved towards the door. Rachel followed him. He stood aside and she went in and began slowly to mount the wooden stairs. When she was at the top she heard the door shut, and then the stairs were pitch dark. A wind had banged the door to after Akbar had gone in.

"Stay where you are," Julian shouted. "I know every inch of this. I'll open the door."

She was still fumbling for the knob when she was aware of him beside her on the dark square yard of landing. His hand stumbled upon hers and she quickly drew it away, aware that her heart was panting like Akbar's tongue. She believed that Julian's was, too. If he knew every inch of the place he was a long time getting the door open. His thigh brushed hers, and she said quietly : " Open the door."

The words were both a confession and an accusation, but their discomfort was at once brushed away by Julian. He flung open the door and shouted : " Voilà ! Entrez, madame."

"How charming ! " she said, and passed in before him. It was a good-sized room, and there was not much in it. The walls were lemon-yellow and all the woodwork was black. Cocoa-nut matting covered the floor. A fire burned in the fireplace of rough red brick. Two wicker chairs, which appeared to have been built for lanky bodies, were before it. There were not many books. A writing-table and a baby grand piano completed the furniture.

Julian showed her a tiny bedroom with two beds, and a tinier bathroom. " And that's the lot," he said. "We feed out. But for odd cups of coffee, omelettes and so forth there's a gas-ring. The efficacy thereof I will now display by making coffee."

" But I mustn't stay," Rachel protested. " I had no intention of coming at all. If it hadn't been for Akbar——"

" The chair on your left," Julian proceeded affably, " is the one more adapted to your build. Gloves and bag may be deposited on the floor, window-ledge, or chimney-piece."

She allowed herself to be persuaded into a chair. Julian opened a door and disclosed in a large cupboard a tap, a gas-ring, a kettle, coffee-pot and crockery. He was soon happily and busily at work. He put the coffee on a small table between the two chairs, and sat himself down, his long legs stretched towards the fire.

"Well," he said, "I didn't think you'd be coming to London so soon. Would you have looked me up, or had you forgotten my poor existence?"

"Oh, I expect I should have called, sooner or later." She kept her tones casual, non-committal.

"Tell me—did you read that book?"

"Yes. I couldn't make head or tail of it."

With a lean forefinger he flicked the ash from his cigarette towards the fire and laughed aloud. "Ah, well," he said, "I shan't puzzle the brains of the public any more. I'm on the right stuff now. Something they'll like, and understand, and pay for." He waved his hand towards the littered writing-table. "There it is—a fortune. Just a matter of time."

"They are so easy, aren't they," said Rachel, "these fortunes that are only a matter of time? But the time is often so long." Her fingers flickered a cynical comment on the vanity of human ambition.

Julian watched her with a curious, concentrated attention. "D'you know," he said, "that you could get quite a lot of money for saying things in just that disillusioned way? Did any one ever tell you that you are a born actress?"

"Oh, yes," she admitted, "often that has been

said to me. You yourself thought I was acting that night when I came down the stairs into the lounge of the hotel at Blackpool. Isn't that so ? "

He remembered the moment—that perfect entrance. " Well ! " he said, " whether it is acting or not, it was superb. Any one who could come on to a stage like that would have the audience where they ought to be. They would be sitting up and waiting for the first words."

" And what are you trying to tell me—are these the words ? " She indicated the littered table. " Are you writing a play ? "

Julian flushed. " Well, as a matter of fact, I am. And I might tell you it's damned good. No high-falutin' nonsense this time. I'm through with that. We all do that sort of thing when we're young. Believe me, this is the goods at last."

" My best wishes," Rachel said with a tinge of irony. She put down her coffee cup and rose. " I must be going."

" Oh, no, please——"

" Oh, yes. What would my husband say—the very day after our marriage ? "

" That was a surprise, you know. I had no idea you and Mr. Bannerman were to be married."

" I had," said Rachel. " Just an idea. I wasn't certain."

" I think you're one of the most astonishing women I've ever met. And the most beautiful." His voice faltered. He put his hand upon the creamy rose she was wearing. " Give me this."

She was carrying her gloves and struck him smartly with them in the face. He stepped back, surprised, and she said : " That is another of the things men do when they are very young. I should like you so much better if you were discreet." She smiled as radiantly as though she had kissed him, not struck him. " You should at least pretend not to take me for granted."

She picked up Akbar's lead. Julian opened the door. " I am forgiven ? " he asked. She shrugged her shoulders lightly and departed.

V

When Maurice had finished his conversation with Mike Hartigan he went into the hall and walked up and down, restless and disturbed, one eye all the time on the window. His day had not gone as he had planned it, but there was still time to mend things. This afternoon he would have out the car and they would have a quiet look round, see all the things that were likely to interest a person who did not know London. They would go through the parks, and see Buckingham Palace and the House of Commons. And then " Oh, hell," he said, " I expect she'd rather walk down Bond Street than do anything else." At least they could go to the theatre at night. Yes ; he would take her somewhere nice for dinner, and then they would go to a show, and after that—— He passed a hand across his perspiring forehead and started as though he had caught himself planning an outrage. There was something so aloof about Rachel. He could not feel that she belonged to him. She was obedient and grateful, but even when she was nearest to him there seemed to be a pane of glass between them.

And then he saw her coming across the square, and his heart ached at the loveliness of her. She seemed at last to have come to terms with the dog. They both blew along with an exquisite willowy grace ; the dark woman and the golden dog. She had a great armful of flowers, though heaven knew the house was full enough of them. White lilac it was ; he could see now. He was sure she was bringing it for him—just as she had brought the flowers from Manchester that day when his heart had been distracted, wondering what had become of her. She had brought the flowers, and he had pulled her down and kissed her for the first time.

Thinking of that moment, he hurried to the door and threw it open. She let go the lead and Akbar dashed up the steps. Rachel was on the pavement waving the lilac and shouting : " Isn't this lovely, darling ?—for you." Then the dog turned to rush back to her. It was in a mad, excited mood. It mixed itself up with Maurice's legs, twined the lead round one of them and brought him down. Mike Hartigan had just come into the hall, hearing the dog's commotion. He and Rachel cried out together. Maurice was aware of the armful of lilac dropping to the pavement as Rachel's hands shot out towards him and of Mike's shout : " Jesus, Maurice ! " Then he was aware of nothing but a stab of pain in the back, followed by a boring torture as though a red-hot gimlet were being screwed between his vertebræ. He groaned in agony for a moment or two, and then was quiet.

It was nearly midnight when Mike Hartigan went to Rachel's room to tell her the latest news. It had been a terrible todo. Maurice was a heavy man and old Bright was too feeble to be of much use as a lifter. A robust taxi-driver hurried across the square to give his services. Mike would not have Maurice shifted far. He shouted for a mattress and blankets to be brought down to the hall, and while Maurice was being placed upon them Bright telephoned for a doctor.

Maurice lay there, his face twitching, his cheeks haggard. Mike Hartigan knelt by the mattress, stroking Maurice's head, while Rachel, with a white drained face, stepped about as delicately as a doe, filled with a sense of impotence and horror.

The doctor came ; there were telephone calls : to a specialist in Harley Street, to a nursing home, to an ambulance dépôt. Then, after the bustle of departure, there was a stricken silence through the house. Maurice had not opened his eyes, had not uttered a word. Rachel turned from the window, where she had stood to watch the ambulance roll silently away on its great cushioned tyres, and found that she was alone.

She went slowly up the stairs, along the corridor to her room. Mrs. Bright came to talk comfortingly to her at lunch-time, urging her to eat, and again at tea-time. But she would eat nothing : she just walked up and down or sat looking at the fire, asking herself : " What now ? "

From time to time a maid came into the room :

to draw the curtains, to make up the fire. The slow day dragged to its end. Moment by moment it shaped more clearly in Rachel's mind the question of what Maurice meant to her. She felt no personal stab. She felt nothing but such horror as fills the mind in face of some impersonal tragedy. And more and more she felt a great weariness, a great boredom and resentment, as though suddenly fate had intervened to rob her of pleasures that had dangled within her grasp. Were they still within her grasp? Bit by bit all her thoughts crystallised round that question. She forced herself ruthlessly to admit that that was what concerned her now.

She took from her breast the rose that she had worn all day. It was wilted; the petals were falling wide open, revealing its heart powdered with gold-dust. Still pondering her problem, she stood by the fireplace, picking the rose to pieces, not knowing that it was in her fingers. The petals fell in a little shower round her feet.

So Mike Hartigan found her. She was so absorbed in her thoughts that she did not notice his head come quietly round the open door. He looked, fascinated, at that repetition of the performance that had repelled him at Blackpool. He could not speak to her. He shut the door softly and went back to Maurice's study, where, alone together, they had been so happy a few hours ago.

Chapter Thirteen

MAURICE BANNERMAN'S name was well enough known in London for the accident to be worth a paragraph in the morning papers.

Charlie Roebuck, in dressing-gown and pyjamas making the morning coffee at the flat in Duck Yard, read the news aloud to Julian Heath, who was still in bed, studying the ceiling. He shouted out the paragraph through the open door, ending with the words : " It is feared that the injury to Mr. Bannerman's spine is serious."

" That's your damned dog," Charlie ended unsympathetically.

" Well, what am I to do with 'em ? " Julian demanded. " Mina will breed the creatures, and she can't sell 'em so she passes 'em on to me. I'm always shoving Afghans off on to some one."

He strolled into the living-room, scantily dressed as Charlie, yawning and rubbing his fists into his eyes like a boy. " This is pretty rough on Mrs. Bannerman," he said, taking up the paper.

Charlie looked at him reprovingly. " Your sympathy's a bit cock-eyed, old thing," he said. " I should say the rough luck was on Mr. Bannerman. First of all an erratic fool smashes his leg in the Lake District. The same charming young person stays overnight in Blackpool in the hope of snaffling the injured gent's young woman. Foiled in this, he sends a wild hound to trip up the old gentleman on his own doorstep, and then calmly remarks that the rough luck is on Mrs. Bannerman. It looks almost as though fate or skilful staff work is playing the young woman into your hands."

"Yes," said Julian, "it does, doesn't it?" He looked very serious, drumming his fingers on the table, while Charlie poured the coffee from the saucepan to the pot. Julian took a long chunk of French bread in one hand and his coffee in the other and sat down before the empty fireplace.

"What do you think of Mrs. Bannerman, Charlie?" he asked.

"My dear boy, I don't think about her. What do I know of Mrs. Bannerman? After the bump, my attention was given to the old boy. You may have forgotten that it was you who snatched the baby and whisked her off to Blackpool. I saw nothing of her. All I know is that you obviously thought her a pick-up."

Julian flushed and did not answer. Charlie took his coffee and bread over to the piano, sat down, and began banging out the tune he had composed the day before. He sang the words with gusto :

> Darling, I don't mind going with you
> If you don't want to go too far.

"Good song this," he shouted, his mouth stuffed with bread. "Going to be a hit, my boy."

Julian got up, stiff with annoyance. "You bloody pierrot," he said briefly, and went to the bathroom and turned on the taps.

Julian Heath and Charlie Roebuck understood one another perfectly and lived together harmoniously. When they were not dissipating some money which luck or enterprise had brought into their hands— harmless and high-spirited dissipation such as they had been engaged on when first they met Rachel Rosing—they worked with a vigour which they themselves considered commendable. Every morning Charlie disappeared out of the flat. He would roar away from Duck Yard in the Sunbeam, or walk in the parks, or stroll elegantly in a small well-defined area that included Bond Street, Piccadilly, Regent Street and Oxford Street, or go and turn over the papers in his club. It depended on his mood and the weather ; but whatever the mood or the weather, he would leave the flat promptly at nine o'clock.

Between nine o'clock and one, Julian would work at whatever enterprise he had in hand. Just now it was the play. At one o'clock he would join Charlie Roebuck at the club and they would take lunch together. Charlie never prolonged the meal beyond two o'clock. Punctually at that hour he would go to Duck Yard and work at his music. One of these days he was going to do the complete score of a musical play that would knock Charles B. Cochran sideways.

Between six and seven Julian Heath would be back at Duck Yard. Then they would change and sally out to dinner and a play or a dance or a music-hall.

"By cripes," Julian once said, "if we are not a Pair of Exemplary Young Men, I don't know where you'll find 'em in London." He stretched his toes to the fire. It was one of those evenings when they didn't want to go anywhere. They had had a bite at the nearest restaurant to Duck Yard, hurried back, pulled their wicker chairs up to the blaze, and took out their pipes. " Sitting here, old horse," said Julian, looking complacently about the small, cosy room, " sitting here with this tobacco-jar between us, last replenished, may I remind you, at my expense, with your cerebration warming one side of the room and mine making this side even cosier, what more can we ask while awaiting the call to name and fame which is but a matter of time ? "

Charlie, hands cupped round a lighted match, drew on a gurgling pipe, and merely grunted.

They were happy young men. Their friends called the flat in Duck Yard the Plague Spot because no one dared go near it. And that suited Julian and Charlie very well indeed. Sometimes, of an evening, Julian would read to Charlie what he had done of the play, and Charlie would sit at the piano and prove that he, too, had not been idle. Yes ; very happy and hopeful young men.

But that morning when he read in the newspaper of Maurice Bannerman's accident, Julian Heath did not feel such an Exemplary Young Man. He made a pretentious disposition of pens and paper about his writing-table as Charlie was preparing to go out. Then he leaned out of the window as Charlie brought the Sunbeam from the garage below, shouted useless advice as the thing roared and made a blue stink in the yard, and, when it was at last gone, turned back into the room and walked up and down with his hands in his pockets. He had wasted yesterday morning, first taking the dog round to Rachel, then gossiping with her in the flat. He was going to waste this morning too. He knew it in his bones. Damn it all, he said to himself, it would be inhuman not to go round, say how sorry he was, see how the poor girl was bearing up. Perhaps he ought to ring first, inquire if she would care to see him. But then he remembered their parting, that flick with the gloves. She might be holding something against him. Then she would tell him not to come.

Well, if she doesn't want to see you, why worry her ?

Because you want to see *her*, you fool.

Very well, then. Don't waste time route-marching about the flat. Get out and see her.

III

Rachel felt dead. It was not grief that had smitten her to the heart ; it was a terrible presage of dread and unpredictable things. Just when safety, security, placidity, had opened before her in vistas seemingly endless, everything was tumbled down, dark and unsure. A lifetime spent with a man condemned to the awful dependence of a cripple, a call upon her for those special devotions that the bed-ridden needed and from which she shrank with all her vital and rebellious soul : thoughts of such things thronged the night and made it hideous.

She did not go to bed. She sat on the great divan before the fire in her room, her dark tearless eyes, hot with terrible emotions. She felt tricked, swindled, hit below the belt by a dirty blow of fate.

At midnight Rose Chamberlain crept in and tried to persuade her to go to bed.

" Go away," she said without looking at her.

" *Please*, madam," Rose pleaded. " When you go to see Mr. Bannerman to-morrow he'll like to see you looking your best."

The thought of a cripple gazing with fond possessiveness at her beauty suddenly sickened her. " Go away," she snarled.

Rose retreated a step or two and considered her thoughtfully. Then she made up the fire to last for hours, approached the divan again, and, saying nothing, took Rachel's legs and swung them up on to the couch. She put cushions behind her, and brought a rug and threw it over her, lifting her up to tuck it under her body. " That's better," she said. " Goodnight, madam."

" Good-night. Put all the lights out."

And she lay there with the firelight flickering upon her for hours, it seemed to her, and then a stirring in the room startled her awake.

She felt dead. It had been a completely unrefreshing sleep. She watched Chamberlain drawing the curtains, and looked with a shudder at the cold, grey grate.

" Your bath is ready, madam. It'll do you a lot of good."

" Oh, God ! What time is it ? I want a cup of tea."

" Eight o'clock. There's a tray in your bedroom. It's warmer there. I've had the electric fire on for half an hour."

Rachel dragged herself across to the bedroom and gratefully took the warm, comforting tea into her bitter mouth.

The bath did her good. She lay in the warm relaxing water and thought of all the things she had proposed to do. What about clothes? She ought to be buying clothes. She had nothing but what she had brought in the trunk. Maurice had given her no money. She thought of cases she had read in the papers and recalled the words : " Pledging her husband's credit." Could she pledge her husband's credit? She supposed she could.

She sat before the long mirror in the bathroom, making herself up carefully. All those sacred jars and boxes and bottles that had been secreted in her trunk at Blackpool were set out on a glass shelf. They looked attractive ; they gave her confidence. If you forgot the bath, Chamberlain had thought, as she lovingly ranged them in place, if you forgot the bath and just looked at the jars and the mirror and the stool before them, you might think you were in a theatre dressing-room. The conceit pleased Chamberlain very much.

It was nine o'clock when Rachel, wearing her bluish tweeds, came into her room again. " I'll have my breakfast here," she said. " And tell Mr. Hartigan that I'd be glad if he could take breakfast with me."

She sat by the fire and waited. Marvellous how everything happened as though invisible gnomes had been at work. An hour ago the room had seemed dead as ditch-water, fire out, everything grey, fusty. Now the bright fire was singing quietly ; a light breeze stirred the curtains ; the flowers had been renewed. She crossed over to the window and saw that the sky was blue, the day dancing. In the garden of the square a few flames of crocus were pricking the sooty grass. My God, she said to herself, how lovely it could all have been if Maurice had not been such a clumsy fool.

There was quite a procession with the breakfast. A maid carried the tray, and old Bright fussed over it, when it was put down, to see that everything was all right. He was very solicitous about Rachel's well-being : hoped she felt better ; was sure everything would soon be all right again. Mike Hartigan came in behind Bright and stood ruffling his hair. The cat Omar came in behind Mike Hartigan.

Rachel was charming with old Bright and sent him away with a message to Mrs. Bright saying that Rachel thought all the flowers were lovely. Then she was alone with Hartigan. She nodded to a chair. "Sit down." He sat down, and the cat leapt upon his shoulder. It curved itself round his neck, its head towards Rachel, its eyes twin green slits fixed upon her.

"I asked you to breakfast. There's only breakfast for one here."

"That's all right, Rachel ; I had mine long before you were up."

"Did Mr. Bannerman," Rachel asked, pouring herself a cup of tea and not looking at him, "omit to tell you that we were married ? "

"Ach, now don't let that be bothering your pretty head at all," said Mike. "I was coming to that. I was going to congratulate you. It was just a bit of an oversight."

" I was not thinking of your congratulations, Mr. Hartigan. I was merely wondering whether you knew that my name was Mrs. Bannerman."

She looked up with a hard spark in her eye as her small white teeth crunched a piece of toast.

Mike put up a hand to stroke the cat, unbared his wide smile and said heartily : " Ah, now, you must get to know we're all friends together. I've always called Maurice Maurice, and why shouldn't I call you——"

" Mr. Hartigan ! " Mike's smile died suddenly as the voice cracked at him venomously. " You will not call Mr. Bannerman anything but Mr. Bannerman when you use his name to me. I wanted you here this morning to ask you one or two questions."

Mike edged his chair a little farther off. " Very well, Mrs. Bannerman," he said.

" Have you been through to the nursing home this morning ? "

" Yes. Mr. Bannerman is much the same. I asked if you might visit him, and they said if you insisted, yes ; but they'd rather you didn't to-day."

" Thank you. Until Mr. Bannerman is well, what am I to do about money ? "

" Money ! You don't want money. There's all you need in the house."

Rachel's face flamed, and as she put down her cup it clattered lightly against the saucer. " Mr. Hartigan," she said, stifling down a wild impulse to throw the tea in his face, " what I want is my business, and it's your business to tell me how my wants are to be met. What am I to do about money ? "

" I don't know, Mrs. Bannerman," said Mike

obstinately. "I am merely Mau—Mr. Bannerman's secretary. I can't do anything without his instructions."

"Well, see to it as soon as possible. And that's all. Except that I don't like that cat. Please don't bring it into my room."

Mike rose, and Omar from his shoulder yawned in her face. "And by the way," said Rachel, when Mike was half-way to the door, "where's my dog?"

Mike turned and stood still, with a scarlet tide rushing to his face.

"Well?"

"I had him shot."

Rachel leapt to her feet, stood upright, taut with fury. "You what!"

"Had him shot."

"What right had you to do anything of the sort? By whose orders did you do it?"

"I did it on my own. It seemed to me if a dog was liable to rush about like that, it was hardly safe the way Maurice is."

They stood for a moment, their eyes defying one another. Then Rachel said: "You have a lot to learn, Mr. Hartigan. Now go away." She remained standing till the door was shut behind him.

IV

She slowly drank a third cup of tea, then walked to the window. Julian Heath was crossing the square. This, she reflected, was her second morning in Portman Square, and this was the second time that she

158

had seen Julian Heath bounding across it at the earliest moment that decency permitted. Bounding was the word. The young man was amazingly alive. His lean figure seemed to belong to the same world as the gay sky and the springing crocuses. But that thought did not enter Rachel's mind. She said to herself that he looked a magnificent dancing partner.

But the spring was gone out of Julian when he was shown into her room. He drooped with sympathy and concern.

" This is terrible, Mrs. Bannerman," he exclaimed, " terrible. Charlie and I were frightfully cut up when we read about it in *The Times*. I had to dash round to hear whether the news is good this morning."

" Sit down," said Rachel.

Julian flopped into the seat that Mike Hartigan had left. Rachel looked at him with interest. " A lot he cares about the news," she was thinking as she said : " We've been through to the nursing home and they say there's no change in his condition."

" I suppose you'll be going round to see him ? "

" They say they'd rather not, unless I very much want to."

" Do you ? "

" No."

A flush came to Julian's cheek. He looked uncomfortable at that clear and uncompromising answer. He fumbled in his pocket. " Smoke if you want to," she said. He held his case towards her and she shook her head rather impatiently. She gazed for a time with darkly smouldering eyes at the fire ; then suddenly she stood upright and declared fiercely, as though he were not there : " I can't stand sickness. It belongs to everything I hate, everything I've had too much of in my time—discomfort, and poverty, and trouble, and uncertainty. I thought it was all ended. I thought everything would be happy and straightforward. And now this! I can't *stand* it. Everything beginning all over again!"

She laid an arm along the mantelpiece and rested her forehead upon it. Her right hand hung at her side, crushing a wisp of handkerchief. "I thought it would all be so different when I had plenty of money," she said fiercely. "And what is it going to be? Can you imagine?" She shuddered.

"You're being terribly honest," said Julian. "I'm sorry. Perhaps I'd better go. You will want to rest and collect yourself."

She swung round on him appealingly. "No. Don't go, please. Don't leave me here to brood all day. I know no one in London—no one at all."

"Well, we can put that right, anyway," said Julian cheerfully. "I'll take you out to see some people. How'll that do?"

"I'd love it. You do understand, don't you? You don't think I'm heartless? I can't *do* anything for Maurice, can I?"

Julian gave her a puzzled look. "No, I suppose you can't," he said. "But look here—what are we going to do? Charlie Roebuck's got the car."

Rachel was brightening. "You're not the only person that's got a car," she said, and, ringing the bell, she gave an order that Oxtoby was to bring the car round at once. She felt better then. After all, there was something in life. She had never before ordered a car to be brought to the door.

Oxtoby lived in a mews behind the square. He had a bedroom and bathroom over the garage, and he took all his meals in the Portman Square kitchen. He had the car—his treasure, his jewel—standing outside the garage door, shining and majestic. He himself, his buttons as brilliant as in the days when he had driven a Staff car in France, was all ready for action. There was nothing to do but pick up the peaked cap and tip it on to his head. He was proud of the car, proud of his job, and was very worried over Maurice's accident. It might mean no work for weeks ; it might mean the end of his job altogether. So he sat there worrying his head about the form of horses, and the prospects of the First League teams, and feeling very vague and restless, when the telephone rang. " Thank God ! " he exclaimed when the order came to take the car round to the house, and within two minutes the Rolls had drawn up at the kerb.

Mrs. Bannerman came down the steps as soon as Oxtoby had leapt from his seat to the door. A young man he had never seen before was with her. He had him weighed up at once. He had had a lot of experience had Oxtoby, in the army and out. " A bit of class," he said to his own mind ; a bit of class looking so much like the best sort of subaltern that Oxtoby's salute became instinctively military.

" Good-morning, Oxtoby," said Rachel. " We sha'n't want you this morning—only the car."

Oxtoby looked dubiously from Rachel to Julian Heath. " I shall drive," said Julian. " D'you think you can trust me with your 'bus ? I've driven her before."

" I can trust you all right, sir," said Oxtoby, and

looking at Julian he felt that indeed he could. " It's just a question of this—I'm responsible for the car, you see, sir, and if anything happened——"

Rachel cut in impatiently. " Nothing will happen. And as for the responsibility, it's on my shoulders."

" Very well, madam."

Rachel nodded curtly, and got into the seat next the driver's. Julian turned his sunniest smile on the crestfallen Oxtoby. " Thank you," he said. " You know how to look after a car. I shall be proud to drive her. She looks lovely."

Oxtoby smiled, too, at that. " Well, it's all I've got to do, sir."

" It doesn't always follow," said Julian, climbing in to the wheel. " Thank you so much. Good-bye."

He raised a negligent hand in reply to Oxtoby's salute, and the car slid away with a beautiful ease. Oxtoby watched it out of sight, and turned away satisfied.

Chapter Fourteen

THE house was called Markhams because it had once been Markham's, but the apostrophe had been dropped for generations. There was a Markham long ago who had no sons and the property descended to his only daughter. She married a Heath, and there had been Heaths at Markhams ever since, and for a hundred years the head of the Heath family had been a Lord Upavon.

Markhams was a lovely house ; the generations, making hay of it so far as architecture went, had given it a character that mere formality could never have attained. Its red brick, stained with ochre lichen, ramped upon by wistaria and clematis and jasmine, its mullioned windows and leaded panes, its tall elaborate chimneys that had smoked upon the Elizabethan scene and that had each its own twist of idiosyncracy, made up a ripe loveliness that sat upon a gentle rise of ground. At the foot of the slope a slow brook was green in summer with the undulation of streaming weed, and crowning the hill behind the house tall beeches drooped their boughs down to the thick brown loam that the years had created out of their very substance. Looking from the house down the slope and across the brook, you saw, nearly a mile away, the smoking chimneys of Markham village.

Standing at her bedroom window, the Honourable Wilhelmina Heath was looking down upon the village that morning. You would have thought her a queer product of Markhams. She was twenty-five years old. Hatless she stood there, with an aureole of red hair upon her head. The face beneath it was small and white and intense as though it were being consumed and the hair the flame of its burning. She wore trousers as wide as a sailor's, made of a stuff ruddy-brown, and you could see that she wore no stockings because her toes were visible within shabby gilded sandals that were on her feet. She had on a nonde-script linen jacket, embroidered with violent colours.

Wilhelmina suddenly jerked up her small shapely arm, looked at her wrist-watch, and exclaimed: " God ! I'll be late." She flickered out of the room, down the stairs, and out of the open front door. She sped to the back of the house where the stables were, and there an old battered two-seater motor-car, that had once been pillar-box red and was now dinted and chipped and dirty as a red-coat after battle, was standing.

" Out, Firdausi ! " Mina shouted. " Out, Judaveh ! " and the two lovely Afghan hounds leapt from the rent and decrepit cushions. They flagged all round her and sprawled their paws upon her, but, after taking each in turn and hugging it, she pushed them away, jammed herself into the driving-seat, and started off with a jerk that threatened to dislocate the white slender column of her neck. The car grated over the clean golden gravel that made a great sweep before the portico of creamy Portland stone, buzzed round the huge circular lawn, and straightened out in the long drive bordered with horse-chestnuts. Already the sheaths were exuding a resinous gum.

The trees would be a grand sight bearing their candles in May. Just beyond the tree-border on either hand was an iron fence, and beyond the fences were meadows that would be gold and silver in June with buttercups and dog-daisies.

Mina loved it all, always had loved it, and always would; but just now she had eyes for nothing but the road ahead as she made the battered car zoom forward like an infuriated dragon-fly.

The village was little more than one long street. Mina's eye noted, as she flashed by, the bills in the butcher's and the grocer's and the general shop which was also the post-office. There was even one on the notice-board of the church. " Be fit, not fat, at forty." And then followed the information that Miss Wilhelmina Heath would conduct, every Wednesday in the village institute, a class for the cultivation of physical beauty. Women of forty and over were invited to attend. As well as posting the bills, Mina had done some personal canvassing. Beauty was her religion. Her own flame-like body gave her a deep satisfaction. She bred her Afghans and gave them away because they were lovely. Her heart was bound to Markhams by the serenity of its face, the slow unhurrying rhythm of its life. The village women, slummocking about the street like cows, at once infuriated and disgusted her. She was fanatical and intolerant. She dragooned them into attending her class, and had even provided the costumes—white shorts and blouses—for those who pleaded poverty.

She had no sense of humour or one glance into the big room of the Institute—her father's gift—would have sent her back to her car rocking with laughter.

A dozen solemn matrons were awaiting her, looking more ghastly in their shorts and blouses than they had ever looked in their Sunday best or week-end worst. Awkward and self-conscious, they stood about, vividly aware of one another's monstrous hams, flaccid calves, and red shining arms. But to Wilhelmina they were no laughing matter. They were her converts, the raw material of jewels in her crown. She banged and locked the door behind her, shouted a cheery good morning, and with great unconcern took off her belt, stepped out of her wide trousers, and displayed a pair of white shorts that were supposed to be like those worn by her pupils. But they were not. They fitted ; they were elegant ; they set her off. She stripped off her linen jacket, displaying the regulation short-sleeved white blouse, and then she was ready.

This was the first class. She had prepared a few words, and she spoke them with great effect. Mina was not afraid to open her mouth. She was an actress when she could get work to do. She had had some good parts, and she was going to have better ones before she finished. So there she stood, and talked to those twelve great gawping jellyfish about beauty, and the joy of health, and the unseemliness of a stomach that needed for its support anything but the iron muscles of a perfect constitution. Only Mrs. Harrison, wife of the landlord of the Spur and Stirrup, had a word to say in reply. She said : " All very well, Miss Mina ; but when you've 'ad twins like me you can't 'elp a bit of a sag. Well, come on and let's see what you're goin' to do. So long as you don't 'ave us all ruptured. . . . An' if you turn Mrs. Mortimer into a Venus,

166

God 'elp 'er. 'Er old man's as jealous as 'ell as it is."

Mina knew better than to bandy words with Mrs. Harrison. The Spur and Stirrup was a free house. The Harrisons were impregnable. It was Mrs. Harrison who had told the vicar that if God lived in a penny roll the bakehouse must be heaven itself, though it was hot as hell.

A dozen mattresses had been brought to the Institute, and soon Mina had her candidates for beauty lying upon their backs, lifting first one hefty leg and then the other. " Gawd, miss ! " Mrs. Mortimer shouted, " there's not 'arf a draught under them doors. I'll bet I feel my lumbago to-night."

" Never mind your lumbago," Mrs. Harrison encouraged. " Think what you'll feel when you're like a twenty-year-old. That's worth working for. If only Miss Mina'll make our 'usbands young, too."

" Don't talk. Breathe deeply and regularly," Mina commanded. " Up. Down. Up. Down. Thank you. That'll do for that. Now rest a little."

The class rested on the mattresses, looking sheepish, hot and exhausted. All except Mrs. Harrison. Mrs. Harrison contemplated with satisfaction her thighs that were thick as elm-boles. " Don't see much off yet, Miss Mina," she announced. " And I'm not so sure as I want to. My 'usband always says as 'e gets into bed on a cold night, ' Ada, thank God for your backside. It's worth two blankets.' "

" Now, up on your feet, please," said Mina brightly. " I want you all to stand in a line, a yard apart. Now, I go at the head. We all run slowly round in a circle, lifting the knees well up. Are you ready ? Off

167

we go. Watch me, and lift your knees just as I do."

" And mind you don't kick yourselves in the eye," said Mrs. Harrison.

So off they pranced, and the ramshackle wooden hut shook and shuddered as it had never done during its wartime service. Twice round the circle went before Mrs. Ames stepped out of the ring, announcing " I'm busted." It was the signal for a general breakdown, a fanning of faces, and great puffing and blowing and catching of breath.

Mina let them rest awhile, then announced : " Well, now, just one more exercise."

" Not for me," said Mrs. Ames. " I'm fair busted."

" Very well," Mina agreed. " Any one who feels tired please step out. The others form a line and watch my action. Then do it after me."

She stood before them and lifted herself on her toes, easily as a flower lifting to the sun. " Now, please."

The ten, twelve and thirteen stoners tried to imitate the simple action. Mrs. Harrison was the first to give it up. She threw herself down on her mattress and shook with laughter. " My Gawd, Miss Mina," she gasped, " we do look a lot of daft coots. If our old men could see us they'd chase us with coal shovels."

Mina did not reply. She suddenly felt deflated, discouraged, slightly absurd. " What the hell can you do for women like this ? " she asked herself fiercely, but did not allow her anger to appear. " All right, dress now," she said. " And any one who's interested be here the same time next week."

She stepped nattily into her wide trousers, snipped

on her belt, pulled the jacket over her flaming head, and gave a general nod round. " Good-bye, then. And thank you all for coming."

She left them struggling into their foul, voluminous clothes. She heard Mrs. Harrison announce : " Girls, I'm writing to Charlie Cochran about our turn."

II

As Wilhelmina's red car approached the entrance to the drive she saw a stately Rolls-Royce coming towards her. It swung into the drive before her, just missing her bonnet, and the sweet gurgling cadenza which the horn emitted did not soothe her annoyance. There was no room to pass a car in the drive, and the Rolls slowed down to a crawl. She followed, fuming. " Some fool doing this just to annoy me," she thought. And she was right. " That's my sister driving the petrol tin," Julian announced to Rachel. " She's a mad driver. We'll teach her manners."

What with those awful village women, and now this, it was with a head seething with various indignation that Mina arrived on the gravel sweep. " Ugly, ugly as sin, ugly as hell," she was shouting in her mind ; and then she saw Julian assist Rachel from the big car. Mina leapt from her petrol tin, stood transfigured for a moment, then exclaimed : " My God, Julian ! What a wonderful woman ! Where did you find her ? "

" Mrs. Bannerman," said Julian, " this is my sister Wilhelmina. You will have gathered from her rude exclamation that she has country manners."

169

The two women shook hands, then stood and looked at one another : the one all flame, the other a smoulder of suppressed fire. It had been necessary to Rachel's career that she should meet many men ; she had never known intimately a woman outside her own class. It had been one of her dreams that some day she would do so ; but never had she pictured those women in anything like the guise that was now before her. This was Lord Upavon's only daughter ; this girl in the abominable trousers, the strange jacket, thé dusty golden sandals. And yet Rachel was impressed. Mina had on no lipstick, no rouge, not so much as a grain of powder, but there was something about her, some-thing about the clear glance of the grey eyes staring out of the white passionate face under the red flam-boyant hair.

"You may call Mina what you like," Julian chaffed. "She has various names : Firelighter, Arson, Spon-taneous Combustion. They all suit her very well. Father has to double his insurance premiums when she is at home."

"Aren't you often at home ? " Rachel asked.

"Only when I've got no work to do," said Mina. "I'm an actress. That means I'm pretty often without a job. Then I mooch about here and look after my dogs and try to do what I can for the village people."

"And the latest, I see," Julian said, "is fitness at forty. Mrs. Bannerman and I saw your bills. You've got a job on, my girl. You might as well try to teach cows to dance a minuet."

"Oh, well," Mina sighed hopelessly.

"You sound as though you'd had a bad time."

"Awful," Mina exploded. "Just awful. Oh, God,

why are people so dreadful? You'd never believe, Julian. I'd never seen them in shorts before."

Julian roared with laughter. " You didn't have 'em in shorts! You didn't! Mrs. Harrison in shorts! Oh, Mina!"

Mina looked at him grimly. " Mrs. Harrison in shorts is no laughing matter," she said. She put her arm through Rachel's. " And then to come home and find you here! That's a compensation. Come in now." She drew Rachel towards the house. " Are you staying to lunch, Julian?"

" I'd rather have it at the Spur and Stirrup if Mrs. Harrison is still in shorts. If she's changed, I'll stay."

" Then you'll stay. There'll be only us three. Father's gone up to town. Another of his old board meetings."

" And that's where you ought to be, my girl," Julian warned her. " How d'you think managers are going to find you if you waste yourself down here?"

" Oh, I don't know," Mina said. " I love the acting, but I hate everything else about it : the pushing for jobs and jealousy and back-biting." The scowl lifted from her face. " Now if I were like you, Mrs. Bannerman, I'd just walk into a manager's office and come out a leading lady."

Rachel shrugged. " I don't suppose it's as easy as that."

She stood in the wide hall and looked about her. She could sense, though hardly explain, the difference between this house and Maurice's house in Portman Square. It wasn't only that falling view across the wide countryside that the doorway framed. It was something in the house itself. In Maurice's house everything looked as though it had been acquired ; here things had the air of having grown where they were. Everything was a little dingier, a little shabbier than at Maurice's, and yet somehow more effective. She wandered with Julian and Mina into the dining-room. The pictures there, like those in the hall, were not, Rachel noted, attractive scenes or agreeable compositions. They were all pictures of people, and you felt that the people had had to do with this place and this family. Mina might dress as fantastically as she liked, and Julian as conventionally as he liked, but about them both there was something that belonged here. She wondered if she could ever feel at home with these people as she did with Maurice Bannerman. He had never daunted her.

Mina, who had been standing, with her hands thrust into her pockets, gazing out of the window, suddenly wheeled round and said, as if in answer to Rachel's thought : " Being beautiful is the only thing that matters."

" Then Mrs. Bannerman wins every time," said Julian. " What about that lunch ? "

Chapter Fifteen

I

AS the car passed out of sight Oxtoby heard his name called, and, turning, saw Mike Hartigan standing at the front door.

" Where's Mrs. Bannerman gone, Oxtoby ? "

" I don't know. She didn't tell me. Just said she wanted the car but not me."

" Who's the young man ? "

" I could hardly ask that, Mr. Hartigan."

" You've got a soft job. I suppose by and by the car will be delivered at the front door, Bright will ring through to you, and you'll come and take it home. An easy day's work, begod."

Oxtoby shrugged his shoulders.

" I shall be wanting to go round to the nursing home soon to see Mr. Bannerman."

" I'm sorry, Mr. Hartigan : there's only the one car. There's plenty of room in the garage, and it might be convenient if Mrs. Bannerman had a small runabout of her own for occasions of this sort."

" Don't worry, Oxtoby," Mike said. " She'll have that all right. It's only a matter of time."

173

Maurice slowly opened his eyes and looked in perplexity about the white room. It was remote, as though
he were imagining it rather than seeing it. The white
net curtains at the open window shivered slightly ;
they seemed to his queer vision like tall living shapes
that were for ever making a sinewy step forward as
though they would invade the room, then deciding,
after all, to stand still and watch.

White everywhere. The walls were white, and the
white chest of drawers with its bulging front was like
a small stubborn iceberg. Maurice was vaguely aware
of himself as something still and white, immobile in
the snowy drift of the bed. He tried to lift a hand,
to see if that were white, too, but found the effort too
much.

With infinite care, he rolled his head to one side,
and saw something which stirred him because it was
not white. It was Mike Hartigan's red face and black
hair.

" Now for the love of God, Maurice, keep still and
don't try to talk," Mike whispered, " or they'll have
me out of this place quicker than smoke. How are
you then, you old devil ? You're not dead yet—not
by a long chalk."

Maurice looked at him for a long time with a
dead, expressionless face. Then he whispered :
" Rachel ? "

" Ach, don't you be worrying about Rachel," said
Mike. " She'd have been spending the whole day
camped down here by your bedside, but they thought

she'd better not come. They won't have you excited
She sent you some flowers."

There was a great bunch of white lilac in a tall vase
on the iceberg of the chest of drawers. Maurice could
not see it till Mike brought it and held it close to his
eyes. Then he lifted a hand and feebly dropped it
again, as though to say " Good."

When Mike was gone, his eyes remained fixed above
the chest of drawers. But he could not see the flowers
for the intolerable whiteness of everything. He
thought it was like being out on a landscape deep with
snow, and then could not dismiss the thought from his
mind. He wandered on and on in snow that fell
thicker and thicker till at last it buried him.

III

Charlie Roebuck stood before the mirror in the
bedroom at Duck Yard, deftly fixing a black tie,
and continued his conversation with Julian Heath,
who was settled down in a wicker chair in the sitting-
room.

" Yes, it sounds as though it's been very gay. By
the way, have you rung up the nursing home to ask
how Bannerman's getting on ? "

Julian thought that no reply was needed to that.
" Well," Charlie went on, " since you *have* been to
the ancestral acres, what news ? Anything addressed
to me from Mina ? Some kind word of remembrance?"

" Not a thing," said Julian with satisfaction. He
wished he could see Charlie's face. " Pretty glum,
I'll bet," he thought.

Charlie came out, pulling on his coat. He smacked open an opera hat and stuck it on the side of his head. " So you stay here and brood ? " he asked.

Julian grunted.

" Very well. Happy dreams." He descended the stairs, whistling his latest.

Charlie, Julian reflected, needn't be so obviously cheerful and unconcerned, just to hide his annoyance. He had had no intention, when he went out in the morning, of not keeping the usual luncheon appointment at the club. Things had just happened, that was all. Here was a young woman without a friend anywhere near, as he had explained to Charlie, and in mere decency he had helped her through a difficult day. " Oh, yes," Charlie had assented. " The sort of thing one does for any girl." And then he had added : " It's not going to stop at a difficult day, is it ? So far as I can see, with her husband on his back, she's going to have some difficult weeks or months. Does your ever-ready sympathy stretch to that ? "

Julian preferred not to face the question. He got up with a grunt, feeling annoyed with himself and Charlie and everybody else, made himself some coffee, and sat down to work. Charlie needn't be so damned virtuous. He was not slacking. He had taken the morning off, it was true ; now to make up for it. But it wasn't easy. Indeed, it was no good at all. He could think of nothing but Rachel. The leading woman in his play became a nonentity, a myth. Rachel took her place. He saw her again coming down the stairs of the hotel in Blackpool. " God ! What an entrance ! " If he could only write a play round a character like that : beautiful as heaven and as cruel as sin ! Oh, yes, he told himself with a self-satisfied smile, he had no illusions about her ; he had Mrs. Bannerman weighed up all right. But all the same, what an actress ! If he could only put her across ! It was fame and fortune for them both. He was certain of it—dead certain.

And so, instead of sitting there scowling at his writing-pad, Julian swept it suddenly into a drawer, took a sheet of notepaper and wrote :

" MY DEAR MINA,—What a little fool you are ! I was cut to the quick—whatever the quick may be —to find you, as usual, wasting yourself this afternoon. Why not let Markham and all the old dames in it go to blazes. You've got yourself to think about. You know that I've always thought you were a damn fine actress, and it's now nearly twelve months since I've seen you in a part. I know you hate London, and so do I. It's the most blatant, gaudy, ruddy mess to be found on the face of the habitable globe, and the most provincial city in Great Britain. But all the same, my dear Arson, setting the Thames on fire remains a pleasant enough occupation. But you can't do it from Markhams. You've got to be on the spot.

" I have a very good reason why you should be —Mrs. Bannerman. What did you think of her? She seems to me to be the whole Hollywood garden in one bloom. And she's *made herself*. I don't know much about her, but putting two and two together, I gather that at the moment she's playing a new part, and isn't she playing it ! I'm going to write a play for her, and you and I between us are going to put her across. I honestly believe she's a *born actress*. There are a few of 'em, you know, and the schools have got nothing to give them. All she needs to learn, you can teach her. Your flat in Panton Street is rotting. Why not come up and take a hand in launching a planet? And you could be looking out for an opportunity to twinkle on your own behalf.

"Do you think I'm gone suddenly mad? Don't you believe it. Julian is on a cert. Charles Roebuck, master melody-maker, sends all the best. 'Od rot him. He's sulky with me.—JULIAN."

And then Julian felt better. He had wanted to do something like that, and now he had confessed it, now he had done it. He decided that a cup of coffee was a rotten substitute for dinner, that he would go and eat something at the Café Royal. On the way he posted the letter to Mina. He played for a while with the idea of ringing up Rachel and asking her to dine with him. No : better not. He had already spent eight hours with her that day. He wondered what Mina would have to say. He believed she would come. She had liked Rachel, and he had succeeded in making Rachel seem a cause, a crusade, into which Mina could throw herself. Mina was a born crusader. Yes ; he believed she would come.

Chapter Sixteen

I

THE evening had turned chilly, and Lord Upavon, who had got home at dusk from his board meeting, stood in the drawing-room with his back to the fire. He was a surprising person to be the father of Julian and Mina. There was nothing of their fine-drawn elegance about him. He was a tall man, but so heavily built that he did not look tall. His face from cheek to cheek across the mouth was much wider than his forehead. He wore a bristling moustache and had an appearance of great good-humour. The appearance was not deceptive. He was good-humoured. His good-humour was the ace he had played all through life. His mentality, like his appearance, was that of a successful pork butcher, but his equable temper, his homely shrewdness, enabled him to do without dazzling gifts. His gruff cheerful voice and ready smile stood him well with the tenants on his farms, the occupants of his immense urban estates, whom it was his habit to visit often, his business colleagues. He was the bluff, no-damn-nonsense Englishman, and it came off every time because it was not a pose : it was good-tempered, unimaginative, immensely rich Lord Upavon.

His heir was like him, and was now with a regiment

in India, doing unimaginatively and with immense concentration and sincerity all the things that officers have always done in India. All the imagination of the family had been poured into the queer mould of Wilhelmina, gifted, intractable, and unstable. All save a small residue which had drained into Julian's handsome and for the most part conventional head. He had just enough imagination to hate sitting on his behind at home, or taking one of the many engaging sinecures that his father suggested to him. His imagination came out as a bee in the bonnet : a determination to live on his own, and by his own efforts ; and in this he was greatly fortified by the knowledge that he could at need fall back on a whole herd of fatted calves.

Wilhelmina was not at all troubled by the knowledge that her father kept her. There had been times when she kept herself handsomely ; and then the unstable link in her make-up would snap, and she would fly home and do nothing. It seemed at one time that she was to have a brilliant career as an actress. She had played a part superbly in a play that took London by storm. When the play ended, she was immediately offered a better part in another play. She said she was tired of London and went back to Markhams. She said she couldn't bear to be away for a moment during the time the cherry blossoms were out. If the production of the new play could be delayed till the cherry blossoms were over, she would take the part. The production was not delayed ; Mina enjoyed the cherry blossoms and was now enjoying the bitter knowledge that the play was still running and that she was being more and more considered an undependable person for whose idiosyncrasies managers could hardly be expected to budget.

Lord Upavon understood nothing of the queer, volcanic composition of his daughter. He was glad when she came home, glad that she was staying home. He liked her about the place. She was all he had, now that Colin was in India and Julian fooling about in London. She seemed happy enough, riding like a boy, painting great daubs and making scenery in one of the barns, now up to the neck with the vicar and all his doings, now setting a damn bad example by staying away from church and telling everybody that she thought it all bunk.

She ought to be married; that was what it all boiled down to, Lord Upavon reflected, as he stood before the fire. He looked very ceremonious. Nothing would induce him to wear a dinner-jacket and black tie. With tails and an elegant white bow, he stood there looking as though something were missing. Then one realised that it was the blue sash of the Garter. The whole man was made for it.

Mina came in. You would not have known her for the girl you had seen this morning. She was wearing a green dress that flowed down to her feet in simple lines and was decorated round the hem with a Greek key pattern in gold. She still wore golden sandals, but now they were new. Her red hair was still untamed. It was one of Lord Upavon's favourite jokes that when Mina was a child she had set fire to a gollywog's hair, and that she had had to wear a gollywog's flaming hair as a punishment ever since.

He laid his hands affectionately under her elbows as she came and stood before him. "Well, well;

what's this, what's all this? We haven't seen this before."

He understood that a man should always notice new clothes on a woman and be interested in them.

"Just something I thought of and made," said Wilhelmina.

"Made, made," said Lord Upavon, who said most things twice in a very hearty way. "Why made, eh? Why made? Don't we allow you enough for dress-makers?"

"Oh, it's just fun. And a dressmaker couldn't make this, anyway—not quite. Are you tired, Daddy? Had a hard day?"

"Well, and what if I have had, eh? What if I have had? Mustn't complain, you know. Work's got to be done."

Lord Upavon had been taken to town in a well-padded Daimler, had attended his board meeting which lasted an hour, lunched at his club with a crony, looked at the papers, then slept till four. Then he called for a cup of tea, and then his Daimler brought him home. "No, mustn't complain," he said, "though it's a bit of a grind, you know, a bit of a grind. Ha!"

The exclamation was caused by the appearance of Curle, the butler, as big and hearty as Lord Upavon himself, announcing that dinner was served.

Mina could never get over the comedy of dinner at Markhams, when she and her father dined alone. It was like a gazelle and an ox trying to be companionable. Upavon was a robustious eater and a connoisseur of wine. Mina could have bought all she needed for sixpence, and drank nothing but water. Nevertheless, her father pressed her for an opinion on every dish at which she had nibbled, and was inclined to discourse lovingly on the wines she never tasted.

" And what have you been doing, eh—what have you been doing ? " he asked, letting the soup linger for a moment on his tongue.

" Nothing much, Daddy," said Wilhelmina, who did not wish ever to think again of Mrs. Harrison and gymnastics. " Julian came to lunch."

" Ought to come more often. Ought to come when I'm here. What d'you think of this onion soup ? "

" I like it."

" They tell me there's very good onion soup at the Café Royal. Quite a speciality. I've never been there. I'd like to know, though, whether this is as good. You've been there ? Do you know the soup ? Is it as good as this ? I shouldn't think it likely."

" I've had it there, but I don't remember."

" Ha ! So Julian came. What's he after, eh ? What's he after ? Curle, that soup's very good. Tell the cook I said so. I don't think it at all likely that the stuff at the Café Royal is anything like so good—not anything like. Mina, my dear, you should try a little of this claret."

" No, thank you, Daddy."

" It's a very light wine, and very delightful. You would like it. It would do you good. You need colour, my dear, you need colour. It's all gone into your hair, eh ? Tell me about Julian."

" He brought a Mrs. Bannerman with him—a most beautiful woman, Daddy. I've never seen a more beautiful woman in my life. She's a Jewess. Jewesses seem to be like that—either repulsive or frighteningly beautiful. Did you ever hear of Rachel, Daddy ? "

" Rachel—Rachel ? Who was Rachel ? I don't think this sole is all that it might be. Do you, my dear ? "

" Rachel was a very famous actress. She was a Jewess, too. I think she must have been frighteningly beautiful like Mrs. Bannerman, when she was young."

" Beautiful Jewesses ? What are we talking about ? I thought we were talking about Julian, or this sole. It's not good—not at all good."

" We were talking about Mrs. Bannerman, who came with Julian."

" Well, why's he running about with beautiful married women ? Why is he doing it ? "

" It's rather a tragedy, Daddy."

" So is this sole. Ha, ha ! "

" She was only married a day when her husband had a terrible accident. They don't know even yet whether he'll be a cripple for life."

" But that's Maurice Bannerman. I know him. I've served on boards with him. Saw the announcement of his marriage in *The Times* and then the next day a paragraph about this accident. I was shocked, shocked. So that's the woman, is it ? How did Julian get to know these Bannermans, eh ? "

" He seems to have met them by accident in the Lake district. What is Mr. Bannerman ? "

" Bannerman ? Oh, everything, everything. You know—the Midas touch. Sprang up out of nothing during the war. And now they tell me he's clearing out of everything. Extraordinary feller—extraordinary. Lives in Portman Square. I was there once. House full of pictures—French stuff. Don't understand it—all bright colours. I was taken into his study, and d'you

184

know what he was doing? Playing the cello—you know, the big feller—zoom, zoom—like a beer barrel. Astonishing feller. Look here, you're eating nothing. This pork's good. It's very good, Curle."

"Sorry, Daddy. I couldn't possibly eat pork after fish. You've got an astonishing digestion."

"So I have, so I have. Well, I don't know; you modern girls, you don't seem to have room for a good dinner inside you."

"He sounds interesting, this Mr. Bannerman. I do hope he'll soon be well."

"Interesting? Yes, he's interesting enough, but a Jew, you know."

"Perhaps I shall meet him. I'm going up to town."

"Town? What d'you want in town? Aren't you happy here?"

"I'm getting restless. I may look out for another part on the stage."

Lord Upavon sighed ponderously. "And leave me, eh? Leave me to stew in my own juice? Restless, are you—restless. That's the trouble. Restlessness. Everybody's too restless. Why don't you get married?"

Mina shrugged her shoulders. There seemed nothing to say.

"Well, if you must go, you must. Come along now. This is where you join in again. Crème caramel. Try a little claret with it."

Mina pecked at her crème caramel and shook her head about the claret.

"None of that stuff for me," Lord Upavon declared. "I'll go right on to cheese. This Cheddar ripe, Curle, eh? Is it ripe?"

He drained his glass, refilled it, and sighed gustily.

" Contentment. That's what we all need. That's what the world needs. Contentment."

" I'd love to see those French pictures," said Mina. " I adore all those people—Monet and Gauguin and all that lot, and Van Gogh. He cut his ear off and sent it in a parcel to a girl."

Upavon, glass to lip, spluttered and splashed the wine upon his shirt front. " What ! Cut his ear off ! His ear ! "

" Yes, he did."

" Good God ! And you want to see pictures by a feller like that ! "

" Yes ; he was marvellous."

" Well, it seems to me a very foreign thing to do, my dear—very foreign."

" I'll call on Mrs. Bannerman and see them."

" Jews, and actresses, and people who cut off their ears—I don't know, my dear. I don't know. Curle, the port. You'd better try some, my dear, and eat a bit of fruit."

" No, thank you. Curle, I'll have coffee in my room. You'll excuse me, won't you, Daddy ? I've got a lot of letters to write. Would you like me to come down and sit with you later ? "

" Yes, my dear, do, do. I am lonely."

He carefully nipped the end of a cigar and Curle held a light. " Too much restlessness," he mumbled ; " running about, shouting, agitating. . . ."

When Mina came down an hour later, he was asleep in a big chair by the fire. His cigar, half-smoked, had been placed carefully in an ash-tray. A balloon brandy-glass, empty, was on the table beside him. Poor dear, he had had a hard day.

Before Julian was out of bed, the telephone bell rang in Duck Yard. Julian slipped on a dressing-gown, looked reproachfully at Charlie Roebuck, and shambled into the sitting-room.

" Well ? " he yawned into the instrument.

" This is Mina. You sound as though some one ought to throw a bucket of cold water over you."

" I expect you're going to do that. You're going to tell me my letter's all bunk."

" On the contrary, it's unusually intelligent. I had made up my mind to come up to town, anyway."

" So you're on ? "

" Absolutely. After Mrs. Harrison, Mrs. Bannerman is a gift from God. I like your nerve, though, saying the schools have got nothing to teach her. Don't you think I'm as good as any blessed school ? "

" You can't give her the team-work, my dear. That's where she'll break down, if anywhere."

" You leave it to me and hop along to Panton Street and see that everything's in order. I'll be there by lunch-time."

" Right," said Julian, and, placing his hand over the mouthpiece : " *No* message for Charlie Roebuck ? Right, I'll tell him."

" That was Mina," he announced, strolling back to the bedroom. " No message for Charlie Roebuck."

Charlie rolled over and covered his head with blankets. " You can make the coffee now you are up, you old jackass," he said. And a moment later, when

Julian had left the room, he shouted : " What did Mina say ? "

" No message for Charlie Roebuck," Julian bawled cheerfully.

" Yes, but apart from that, half-witted one ? "

" She's coming to town."

" To stay ? "

" For some time. Arriving about noon. Wants me to see the flat's in order."

" You can't do that." Charlie put on a dressing-gown and rambled out after Julian. " You've got to work. You must let me do it."

" Looking after me, aren't you, little brother ? " Julian sniffed hungrily over the steaming coffee. " Well, perhaps you're right."

" Of course I'm right. You've done nothing for two days."

"And God made the whole world in seven. Well——"

" Well ? "

" Right-o. You look to it. And good luck to you, little brother."

" I'll need it."

" You will," Julian assented heartily.

III

From Duck Yard you can easily get into Bond Street by way of Brook Street. Along those cheerful thorough-fares Charlie made his way that bright morning of early spring. It ought to be said that he had dressed with unusual care, but it would not be true to say it. His

188

usual care was enough. Both Charlie and Julian had a deceptive appearance of wealthy unemployment. It took in everybody save their friends who knew the mania for success that consumed them both.

Wearing his neat grey suit, faultlessly pressed, his brown shoes, a light green tie and a grey hat, Charlie went elegantly along Bond Street and thought of Mina. He had thought about her a good deal off and on throughout his young life. He could remember very clearly the first time he had seen her. He was fourteen and had come to Markhams to spend part of an Easter holiday with Julian. They were at the same school, completely taken up with one another from the beginning. They had travelled by themselves to the station nearest the village. It was five miles away. A car had met them there, and as they went up the long drive to the house, under the fresh green of the chestnuts, touched here and there with bloom, Charlie saw a girl in the meadow on the right. She was riding a pretty pony hell-for-leather, going for a home-made hurdle of furze. She looked a little fury, with red hair blazing upon her head.

"That's my sister, Mina," Julian explained; and at precisely the wrong moment let out a yell. "Mi-i-na!" Mina slewed her head round, she and her mount between them made a mess of things, and as the car sped by, Charlie saw Mina pick herself up and hobble in pursuit of the pony.

"Now she'll be mad with me," Julian promised; and she was. She told him in a brief torrent of words what she thought of him; and for the rest she had as little to do with him and Charlie as she possibly could. Whenever Charlie passed the meadow, she seemed to be there, demonstrating again and again how easily she could clear the hurdle.

Charlie and Julian went on to the same public school and to Cambridge ; and through all those years Mina appeared from time to time, bright and untamed. Charlie could recall handing pink cakes to her as she and Lord Upavon sat at tea on the lawn during a summer half-term. He could recall making a duck in the boys versus old boys cricket match, and going back feeling sheepish as Upavon shouted, " Hard luck, sir," and gave a perfunctory clap, while Mina put out her tongue and whispered, " Sucks-boo," as he went by. He sat on the pavilion steps when he had taken off his gloves and was conscious of nothing but her hair burning against the fresh green grass on which the white players scuttled to and fro.

Oh, innumerable little things Charlie Roebuck remembered as he sauntered through Bond Street, and most clearly he remembered a day when he had punted Mina along the river to the old orchard at Grantchester, and they had had tea at one of the little tables in the long grass. The apples were ripening on the bowed, mossy trees, and the air was full of a sharp anger of wasps. There was not a cloud in the sky, and they were content to sit there talking of nothing much, absorbing the good warmth as the sun fell down and down. They stayed so long that the sky in the west was a saffron smother as they got into the punt, and mist was trailing in milky veils on the river and in the meadows. Mina lay full length. You could see her white face, and around that the frame of her red hair, and around that the green of a cushion. It was so quiet that Charlie could hear the silver dribble of water from the pole's end and the wrenching of grass by the beasts that were knee-deep in the smoky drift that hid the fields. And you could hear the water voles paddling their tiny craft from bank to bank and smell the heavy odour of mint and meadow-sweet and rotten river mud.

They did not speak for a long time, and then Mina said in a very quiet voice : " I suppose Rupert Brooke is just a sentimentalist already. Never mind. His ghost is on the river to-night. His ghost will always be on this river. D'you think there'll ever be another war, Charlie ? "

" God knows."

" D'you think there *is* a God ? "

" No."

" Neither do I. I wish we could get rid of God and the Devil and realise that good and evil are in our own hands. Then we might get somewhere."

" I doubt it."

" Why ? "

" Because I see no reason why good and evil in our hands should work out any differently from good and evil in the hands of God and Devil."

" Then you don't think we'll ever get anywhere ? "

" Nowhere much."

A queer, pessimistic little conversation, folded round by the beautiful melancholy of the evening ; and all the time Charlie was thinking : " Oh, if only I could get down there beside you, and put my arms around you, and kiss that white fierce little face, I should get as near to heaven as any god is ever likely to take me."

They lapsed into silence, said nothing at all till they had put the punt in at the landing-stage and were walking up the lane from the river. They were between high buildings, in a corridor roofed by the deep violet of the sky. Mina said : " I wonder what's to be *got* out of life ? Everything is so beautiful, but we seem to be only looking at it. We don't seem to be part of it."

Charlie stopped suddenly and took her by the elbow, thought with a sharp pang how small and thin it seemed. " Oh, my darling," he said. " Mina, you love, you darling ! You sound so lonely."

Her white face looked up into his. It glimmered below his eyes as pale as a dog-daisy in the dusk. " Yes, Charlie, I am," she said simply. " Terribly." She took herself quietly from his grasp and they went on.

Chapter Seventeen

I

MINA'S flat was over a tobacconist's shop in Panton Street, quite a commonplace little shop where a lot of commonplace business went on all day. The shop was run by Billy Eckersley, who was born at Wigan, graduated from a Saturday night sing-song in a Manchester pub to a northern music-hall circuit, and had the makings in him of a first-class comedian. But Billy Eckersley did not have the sense to wait till army concert-parties were formed ; he rushed into the infantry, and in the same afternoon lost half a leg, which put a stop to his clever clog dancing, and inhaled enough gas, as he lay out waiting for a stretcher party, to put an end to his singing. Billy could still sing a bit, but he never knew when a choking fit would break him off short. He was an indomitable person, surprised everybody at the orthopædic hospital by the quick mastery he made of his artificial leg ; and when he was discharged he did his best to get back to the music-halls, working the cough into his business in the manner of George Formby. But it was too painful. He had to give it up. He married a V.A.D. nurse who came from London. She declared that she would perish in Lancashire, so Billy, who had always been a saving man, bought the business in Panton Street.

It was a three-story building. By day, Billy laboured

on the ground floor. When business was over he retired to the top story, where he and Mrs. Eckersley had their quarters. Between these two stories was Mina's flat. It had been decorated and furnished by Lord Upavon as a twenty-first birthday present. Mina was then a student at the Academy of Dramatic Art. Her father was shocked at the place she chose to live in. He wanted her to go into a great block where everything was spick and span, hygienic, furnished with lifts and " service." Mina said she would hate it. She wasn't the bee type and would not live in a compartment of a hive. Nor would she allow Lord Upavon to do all the drastic things he wanted to do in Panton Street. And so she had a sitting-room and a bedroom and a bathroom, all decent and homely ; and she had the joy, which she greatly esteemed, of Billy Eckersley's occasional company and Mrs. Eckersley's most efficient housekeeping and cooking. There were no young Eckersleys. " Nay, lad," Eckersley would declare. " Not for me and t'missus. Spend all wer brass on summat as'll be blown to bits next time t'bloody fooils get loose ? Nay, we've got more goomption."

Mina's request that the flat be got ready was unnecessary. Charlie knew enough about Mr. and Mrs. Eckersley to be aware that the flat was always ready. Mina's rather fragile, but for a time brilliant, attachment to the stage gave her in Billy Eckersley's eyes a romantic radiance ; and, for Mrs. Eckersley, no less radiance showered from the fact of her being Lord Upavon's daughter. Between them, they thought a bit of Mina, and Mina liked them and got on with them splendidly. Once, when she had a few friends in, one of them burst out : " Oh, Mina, do have up that funny

194

little man from the tobacconist's shop. I'm told he's no end of a comedian. D'you think he'd do a turn for us?"

"No, I do *not*!" Mina answered firmly. "He's done a turn in this room more than once, and that's because I like him and he likes me, but I'm not asking him up like a performing dog to amuse a pack of people he's never set eyes on."

So Charlie took his time. It was noon when he arrived at Panton Street with an armful of flowers which he had bought in Piccadilly Circus. He looked into the shop to fill his cigarette case, and there found Billy with four piles of tobacco on the counter, about to compound them into what he called " Hippodrome Mixture " in memory of a week which was very precious to him when he and Little Tich and Harry Weldon had all been on the same bill at the Hippodrome in Manchester. Billy was pale and solemn looking, as so many Lancashire comedians are, but he had a lift of the eyebrow which could transmute mere simplicity into a tremendous innocence. It made him look a babe in the wood of this wicked world, and all his songs had given point to that look. They had celebrated the sad lot of the northern lad in the grip of the metropolitan harpy, getting out of tight corners with little left save a pair of boots for the walk back to Wigan. But Billy's looks were deceptive. He was sprightly enough in conversation.

"Good-mornin', captain," he greeted Charlie. "Don't often see you around when Miss Heath is not about."

"You've got it in a nutshell, Billy. Miss Heath is going to be about. She's coming to-day."

"Lummy. Ah'd better send oop and warn t'missus. Is she staying long? She hasn't been here, not above an odd few days now an' then, for nearly a twelve-month."

"I don't know how long she's staying. But don't you bother, Billy. I'll go up and tell Mrs. Eckersley."

"Reight. Ah don't suppose there's more than a spit and a rub wanted, onny road."

And, indeed, not even that seemed necessary. It appeared to Charlie that Mrs. Eckersley strode vigorously through the rooms and that everything was then in order. He was left alone in the sitting-room. He took into the bathroom all the vases he could find, filled them with water, and soon had the sitting-room gay with flowers. Not that they were needed to make it gay. It was a gay enough room before they came. Charlie switched on the electric fire and looked pleasurably about him, though he knew it all very well. Although Mina had used it so little, it had a lived-in look. There was none of the cold discomfort of the modern fashion. So far as there had been any attempt at a "scheme," it consisted merely in all the walls and all the paintwork being enamelled a creamy white and all the fabrics—curtains and upholstery and carpets—being a rich crimson. The pictures were reproductions of work by those painters whom Mina had told her father she liked so much. Their colours flamed against the white of the walls. In the place of honour over the mantelpiece was a big copy of Van Gogh's sunflowers. There were two easy-chairs, a cabinet gramophone, a writing-desk, and a gate-legged oak table whose surface Mrs. Eckersley kept so resplendent that the daffodils which Charlie had placed upon it looked as though they stood over their reflection in a peaty pool.

Charlie turned over a pile of records that were on the floor in a corner of the room. He found to his delight one of his own compositions—his one undoubted " hit " thus far. It had been sung in every pantomime that Christmas. Everybody in England had sung it or whistled it, but that, to Charlie Roebuck, was no reason why he should not hear it once again. There was no pretence about Charlie; he liked to hear his own stuff; and now he put on the record and began to shuffle about the room to its rhythm. It was a quick fox-trot. The sound of it prevented his hearing Mina's footstep on the stair. He was first aware of her when she stood in the room, smiling at his infatuation with his own work. He did not speak, but solemnly took her right hand in his left, put his left arm upon her waist, and drew her into the dance. Round the table they went, in and out of the chairs; not a smile on Charlie's face; only the dead solemnity he accorded to his own work. The record wound to a close and Charlie clapped. " That was pretty good," he said.

" Good-morning," said Mina, throwing a short fur jacket on to a chair.

" Oh, good-morning."

" I expected to find Julian here."

" Julian's where he ought to be—at work. He wasted all yesterday and most of the day before on the Bannerman woman. I insisted on his staying in this morning."

Mina smiled. " How you two look after one another ! You sound as though you don't approve of the Bannerman woman."

197

" Do you ? "

" I think she's amazingly beautiful. Her face and body are perfect and she walks like a doe. Don't you think she's lovely ? "

" I know very little about her. Julian and I butted into their car up in the Lake District. There was all the excitement of the moment, old Bannerman pretty badly hurt, it was raining like stink, and altogether, believe me, I saw little enough of the woman. She was as white as paper, and trembling, and Julian was gallantly holding her up. That's about all I noticed. I haven't seen her since."

" That makes your prejudice the more unreasonable. Because, clearly, you are prejudiced. You don't like her. I can tell it from every word you say and every accent you use. However, what about sitting down ? "

Charlie pushed a chair up to the fire, and when Mina was sitting he continued to stand, one elbow on the mantelpiece, his head resting on his hand. " The floral decorations, I take it," he said, " are worthy of passing mention ? "

" Thank you, Charlie, they're lovely."

" May one who is faintly interested in your well-being inquire what has brought you to town and whether you are staying long ? "

" Work, chiefly, Charlie—work. It's time I got a job again. And while waiting for that, I intend to take Mrs. Bannerman in hand. Julian thinks she'll make a grand actress, and I'm not sure that he's wrong. He's writing a play for her."

Charlie came away from the mantelpiece and strode down the room. " Oh, God ! " he groaned. " That woman ! Why didn't we kill her while we were at it ?

We could have got away with it. You get nothing for murder on the high road."

"You *are* prejudiced, Charlie." Mina lit a cigarette and looked at him with amusement.

"Well, it's a bit thick to find *you* in it, too," Charlie complained. "Here's a woman who's married one day, whose husband is knocked out the next, and who is found the day after that gallivanting about the country with a young man she has seen for five minutes. Do you like it, Mina? Honestly, do you like it?"

"You'd better take me out and give me some lunch."

"Will I not! Julian dropped me yesterday. He can whistle to-day."

"That's the spirit. Come on."

II

They had not far to go. Stone's chophouse in Panton Street was but a step away. "I love the waiters there with the red waistcoats," said Mina. "They look as though they might shout 'View hallo!' at any moment and drop the soup and pursue a fox into the Haymarket."

"And they have a guaranteed real Indian to make curries," said Charlie.

"And there will be no celebrities there except us," said Mina. "Have you got a notebook and pencil? I want to make a note of everything I eat, and of all the flavours. Daddy's sure to want to know, and I never remember what I eat unless I write it down. Don't you think there's an awful lot of nonsense talked about food, Charlie?"

" And about wine."

" And about women. About Mrs. Bannerman now . . ."

" In the name of suffering humanity, I protest," said Charlie. " Did you bring me here to talk about that woman ? "

" What else ? You don't think, do you, that I'd allow you to break your solemn oath and covenant with Julian except for something special ? Now, Charlie, I want you to be reasonable. I shall probably be seeing a lot of Mrs. Bannerman, and therefore, I dare say, you will be seeing a good deal of her too. Can I trust you to be intelligent ? "

" Very well," said Charlie rather sulkily.

" That's my brave boy."

" Oh, hell, don't rag. What are you going to do this afternoon ? "

" I want to get a good feel of London again before I settle down to anything. So I think I'll let you take me for a walk."

" Really ? "

" Yes, really. If you don't work this afternoon, Julian will feel morally quits with you. Then you'll get on all right again. It will be a splendid thing for you, Charlie, to stop being earnest for a day."

" Well, a man's got his career to think of. . . ."

Mina waved a hand with faint annoyance. " Yes, yes," she said. " D'you know the silliest thing I ever heard ? It was at a Book Society luncheon. A very highbrow novelist, who looked rather like a piece of the Parthenon frieze, reproduced in lard, said in pained tones : ' After all, one is an artist or nothing.' My God ! I would have hurled my rice pudding at him only I was hungry. Don't get like that, Charlie."

" Oh, my stuff isn't highbrow."

" It's not the stuff ; it's the attitude. Come on now and smell the air."

So they went through the Haymarket and into Trafalgar Square and down Whitehall, and thence they launched themselves into the green heart of London. They wandered about in St. James's Park, and Mina said that the fat pigeons with their puffed-out chests were the spit and image of Lord Upavon. The crocuses were out, and here and there a stray daffodil had broken a golden banner over the tall spears ranked about it. Mina was entranced to find a few green feathery leaves on the low branches of a hawthorn. She took off her small wool hat, pushed it into Charlie's pocket, and shook out the flames of her hair to the sunlight.

" You are like Salome," said Charlie, looking at her tense white face. " I'm sure Salome had red hair."

" Salome was a bitch," Mina said simply, " and she didn't have hair like mine. No one in the world has ever had hair like mine."

She danced ahead, fluffing out her hair with her fingers till it was a dazzling nimbus. Charlie's heart ached. She did not care what the passers-by thought. He was sure she did not care what he thought. She looked detached, marvellously free.

They went up Constitution Hill, Mina very subdued. " I always *creep* past the King's garden wall," she said. And so they came to Hyde Park corner and went right through to the Marble Arch, and then they made a big sweep through Hyde Park and came out in Knightsbridge. They had tea there in a small café that had no other customers. It was very cosy, with a fire burning and a shaded lamp on their table. The evening darkened as they sat there. The lights bloomed in the road without, and between their haven and the wide dimming spaces of the park the traffic shuttled with blaring horns and flashing lights.

Charlie felt indisposed to venture from the quiet fireside to the maelstrom of the street. It had been a glorious afternoon. Not for long had he had Mina to himself for hours and hours. They had both sat silent for some minutes, occupied with their own thoughts. "What are hers, I wonder?" Charlie asked himself. There was nothing to help him to an answer. Occasionally her grey eyes looked at him with a friendly smile, then they would shift on to the roaring commerce of the street. Her hand lay on the table, almost under his own, white like all her skin, the nails faintly pink, like shells, unstained. He longed to put his hand on her hand and to tell her what was in his heart. As if divining his thought, she rose abruptly. "Well," she said. "That was good, Charlie. Thank you. I shall remember this afternoon."

"So shall I," said Charlie, thinking how many afternoons there were that he remembered which yet lacked the grand thing that would be the crown of all remembrance.

Chapter Eighteen

I

RACHEL was surprised and enchanted when, that evening, Wilhelmina Heath rang up to ask if she might call in the morning. The inquiry came at just the right moment. Rachel was feeling miserable and forlorn. She had braced her nerves, summoned Oxtoby, and called at the nursing home. It was only ten minutes' walk away, but Oxtoby did not mind the absurdity. He seemed pleased to have something to do.

Rachel was taken to the white room and warned on the threshold by a stiff, creaking nurse that she must not stay long and not excite the patient. Then she was left alone with Maurice. He was awake and conscious of her presence. She bent and kissed him, but felt his lips unresponsive. Only his eyes made her aware that he knew she was at his side. She spoke some commonplace endearments in a low tone, but he could not answer her. She took his white hand in hers and squeezed it gently, but felt no answering pressure. She smiled but was rewarded by nothing but the dumb stare of Maurice's dark eyes. It was horrible, beyond words—ghastly. It was like coquetting with a corpse in a morgue. She could not stand it, and suddenly a fit of sobbing took hold of her, shook her violently. She had to let go his hand in order to press a handkerchief into her eyes. When she at last regained possession of herself, she saw that he was aware of her distress, that behind the brown eyes there was a terrible clamouring for expression such as you see sometimes in a dog's, gone almost mad with emotion. At last he gasped, "Not to cry—for me—Rachel."

For you ! Ah, God, yes. I suppose you ought to be cried for too ; but I was crying for myself.

She was glad when the nurse came and took her away. The matron was sympathetic. Would she like some tea ? No, she would not ! Not in that place. There was something refreshing in Oxtoby's healthy, pink face, soothing in his respectful deference.

" Drive me somewhere—anywhere," she said. " Be back at home in a couple of hours. Put up both the windows, please."

" How is Mr. Bannerman, madam ? "

" Very bad indeed."

Oxtoby said no more, but his look was all grief and solicitude which he expressed in the only way he knew, by handling the car with a tender virtuosity—no jolts or jars or sudden swerves. Rachel felt soothed. It was warm in the car. It was as comfortable as a travelling boudoir. She pulled the rug closer about her knees, settled deeper into the cushions, watched beyond the window the procession of the abomination of the Great West Road. The rhythm of the car's movement lulled her, and soon she slept.

When she awoke she had no idea where she was. All she could see was that the car was still travelling over a great wide stretch of concrete, treeless and desolate, passing here and there through cuttings where the earth was as raw as new wounds. Presently, a building as vulgar and offensive as the road itself appeared ahead, and the word " Road House " on a hoarding caught her eye. Rachel had heard of road houses, but she had never been at one. This, she thought, will be a better place for tea than a nursing home ; and she called through the tube to Oxtoby to stop.

" I shall have tea here," she said. " You'd better have some too."

She loved the great central room of the road house. The place was called the Cockatoo ; and cockatoos dominated the decoration. They crowded the walls, they appeared, neatly embroidered, on the waiters' lapels, they were printed on the menu cards, and, in the flesh and feather, they were strident in cages that swayed here and there, hanging on chains from the ceiling.

The floor was for dancing, and the chairs and tables, twisted tubes of metal, were ranged round it. Rachel would have loved to dance. She felt that it would help to lift from her mind the hellish depression that had settled there. But no dancing was going forward, though an orchestra's chairs and music stands were arranged on a little dais, with a drum emblazoned with a cockatoo. However, the wireless was blaring away, and that was something.

The cheap and vulgar effrontery of the whole place seemed good to Rachel as she sipped her tea from a cup on which a cockatoo was printed and spread upon her toast a pat of butter on which that same bird continued its insane iteration. She had not felt strange in Portman Square ; Markhams had not got her down ; but she could like the Cockatoo also. It was not dirty ; it was not poverty-stricken ; it had its defiant if banal gaiety. And that was what mattered to Rachel. Her shaken spirits rose a good deal in that absurd place ; and then suddenly they shot down again, leaving her deathly cold.

"Anything more, madam ? "

"No, thank you."

The waiter began to make out the bill, and Rachel remembered that she hadn't a penny. Maurice had done nothing about money ; Mike Hartigan had been offensive about it ; and the last shilling of her own had been spent on lilac the morning when Maurice fell.

The waiter put the bill on the table and walked away. She sat there burning with shame. She recalled an occasion years ago when she had been in a café in Manchester and found, when the bill came, that she had lost her purse. It was horrible, humiliating. She could still feel the burn of it in her cheeks—all those cheap oily-headed Jews watching the little scene. "You had better come with me and see the manageress." As if you had been trying to get away with something. " Perhaps you have some friend in the café who might lend you the money ? " No ; no friend. " Well, your name and address——" Rachel remembered it all, remembered that the bill was for sevenpence halfpenny. All that shame and public exhibition for sevenpence halfpenny ! Oh, it was hell being poor. It was out of that and such-like incidents that Rachel's fight began.

And now to be back in just such a situation ! If Rachel had never felt the fangs of the most abject poverty, she would have laughed. As it was, she had her moment of quick panic, her hot flush of fear, before she saw the absurdity of fear and panic.

She called the waiter. " Tell my chauffeur I would like to speak to him."

" Oh, Oxtoby, I'm sorry, but I've no money. I've come out without a single penny." She smiled at a situation so ridiculous.

" Well, madam, we can soon put that right," said competent Oxtoby. He produced a wallet, talking as he did so. " My last employer was a warning, madam. I'm never without a few pounds now. He never had a penny to buy an evening paper."

Rachel permitted the waiter an amused smile. " You see what we employers are," the smile said.

" Thank you, Oxtoby. If you'll just settle the bill and see that the waiter has something—— ? I'll get back to the car."

But the old shame somehow haunted her mind. All the way home it was there. She ran into Mike Hartigan in the hall. " Mr. Hartigan, Oxtoby paid for my tea. Will you settle with him, please ? And the sooner you look into the question I mentioned the other day the better."

She did not wait for Hartigan to answer. She ran up swiftly to her room in a bad temper that did not lift till the call came from Wilhelmina Heath.

II

And there Wilhelmina was. Near to the fireplace in Rachel's room a small table was prepared for breakfast. Across the coffee-pot and the thin curly rashers of bacon, the toast and marmalade and fruit, Rachel radiantly looked at her visitor. She had been so overwhelmed by Mina's telephone call, coming when she felt as low as she had ever felt in her life, that she blurted out her urgent invitation. " You *must* come and have breakfast with me."

Mina's clear laugh rang into the instrument. "You've got me weighed up, Mrs. Bannerman. You think I'm one of those tomboys who are out of bed and rushing about in the morning dew."

" Well," said Rachel gravely. " I can assure you that I don't face the day before I'm ready, and I'm ready at nine."

" Very well, then. Breakfast at nine."

As she waited for her visitor Rachel would have sung had she been in the habit of singing. She felt tremendously uplifted by the knowledge that some one was coming to dissipate the awful sense of frustration and loneliness that had filled her mind since Maurice's accident. Not a soul she could call upon in London, except Julian Heath. She knew that she could have all she needed of him ; but the voice of caution told her that she must not rush in too freely there. But Wilhelmina was another matter ; and, if it came to that, Wilhelmina might make it easier for her to see Julian if ever she wanted to. It was while she was dressing that she thought of that, and she paused, one leg crossed over the other, a stocking in her hand. Did she want to ? She was surprised and a little disturbed by the sudden quickening of her pulse at the thought of Julian. She had experienced it before when she had stood at the window watching him bound with beautiful ease across the square. Her pulse had never quickened at the thought of Maurice ; he quickened nothing but her wits. She pushed the whole thing out of her mind. Be practical. Everything's too dark at the moment. You don't know where you are.

From the window of her room she saw Mina arrive in that dreadful little stinking car that she had driven at Markhams. Mina came up to the room, Bright himself conducting her with a deference that Rachel found surprising. But then Rachel was not so well instructed as Bright in genealogy. Mina carried in her arms the cat Omar, and her first word was a cry of delight. " What a gorgeous cat, Mrs. Bannerman ! I found him on the stairs."

Omar exuded self-satisfaction. He gave himself up to Mina's approval with a deep secret knowledge of his own beauty. He lay along her arm, turned himself over on his back, and exposed the rich honey colour of the fur on his belly. His tawny eyes went swoony with abandon ; then he leapt to the floor, flicked his tail contemptuously at Rachel, and arched his body against Mina's leg.

" That cat seems to like everybody but me," said Rachel. " Yes, Mr. Hartigan ? " Mike had appeared at the door.

" The cat, Mrs. Bannerman. He's forbidden this room, I understand."

" Oh, I'm sorry," said Mina. " I didn't realise I was breaking a law."

" I should be glad, Mr. Hartigan, if you would allow the cat to stay," Rachel said frigidly. " If Miss Heath would like to have him."

" With the greatest of pleasure," Mike assented heartily, " so long's you'll not be stuffing him up with dollops o' slops."

" Thank you," Mina said. " I think I know how to

treat animals. I bred that Afghan that my brother gave to Mrs. Bannerman, you know. You can't complain about *his* condition, can you ? "

" You'd better ask Mr. Hartigan." Rachel looked cruelly at Mike, standing in the doorway teasing his thick black curls. The affable grin had gone from his face. He trembled for words.

" Well, Mr. Hartigan ! " Rachel prompted him unpityingly.

" Ach, it was a disastrous calamity, Miss Heath," said the unhappy Mike. " You see, we——"

" We ? "

" I, then, Mrs. Bannerman. I thought the dog was not to be trusted. After bringing Mr. Bannerman down like that. So I—I——"

" I wish you could explain your deeds as quickly as you carry them through," said Rachel. " We're waiting to get on with our breakfast."

Mina looked from Rachel standing erect and implacable, beautiful and pitiless, behind the breakfast table, to the man dithering for speech in the doorway. " She's torturing him," she thought, " knowingly and deliberately. I wonder why ? "

To Mike she said : " All right, Mr. Hartigan. I think I understand. You were no doubt terribly upset at the time. But I wish you'd waited till you were calmer. He was a lovely dog."

A smile that went to Mike's heart took the mild sting from the reproof. " I see that now," he said. " I'm terribly sorry——"

" All right, then. Your cat will be safe with me."

" You let him down very lightly," said Rachel, when the door was shut.

" He looks such a nice man. Who is he ? "

" My husband's secretary."

" And I've no doubt he's very fond of your husband, and that explains everything. I only hope Akbar was put out properly."

" He was shot."

" Ah, well——" A little sigh, an intensification of the pallor round which Mina's hair flamed, and she seemed to shake the whole thing from her mind. But she did not so successfully dispose of the memory of Rachel's face, lovely and venomous, or of Rachel's voice playing on the nerves of that hapless man. Mina hated it ; and yet she said to herself, " How intensely she did it ! She does nothing casually. I believe Julian's right about her. She's a born actress."

III

" Of course, you know," said Mina, " I had heard a lot about Mr. Bannerman before I met you. Daddy and he have had a good deal to do with one another. Business affairs. Daddy's been here, in this house, and he tells me that Mr. Bannerman has a lot of pictures that I want to see. That's why I've come—pure selfishness. That's a beautiful one over your fireplace."

She was half a head shorter than Rachel. She stood on tiptoe before the fire, her white, pointed face lifted towards the Monet. " You'll take me round to see the others, won't you ? "

And then it occurred to Rachel that she herself did not know this house of which she was the mistress. Misfortune had struck at her so swiftly that she had recoiled like a snail withdrawn into familiar security. Just this room, her bedroom. Maurice's study and the dining-room ; that was all she had seen.

She apologised to Mina. " I don't know the house myself," she said, " and I'm sure I know nothing about pictures. I'd better get Bright to take us round."

Bright was only too pleased. It was evidently no new task for him. " I've shown lots of people round, madam—art students, collectors, all sorts. Yes. Mr. Bannerman's pictures are very famous."

And so they made the rounds, and Mina was aware, as Rachel was not, of the beauty and importance of the pictures which Maurice Bannerman had gathered together. What impressed Rachel more than the pictures was the house ; and when Bright paused before lovely folding doors of mahogany, and said : " I'm sure Mr. Bannerman would have wished to show you the ballroom himself, madam," she only made an impatient gesture to him to fling open the doors.

It was a lovely room. Mina saw at once the splendour of its proportions, the perfection of its decoration. Rachel, with no knowledge to tell her why, just felt that it was right. The icy crystal bunched here and there in chandeliers, the long planished floor—at once she imagined it illuminated and pulsing with a throng of splendid people.

" What a glorious place for a ball," she exclaimed. " Has Mr. Bannerman ever given a ball here, Bright ? "

" No, madam. It hasn't been used for that purpose since Mr. Bannerman came into the house. He uses it as his picture gallery."

Mina had glided away, leaving them in the midst of the floor. " Please, don't wait for me," she exclaimed to Bright over her shoulder. " I shall be a long time here ! "

" Very well, madam. This is the last room."

Rachel sat down on a divan against the wall and soon forgot Mina's presence. She was overcome. She felt frustrate and weak, ready to break her heart at the sight of the splendour that lay just beyond her grasp. She felt like a child given a magnificent toy that must be kept behind a glass door. There it was—to be looked at. And there all round her was this magnificence that could never blossom into the vivid pageantry she imagined in her heart—never, so long as Maurice was lying on his back.

Then she was aware of Mina standing before her— Mina whose eyes were bright with the beauty they had fed upon. " It's wonderful—wonderful ! " she cried. " I didn't know there was such a marvellous private collection of these Frenchmen anywhere in England. I do hope I shall meet your husband soon. He must be a grand man—to recognise how worth while all this is, and to take so much trouble to collect it. I shall love him."

Rachel looked stonily before her.

" Don't you think it's a grand bat in the eye to all sorts of silly people to keep this room for a gallery instead of having hordes stamping about in it ? " Mina persisted.

" I don't know," Rachel answered. " I was just thinking a dance in here would be glorious. Probably," she added with great bitterness, " Maurice has collected all these things "—waving a light dismissive hand— " because he knows he'll be able to sell them for more than they cost."

Mina knelt swiftly at Rachel's feet and took the long hands that were lying in her lap. "My dear," she cried, "are you unhappy?"

Rachel pulled herself upright with a sudden effort. "If I am," she said, "help me not to be such a fool as to talk about it." Raising Mina gently to her feet, she said: "Get up, please," like a queen addressing a subject. With her long sinuous stride she led the way from the gallery.

When they were back in Rachel's room, Mina said as casually as she could: "Are you interested in the theatre at all? Have you done any amateur acting?"

"No," said Rachel, lighting a cigarette, "never."

"But you've been to the theatre a lot?"

"No. I've only been once or twice, when I was taken. In Manchester. You know I've lived there all my life till a day or two ago? Cochran always tries out his shows there. That's the sort of thing I've been taken to see—once or twice."

"You've never been to an ordinary straight play?"

"Never in my life."

"I should like to take you to one. It's terribly hard luck, what's happened to you—Mr. Bannerman's accident as soon as you were married. It'll help you, it'll cheer you up, if I take you out a bit."

Rachel, leaning on the mantelpiece, looked down at the red golliwog fuzz below her eyes. She liked the girl.

"It's good of you," she said. "I'd like to. But what about clothes?"

Mina laughed aloud. "I'm not going to blue my money on the dress-circle," she said. "Never mind clothes. Let's have dinner somewhere to-night and wander into a pit. I think I know a play you'll like."

Rachel looked a little crestfallen. Often she had pictured the London theatre—jewels, furs, diamonds sparkling in shirt fronts. So it had always seemed to her. What was to happen behind the footlights hardly came into the matter. And now, " We'll wander into a pit." Lord Upavon's daughter too !

" Right," she said.

" Splendid. At my flat at seven." She wrote the address. " Shall you be able to find it ? "

" I expect my chauffeur will," Rachel said grandly.

Chapter Nineteen

1

MINA had hardly left the house when the telephone bell rang. The call came from the nursing home. Mr. Bannerman was asking to see his wife. "Yes," said the matron. "I'm glad to say he's very much better. He asks that Mr. Hartigan should come round too."

Ten minutes later the car was at the door. As Rachel crossed the hall to go to it, she said casually to Bright : " Mr. Bannerman is asking to see Mr. Hartigan. Tell him, will you, to get round there at once ? "

She would not, she said to herself, she would not have that man in the car with her. The thought of that night in Blackpool when he had picked her up made her cheeks burn. He had done her a good turn ; stood her a dinner and a blow on the sea ; and she could have destroyed him for it. Let him walk.

Five minutes later, fuming in a traffic block, she saw Hartigan tear past, hatless. He was already at the nursing home when she got there. And she hated him for that too.

The matron took Rachel into her sitting-room, and there she found a short, clean-shaven, bull-necked man, with big strong hands like a butcher's. " This is Sir Aubrey Anderson," the matron murmured, and left them together.

Sir Aubrey was a surprise to Rachel. She had heard the name of the famous surgeon, and she had imagined something different from this rather shabby being. The hands, in particular, surprised her. She knew the expression " surgeon's hands " and associated it with fine, thin, white hands rather like her own. When Sir Aubrey took her hand in his she felt her bones crack.

" Sit down, Mrs. Bannerman," he said. " We've got some good news for you."

She murmured that she was glad, and took the chair he moved towards her. " Maybe, Mrs. Bannerman," he said, " you've heard of such a thing as an osteopath ? "

Rachel shook her head. " Never heard the word," she said.

" Ah, well," said Sir Aubrey, " you'll hear it a bit more often in the future. It's one of those words we surgeons only whisper. For our own sakes, the less we say about it the better." He surprised Rachel with a twinkle that was as good as a wink. " Our trade union doesn't like 'em. But when I've done all I can, and I see it's not enough, then I sometimes call in an osteopath. On the strict q.t., you know. Not a word to any one, eh ? Well, that's what we've done this time. You'll find Mr. Bannerman better. Keep it to yourself and thank your God he didn't fall into the hands of some of the stick-in-the-muds. Good-bye to you."

He held out his hand abruptly, opened the door for her, and left her to the care of the hovering matron.

" He's wonderfully better," said the matron ; " but no excitements, please, Mrs. Bannerman. Don't stay too long. I'll call you in ten minutes. Mr. Hartigan has seen him and gone."

Maurice could speak. That was the great difference.

She saw at once, as she crossed the soundless carpet of the white room, that he was inert as ever. Pain was written on the face that lay upon the pillow, but the eyes were clearer.

"Darling," said Maurice. "Good-morning. Good-morning."

She bent over the bed and kissed him. "I'm so glad, Maurice," she said. "I've just seen Sir Aubrey Anderson. He says you will get well."

She sat in a chair at the bedside and pushed the dark heavy hair back from Maurice's forehead.

"Yes," he said. "I shall get well, Rachel. It will be all right, after all. And I thought it was finished." He stared straight before him at the white chest of drawers which no longer looked like an iceberg. He could see the white lilac upon it. "Now I shall be able to make you happy, darling," he said. "Have you been lonely—unhappy?"

She nodded her head.

"I shall be here a long time," Maurice said. "I shall get well, but I shall be here a long time. You must be happy. You must enjoy yourself. You must have money. I have spoken to Mike Hartigan about that. That will be all right now. You will buy beautiful dresses—eh?—and come here every day to see me. I will see you looking more and more beautiful. But now that is enough about me. Tell me about yourself. How are you—eh? What do you want? What can I do for you?"

"But you've done everything, darling. If you've told Mr. Hartigan about the money, I can look after myself, can't I? I can get all I need. That was kind of you, Maurice, to think of that."

"Oh, money," he said impatiently. "I didn't mean money. No——"

She smiled at him sweetly. "You've had so much money, my dear, and you've had it for so long, that you've forgotten what it means to some one like me. A man who gives a woman money, freely and gladly, gives her an awful lot. Believe me, my dear, I know."

A nurse knocked at the door, appeared on the threshold. Rachel rose and bent over Maurice once more. His pain-filled eyes brimmed with happiness as her face swam above him ; her deep, enigmatic eyes with their long, black, silken lashes, the ivory prominence of her cheek-bones, the dark lustrous beauty of her hair. He raised his hand and drew a finger along the curve of her lips. She felt it tremble with desire and, stooping, kissed him hurriedly. "Good-bye, darling. Good-bye," she said. He saw the door shut silently behind her, and closed his eyes, feeling empty and bereft.

II

When Rachel stepped outside the nursing home door, the day waved in her face like a banner. It was a gay, alluring day. She had not noticed it before. You didn't notice those things in a car. But now it was all about her. The sky was a cloudless blue ; the air was warm ; people going by seemed to have a lilt in their steps. "I shan't want the car," she said to Oxtoby, and she stood there as he saluted, jumped to his seat, and moved silently away. She wanted to be alone, to think, to chew greedily on the thought that she had money—money of her own.

In two minutes she was in Wigmore Street, gay with florists' shops, rich with old pictures, and carpets, and furniture, and lovely glass. She passed a café and felt that she would like to go in and drink coffee and hug her happiness. She laughed to think that she hadn't the necessary sixpence. She could afford to laugh now, because the thing was done. All the sixpences she would need would soon be hers.

And then she saw Mike Hartigan coming towards her. Still hatless, he raised two fingers in a half-salute. She was about to pass on with a curt nod, but on an impulse she stopped. " Mr. Hartigan," she said, " I should like a cup of coffee. It would be a good oportunity to speak to you about my conversation with Mr. Bannerman this morning."

" About the money," said Mike bluntly.

" Yes, about the money."

They were alone in the café. " It's ten thousand pounds," said Mike curtly. " A coffee for this lady, please."

Rachel's heart hammered her ribs. Ten thousand pounds ! " Aren't you having coffee ? " she inquired tranquilly.

" No, thank you."

" Well—can you explain this business to me ? "

" There's nothing to explain. I wrote a letter to Maurice's—Mr. Bannerman's—bank manager instructing him to credit ten thousand pounds to an account to be opened in your name. Mr. Bannerman signed it. I've just been along to the bank, where they know me well enough to realise that everything's in order. You'll have to go round and give 'em a sample signature.

That's all there is to it. Here's your coffee. I'll take that bill, miss."

Mike rose to depart. "Perhaps, before you go, you'll tell me the name of the bank," said Rachel.

Mike told her. "And perhaps," Rachel added, "you will be there in half an hour, so that when I give my sample signature you can guarantee that I'm the person concerned. I don't suppose even a bank manager would be so simple-minded as to take my word for it."

"I'll be there," said Mike.

"You will, indeed," Rachel commented grimly to herself. Not again would she find herself in one of those damnable situations. "Perhaps you wouldn't mind waiting a moment, madam," while people telephoned and eyed her, and made discreet inquiries. No, never again, once she had ten thousand pounds.

And that evening Oxtoby, meeting Mike Hartigan, said : "You were right, Mr. Hartigan, about that car."

"What car?"

"That car you said Mrs. Bannerman would be having—a car of her own."

Mike grunted. "Of course I was right. Why wouldn't I be?"

"Ay, she's been on to me about it this afternoon. A sports model to drive herself. And me to teach her."

"That's about all you can teach her."

Oxtoby nodded with morose understanding. "I should say so, Mr. Hartigan."

"This is nice. This is charming," Rachel said, looking round Mina's flat. She was in an altogether better mood. She had been received at the bank with deference. She had understood for the first time what it was to be married to Maurice Bannerman's money. She had watched the erection of the ten-thousand-pound barrier between herself and destitution. A few scratches on paper and it was done. Never before in all her life had she felt safe, secure. When asked for her signature she had absent-mindedly written Rachel Rosing. Then she amended it to Rachel Bannerman. "That's better," the bank manager said. Yes, thought Rachel, that is altogether better.

And then there was that agreeable talk with Oxtoby about the sports model. They were to go out to-morrow and find something that she liked the look of, and that he approved.

So Mina found her better spirited, quick, receptive; and that suited her purpose excellently. From her unusual height Rachel looked down at Mina stretched in a chair. "I have kept my car," she said grandly. "It can take us wherever we are going for food."

"Oh, my dear, send it away," Mina begged her. "In the middle of London you're much better off on your legs, unless you're all dolled up. And I hate being dolled up—don't you? It nearly broke Daddy's heart when I would not go through all the tomfoolery of being presented at Court. You've got to put your foot down somewhere, haven't you?"

"I rather like all that sort of thing," said Rachel.

Mina got up and shuffled into a coat. " Very well, then. We'll let you keep your car just for once. And now we'll find somewhere nice and quiet to eat. I can't stand these flashy restaurants—can you?—all glass and glitter, and high prices, and men from Manchester looking cock-eyed for celebrities. Let's go to Rule's. It's a bit off our track, but that'll justify the car."

She marched Rachel downstairs as she talked, and merely murmured " Rule's " to Oxtoby. Oxtoby seemed to know all about Rule's, so Rachel supposed it was all right. But her preconceptions were to have another shock. Just as she had imagined the London theatre under very high lights indeed, so her mental picture of her first meal out in London had been a dramatic composition of bands and waiters saying " Sair ? " and opulent white-shirt-fronted men, and ladies gloriously and scantily arrayed. Champagne bottles in buckets of ice were in the picture too, and orchids on the table, and gilt everywhere.

They alighted from the Rolls in a dark, narrow, and somehow nefarious street, and when Mina had suggested that the car might be back for them in three-quarters of an hour, she led the way up a shabby, cramped stairway and pushed open a door. Immediately before her Rachel saw a fireplace and a waiter standing by it, warming his tails. There was a small bar at which a few men were conversing in quiet tones and at small tables there were a lot of seats upholstered in red plush, looking very mid-Victorian. The whole place was mid-Victorian, deeply decorous, hushed and tranquil. The dark panelled walls were hung thick with old play-bills and prints of famous players. The subdued

223

murmur from the bar and the tinkle of the cheerful fires in two grates were the only sounds that broke the stillness.

Mina sank into a red plush seat in a cosy corner and tapped the place beside her. There was room for two on the seat.

" This is one of the few civilised eating-places in London," she said. " I don't like eating to be a public exhibition."

Rachel looked about her, feeling that there was no end to life's disillusions. She didn't like this half so well as the Cockatoo, but Mina seemed to think it was all right, and Mina was Lord Upavon's daughter, so it must be all right. The only other diners were a lovely girl and a youth. The girl wore a velvet dress of the deepest blue and a huge picture hat of blue velvet that sloped across her face. The young man had a disordered thatch of lint-white hair, a red face and a wild blue eye. His clothes were anything, put on anyhow. The girl in blue gave a grave deliberate attention to the business of eating, while the youth, in a high, cultured voice, assailed her with verbiage. Strange words fell on Rachel's ears as Mina assisted her in the choice of a simple meal. " You know what Chekhov said to Gorki : ' Teachers ought to know everything—everything, my dear fellow.' Extraordinary mind Gorki had. He once dreamt that he saw the sky scrofulous, putrescent, greenish-yellow, and the stars in it were round, flat, without lustre, like scabs on the skin of a diseased person."

The young woman in blue velvet did not raise her eyes from her plate. She went on eating with a sort of imperial determination. But Mina shouted : " Oi !

We're just going to have dinner. Don't turn our stomachs."

The youth looked at Mina as though she were some curiosity he had not till then observed. Then he came and stood beside her, examining her flaming hair with close attention. "Marvellous!" he said. "It's natural," and returned to his seat. "It was Andreev," he shrilled, pushing aside a full plate, "it was Andreev who said a man who has not tried to kill himself is very small beer."

His companion at last raised her lovely head, very slowly, and pronounced in a cool, replete voice : "Your conversation is too abstract."

She picked up the menu, and said to the waiter : "I'll have a pancake—no, two pancakes."

"There's an answer to that," the young man shouted. "There's an answer to that too, and Chekhov gives it to you. He had been discussing rather deep things with some women who took just the attitude that you do, and suddenly he said : 'I love candied fruits, don't you?' That's the answer to that. Let us discuss candied fruits. We find our level."

The girl dropped her eyes again to the table on which the waiter had placed the pancakes. She began steadily, like a machine, to destroy them.

"We are witnessing a not very successful courtship," Mina whispered under her breath. "This is one of my lucky nights." But Rachel was baffled and did not see where the luck lay.

In the pit of the Hogarth Theatre Rachel sat at Mina's side waiting for the curtain to go up. It seemed there was to be no end to her disillusions that night. She had not imagined that a London theatre could be small and dingy. But the Hogarth was both. You could drop it, she reflected, into the Palace or the Opera House in Manchester and still leave room for a football field. She could see a sprinkling of evening clothes forward in the dress-circle, but even there many people had not bothered to dress. But the house was full and there was a sense of expectancy which she could not but feel.

The curtain swung up, and Rachel, who had never before seen the rising of the curtain reveal anything but a row of swaying legs, saw a library with but little furniture and a window opening out of that dark room upon a blue oblong of moonlight. A woman's figure, dimly seen, was in the room. She held a telephone receiver to her ear and was nervously and impatiently clicking at the instrument on the table. Out of the darkness her voice came, anxious, supplicating, very low and furtive. " Hallo ! Hallo ! " A stock opening.

The act ended, and Mina turned anxiously to Rachel. " Well ? "

Rachel's eyes were shining. " That was good," she said ; " very good. But it could be better. When Lady Constance admits the theft she says, ' *I* am the thief ! ' tapping herself on the chest. She should not do that. She should just throw up her head, high, like this, very proud, and say the words. It would make all the difference."

Mina looked at her in amazement. It was right ; it was sound ; it *would* make all the difference.

"Well," she said ; "whether she's doing it badly or not, that girl's getting a hundred pounds a week for doing it. Like to meet her ? "

"Could I ? " Rachel glowed at the prospect, and followed Mina, scrambling over legs, and presently finding herself on draughty stone stairs. "I would like to show her," she said, "how that bit should be done."

Mina stopped in her eager pelting stride. "My God, Rachel," she said, "before you go a yard farther promise me on your soul to do nothing of the sort."

"But why ? It is an improvement."

"My dear woman, when one of the most celebrated actresses in London has been doing something every night for the best part of a year, you do *not* tell her how to improve it. Not on your life ! "

So Rachel found herself for the first time in a theatre dressing-room, and if Mina had any doubts of her skill as an actress they were quickly scattered. Joyce Willows was lying in an easy-chair, wearing an exquisite dressing-gown and smoking a cigarette. She stood up, and Rachel, overtopping her by inches, outshining her in loveliness, extended a white hand as timorously as though she were meeting a queen. "I have not seen you before in that part, Miss Willows," she said. "It is amazing how you get that finish— that perfection."

"Practice, my dear," said Joyce Willows in a bored voice. "Have a cigarette."

She pushed a silver box across the table, and turned from Rachel to rag Mina.

"Well, you lazy little slut, when are you going to work again? Or are you going to suck on to Daddy for the rest of your life?"

Rachel left them to it. She covertly studied and appraised the woman who could earn a hundred pounds a week, her clothes, her room, the brushes, combs, pots and bottles set out on the dressing-table. Mina wrangled with Joyce Willows and watched Rachel out of the tail of her eye. She could see what was in her mind. "All this is very nice, and I don't think much of this woman. I can do anything I have seen her do to-night."

Suddenly Rachel said: "Do the people worry you, Miss Willows—the audience, I mean?"

"Good gracious, no. When the footlights are up it's easy to forget 'em." She broke into a laugh. "Why? You're not stage-struck, are you?"

"Oh, no," said Rachel modestly. "A show like yours would knock that out of any one's head. I was just wondering."

"No harm in that," said Miss Willows complacently. "Have another cigarette."

Chapter Twenty

I

LORD UPAVON was a staunch traditionalist. What had been done at Markhams in the past must continue to be done at Markhams. The annual play had been done for so long that it was sanctified. It was Upavon's grandmother who began it, the lovely Georgiana Shadbolt who had sprung from God knows what obscure beginning. The beautiful barnstormer had ended as the great lady whose pictured elegance was resplendent in the long dining-room. The annual play had been Georgiana's device for gathering her old associates about her once a year. Distance and death lopped them down one by one, but the play went on, young amateur Heaths taking the part of the old professionals. It was surprising that the family did not give more talent to the stage. Till Mina came along, there had been no professional since Georgiana, though it was said that there was something stage-struck about most of the Heath women. Julian too, had a touch of the virus. He had played occasionally ever since he could remember, and he and Mina had spent weeks on end in the big barn at Markhams making properties and painting scenery and designing costumes and fiddling with lighting. When he came to the writing of his play, he had a background of tradition and much practical experience to go on.

And yet, with all that, the great idea came to him as a sudden inspiration. A letter had come from Lord Upavon, saying that he would be in town that day and that it was high time something was decided about the annual Markhams play. " Bring Charlie Roebuck along," said Lord Upavon, " and let's get the thing settled. We'd better all be at the Café Royal at one. I've asked Mina to be there. I don't know the place, but I'll find it. I've heard a lot about their onion soup."

Julian tossed the letter to Charlie, a safe buttress of the Markhams plays these many years. " Any ideas, old horse ? " he demanded. " And for God's sake don't say *The Dover Road*."

" Time the damn' thing died," Charlie grumbled. " All very well in granny's day when every family could furnish a platoon for an army or a cast for a play. But what are you going to do with it to-day ? Same old crisis that we've had for years past—no women. You'd better rake in that Bannerman woman this time. She'll be useful for once. She's ornamental."

Julian put down the coffee pot and banged a fist upon the table. " By cripes ! " he shouted. " You've said it ! Did you know I was writing a play with that woman in mind ? Did you know it ? "

" Well, considering that it's been leaking out all over the flat for the last month——"

But Julian was by now genuinely excited. " By God ! " he shouted. " For the first time, the Markhams play will be written by a Heath. D'you know that that play has gone amazingly, my boy ? D'you know it's nearly finished and that it's good ? "

" I shall know nothing till I've read it," said Charlie

doggedly. " Go and have a run this morning, though it's your turn to work. Leave me here with the play, and I'll tell you what I think of it when you get back. In the meantime, you can be seeing whether the Bannerman will join the conspirators at lunch. Go on. Buzz off. I'll wash up."

Julian was clearly too excited to be entrusted with crockery. He took up his hat, slapped Charlie on the back, exclaimed : " There's a treat coming to you, my lad," and ran whistling out into Duck Yard.

Charlie was not so sure about the treat. He washed up methodically—almost Methodistically Julian had once said—and then, in no mood of excitement, took up the neat typescript that Julian had laid on the table. It was Julian's habit to take each day's writing to a typist, and so Charlie had a tidy, easy bit of work to consider. He lit a pipe, threw himself into a chair, and, prepared to be tolerant, began to read—*Thin Ice*.

At eleven o'clock Charlie was telephoning to Mina. " No, I'm not ragging. Never more serious. The boy's written a grand play. You come round here at once and read it. Then we shall all know what we're talking about when we meet your father."

He put down the receiver and turned again to the typescript, looking curiously solemn. He knew in his bones that Julian had done something important. For years now they had striven enviously towards their goals. Well, Julian was there first. Good luck to him. He, in his own line, had never done anything that was in the same class as *Thin Ice*, a cynical modern comedy of a social climber who pulled everything off by a superb assumption that she was as good as the next.

" He's made," said Charlie to himself ; and a sudden intuition came to him that the days in Duck Yard, the hard work together and the friendly bickerings, the happy buzzing about the country in a second-hand car, would soon be over.

At that moment Julian, unaware that a stern if friendly critic had awarded him a crown, was inserting his long, slim body into a two-seater car alongside Rachel Bannerman. A month had passed since Rachel and Oxtoby had bought the car, and Rachel had found that what Oxtoby called road sense came to her like the air she breathed. So now Oxtoby languished in his room above the garage. The Rolls was never out ; his only occupation was polishing the scarlet sports car till it shone like a fire engine.

It had been a grand month for Rachel. With no introductions, she had discovered the dress-shops and the shoe-shops, the milliners' and the hairdresser's, and life was beginning to fashion itself more along the lines which she had imagined. Rose Chamberlain was the happy custodian of an extensive and beautiful wardrobe. The only thing which Rachel felt she needed to make her happiness complete was a taste of the night-life which she glimpsed here and there but could not share. She had discovered everything except friends. Mina Heath, it is true, was always at hand when wanted, but the one thing Mina would not do, even to gratify Rachel, was to razzle. She would not dress for any occasion if she could help it. Rachel was confronted with the problem of a companion who instinctively preferred the obscurity from which Rachel had emerged to the electric glare into which Rachel wished to enter.

They went often to the theatre. Mina was enchanted to discover that the theatre had a profound fascination for Rachel. She took care to let her see the actresses whose work was of the sort which Rachel might herself in time attempt. And always Rachel seemed to understand the artifice behind the art. Once Mina tried a small experiment. She bought copies of a play which she and Rachel had seen. It contained a long passage between two women, and in Mina's flat Mina and Rachel read it over.

" D'you think you could learn that part and do it without the book ? " Mina asked.

" Easily," Rachel replied with confidence.

" Well, when you're ready, let me know and we'll try it."

Rachel was ready by the next evening. It was a grand game to her, and completely without self-consciousness she threw herself into the part. She was surprised by Mina. She knew, but had never realised, that. Mina was an actress who had achieved fame ; and when, in that little scene, Mina unmasked all she knew, drawing Rachel on, Rachel was hardly prepared for the flaming passion that Mina could command. But she was not over-balanced. She clung instinctively to a realisation that all that passion had to be countered, on her part, by a complete self-command, a deadly, precise refusal to be passionate, and Mina could not throw her out of gear. It was a successful and revealing little performance.

All this was very delightful to Rachel ; but her entreaties that they should take their pleasures more royally, dress up for the theatre, dine resplendently before the show, or go to some popular place for supper afterwards, did not move Mina. The cherry blossom would soon be out at Markhams, and for two pins she would fly back to it.

Rachel had plenty of leisure to review her position during that month in the great house in Portman Square. She realised with a disturbing clarity that Maurice had faded away into the background of her life. Her daily visit to the nursing-home was a disagreeable duty to be disposed of before she plunged into her new and pleasurable occupations. Maurice was improving. The cloud of pain that had masked their first meetings was thinning away, and he was able to talk freely. The earliest opening of Rachel's eyes concerning Maurice came when the matron said : " Well, Mrs. Bannerman, you will be able to extend your visits now. You can stay for half an hour this morning, and soon we'll take off the time-table altogether."

Rachel was aware that her heart missed a beat, as though she had heard bad news ; and she was realist enough to face all the implications of that fact.

Maurice was still on his back. He could move his head and his limbs freely, but he must still lie down. It was Rachel's custom to bend over the bed and kiss him when she entered the room ; and on that morning when Charlie Roebuck read *Thin Ice* Maurice had put both arms round her waist as her face came down to his and had held her in a tight embrace.

He kissed her passionately on the hair and the eyes and the mouth and whispered eagerly : " Lie down, Rachel, lie down on the bed."

She drew herself quietly but resolutely away, masking the alarm that suddenly surged through her.

"No—darling—please, it is almost public here," she said. "Any one might just knock and come in."

He let her go, loosening his arms reluctantly. "It is so awful," he said, "to be always dreaming of you and not having you."

She was horrified at herself—at the thrill of disgust that had gone through her. His big face was pale and flaccid, his eyes were cavernous. She could not bear to think of more than that perfunctory, accustomed kiss. She brought the visit to an end as soon as she decently could, and took down great gulps of the sweet air when she got into the street.

Oxtoby would have her car waiting in Portman Square. The new thrill of driving as quickly as she could, all alone, along the high roads of the Home Counties was something she had come to look forward to as a stimulant after the depression of the nursing home. But that morning she did not drive alone. Julian Heath turned up just as she was about to start. She had not seen him for some time. Her heart leapt out to him as though to a friend met in a sunny street after one had come from identifying a corpse.

"Well, well," said Julian. "So that knocking about we gave you in the Lakes has not been a warning! You're taking to the road yourself?"

"And enjoying it," said Rachel. "Are you going to sample this car?" She swung open the door invitingly.

"I must be back to lunch," Julian said. "As a matter of fact, what I came for was to ask you to take lunch with me and my father, and Mina and Charlie Roebuck."

"We can talk about it as we go."

He climbed in. He thought she looked what he called to himself very fetching. Her coat and skirt were both of sage-green suède. On the coat was a pocket of willow-green, almost yellow. Her beret was of the same colour. He noticed that she had a wrist-watch that looked to him expensive. He thought that on any other woman the clothes she was wearing would look a trifle aggressive; but she had the personality which reduced clothes to mere decoration. What she was would always dominate what she wore.

It was a close fit in that little car. Rachel was intensely aware of the warmth of Julian's thigh pressing against her own. She laughed a little nervously. " Don't be too critical," she said. " This is all very new to me."

" One would never guess it."

" Tell me if I make a fool of myself."

" Right. You are doing very well so far. You have remarkable self-possession. When are you going to have dinner with me ? "

" I thought it was lunch to-day."

" Oh, that. No ; I don't mean a mass meeting. Honestly, can't we go somewhere and eat and dance ? You must dance beautifully."

" Yes, I do."

" Well, then."

For a while Rachel did not answer. She kept her eyes on the road ahead and a light, steady hand on the wheel.

" I don't think I ought to," she said at last.

" Why not ? "

" I shouldn't mind if it were Mina. I've asked her

again and again to take me somewhere gay, but she won't do it."

Julian laughed. " Mina won't lead you down the primrose path," he said. " You're lucky if she hasn't dragged you to the National Gallery and the Tate."

" Well, if she won't take me out, I must stay at home."

" But why ? I don't see it."

" You see it as well as I do. I told you, when you asked me to dine with you at Blackpool, that I didn't think Mr. Bannerman would like it. I don't suppose he'd like it any the more now that we're married and he's laid up."

" You're a Puritan," he said lightly.

At that, she flamed at him suddenly. " Damn it, man, I'm no more a Puritan than you are. Don't you realise that I'd like to come, that I'm longing to come, only——" She bit her lip, annoyed that for once she had lost her self-control. She slowed down the car. " Now, go on," she said bitterly. " Do as you promised to, and tell me I'm making a fool of myself." She brought the car to a standstill.

" I'm sorry," said Julian awkwardly.

She turned towards him, took him by the shoulders, and shook him. " My God ! " she said. " You well-bred men ! You sit there with your nice pink face and tailor's-dummy clothes and say ' I'm sorry.' Don't you know when a woman's told you she loves you ? Don't you *do* anything about it ? Don't you understand ? "

" But—Rachel ! " he cried ; and then said no more. He took her vehemently into his arms, crushing his mouth upon hers till she fell away from him exhausted.

237

" Oh, Julian," she cried, " you are so young—so young and beautiful."

He did not give back her tender words, but that was something she was too infatuated to notice.

II

When they got back to Duck Yard they found a note saying that Mina and Charlie had gone on to the Café Royal. It had been difficult after that passionate kiss, and in the light of all that it implied, to talk about the play at Markhams. Julian had rather excitedly explained to Rachel what it was all about. A great annual affair. Everybody in Markham village turned up, and sometimes the villagers provided a player or two. The play was given in the great barn where there was a really good stage. He and Mina and Charlie Roebuck had worked at it for years and there were plenty of theatres not so well equipped as the Markhams barn. It was a social event as well as a village event. The people came from the big houses for miles round. The biggest pots came to dinner at the house. And the best of it all was, said Julian, that Cecil Hansford, the theatrical manager, who had a place a few miles from Markhams, always made it a night out. " When he sees this play," Julian said excitedly, " it's for the West End as sure as God's in His Heaven and all's well with the world. There's only one curmudgeon who's going to cry the play down, and that's Charlie."

That being Julian's expectation, all the greater was his surprise when his father greeted him with a hearty buffet in the back and a genial broadside : " Well, Julian, what's all this I hear, eh ? What's all this I hear ? A genius in the family, eh, a genius ? Charlie says you've written something remarkable—don't you, Charlie ? "

" It's a fact, sir," Charlie agreed. " You've done it, old boy. Mina's read the thing, too. I had to get her round at once. She agrees. You've done it. Hasn't he done it, Mina ? "

Mina merely nodded gravely. " Yes, I think it's good, Julian."

" So this is Mrs. Bannerman," old Upavon fussed. " Now you sit here by me, Mrs. Bannerman. I was upset, dreadfully upset, about your husband. An old friend of mine, and a clever man. How is he, eh ? How is he ? "

" Recovering slowly," said Rachel. " He will get better."

" That's fine. That's fine. Ah, waiter ! Now, Mrs. Bannerman, they tell me there's remarkable onion soup in this place. I don't know. I shall pass judgment later. Let's try it, shall we ? We'll see what we think of it. We'll take nothing on trust, eh ? Now, you boys, what are you going to drink ? Don't you think the occasion calls for something ? He put on his pince-nez and ran his finger down the wine list. " Um—yes. No vulgar champagne. This hock, eh ? Yes, I think so."

He was brisk and happy, in command, while the food and drink were being ordered ; and then the others took control. There was little for them to argue about. All three were of one mind as they had never been before when the Markhams play was on the

239

carpet. " Then it's to be *Thin Ice*, with Mrs. Bannerman as Iris Mearns ? " said Julian.

" Carried unanimously," said Charlie, and Mina nodded.

Upavon raised his glass. " Julian, my boy, to you and *Thin Ice*. Mrs. Bannerman, to you as leading lady."

They all drank. " *Thin Ice*," said Charlie Roebuck. " Julian and Mrs. Bannerman."

Chapter Twenty-one

I

THAT was a Friday. During the week-end Julian Heath worked with passion to finish the play. He put in his customary spell on Saturday morning, and during lunch at the club told Charlie Roebuck that he intended to work through the afternoon.

" That's commendable," said Charlie. " My piano won't disturb you ? "

" Oh, blast ! " Julian exclaimed peevishly. " I'd forgotten your thumping."

" It's of no importance—none whatever, but I think I'd better keep it up."

Julian pondered, scowling. " There's only one thing to do—I'll have to find a flat of my own."

" Obviously," Charlie agreed. " A successful dramatist won't want the half share of a flat in a mews."

" Looking a bit ahead, aren't you ? "

" Not so far. If you want a flat, find one. You're not surprising me. I've seen it coming ever since I read that play."

Julian continued to scowl. " All right. Run away home and tinkle Nelly Bly. I'll work here—for this afternoon, anyway."

Charlie left him, and he went to the writing-room, but for a long time he did not write. He stared at the paper, sitting with his hands in his pockets and his chin on his chest, while in his head the words repeated themselves : " A flat of my own." They meant more than appeared on the surface. They meant, he at last admitted to himself, Rachel Bannerman.

He finished the play at two o'clock on the following Monday morning. Charlie Roebuck, in dressing-gown and slippers, stayed up to see the child finally delivered. Julian had assured him that the great moment would come during that night ; so Charlie stuffed a wad of paper into the telephone bell, kept the fire bright, brewed fresh tea now and then for the sustenance of the stylist, and obliterated himself as completely as possible behind a novel. The flat was as quiet as a midnight graveyard. He could hear Julian's pen scratching across the paper, an occasional suck and gurgle of Julian's pipe, and when at last Julian drew a great slanting stroke beneath what he had written, threw down his pen, and said prosaically : " Well, that's that," Charlie was strangely moved, as though he had been privileged to see the first dawn of a comet, destined to move with growing brightness across the sky. And, as it happened, that was about what it came to. Even to-day *Thin Ice* is a safe play to " revive."

II

That same Monday morning Maurice Bannerman came home. Mike Hartigan wheeled him in a long wicker contrivance. It was possible now for Maurice to bend his spine a little. He had not to lie with his face skyward. A pillow at the top of his wicker carriage eased up his shoulders, and he was able to turn his head and look about him. This seemed to him almost in the nature of a miracle. He insisted on Mike wheeling him twice round the big garden in Portman Square. He looked at the plane trees, now greened all over, and at taxicabs and house doors and window-boxes, and at the light spring clouds puffing across the blue sky, and they seemed to him equally to possess ineffable attributes.

" Begod, Maurice," Mike shouted, " d'you remember I said at Blackpool we'd cause a sensation if I wheeled you along the front in a pram ? Well, here we are. Give me a Norland Institute uniform and I'm the complete nanny. Come on in now and have your titty-bottle."

Maurice gave a slow, lugubrious smile. " Once more round, Mike, if you please." He moved a weak arm towards trees and houses. " This is fine. This is good."

So they went round again, and then there was Oxtoby waiting at the door to assist Mike Hartigan in taking the carriage up the steps ; and there was that very taximan who had run up to help the morning Maurice fell and he now all anxiety and solicitude to know how the patient was faring ; and inside was old Bright, grave and glad, yet not strong enough to do much ; and Mrs. Bright, her hale face smiling a welcome and the flowers she had arranged twinkling everywhere. Every one seemed to be about, helping Maurice to come back into his house under the compassionate red-hawed eyes of the old Jewess that Rembrandt painted so long ago. Every one seemed to be about. . . .

"Where's Rachel?" Maurice asked, turning his head slowly towards Mike Hartigan.

She glided down the twisted stair as silently as a shadow, and very slowly. She had been standing there at the top as they helped him in, her slim hand on the dark polished mahogany of the rail. Her face was as still as something carved in ivory, and in the stillness her eyes were large, dilated as though with horror. She did not move as they brought the carriage through the door and trundled it to rest by the fireplace. When she heard him ask for her she began slowly to descend the stairs, one hand brushing the rail lightly. Bright and his wife, Oxtoby and Mike Hartigan, instinctively faded away as they saw her come. She was wearing black, which made her pallor extraordinary. She bent over the wicker carriage and kissed him.

"So you're back," she said.

"Yes," he answered. "Thank God, I'm back, Rachel. Now it will not be so bad—to be ill—now that I am back—now that I am with you."

He took her hand and put his lips hungrily upon it. "That has been the worst, my darling," he said, "not to be with you."

She left her hand resting lifeless and unresponsive in his, and, turned sideways to him, gazed into the fire.

"But you will get well?" she asked.

"Yes, in time, I hope. But it will be a long time."

"We must make the best of it."

"Yes. It will not be so bad."

She crumpled suddenly to her knees, buried her head in his lap, and cried: "Oh, my God!"

Maurice smoothed the black sleekness of her hair.

"Rachel. My darling. My little Rachel," he murmured.

She gradually ceased to sob, got to her feet looking
whiter than before, and said : " What do you want
to do, Maurice ? Will you stay here for awhile ? "

"No," he said. " I want to see my pictures. Ask
Mike Hartigan to come."

She touched the bell beside the fireplace. She stood
gazing into the fire as Mike wheeled Maurice away.
Then she went slowly and tragically back up the stairs.

III

Mike Hartigan wheeled Maurice slowly round the
ballroom which was a picture gallery. Now and then
Maurice called a halt so that he might gaze at this
and that : an elongated face by Modigliani, a lucent
haze of tiny confetti composing a landscape by Seurat.
But Maurice's mind was not on the pictures. " Mike,"
he said presently, " you can clear out when you
like."

Mike brought the carriage to a standstill and came
round to face Maurice. "Altogether, I mean,"
Maurice said.

"Now what in hell are you talking about this time,
Maurice ? " Mike demanded.

" I'm telling you to clear out, to go and find another
job. You don't *like* being a nursemaid, do you ? I
can hire a male nurse. That's what they wanted me
to do at the nursing home. I've got to be put into bed
and taken out again, and washed and shaved, and
God knows what. Clear out and leave me to it."

245

He glared at Mike defiantly. "That novel-writing business that we talked about in Blackpool, that's finished. It was probably all damn nonsense, anyway. But whether it was or not, it will be a long time before I put pen to paper. So the secretary's job doesn't exist any more, Mike. You can clear out."

"Have you finished?" said Mike.

Maurice nodded briefly. "Then don't let's hear such damned nonsense again, Maurice. What d'you shave with—a safety razor or a cut-throat? That's the only thing I don't know about you."

"Thank you, Mike," said Maurice. "I told 'em at the nursing home they could keep their damned male nurse. I hoped it wouldn't come to that."

"I should think not, begod."

"Mike, I've got into a bad habit. I've learned to smoke cigarettes. They wouldn't let me have cigars. I'm not supposed to smoke many cigarettes, either—just a few a day. I feel like one now."

Mike produced a cigarette, put it to Maurice's lips, and lit it for him. "Smoke your pipe, Mike, if you want to. It won't hurt me."

So they smoked contentedly for awhile, and presently Maurice said : "It feels better to be home now. I know where I am. I'll have that bone-setting feller coming in every morning, but apart from that we shan't be worried, Mike. Tell me the news now. How have things been going? How is Rachel settling down—poor girl."

Mike kept his face unmoved. "She's been going round a lot with Mina Heath—you've heard of her, Maurice? She's an actress, Lord Upavon's daughter."

Maurice nodded his head. "Yes, I've heard of her

and seen her. Ginger. Fiery little devil. She's a good actress. Surprising daughter for Upavon. Dull old man."

"Well, she and Mrs. Bannerman are as thick as thieves. She's here most days and they go to the theatre together. Not that Mrs. Bannerman tells me anything, Maurice. She doesn't like me, and that's all there is to it. I'm reconciled, so don't worry. I get it all from that daft little hussy Rose Chamberlain. She gabbles as if she were a society journalist and Mrs. Bannerman a leading lady."

Rachel came into the room. She was drawing on gauntlets and had changed from her black into the green suède which she liked for motoring.

"Darling," she said, "I am going out. I must have a little air. You can do without me till lunch-time?"

Maurice took one of her gloved hands and held it. "Do as you please, my dear," he said. "Don't think because I'm chained up by the leg that I want you to be about the house always. No, no, Rachel. You must enjoy yourself."

"Well, good-bye. I'll be back at lunch-time."

"You will have to lunch alone, my dear. I'm not fit yet to sit at a civilised table. I have to be fed. Mike here will look after me."

"Well," said Rachel flippantly, "he owes it to you."

"It does not always follow, Rachel, that men pay what they owe. Still, that is not the point. The thing now is that you should get about and see all you want to till we can get about together again."

Mike had strolled to the end of the room. Rachel

247

bent and kissed Maurice, with tears stinging her eyes. "You are so good, Maurice," she murmured, "so patient with me," and she went swiftly from the room, torn by the perplexity of goodness which could only make her feel humiliated, not humble, which awakened in her no responsive thrill. Maurice lay quite still till he heard the roar of her car, the swift powerful rush of its starting, so different from his own opulent and leisured handling of a motor-car. He sighed and called Mike Hartigan to him.

"Mike, do you think she's happy?"

Mike fidgeted, relit a cold pipe, and answered reluctantly as the smoke puffed through the cage of his fingers: "Ach, she's as happy as it's in her to be. What more can any of us want, Maurice? Or, anyway, what more can we get?"

Maurice could think of no answer to that. "Let's get into the study, Mike," he said; and, still smoking like a kitchen range, Mike got behind the carriage and pushed.

IV

Mina Heath had breakfasted in Duck Yard with Julian and Charlie. Before she was out of bed her telephone had rung and Charlie had told her that *Thin Ice* was finished. He was more excited than Julian. Indeed, Julian was still asleep, and Charlie was as solicitous as a mother whose child had exerted itself beyond its strength overnight. He spoke quietly into the telephone, and then went quietly about the business of bathing and preparing breakfast. Only when everything was ready and Mina had arrived did he wake Julian, who was permitted to sit at the table in pyjamas and dressing-gown.

The three of them combed through the last act of the play together, decided that it was good, and had a preliminary discussion concerning the cast. Lord Upavon liked to appear in the annual Markhams play. That was always a difficulty, because he could never be anything but himself, and the range of plays was therefore restricted to those which contained a pompous old gentlemanly character. Julian had written a part which would do very well ; and there were parts for himself and Charlie and Mina. There was Iris Mearns for Rachel Bannerman ; and it was decided that the part of a comic, free-spoken house-keeper should be offered to Mrs. Harrison of the Spur and Stirrup. That left only one part to fill : that of an elderly bishop from overseas, and it was agreed that the Rev. Justin Wyndham, the vicar of Markham, would probably be flattered by translation. He had played before and was considered not bad at heavy stuff.

So Julian wrote on a sheet of paper :

THIN ICE

A Modern Comedy
By
Julian Heath.

The whole action takes place in the library of Matcham Manor.

Act I.—6.30 p.m. on a January evening.
Act II.—After dinner the same night.
Act III.—Before breakfast the next morning.

Cast :

Sir Edward Barlow, Bart.	.	LORD UPAVON
The Bishop of Boomerang	.	THE REV. JUSTIN WYNDHAM
George Barlow	. . .	JULIAN HEATH
Henry Lorrimer	. . .	CHARLES ROEBUCK
Mary Sinclair	. .	WILHELMINA HEATH
Mrs. Oddy	. . . .	MARY HARRISON

and

Iris Mearns .	. .	RACHEL BANNERMAN

" No," said Julian, looking critically at what he had written, " that won't do." And he scratched out the last word and wrote " Rosing " instead.

" Bearing in mind," he said with a grin, " that this play is destined for the West End and that Mrs. Bannerman will appear in it there, we'd better have the details right. And don't you agree with me ? Don't you think ' Rachel Rosing ' is a better name than ' Rachel Bannerman ' to play under ? "

They agreed that it was, and, after some talk of this and that, Mina took the manuscript of the last act to the typist's in Baker Street. " And the sooner we get to work, the better," she said. " The show is in a month's time."

When she had left the typist's, Mina crossed the road into Portman Square. She was the only one who was troubled by any doubts about Rachel. Julian and Charlie Roebuck seemed to take it for granted that Rachel would be able to give to the play all the time they demanded. And, Mina knew, it would be a lot of time. It had been the custom, as long as she could remember, to make a house-party of the cast, barring those who lived in the village, for the last fortnight or so, in order that rehearsals might go on intensively. All very well for the rest of them. But Rachel had a husband lying on his back. There were several things which Mina thought should be cleared up. She was hurrying towards Rachel's house when Charlie Roebuck's voice hailed her.

" I've left Julian in the bath. I thought I might catch you up."

Mina sighed. For how long had not Charlie Roebuck been devising excuses for catching her up? He was looking very young and fair and handsome, and, Mina thought, terribly good tone and public school. How awful to like a man so much as she liked Charlie and yet to feel that if he uttered one word of love to her she'd scream. It would be, she reflected, as if those handsome men in the advertisements suddenly forgot that they had to talk about nothing but where they bought their vests and pants.

" Well," said Charlie, " I thought possible we might bait up on coffee and biscuits."

" Come along then," Mina answered, resigned.

They went back into Baker Street and climbed the stairs to a tall room over a French pastrycook's shop. They nibbled little biscuits and drank excellent coffee, while the ceiling above them shuddered beneath the leaping of a class in ballet dancing. It was otherwise a quiet place. There was no one else in the room, and Mina didn't want Charlie to improve the moment.

" Look here," she said. " What makes you and Julian think that Mrs. Bannerman will be able to leave her husband in order to put in all the time we shall want on this play ? "

"Well, won't she? I've just been taking it for granted. Really, I know next to nothing about her."

"Yet the little you do know leads you to take it for granted, as you say, that she'll abandon a husband who's just married her and probably be desperately anxious to have her about."

Charlie shrugged his shoulders and munched a biscuit. "I get all I know from Julian. It seems she was as poor as a church mouse."

"Well?"

"Well, now she's got him."

"I'm damned!" said Mina vehemently. "What a filthy view to take. You ought to be ashamed of yourself, Charlie."

"Well, there it is," Charlie said. "So far as I can make out, ever since her husband's accident she's put in the minimum of time with him and the maximum with you or Julian. Not that I care a hoot, my dear. If she's a good actress—and you all seem to think she is—then she's what we want, and I have no doubt she'll find the time. Surely she would have told us if she expected to meet difficulties."

"Perhaps so. But I'm going along now to see her. Thanks for the coffee."

But Mina did not see Rachel. Instead, she saw Maurice Bannerman. Maurice was still in his study. He had sent Mike Hartigan away. For half an hour he had been reflecting on Rachel's tears. Were they for him or for herself? Was it absolutely necessary that she should rush out of the house as soon as he entered it? Fear began to cloud his mind. His home-coming, after all, had not been what he expected. It could have been if Rachel had wanted it to be. He brooded miserably ; he prayed that his premonitions might prove unfounded ; yet he was too much of a realist to allow easy hopes to lead him astray.

And then Bright came and asked if he could see Mina Heath, and he said " Send her in."

As Mina came into the room she pulled off the beret she was wearing, and her hair, suddenly released, sprang into a dramatic halo round her white face. Maurice laughed : it was so like a trick, like a Jack-in-the-box leaping to view at the touch of a spring.

" How nice to find you can laugh," said Mina. Her voice was clear, direct and musical, different from Rachel's controlled and rather languid tone. She was altogether extraordinarily alive ; she seemed in a flash to have made the sober room more cheerful.

" Well, sit down now," said Maurice. " You know, I haven't had much to laugh about lately. I really think that is the first time I've laughed for weeks."

" That makes me all the more glad I came," said Mina. " Really, I came to see Rachel. I had no idea you were at home. You do forgive me for bursting in, don't you ? I sort of know you. I've heard my father speak about you."

" And I know you," said Maurice. " I've seen you act. So we may consider ourselves a sort of friends— eh ? "

" Yes, of course. And I wanted to thank you about the pictures. I came the other day and was allowed to look at them all. But what a marvellous collection ! "

" Not so good as Courtauld's," Maurice answered with a smile, " but not bad."

" Not bad ! I should say not. Aren't they splendid,

all those people ; the way they busted up the dull
old buffers."

"You know," said Maurice, "the first thing I did
when I got home this morning was to have a look at
the pictures. Already you make me want to see them
again."

"Why not ? I should love to see them too. Those
lovely ships of Boudin."

"Come on, then."

"Good. I feel like a bath-chair man," said Mina.
She got hold of the carriage and pushed. "This
way ? "

For half an hour they looked at the pictures and
talked about them ; and then Maurice sent for Mike
Hartigan and got him to bring some bits of porcelain.
Mina knew nothing about that, but she found Maurice
fascinating on the subject. His thick hands, gone very
white, held his precious pieces fastidiously. He talked
of biscuit and overglaze and underglaze, of lustre,
stoneware and celadon, opening for Mina a dainty
world. Some colour came back to his pale face ; his
dark eyes glistened. All about the wicker chair there
was a regular show, set out on occasional tables, when
he had done.

"Now don't you be tiring yourself, Maurice," Mike
Hartigan warned.

Mina jumped up, instantly apologetic. "I'm sorry,
Mr. Hartigan," she said. "You do right to drive me
out."

"It's been charming to have you," Maurice protested. "You've livened me up. You must come
again. This is too much like a museum. You make it
more like a——"

He was going to say "like a home." He fumbled and left the sentence unfinished.

Mina was on the other side of Portman Square when she saw Rachel's red sports car stop at the door. That reminded her that she had intended to talk to Maurice Bannerman about Rachel, and that the strange attractive creature had driven all thought of Rachel out of her head.

Chapter Twenty-two

RACHEL ROSING could not remember a time when she had not used people to further her own ends. The poverty in which she had been born filled her with a passionate resentment. It was not the kind of resentment that drives people into parties that promise reform. She had no more taste for the rough and tumble of politics than for the rough and tumble of the Blackpool Pleasure Beach. She did not give a hoot for reform. The quarrel between her and society was personal. From infancy she had observed with envy that there were thousands of people living in luxury. She wanted to enjoy what they enjoyed. That was all it came to. Once she was up, it would not matter to her who was down, and she had always been prepared with complete unscrupulousness to use wealthy people. So, playing her ultimate card, she had wed Maurice Bannerman.

It had never occurred to her till now that she might herself have qualities that would bring her wealth. But now Mina and Julian Heath kept on and on with this story of her being an actress who might easily become eminent. And that might mean wealth—wealth earned by her own talents, not diddled out of a rich man.

The thought altered the whole of Rachel's attitude to Maurice Bannerman. She did not love him; she had never deceived herself about that; and now she might not even want him. She was saddled with a cripple at a moment when, with luck, she might soon be a wealthy woman by right of her own qualities. And at a moment when Julian Heath was occupying more and more of her thought. A month ago, her wiliness, acute as a serpent's, would have warned her to go slow with Julian Heath. Had Maurice, then, cast her out, what hope had she that Julian would take her in? But she could imagine that a successful actress as beautiful as herself might seem attractive enough to Julian Heath.

Her copy of *Thin Ice* had reached her, and a few mornings after Maurice had come home she took it into the study where he was lying reading the morning paper. He held the paper high above his face. He said jocularly to Rachel as she came in that it would be more convenient if Mike Hartigan pasted the sheets to the ceiling.

" I've no doubt he'd be glad to do it," said Rachel. " He's taken you off my hands entirely. There seems nothing left for me to do." She said it with a fine air of affliction. There was she, a loyal and devoted wife, only too anxious to serve, and all the little duties which she would have liked to take on her shoulders were snatched from her.

" There's one thing, my dear," said Maurice gently. " If you could give me a little more of your time—if you could come and sit with me sometimes. And when Mike takes me out, if you could walk with us——"

" I hate walking," Rachel said briefly.

" I wonder if you realise how much just now I should love it? "

The frank appeal to sentiment did not touch Rachel. "As a matter of fact," she said, "seeing that Mr. Hartigan is looking after you so well, I was going to suggest that you might do without me altogether for a fortnight."

Maurice was so startled that he nearly sat up in his carriage. "What do you mean? You don't want to go away?"

Rachel explained it all very slowly and patiently. "So you see," she said, tapping the typescript she held in her hand, "it would mean my being at Markhams for the last fortnight before the play's presented."

"But surely," Maurice protested, "Markhams is no distance in these days. Oxtoby could run you there and back every day, or for that matter you could run yourself."

"But it's the fun of the thing—the house-party," Rachel persisted.

Maurice took off his big horn-rimmed spectacles and rubbed his eyes. He allowed the sheets of the paper to fall to the floor. "I see," he said wearily. "The fun of the thing." For a moment he was silent, then he said: "This has been going on for some time, then? It would have interested me very much. I should have liked to read the play, to know something about it. Why do you not tell me about things like this, Rachel? I like to know what you are doing. After all, you are my wife."

For a moment Rachel was silent. "Am I?" That was the retort that was quivering on her tongue. But she did not utter it. She knew that once those words were out they ended everything. And she did not want everything to end—yet. So she said, with a

258

gentler manner : " Well, here it is, my dear. I've brought it for you. I've only had bits of it till now."

" Thank you," said Maurice. " Stay now, and let us read through it together."

Rachel was gracious, and stayed. It would be interesting, after all, to see what Maurice thought of *Thin Ice*. She had never doubted his brains. His absorption in the play from the first page looked good, and when at last he came to the end and took off his spectacles with a characteristic flourish, she found herself really excited to hear his opinion. No one, save Julian's own gang, had seen the play. An outsider's view was important.

Maurice tapped the typescript impressively with his spectacles. " This is good," he said. " Yes, this is all right." She had come to know that he never spoke more highly than that of anything. That was the way he talked about the finest pictures he possessed. He looked at Rachel thoughtfully. " You have here, my dear," he said, " a hard job. This woman,—this Iris Mearns—it will be no joke playing that part. If you can do that you are a great actress."

" Julian Heath and Mina and Mr. Roebuck all think I can do it."

" I should be very proud of you, Rachel."

He was not thinking of the barn at Markhams. Like the rest of them, he had allowed his mind to go beyond that. He saw at once the possibilities of success in *Thin Ice*. He was seeing Rachel treading a West End stage.

" You must do what you like about this, my dear," he said. " If you want to go to Markhams for a fortnight you must go. This play surprises me. I apologise

259

to Mr. Heath. I have only read that book, you know —the one you lent me—*The Pillars of Hercules*. I did not think he had this in him. You know the work of Noel Coward, of course?"

"It's just a name to me," said Rachel.

"Well, this is the sort of play he writes. Except, perhaps, this comic, commonplace woman. I don't think he could have done her. Your Mr. Heath is going to make a lot of money, my dear." He handed back the typescript. "Give all your mind to this, Rachel. It will please me, and it may be very important for you."

Rachel gave him the perfunctory kiss to which he was becoming accustomed but not reconciled. She ran up to her own room, and stood looking out into Portman Square with her head in a whirl. She valued Maurice's opinion more than Julian's or Mina's or Charlie Roebuck's. For the first time she began really to believe in the play. And yet the very steadiness of Maurice's belief in *Thin Ice*, his conviction that Julian was a dramatist with money in him, was a nail in his own coffin. She wanted to see Julian, to tell him at once that there was another convert to the group who believed in him. She was wondering whether to go round to Duck Yard when Rose Chamberlain knocked at the door and came in.

"Your dress has come, madam, from Rosabelle."

"I'll see it in a moment," said Rachel.

She remained looking out of the window. In the garden that filled the square the daffodils had come and gone. They were brown husks tinkling under the plane trees and under the cherry trees whose starved blossom was a thin powdering of snow. There were a few magnolias, too, their waxen blooms, flushed with pink, not doing well in the city air. Rachel did not see these things that were before her eyes ; she saw the little shop in Market Street, Manchester, where she had painfully haggled over prices with her customers and whence she had herself sallied out many a day carrying dresses to buyers. And now the great Rosabelle had sent a dress to her. It was the first thing she had bought from Rosabelle, who had been rapturous about her figure. Even now, when she was becoming accustomed to luxury, the price of the dress caused Rachel a slight uneasiness. But the uneasiness was swallowed up in the savouring of that simple announcement " The dress has come, madam, from Rosabelle," in that beautifully concrete assertion of her changed status.

It was the dress she had chosen for the first two acts of *Thin Ice*. She went slowly into her bedroom where Rose Chamberlain had laid it out. Rose was regarding it with ecstatic eyes. She had been told it was to be worn in a play. That invested it for her with sanctity.

Rachel put on the dress. It was of deep red velvet, a sheath to the hips, a flat line to the feet, and an exquisite downward and outward flowing line into a train behind her. It left exposed the topmost swell and deep division of her breasts and the burnished ivory of her back, supple upon the long jointed pivot of her spine.

Chamberlain adjusted a line here and there, stood back with hands clasped, and said : " Oh, madam ! "

" The shoes, you fool," Rachel said in a voice husky with emotion.

She sat down and Chamberlain took off the shoes she was wearing and put on the golden sandals that went with the dress.

"Draw the curtains and put up all the lights."

Then she looked at herself slowly and appraisingly in the mirror, took a slow step or two, swinging with her foot her train this way and that.

She motioned to Chamberlain to leave the room. She was unable to trust her voice. She sat down, feeling queerly moved. It was a ritual moment in her life. When Rachel dressed, she dressed to kill; and she knew that she had never before dressed like this. This was Beulah: she looked forth on worlds to conquer.

Chamberlain tapped at the door. "Mr. Julian Heath, madam, is asking to see you."

Rachel's dark eyes burned for a silent moment upon the girl. "Send him in."

"In here, madam!"

Rachel did not answer, but the dark eyes seemed to light with angry sparks. Chamberlain backed away, submissive. "Very good, madam."

Rachel stood at the dressing-table, her back to the door, and in the mirror she saw Julian come into the room and the door shut behind him. She could read in his face his surprise at the curtained windows, the lights; she could see his nostrils flaring the scent of woman's clothes and cosmetics. She turned towards him, shifting the lie of her train with a practised kick. She did not smile. Her face was set in a mask of beautiful dark gravity. She said simply: "Iris Mearns" and pivoted slowly before him, her arms lifted out a little from her sides.

" My God, Rachel," he said, " you startled me."

And still she did not smile. " This is intended," she said, " to be a startling effect. It must startle everybody."

She turned again slowly to the mirror, and left him staring at the provoking loveliness of her back. He took a sudden step forward, spun her round, and buried his face between her breasts. Her head came down swiftly upon his, her rounded creamy chin pressing hard into the fair curls of his head. He kissed her and kissed, and she snuffed eagerly the clean male scent of his hair.

Then she said hoarsely " Stop ! " He raised his head, still holding her about the waist, his face a burning red, and saw that now she was smiling. " Go," she said. " Go at once. Whatever will that girl think."

" But——"

" Go now. The dress is perfect. It has been christened. It is the right thing for a bad woman."

Neither of them thought of what it was he had come to say.

Chapter Twenty-three

IT was always in May that the Markhams play was produced. May weather can be anything. There was an unlikely tradition that once, in the glorious Georgiana's day, braziers had flamed all along the great barn, sending up their incense to the roof that was high and dim as a cathedral's, and that after the show the house-party skated on Markham Lake under a sky that crackled with frosty stars.

But that May was beneficent. The big double doors at the western end of the barn were open wide, letting in the afternoon sun that shot level spears through the building. The dusty golden light fell on Charlie Roebuck and Julian Heath, wearing battered flannel bags and polo-collar pullovers as they worked with plane and hammer and chisel on the properties ; on Mina, whose halo was irradiated like a pale saint's as she laboured, wearing flannel trousers and a green jersey, on the canvas of a set ; on Harrison of the Spur and Stirrup, a noted amateur electrician who was to control the switchboard on the great night.

No one was speaking. Mina would dab and stand away, legs apart, cigarette in her lips, considering an effect. Now and then she would stoop and pat the Afghans, recumbent at her feet, now listen to the bursts of song from blackbird and thrush that poured into the barn ; and all the time she was thinking how glad she was that Maurice Bannerman was arriving that afternoon.

Julian and Charlie, puffing at pipes, trimmed and chipped, apparently absorbed in their job. Julian was thinking of the fireworks over at Pagham, and Charlie was thinking how like a pale saint Mina looked, and how frigidly saintly she had been that morning when he had come wading out into the dew before breakfast and had found her wandering under the white domes of the cherry orchard.

Harrison was thinking he'd better get this blasted wiring done quick or opening-time would be on him before he knew where he was ; and Rachel, leaning back in a bamboo chair filled with cushions, which Julian had carried into the barn, was just being decorative and running her part over in her mind. The house-party, small enough this year, had been assembled for a week. In another week the play would be performed.

The house-party, indeed, was altogether too small for Lord Upavon's liking, and that morning at breakfast he had been puffing and grunting about it. "Too bad, Mrs. Bannerman, too bad," he said, carving himself some ham at the sideboard. "We mustn't separate you from your husband like this, eh? We mustn't do it. Let me give you some of this ham. Now what about telephoning him, eh? What about telephoning him?"

Rachel, declining the ham, and nibbling at Swedish bread and fruit, murmured that she feared Maurice would find the journey impossible to make.

"We'll see, we'll see," old Upavon grunted, sitting down to his ham with a bright anticipatory eye. "Telephone him after breakfast."

265

Julian glanced across the table at Rachel, but she did not vouchsafe him a look. He had tried since the house-party assembled to find some excuse for bearing her off after dinner, and the fireworks at Pagham were a godsend. No one else wanted to go. They laughed the idea of fireworks out of existence, but Julian persisted that he at any rate had a passion for fireworks and would not miss them on any account. Would no one be persuaded to come? And Rachel, who could take a cue with the best, reluctantly agreed to give him her company, since he seemed to be set on going. And now here was Upavon threatening to bust the whole idea by bringing Maurice along.

Maurice had improved greatly. The cushions behind his back had been gradually increased, and now, for some time each day, he was allowed to sit almost upright. But all the same, his surgeon and his bone-setter were not easily persuaded. It was only after Mike Hartigan had received a detailed lecture on the care of his master and Maurice himself had promised the most discreet behaviour that he was permitted to go. He hired an ambulance for the journey, and the wicker carriage was strapped to its roof.

Lord Upavon came puffing into the barn, volubly shattering its peace. "That's fine, Mina, my dear, that's fine. 'Pon my soul, we're going to make this the best play Markhams has ever done. Well, you boys, I've just asked them to send some tea out for us all. Welcome, eh? Welcome?"

The tea arrived at that moment. "Now, Mrs. Bannerman, here we are. Refreshing. Refreshing. And you, Harrison, come and have some tea. Or would you rather have something else?"

" Well, my lord, if I could have a glass of beer an'
keep on with the job——"

So beer was brought for Harrison while the others
made a picnic tea on upturned boxes, and Upavon
chattered of the arrangements he had made for Maurice.
He was never happier than when fixing up difficult
details of hospitality. " He'll sleep on the ground floor,
Mrs. Bannerman. No stairs. Had a nice little bedroom
fixed for him, with a small room for his man next door.
Oh, and look at this, Julian. Some little bird's been
talking already."

He produced a London paper open at the society
chit-chat. Julian read aloud. " They were talking
last night at Lady Wreckage's about the Markhams
play, always the occasion for an intimate society
gathering. I hear that the play this year has been
written by Lord Upavon's tall, literary son, the Hon.
Julian Heath, and that the author's sister, as reticent
in society as she is famous upon the stage, will play a
part. She has the most enticing hair, which has been
compared with the lovely Mrs. Bunck's. There is
some talk of a great surprise which the play has for
us this year in the shape of an actress who has not
been heard of before but is likely to make something
of a furore. Lord Upavon will himself, of course,
grace the occasion."

Julian threw the paper to the floor. " I'm glad they
were talking about it at Lady Wreckage's," he said.
" I telephoned the paragraph myself, though I didn't
say anything about Mina's spontaneous combustion
or that crashing outsider the Bunck woman. Another
paragraph is due in a day or two. We shall then divulge
the name of the actress who, God help us, is to make

something of a furore. Come on, Charlie. Get hold of that jackplane."

"There's a car," said Mina. "That'll be Mr. Bannerman." She clattered her cup into the saucer and ran to the door to see the ambulance coming up the drive.

II

Upavon had gone with Mina towards the door of the barn. Charlie Roebuck was already working at his bench. Julian stood behind Rachel's chair. He said in a low voice : " Father and Mina have gone to meet Mr. Bannerman."

"Thank you," said Rachel. She had been drowsily content. She got up and faced him, yawned, showing him her red tongue curled among the white seeds of her teeth. Like a cat's yawn, it was to hide embarrassment. She was embarrassed because Julian had found it necessary to remind her to watch appearances. She remembered how Maurice had done the same thing not so long ago. "My dear, Oxtoby is wishing us luck."

My God, she thought, smiling with all the lustre of her eyes into Julian's face, was that only a few weeks ago ?

Mina was waiting for her at the door of the barn. Upavon had gone on towards the house. " I'm so glad your husband has been able to come, Rachel," she said. " I thought we were awful beasts separating you for so long."

"But I've found everything here so fascinating," said Rachel.

268

"Oh, yes, it's been all right for you. I was thinking of Mr. Bannerman."

There was something forthright and challenging in Mina's tone. She strode fiercely ahead, her hands in her trousers pockets, her hair having a bristling, provocative look. "Round and round Portman Square in a perambulator isn't terribly thrilling," she said.

Rachel gave Mina a sidelong glance. The girl's hard defiant tone interested her. Her agile mind quickly supplied all its implications, but the faint tolerant smile did not leave her face. "At any rate," she said, "Maurice should be happy here. There will be all your pictures for him to look at."

"Oh, those," said Mina scornfully. "Stuffy family portraits. A fat lot he'll care about them."

"Well, we shall see. I couldn't have said whether he would like them or not. I didn't know you were at all acquainted with his tastes."

"I spent an hour with him ten days or so ago. I called to see you, and you were out."

"You weighed Maurice up well in an hour, my dear."

"Sometimes you can."

"He said nothing to me about your call. Nor, for that matter, have you done till this moment."

She felt a sudden pang of jealousy at the thought that Mina and Maurice had passed an hour together without her knowing about it. "Well," she said, with the ghost of a sneer, "I see Maurice need not have a dull time here. He will be in understanding company."

Mina stopped sharply in the path and turned towards Rachel. Her face was deathly white and her

269

grey-green eyes glinted with anger. "Look here, Rachel," she said. "I want to give you a straight tip. We Heaths are divided into fools and those who are not fools. So far as I can make out, we always have been. Don't take my dear old father as a sample of what a Heath can be. He's a fool if ever there was one, and there's no one on earth I like better. But I'm no fool. I just want you to be clear about that. Don't be surprised at anything I do. And another thing you want to be clear about is this : Julian's no fool."

Rachel had stopped, too. She looked curiously at the faint flush of red that began to stain Mina's cheek. Her own self-possession was completely unshaken. But she was shaken below the surface. She merely asked coldly : "What has it to do with me whether Julian is a fool or not ? "

"Nothing, I hope," said Mina. She called her dogs and ran towards the house. Rachel followed, slowly and thoughtfully.

III

"Sorry you can't have dinner with us, Bannerman," said Lord Upavon. "There's something rather special the cook's turning out to-night. I should have liked your opinion on it. But you can come along to the library after dinner, eh ? Can you manage just an hour's chat and a cigar ? "

Maurice said he could. He was allowing himself one cigar a day and had not yet smoked it. "But I must be in bed by ten—mustn't I, Mike ? "

"That'll be all right," Upavon said. "You come to the library and take him away at the proper time,

Mr. Hartigan. We've got to do him some good here. I may be asleep myself at ten. Not like these youngsters. Fireworks ! I'm sorry about that, Bannerman. It was all fixed up before we knew you were coming. Otherwise, I'm sure Julian wouldn't have dreamed of taking Mrs. Bannerman away."

Maurice's calm eyes looked at the old fuss-pot toddling to and fro, dressed for dinner : tails, white tie, twinkling little shoes. " I wonder," he thought to himself, " whether he realises that neither his son nor my wife gives a damn about my feelings ? " Aloud he said : " Well, we must manage to spare them for one night. Now, please don't let me keep you. I'm comfortable here and have everything I want. You have been most kind."

" Well, after dinner, eh ? After dinner." And Upavon ambled away, making disgusted noises about pap and broth, and the other abominations that Maurice must eat.

Julian and Charlie Roebuck had not risen to Upavon's height. They wore dinner jackets. Rachel was wearing the dress she had bought in Manchester for her first dinner with Maurice. Mina, with a silken-headed Afghan stretched on either side of her chair, was wearing a dress the colour of beech-leaves when they are still an early wonder in the woods. She looked herself like something you might come on with surprise, racing wildly down the grey aisles of a forest.

" Julian," she said, sipping water as delicately as though it were the finest wine, " if your play goes on in the West End, what are you going to do about the cast ? Are you taking the whole family party with you ? "

"Not me," said Upavon. "My God, child, it's unthinkable."

"So is Mrs. Harrison," said Julian, "and so is the Vicar. His Bishop would hardly approve."

"So am I," said Charlie Roebuck. "I'm an amateur, and I stay one."

"I was really thinking only of myself," said Mina. "Will you give me a chance? I want to act again. I want to do something good—to *be* some one once more."

"It's not my experience," Julian said, "that the poor author is consulted in these matters. He's just the bloke who writes the play and gets his name on the bill with luck. But they darned well won't get this play unless you and Mrs. Bannerman and myself are in the show."

"Thank you," said Mina. "I'm set on it."

"Why do you suddenly want to be famous?" Rachel asked.

Charlie Roebuck intervened. "But Mina *is* famous, Mrs. Bannerman. You know that, don't you? She was as much talked of as any actress in London not so long ago."

"Yes," Mina smiled; "not so long ago. But I'm tired of being an intermittent celebrity. I'm going to be famous all the time now. Because famous people can do things and get things that others can't. It's a great advantage in any game you choose to play. Beauty or celebrity; a woman must have one or the other, don't you think, Rachel?"

Rachel considered her gravely for a moment, as though assessing her looks and reputation. "You already have both, Mina," she said then.

"Hear, hear, Mrs. Bannerman. That's well said, well said indeed," Upavon cried. "And if your own success is as great as your beauty, why, then, you and Mina will be a marvellous pair. Eh, Julian? Eh, Charlie? Well, here's their jolly good luck, anyway." And the old boy, who dearly loved to toast something, rose gallantly, glass in hand. Julian and Charlie followed his example rather sheepishly. "Reigning toasts" were neither of their generation nor to their taste.

IV

Rachel went to her room and changed. "Go to bed when you like. I shall be late," she said to Rose Chamberlain, that pert piece whom Mina despised. Mina got along very well without a maid, both in London and in the country, and that Rachel should have thought it necessary to bring the girl to Markhams seemed to her sheer snobbery. "As if she couldn't put her own pants off and on," Mina commented vulgarly to herself. Her admiration for Rachel as an actress had suffered no set-back; it had, indeed, been enhanced; she marvelled that such a natural mastery should have gone for so long undiscovered; but in a dozen trivial ways Rachel was getting on her nerves. And she found to her annoyance that her nerves were more susceptible since she had known Maurice Bannerman.

Julian, wearing a light overcoat over his dinner-jacket, had brought Rachel's red car to the door and was waiting in it when she came down. It was nine o'clock, and a beautiful mild evening. Maurice, whom

Mike Hartigan had wheeled into the library, heard the slam of the car door, the opening roar of the engine, the diminishing drone as the car flashed down the drive towards the village of Markham. Lord Upavon, Charlie Roebuck and Mina, were all in the library too.

" I'm going down to the barn to overhaul the lighting," Charlie announced. " Dress rehearsal to-morrow night. I must see that everything's in order. You coming, Mina ? "

" Sorry. I've got to finish Mrs. Harrison's dress. She's marvellous with a beer-engine but hopeless with a needle."

" Bring it down here," said Lord Upavon. " She can bring it down here, eh, Bannerman ? "

" That'll be fine," Maurice agreed, " if Miss Heath can put up with us old men."

" Old fiddlesticks," Upavon grunted. " I don't call myself old, and I can give you twenty years. Try this port. This *is* port—not the stuff they make out of stewed typewriter ribbons."

Maurice shook his head. " One cigar a day. No drink."

Upavon filled his glass and pierced a cigar for Maurice. Mina went out to get her sewing. Charlie Roebuck was waiting in the hall. " You're giving me the pretty cold mitt, aren't you ? " he grumbled.

" Don't be a child, Charlie," Mina answered brightly. " I tell you I've got work to do, and it's got to be done to-night."

Charlie kicked at a rug. " I call this the most stinking visit I've ever made to Markhams," he said.

" That's unfortunate."

" There's Julian gallivanting off with that Bannerman woman, whom I should like to see simmering gently in a casserole on the hobs of hell——"

"Charlie, you're being romantic. If you were at all practical, you would know that a camisole, not a casserole, is Rachel's environment."

"Oh, well. Damn the lighting."

"Right. Damn the lighting. And if it will help your feelings, blast it also."

"Let Julian see to it to-morrow."

"Yes. Let Julian see to it to-morrow."

"You're being very annoying."

"Why! I'm agreeing with all you say."

"We haven't had a moment together all this week."

"It's been a very busy week, and I've still got Mrs. Harrison's dress to finish."

"Well, I'll go and see to the lighting. I hope I electrocute myself."

He did not go, however, but stood there kicking sulkily at the rug. Sulky and handsome and rather flushed. A great pity for him filled Mina's heart. She knew that sooner or later she would have to deal him a harsh cut. Get it over.

"Charlie," she said, "why don't you put me right out of your head? I could never marry you, you know."

Charlie started and his flush deepened. "But, Mina, I've never had the nerve to dream of such a thing!"

"Now, Charlie, don't let's pretend, there's a dear. You've dreamed about it for years."

"Well——" He moistened his lips and fiddled with his tie.

"Well, it's no go. Perhaps I know you too well; perhaps I like you too much. Or perhaps I'm just a plain fool. But you don't *excite* me, Charlie. You don't intensify everything that I am. Oh, dear! Does that all sound plain rot? Do you guess what I mean?"

"Yes. I'm not so dense as that, Mina."

"Isn't it better, then, that we should get this all said and done with?"

"Yes," Charlie agreed miserably. "I suppose it is. Well, go and get your knitting, or whatever it is. I'll go and see to the lights. Give my apologies to your father and Mr. Bannerman. I shall go to bed when I get in."

Mina ran up the stairs before he could say anything more. She slammed the door behind her and sat down because her knees were trembling. She had begun so casually on the quashing of Charlie, but it had churned her up more than she expected. She fanned her burning face with a handkerchief and presently felt calmer. She heard her father's voice. "I can give you twenty years." That would put Maurice Bannerman in the early forties. She was in the early twenties. Then the turn of her thoughts startled her. "Oh, God! Oh, God!" she exclaimed angrily. She seized her sewing as though it were a neck to wring and walked resolutely down to the library.

V

When alone, Upavon made no bones about it: he paid tribute to the excellence of his dinner and the perfection of his port by falling asleep in the library. For a week now the presence of his family and his guests had interfered with that easy habit. But that night,

276

with Julian and Rachel away, with Charlie Roebuck engaged elsewhere, with Mina unusually silent over her work, and Maurice Bannerman inclined to be taciturn, he slipped towards oblivion several times and recovered with a " grumph " on the brink. At last he slipped and did not recover. Mina, sitting at a little table drawn close to the fire, went quietly on with her work, her red head bent over her needle. The curtains were drawn ; the fire purred ; Maurice, half-sitting, half-lying, watched the busy hands.

Presently Mina raised her head and looked at him with a smile. She noted anew the terrific force of his great blue-black chin, so strangely in contrast with the dark eyes that now looked almost mild.

" Comfortable ? " she asked.

" Yes, thank you."

" It must be very boring for you to be laid up like this after the tremendously busy life you've led."

" I shall get over it," Maurice said confidently. " It's a rest. It gives me time to think. I had given up my tremendously busy life, anyway. I've had all I want of that."

" And what do you want now ? "

" Oh, a new heaven and a new earth," Maurice smiled. " Theatres, concerts, picture galleries, libraries, instead of board meetings, mergers, dividends and directorates. Those were the things I wanted first. I've always wanted them most. Now I'm going to have them." He stuck out his chin impressively.

" You say that as though you always got what you wanted."

" Generally speaking," said Maurice, " I do."

" It's a nice night for the fireworks."

"I suppose it is."

"There's a grand moon coming up." Mina had put down her work and moved to the window. She stood with the curtains held back, her nose against the glass. Maurice did not answer. "I think I'll step out on to the terrace for a moment. It's so stuffy in here. Father *will* have a fire."

"You'd better put on a coat."

"Yes." She turned from the window and looked at him steadily for a moment. "Wouldn't you like to come too?"

"Me!" said Maurice, startled. "Why, I shall be getting trundled off to bed in five minutes. Ah, here's Hartigan now. Mike, Miss Heath wants me to sit on the terrace watching the moon come up. What do you say to that?"

"Why," said Mike, "I'd say praise God for an intelligent woman's lovely thought. Get your coat on to you, Miss Heath, and I'll put an extra rug round him."

When Mina came down, Mike had already wheeled Maurice on to the terrace and left him there. The carriage was pushed close against the balustrade. Mina leaned on the parapet and, looking out into the pale mesh of the moonlight, she imagined rather than saw all the familiar landmarks that she had gazed on from that spot ever since her eyes were higher than the grey stone coping. She could catch here and there a glint of the stream in the valley bottom, and the square, stubborn little tower of Markham church blocked darkly into the sky. The barn was in darkness. Charlie had finished with the lights and no doubt was gone to bed. Mina did not want to break the silence. Maurice did it for her. "This is a lovely place, Miss Heath," he said tritely.

"Yes. But could you stand it for long?"

"No. I don't think so. I have always lived in some great city or other. I think now I always shall."

"I can stand it for a long time," said Mina, "and then I run away. I can't stand the thought of anything going on for ever."

"It all depends. I think you should have gone on for much longer being an actress." She could see his faint smile in the moonlight. "You don't mind my saying that?"

"No, I think your opinion is worth having."

"Well, then. I saw you more than once. You were very good, you know. There are so many actresses—just clever—competent. You are better than that."

"You haven't seen Rachel act yet?"

"No. I am looking forward to that."

"You had no idea she was a great actress?"

"Great?"

Mina struck a match and lit a cigarette. He saw her face catch the light like alabaster. "Yes—great," she said. "I know what I'm talking about."

"No. I had no idea. She was—well, nobody."

"She's going to be somebody."

Maurice pondered. "It will be strange," he said. "I gave up what I was doing because I wanted to be somebody myself. . . ."

"Oh, you're somebody."

"My dear Miss Heath, you only mean I'm rich. But that is not much of a thing to be. A little luck to begin with, a good deal of ruthlessness to go on with : there you are—that's the short biography of most rich men. No. I meant something else. It will be amusing if, after all, I can do nothing and Rachel turns into a famous woman."

"I tell you, Mr. Bannerman," said Mina earnestly, "there's no 'if' about it. Before a year is out, Rachel will be famous. If you think that's amusing, God help you."

Her own swift vehemence appalled her. For a long moment she stood silent, her face aghast. Then she exclaimed : "Oh, how could I ! How could I say that to you !"

Maurice had finished his cigar. He considered the end without speaking, suddenly threw it in a bright parabola over the parapet.

"I know what you mean," he said quietly.

"What can you do ?"

Again he did not hurry to answer. Then he said : "What *does* an intelligent man do in such a case ? Shout ? Cry ? No. One does—nothing."

"But it's terrible."

"Many things are terrible. But there they are."

"Have you no feelings ?"

She regretted at once the foolish question.

"Yes," he said. "That is how I know that this would be a terrible thing."

"You really loved her ? You love her still ?"

"Yes," he said very simply, but she felt the great depth of his emotion behind the word. After a moment he added : "Now I must go in."

Mina wheeled him into the house.

For once Rachel was content to let Julian drive. Usually, she liked to do it herself. To be driving her own car was still a new, exciting, rich sort of thing to her ; and, besides, she had the true touch and loved the feeling of power under easy control.

But now she stretched her legs down luxuriously to their furthest reach, resigned herself with content to be hurried through the countryside on which the night was settling deeply. There was still a flush of dusky red along the western sky ; night was already in possession of the zenith and had lit a few stars.

They did not speak as the car swung along negligible roads, little more than well-paved lanes, the headlamps throwing a leaping light upon trees and hedges, making with its exaggerated glare every corrugation of the road look like a chasm, every small creature rushing to safety look like a small actor playing a lively part in a flashing spotlight. They tore through quiet hamlets where a few yellow lights stained the white façades of dreaming houses, and once, rushing downhill, they came full tilt upon a water-splash. The red car zoomed through it like a plough turning up a great furrow that for a second shone white through the darkness. Then they were climbing the opposite hill, and suddenly above the hill's crest, a serpent of fire slowly soared into the sky. It hovered for a moment, then with a soft concussion its head burst, and the sky was adorned with a great dome of golden light that shone incredibly beautiful for a brief moment between darkness and darkness.

In that moment the car reached the hilltop. Julian brought it to a standstill, and turned to see Rachel's face catch the luminescence from the sky, glow like a golden flower, and fade again to an oval of pallor at his side. He pulled the car close in to a hedge. Beyond the hedge a field dipped steeply, and through a gap they could see a roped-in space where the set pieces of fireworks were rigged.

Julian slipped an arm round Rachel's waist. She took the hand in hers and pressed it to her breast. " Do we really want to see fireworks ? " Julian asked.

" Yes, that's what we've come for."

They never knew what was the occasion that had called for the jubilation at Pagham. They remembered a long wall of people, dimly seen for the most part, but thrown every now and then into startling clarity, a frieze of white staring faces turning slowly up in growing light and slowly down in growing darkness. They remembered, beyond that, a little tent, brightly lit within, the red and gold roof-stripes a warm constant glow through all the alternations of darkness and light. They remembered the gleam on the brazen instruments and scarlet jackets of the bandsmen in the tent, and the sweet sentimentality of ancient waltz tunes that oozed out upon the warm air, and the elms majestically unmoved amid the coruscations that burned like brief diadems upon their brows.

That was what they long remembered of Pagham ; that and the occasional set pieces, fierce whirls and vortices of flame, red and green and yellow, sizzling and consuming themselves in a swift blaze of passion ; and they remembered how the full-faced moon slowly climbed out of the east, making the whole show suddenly intolerable. Without a word, Julian started the car, and soon there was no reminder of all that fret and combustion ; there was nothing but the equable milky radiance of the moon falling on field and farm, and on all the gentle convolutions of a sleeping world.

Julian allowed the car to purr quietly along. He was subdued by the peace and silence of the night, and by the beauty of the woman at his side. He was in no hurry to be back at Markhams. It was eleven o'clock when they got there, and everybody had gone to bed save Curle the butler. Julian was in no mood for sleep. He undressed slowly, put on his pyjamas and dressing-gown, and leaned at his open window, smoking a cigarette. Then impatiently he stubbed out the cigarette on the stone window-sill, the better to savour the scent of wallflowers that came up heavily from the garden. Beyond the garden the cherry-orchard lay under the white light of the moon, a spume of phantom blossom, like a midsummer ground mist. A few owls were calling with forlorn fluttering voices, and he leaned far out of the window to see if he could catch sight of them against the whiteness of the trees.

And then with a leap of the heart he saw that Rachel too, was leaning from her window. There was an unoccupied room between his and hers. Her face, turned towards him, was white in the black mesh of her hair which poured about her shoulders. Her hand beckoned, and she vanished.

Julian turned back into his room. He could feel the blood pounding in his veins, feel the trembling of his hand as he passed it nervously across his face. There was not a sound anywhere. He and she might have been the only two people alive in a house dead under the pallid radiance of the moon. He switched out his light and stepped noiselessly into the corridor. He turned the key in the lock and slipped it into his dressing-gown pocket. Rachel's door was on the jar, her room dark save for moonlight. He turned the key behind him and saw her silhouetted against the long luminous oblong of the window. She was naked, her black hair cascading about her thighs.

" You called me ? " he whispered.

Rachel did not answer. She took one lithe step across the room and gathered him silently in her arms.

Chapter Twenty-four

I

IT was not till the next day that Maurice saw how complete a theatre was established in the barn. It was Julian who showed him round. Julian was feeling shaken by the experience of last night. Before any one else was stirring in the house, he had risen from a sleepless bed, bathed, and gone striding out into the fields. He still felt slightly shocked by Rachel's passion, fierce and possessive. She had taken him, not he her. He was no virgin, but he was crude and callow ; he had not known anything so avid and elemental as she had shown him. The moon was setting, a white exhausted disc, staring levelly through the window, as he lay, tired but wakeful, looking at Rachel's face sleeping within the crook of his arm and in the disordered loveliness of her storm-tossed hair.

He was able to look at her then dispassionately, to marvel at the smooth perfection of her face, unmarred by the stress of her loving. She lay on her back, her lips parted by ever so little, as though she were still in the wonder of ecstasy. He could just see her small white teeth. The line that began beneath her lips and ran round her chin, down the slender column of her neck, was the purest he had ever seen on any woman. Her breasts were bare, tilted up towards him, and upon one of them her hand lay. In the pale light the lids of her eyes looked blue like the transparent petals of chicory flowers.

Julian could not disentangle the mixed skein of his feelings. She had protested to him with sweet tears and with passion that she loved him, and he had murmured back endearments. But he knew that he did not love her. He felt that he could as soon love a black panther. And yet, love or no love, she had given him something memorable. Marry her? Not even if she were free. What else, then? Well, he would let that wait on events. He was not going to pretend that this stolen fruit was not sweet.

Ever so gently, he disengaged his arm, stepped out of bed and slipped into his dressing-gown. Rachel stirred in her sleep, smiled, and murmured some words he could not catch. He pulled the bedclothes up about her shoulders, and stole back to his own room. The moon was gone. Already there was light in the east. He heard a sudden stirring outside his window. It was as though innumerable wings had with one motion unfurled themselves. Then all the birds in the world started singing together—one great chorus to the dawn ; as suddenly, all were silent again ; then, one by one, they began their several songs.

II

When Julian came back from the fields, his shoes soaked with dew, everybody was at breakfast. Even Maurice Bannerman was there. Upavon was very proud of that. " Look at him, Julian," he cried. " We're curing him—eh ? Making a new man of him."

286

Maurice was sitting almost upright in his chair. He was not eating much. Mike Hartigan, who was at the table, was seeing that he got the little he required.

Rachel was taking the rind from an orange. She looked calm and beautiful. She split the orange into sections and brought some of them to Maurice. " This is lovely," she said. " Try it."

" Thank you, my dear," said Maurice. " How did you get on last night ? It was a beautiful night for you."

" Yes," Rachel answered quietly. " It was. Most beautiful."

It was then that Julian broke in. " Could you have a look at our little theatre this morning, Mr. Bannerman ? Mr. Hartigan has told me that the stage interests you. I should like to know what you think of our show. We've been working on it for years. What about you, Rachel ? "

" The dress rehearsal is this afternoon, is it not ? I must be ready. It is most important. I shall drive myself about for an hour or two—get some air. Then I shall rest and think. I shall not want any lunch."

" Already the leading lady with emotions and a temperament," said Mina rather sharply ; and she alone heard Charlie Roebuck's whisper in her ear : " For God's sake say nothing to stop her. Let her go."

So after breakfast the party split up. Rachel unceremoniously zoomed away. Mina got into her disreputable car and went down to the village to take the dress to Mrs. Harrison. Charlie Roebuck, to his surprise, was permitted to go with her. Lord Upavon took an ash stick and said he would potter round. And Maurice, with Mike Hartigan pushing, and Julian in attendance, set off for the barn.

"I have read your play, you know, Mr. Heath," said Maurice. "It is good. I am looking forward to seeing it."

Julian murmured an author's conventional disparagement of his own worth.

"Now, what about the West End?" said Maurice. "Please don't think I am just a mass of stocks and shares and dividends. I know something about the finance of the theatre. Oh, yes. This is a small cast you have, and the scene is not elaborate. It is not going to be enormously expensive to put on. Now, what about the money? Do I come in there?"

Julian broke into a cold sweat and suddenly his knees trembled. Maurice's offer was generous; it took him by surprise; but the idea of being beholden to a man so little beholden to him made him feel inexpressibly small. He mumbled a refusal.

"But I shan't lose money, you know." Maurice smiled. "I'm a financier, and I've calculated that this is a safe thing. I should be making, not losing. It's not a favour I'm offering you. But, naturally, I should like to finance a thing with Rachel in it."

Julian at last found his tongue. "It's very good of you, Mr. Bannerman, but there's already a bargain about this. You probably know Cecil Hansford, the manager? Well, he's a very old friend of all of us here. He's keen on my writing and Mina's acting, and he promised long ago that if ever I wrote a likely play, he'd finance it."

"Well, that answers that," said Maurice; "but, remember, if anything goes wrong, the offer holds."

They reached the barn, and Mike Hartigan, Julian and Harrison, who was having a last look round, managed to get Maurice's carriage up on to the stage. Thence they surveyed the auditorium, fine and spacious ; and then Harrison gave a display of the lighting which Julian claimed with justice to be the most efficient in any private theatre in the country.

Julian began to realise that Maurice Bannerman did know what he was talking about when a theatre was in question. He understood the value of the fine, deep stage and the value of the hard work that Mina and Charlie and Julian had put in on the set.

" If you go to the West End," he said, " you must take all this with you. You've all put something into it—something that a professional scene builder might easily miss."

" There's no ' if ' about it, Mr. Bannerman," Julian answered. " We're going to the West End all right."

Maurice remembered that Mina too, had said there was no " if " about it. They were sure of themselves, these young Heaths.

They inspected the dressing-rooms, and excellent they were. On the door of Rachel's they found a notice—" Miss Rachel Rosing."

" Good God ! " said Julian. " Who's done that ? "

Rose Chamberlain was in the room, fussing about at the dressing-table. She looked superbly happy. " I'm just seeing that everything is ready for madam," she explained.

" Did you put that notice on the door ? " asked Julian.

" Yes, sir. I thought it looked so professional."

They withdrew quietly, leaving the acolyte in the temple.

" Well, there it is," Julian said. " You see, you can

really tell here what a show looks like. It's not just a drawing-room entertainment. Our family have been barmy about that sort of thing for generations. But I do feel, you know, that nothing has ever been done here before so good as we're going to do this time."

Maurice looked at the young proud face—no conceit or arrogance in it, but a supreme self-confidence. He knew that Julian was right, that something very good indeed was going to happen, and that for Julian it was going to mean the sort of fame he had for so long himself secretly and passionately desired. He felt a brief pang of anguish as he looked at the handsome young man, so confidently on top of the world.

" And I," he said, " what shall I do this afternoon ? "

" I wonder whether you'd hold the prompt book ? " said Julian. " We haven't arranged for any one to do that. Would you ? It wouldn't tire you ? "

" Oh, no. Do let me." Yes ; he could at least hold the prompt book as Rachel and Julian trod the stage.

Then Mina and Charlie Roebuck arrived. They had loaded the car with old books from the library, and now everybody save Maurice fell to the work of preparing the one scene that the play required. They packed the books into the bookcases, put the furniture into position, laid carpets, arranged chairs and tables, hung pictures, put up stag's antlers above the painted oak wainscoting, and fixed the grandfather clock so that when the play opened it would be telling the appropriate time. When everything was done, they dropped the curtain, went to the back of the barn, and waited while Harrison switched on the footlights. Then Julian shouted : " Now, Harrison, up with her ! "

The great curtain swung back, and for a moment they

all stood in the silence of complete satisfaction. It was perfect. The sconces on the walls and a tall standard lamp near the fireplace glowed tranquilly on rows and rows of books. The fire shone in the great stone fireplace. A bowl of flowers on the centre table was a fine pictorial focus. The whole setting was what it was intended to be : rich, lulling, complacent.

Julian broke the silence. " Yes," he said. " That's it. Everything ordered and old and established. And then Iris Mearns comes along and smashes it all up. It's just as you see it now, Mr. Bannerman, when the curtain goes up. No one in the room. Then Iris Mearns comes in by that door up there in the gallery on the right. She comes very slowly down those stairs. She's got to make an instant impression. And, by God, Rachel will do it. That dress she's got, to begin with——"

" I haven't yet seen it," said Maurice.

II

Lunch was an uneasy affair. Mrs. Harrison and her husband had theirs in the kitchen. Lord Upavon, as irritable as a leading lady, tried to be agreeable to the vicar, who was himself not at all in an easy mood. Mina, Charlie and Julian were fairly self-possessed, though there was a feeling of terrible strain behind Julian's calm. He was like an owner with every confidence in his colt but admitting, nevertheless, that he will be glad when his first race is over.

Maurice was eating in his own room, and Mike Hartigan was snatching a bit of food with him. Rachel, true to her promise, had not been seen since breakfast. She drove wildly about the countryside for nearly two hours, returned at eleven o'clock when everybody was in the barn, and went straight to bed. She did not sleep, but lay there completely relaxed, her curtains drawn. She did not hear the bird-song without or smell the scents of the spring morning that wafted in through the curtains. She was wrapped in a world of her own. Her hands behind her lovely head, she was already wearing the glorious dress that Rosabelle had made ; she was already entering into the skin of Iris Mearns, exchanging with Julian Heath the sharp destructive words that he had written for her to say. Scene after scene went through her mind, absorbed her into the very essence of its point and meaning. She felt, as she had felt before, with a wonder that not till this last few weeks had the gift been revealed to her, that she was slipping out of her own personality, that she *was* this rich, strange, disturbing creature who could touch happiness with a little finger and see it wither.

Rose Chamberlain, sick with happiness, came to her at two o'clock and helped her to dress. Rachel did not open her mouth. Seeing her in that repelling mood of an automaton, Chamberlain did not dare to open hers. With no word to any one, quietly rapt in the illusory destiny of Iris Mearns, Rachel walked to the barn and went to her dressing-room. Then she smoked one cigarette before motioning to Rose Chamberlain to bring out the dress in which Iris Mearns was to make her entrance.

Maurice was comfortable in the wings. Propped up in his carriage, with screens behind him and at the sides, and with Mike Hartigan sitting near, he waited for the play to begin. He loved being in a theatre. Though he had much money profitably invested in films, he did not visit a cinema more than two or three times a year. He preferred to see the poorest flesh-and-blood show to the most gorgeous company of vocal phantoms that the studios could produce.

Now, with so personal an interest in the play about to be performed, he was more keenly excited than he remembered being since the far-off days when the theatre seemed to him the grandest thing in the world, and, with his fiddle under his chin, he sawed away at the music which preluded the curtain's rise at the Manchester Grammar School.

From where he sat, prompt book in hand, he looked right across the stage to the gallery from which Rachel would make her descent. It was a grand part that young Heath had written for her. Would she be as good as they all thought? Well, he would soon know. He could hear Julian shouting, " Is everybody ready? " And then, " Well, let it go. As soon as you like, Rachel."

Maurice was aware of Rose Chamberlain creeping out and standing near him, of Mike Hartigan silently shoving a chair towards her, and then he saw the door on to the gallery open and Rachel come through. She stood for a moment looking down into the empty room. Then she lit a cigarette, pondered a moment, crushed it out, and, as though taking a sudden resolve, came down the stairs rather quickly. She crossed the room in a lithe stride or two, threw up the lid of a writing-desk, and began to rummage among the papers. She took out a letter and threw it into the fire. She strode back to the desk and was busy again with its contents when Julian entered.

"Hallo, Miss Mearns." Then seeing what she was at : " I say, that's my father's desk."

His eye fell on the burning letter in the fire. He moved to snatch it off, when she seized him by the wrist and held him firmly till the letter was consumed. Then she went to the desk and closed it carefully. "Now," she said, "suppose we sit down and talk about it."

"I'll be damned if I do."

"You'll be damned if you don't."

"Yes," thought Maurice, "that was all right." Rachel had made her instantaneous impression—the impression of a superb, ruthless woman, swift and feline. It was not the action she had performed or the few words she had spoken. It was the way she had performed the action and spoken the words, the way she had taken in hand a dangerous situation, imposed herself on the sudden intruder. She was an actress.

The act ran on, and Maurice watched with growing excitement as all that Mina and Julian had said about Rachel was made manifestly true before his eyes. Oh, she was great ; she was great !

She grew in stature as the act proceeded, an adventuress of superb proportions, indomitable, resourceful, beautiful and cool. There seemed never a slip in her conception of the part. She built it up with a hundred gestures and intonations. Even her fellow-players had not expected the complete annihilation of herself which they were witnessing, the complete creation of a being who led them all on to do even better than they had hoped to do. The act ended with every one on the stage, and when the last words were spoken they all spontaneously stood round Rachel and clapped. Even Mike Hartigan's hatred of the woman was forgotten for a moment. Standing in the wings, he joined his cheers with the others, and Rose Chamberlain exclaimed rapturously under her breath, " Oh, madam ! "

Only Maurice did not cheer. He was too moved, too torn by conflicting feelings of admiration, doubt and love, to do more than stare in bewildered regard at Rachel.

Rachel was unstirred by the enthusiasm. She smiled coldly from one to another, then walked towards the wings. Seeing Chamberlain standing there, she asked : " Where is my cloak ? "

Chamberlain had forgotten the cloak. " Get it ! " said Rachel. " I told you to have it ready at the end of each act." She did not move towards the dressing-room till the cloak was upon her shoulders.

IV

When it was over, they all had tea upon the stage. They were happy. It had been a grand success. Congratulations showered on Julian and Rachel. Julian was rather flushed, rather excited ; and, indeed, he had reason to be. He knew more than most people did about the chanciness of the dramatist's job, but if ever a play had had success written all over it, his had had it that afternoon. And he had all the money he needed to put it on and knew plenty of people who would help to push it towards success. He had good cause to feel on top of the world.

Rachel took it all calmly. She complained that she was tired, and for once she was not playing a part. She felt tired to death. She was Iris Mearns no longer. She was Rachel Rosing, exhausted, realising for the first time that her gift had its penalties as well as its pleasures. She wanted to go and sleep, and wondered if she could politely manage to excuse herself from dinner. It was Maurice who suggested that she should rest. "Come along, Rachel," he said. "All these excitements will be too much for me. I must get back to my room. I'm sure every one will excuse you, too."

Mike Hartigan pushed him to the house. Rachel came into his room, which she had not before entered. Mike shifted the pillows, so that Maurice might rest at full length, and then Maurice signed to him to get out. Rachel stood by the carriage, looking down at him. He reached out and took her hand. "My darling," he said, "I do not know how to say what I think. I feel so proud of you. I did not know, when I asked you to marry me, that you had it in you to be a famous woman."

"No," she said. "You knew nothing about me—nothing."

"Only one thing," he said. "That I loved you." He fondled her long white hand, pointed with red, and raised it to his lips. "Go and rest now, darling," he said.

He waited for some sign from her. She bent and kissed his forehead. " Yes," she said, " I must rest. I'm terribly tired. I didn't know it would take it out of me like that. I wonder whether work for the films is so exhausting ? "

When Rachel was gone Maurice took from his pocket a letter he had received that morning. It was from a firm of private inquiry agents, and it told him that the woman named Oxtoby who had married Morris Fahnemann so long ago had been dead for years. Maurice had said nothing to Rachel, but had set the inquiries afoot as soon as she had promised to marry him. It had cost him a lot of money, and in a way there was small satisfaction in the information now that he had obtained it. It brought Rachel no nearer to him, though she was, in fact, and beyond the law's interference, his wife. He was glad that in the marriage register in Manchester he had inscribed himself, " Widower." Everything was in order. Everything except the main thing.

v

Mina went back to her dressing-room when tea was over. Mrs. Harrison was beyond herself, clucking like a bawdy old hen. Mina wanted to be shut of her, to have a moment's quiet. She had changed into her flannel trousers and green pull-over, and sat with her feet on the dressing-table, her chair tilted back, her hands joined behind her head, a cigarette in her mouth. She felt deeply stirred. She felt that most of those who had been concerned in the play that afternoon were on the brink of great events, great changes. Julian's days of obscurity were over, to begin with, and so were Rachel Rosing's. Any one who now doubted that the woman would be one of the greatest actresses of the day was a fool. Once *Thin Ice* had run for a week, the world would be Rachel's. The theatre, the films—everything. For herself too, this was going to mean a lot. Her part was a good one, and with Rachel as the perfect foil that she had been that afternoon, it could be made one that would attract more attention than she had ever had before.

What was it all going to mean for Maurice Bannerman? Mina had been doubtful how serious Julian was about Rachel. She did not imagine that he would allow himself to be deeply complicated with what Charlie Roebuck contemptuously called a " pick-up " or even with a pretty good actress ; but with an actress who seemed to grow in importance under your eyes it might easily be another matter. And Maurice Bannerman, dear simple soul, would do nothing about it. " What does an intelligent man do ? Nothing." By God, thought Mina with sudden vehemence, I'd give her nothing ! I'd break every bone in the bitch's body.

She sprang to her feet, taut and quivering, and stared sightlessly out through the small window. Her arms hung at her sides, her hands clenched till the knuckles looked as though they would burst through the skin. Her eyes glinted with fierce green flecks. " By God ! " she said again. " If she goes too far I'll deal with her myself." Her little breasts rose and fell under the pullover. Through the lovely young green of the trees she could see the house, and suddenly at her window on the first floor Rachel appeared. She was a long way off, but Mina could see that she was wearing some elaborate negligée ; she saw her stretch her arms indolently above her head and then withdraw. Mina shook her fist towards the window, looking like a beautiful, fierce little witch. " Look out," she muttered. " Look out ! I'll get you one of these days."

Chapter Twenty-five

I

THE delightful snobbery of the London press always ensured a notice for the Markhams play. The play was, in its way, an historic affair, but that it was performed at a nobleman's country seat was the main thing. After all, Upavon was an M.F.H. That meant that all the hunt members would be invited, as well as all sorts of other swells from town and country. Drama produced under auspices so august could hardly be neglected. And so, usually, the occasion got into print for its social rather than its artistic value ; but that was altered the year when *Thin Ice* was produced.

There were three performances—on Monday, Tuesday and Wednesday. It was for the Monday that Upavon invited a great company of guests to dinner. Cecil Hansford, the theatrical manager, was among them. Julian counted on Cecil Hansford, and he did not count in vain. When the show was over, and the storm of applause had died down in the barn, Hansford slipped round to the dressing-room where Curle, the butler, was squirting soda into glasses. Lord Upavon, the vicar, Julian and Charlie Roebuck were watching him critically, feeling that they deserved well of the republic.

" Another glass, Curle, another glass," Upavon fussed. " Well, Hansford—well, pretty good—eh ?

The talent of the Heaths didn't die with Georgiana—eh?"

Hansford raised his glass. "Good luck, Julian. You've done it, my boy."

Julian blushed and smiled. Hansford gulped down his drink. "I must be off. But I couldn't go without offering my congratulations. One word in your ear. Play up like hell to-morrow night. And tell your leading lady to do the same. God! Where did you find her?"

Without more words, Hansford vanished. He was on the telephone the next morning to two or three critics of note. He spread the news. A play with a kick in it. A new actress who had beauty and brains and was going to knock 'em in the West End. Hansford had never been known to tip a wrong 'un. The critics came on Tuesday night. On Wednesday morning *Thin Ice* and Rachel Rosing were proclaimed by several people who mattered to be the most interesting play and the most moving actress of the moment.

"Which," said Julian, turning the pages at the breakfast-table with a grand pretence of indifference, "is as it should be. Lucky thing, Rachel, you remembered to tell these people they could get your photograph from Portman Square. Doesn't it look fine?"

It did, indeed. A perfect profile, to turn the heart with its beauty. But it was Maurice, not Rachel, who had thought of that, and it was no West End photographer but a man in Blackpool who had taken the picture. Maurice had had it done before he married Rachel. He had thought of publicity before the others,

301

and, ringing up Blackpool days ago, he had ordered a dozen prints to be sent to Portman Square so that they would be on hand for the London press. The picture appeared in several papers together with Julian's. " Peer's son writes play. Financier's wife as actress." Their names began to be linked together. Julian Heath ; Rachel Rosing ; *Thin Ice*. Two of the weekly illustrated papers sent photographers to Markhams. They took pictures of Julian and Rachel in front of the house. Several papers of the sort that make up for having no news by being exceedingly newsy contained fag-ends of gossip and tittle-tattle. Rachel loved it all. Mina said nothing and ground her teeth.

II

On Thursday morning—the day after the last performance of *Thin Ice*—Maurice received a letter from his bone-setter who was getting very nervous about his patient's long absence. He announced that he would come to Markhams that day—he hoped to be there by noon—and he ended with a hint that if Maurice had been behaving himself and observing all the precautions, it might be found possible for him to stand up with a couple of sticks and try a step or two.

Maurice read the letter at the breakfast-table. Mike Hartigan looked at him as fondly as a mother on a child about to essay first steps in public, and Mina clapped her hands. "Oh, that will be great, Mr. Bannerman," she cried. "Aren't you excited, Rachel?"

Rachel looked up calmly from a letter held in her hand. " Naturally. I shall be delighted when Maurice can walk again," she said.

" Aren't you all on pins for this old bone-setter to come ? " Mina persisted.

" I'm afraid I shan't be here to welcome him."

" Oh, but surely——"

" My dear Mina," Rachel said with icy reproof in her voice, " I may be allowed to decide such a matter for myself ? "

Mina did not answer. She bent her furious humiliated face over her plate. " This letter," Rachel pursued, " is from Mr. Hansford. He asks me to lunch with him to-day. He would like you to come too, Julian."

" Ah ! " Julian's face lighted with swift understanding of what the invitation might mean.

" Surely," said Mina with cold malice, " any one so famous as Rachel is not obliged to hop at the first crook of a finger. Couldn't another date be suggested ? "

Maurice intervened. " But why ? I shall be all right. I am well looked after. There is Mike here. And, anyway, I don't suppose my bone-setter will want a public audience. No. You must go, Rachel. I can see that this may be something very important for you." He smiled. " I hope to-day will see a first step for both of us."

Mina watched him closely as he waved his plump shapely hand, dismissing the matter. She was aware of the anguish under his gay pretence. He did not want Rachel to go. He was shocked that she was going. But he would be damned before he asked her to stay. That was how Mina saw it.

" I'll tell you what," said Julian, finally relieving

303

the tension. "We'll ring you up from Hansford's after lunch and swap glad tidings."

"That will be fine," Maurice agreed.

After breakfast Charlie Roebuck brought to the door the battered car that was jointly his property and Julian's. He felt flat. The show was over. If it ever went on professionally, he was out of it. He wanted to get back to work. He was sure Julian was going to come a cropper over that dark enchantress. There was more going on than met the eye. And Mina these days was as stimulating as Monday's mutton. He was glad to be off. He said his farewells. "See you soon, I suppose, Julian? Sorry to take the bus, but I suppose Mrs. Bannerman will give you a lift. Anyway, a celebrity like you wouldn't be seen dead in a thing like this. You'd better make over your half-share to me in memory of a life's friendship."

"Memory my foot," said Julian. "Take the old dust-cart and be damned to it, but there's a lot coming for you and me, Charlie." He went off whistling, to find the copy of *Thin Ice* which he was sure Cecil Hansford would want to see. No one was left on the step except Mina. Charlie looked back over his shoulder to wave to her, and thought she looked a tragic little slip of a thing. What in hell had happened to them all lately, he demanded savagely, making the old car jump and jangle down the ruts of the drive. They were all at sixes and sevens ; none of the old joy and contentment anywhere.

Mina was feeling as forlorn as Charlie thought she looked. She, like him, was suffering from the emotional slump that followed the end of all their effort. There was no one about. Her father had gone off for his daily

304

"potter." Maurice had retired to his room, saying he was going to rest so that his bone-setter should think him a good boy. Rachel, no doubt, was "resting." Astonishing how much rest she needed lately; and Mina was tortured by doubts about Julian's part in assisting the process of rest.

Mina strolled moodily round the house, called her Afghans, and gave herself up to the identical mood that was gnawing Charlie Roebuck. All on one another's nerves; all distrusting one another; and they had all been so happy before this blasted Jewess came with her fatal beauty. Mina stopped at the door of the barn and looked in. Nothing had been touched. The chairs in the auditorium stood in close rows; programmes littered the floor. The scene was still set, she knew, though the curtain was down. The whole place had the forlorn, haunted air of an arena whose play is over. Wandering with no conscious object, Mina entered the high, dim building. The dogs hated the place. They stretched themselves out to wait in the sunshine at the door.

She went up the long aisle between the chairs, turned to the right, and climbed the few steps that led to the stage. The curtain kept the stage in a heavy twilight. Julian was sitting on the couch drawn up near the fireplace with Rachel on his knees. His lips were pressed to her breast. Her head was thrown back. She was completely abandoned. The back of the couch was towards Mina. They neither saw nor heard her. She stood for a moment, her hands in her trousers pockets, regarding them with an indifferent irony and contempt that was the last emotion she would have expected to feel at such a moment.

When they came out, they found her sitting at the great door of the barn, with the dogs at her feet. " Hallo, Mina ! " Julian cried affably. " Enjoying the sunshine ? "

" Don't you think," said Mina, " it's sometimes wise either to have a doorkeeper or to lock the door ? "

Rachel gave her a look of black hatred and said to Julian : " Come along. It's time we started off for Cecil Hansford's."

III

From the secondary road on which they had passed nothing for a long time Rachel, who was driving, suddenly switched the red car into a mere lane.

" Hallo ! Where are we going to ? This isn't the way," Julian cried.

" We are going half a mile or so up this lane," said Rachel. " We can talk there. We've plenty of time to get to Hansford's by one o'clock."

She said no more as the car jolted and bumped along the lane. It was a cart-track. Creamy waves of fools-parsley washed along it on either hand, stained here and there with the red of campion. Rachel put the bonnet into a gate, turned the car so as to be ready to continue their journey, and then said, when the engine faded out : " Now I reckon we're in a bit of a fix. Mina must have seen us."

" Mina doesn't babble about all she sees."

Rachel looked at him and could have struck him. He was so undisturbed, so sure of himself. His perfect grey suit and brown suède shoes, his curly golden hair and blue eyes and small crisp moustache, his well-kept hands with a blue cuff falling over the wrist and the wrist-watch : it all looked so collected and urbane and free from passion that she could have shrieked. But she did not shriek. Far from it. She smiled bewitchingly, and her heart melted in her as he smiled back, his red lips parting under the gold of the moustache to show his white teeth. He was beautiful, and he would be famous, and he would be rich, and she loved him. But it was not his fame or his riches she loved. For the first time in her life she had met something that struck at her self-interest and destroyed it. She wanted to throw her arms about him again, but his smile held her off. It was so easy and complacent and damnable, that smile. It was content to possess her, and she knew that he himself was not possessed. He stretched out a hand to fondle her breast, and she said : " No, Julian, please. Not now. About Mina. How can you be sure she'll say nothing to Maurice ? She likes Maurice. She talks to him."

She wanted to alarm Julian, but he refused to be alarmed. " Oh, you know," he said easily, " tittle-tattling with a wronged husband isn't exactly Mina's line. Oh, no. By cripes, no."

Oh, God, she cried to herself, could nothing move him, could nothing bring her nearer to him than this ache in her which evoked no ache in him.

" You don't love me," she said.

" Oh, Rachel, my darling." His hand went out towards her again, but she held it off.

" No," she said. " You enjoy me, and that's all you want—to enjoy me."

Julian shifted uncomfortably in his seat. " This is a

307

damned nuisance," he was thinking. He looked down the lane, bursting with spring sap, and at the swifts rushing with shrill whistling against the blue sky. The air was heavy with the scent of hawthorn and vibrant with the song of birds. " God knows," he thought. " This is a setting for a love scene. If she'd let me get hold of her, I could soon make her quiet."

But she would not. " This is not only a nuisance," he reflected, " this is serious. This woman is going to make my play. I can't afford to put her out of sorts. You're in a jam, my boy. Watch your step." But nothing of Julian's cynical calculation was reflected in his fair young face. He succeeded, indeed, in looking deeply abashed as he turned to Rachel.

"Look here, darling," he said soothingly. "You may be absolutely certain that nothing Mina has seen —if she has seen anything—will reach your husband."

And then Julian got the shock of his life. "He's not my husband," Rachel said.

Julian felt as though he had been knocked endways. "But, Rachel, my darling, what do you mean?" He wondered for a moment whether hysteria had overcome her, but saw that she was calm enough, though slightly flushed. No ; he could not imagine that in any circumstances Rachel would become hysterical. "What's the joke?" he said. "Didn't I see the announcement in *The Times*? Didn't I send you a wedding present? And I know more than that too, my lady. I've had a good many talks with that nice chauffeur of yours. He told me that he brought you away from the registry office in Manchester."

"Yes, yes," said Rachel, " that's true enough. But all the same, Maurice Bannerman is not my husband."

Julian lit a cigarettte with desperate calm. " Had we better get along ? " he asked.

" Oh," said Rachel, with a sharp flush of anger, " you're going to take the pitying, forbearing attitude, are you ? You think I'm talking through my hat. I'm not. I could put Maurice in gaol to-morrow, if I wanted to, as a bigamist." A sudden need to justify herself took possession of her. " Now you see the sort of man I'm fixed up to. I suppose you thought I was just some corner piece running after you. But I'm justified in dealing with Maurice like this—am I not ? "

She looked at him with her splendid eyes flaming darkly, a slight flush seeming to shine through her skin. She plunged deeper into her sudden impromptu deception. " I don't owe much, do I, to a man who's let me down like that ? "

Julian took her hand and stroked it. " This is surprising," he said. He felt a sudden gleeful leap of his own pulse. He clutched at a justification of his own meanness in taking in his father's house the wife of his father's guest.

" You're not Maurice's wife," he said, musing over the words and the comfort they gave him. " But, my dear, how long have you known this ? "

" Almost from the beginning," she said. " I dare say I should never have known if the accident hadn't happened to Maurice. Naturally, left alone in the house with nothing to do, I wandered about looking into this and that. I found papers—letters—in Maurice's desk. . . ." The lies improvised themselves upon her tongue. She found she hardly had need to think them.

Letters—in Maurice's desk.

The opening scene of *Thin Ice* recurred to Julian's

mind. He could imagine her swift, deft fingers, her darting glances. He found he was not liking her any better.

" Does your husband——? "

" He is *not* my husband."

" Does Maurice know that you made this discovery? "

" No. But don't you see, darling, that's why I avoid him, that's why I can love you? You must have known there was some reason. You couldn't suppose that if Maurice and I had been married only a few weeks I could let you love me? You couldn't think that of me, could you, darling? You see, I'm free." She put her arms round his neck and pulled his head down on to her shoulder. In a whisper she said in his ear : " Maurice has never had me, lovely one. Only you. No one but you. I'm always yours. You believe that, don't you? "

" You dear one," said Julian. He kissed her fiercely, then said : " Don't worry about Mina. She's not a babbler."

" I won't then, my love."

" And now we must go on. Hansford is important to us both."

" Right," she said. " Will you drive, darling? I am exhausted." She was silent after that, pondering what she had said and done, seeking a next step. Only one thing she said as they were nearing Hansford's house : " You won't say anything about this to Maurice—or any one else? "

" Not I," said Julian, with deep conviction.

Chapter Twenty-six

I

MAURICE did not go back to Portman Square in the ambulance that had brought him to Markhams. He had walked a few steps the day when Rachel and Julian had had their satisfactory interview with Cecil Hansford. Hansford wanted to put *Thin Ice* on in September. Rachel, Mina and Julian were to play in it. Julian, drawing two salaries, as author and actor, would do very well. Rachel would get as much money in a week as she had ever before cleared in a year, Mina's salary would be nothing to sneeze at.

It was all very cheering, and Hansford was as cheerful as anybody. He had an infallible nose for smelling money in a play. He was one of the few managers who could say that never yet had he lost money in the theatre. He was sure he was not going to lose it this time.

A cheering day for Maurice too. He walked, and felt as elated as if he had flown. The next day he walked again ; and the day after that he went home comfortably cushioned in his own Rolls-Royce. He would still have to use his carriage for most occasions, but for a lengthening period each day he would be allowed on his feet.

Mike Hartigan rode in front with Oxtoby, and Rachel with Maurice. Julian promised to drive her car up to town when he came, which would be in a day or two. It was a grand day, reaching out towards June. Maurice was profoundly content. He felt that now that he and Rachel could be together in their own house, things would have a chance to go well. He was beginning to indulge himself again. He was smoking several cigars a day. He was smoking one now, leaning back in his cushions, rather abstracted, patting Rachel's hand and saying little, as was his way when his mind was tranquil.

Rachel was anything but content. An unappeasable pang was in her heart as soon as the car had left the drive of Markhams. Julian, smiling and debonair, had stood on the front steps, waving, looking as though life could not be sunnier—and, indeed, that was how he was feeling. And again Rachel felt that something akin to hatred was bound up in the strands of her love for him, hatred that he could see her go and smile and smile. She feared what was before her. God alone knew what Maurice might want of her now that he was getting on his legs again.

She flew up to her own room as soon as she reached Portman Square, and rang her bell furiously for Rose Chamberlain who had been sent on the day before. Still dressed in her travelling clothes, she stood before the cold fireplace, livid beyond proportion to the cause of her annoyance. "That cat, Chamberlain," she flamed. She pointed a long trembling finger at Omar, the golden Persian, a warm, oblivious ball curled on her couch. "Haven't I told you again and again that I won't have the creature in this room!"

She was drawing her gloves through her fingers, and suddenly she bent towards the cat and struck him with them sharply. " Go ! Go ! " she said. " Get out ! "

Omar at the stroke leapt to sudden life. Back up, tail swaying dangerously, mouth open to show snarling teeth and clean pink tongue, he watched intently with alert and lovely eyes. " Go ! " cried Rachel, and struck again, but Omar struck quicker. His heavy pad made one lightning rip, and Rachel drew back, white with anger, and examined the red scores from which the blood oozed slowly down the back of her hand. Omar spat once, then leapt from the couch and went from the room with dignity. In the bathroom, Rachel poured witch hazel into her wounds, and then went down to lunch feeling extraordinarily shaken. The cat's maleficence, the transformation in one second of that bundle of warm placid fur into a thing that struck and wounded as she had never before been wounded, startled and alarmed her. She had never supposed that one need be afraid of a cat ; now the cat took on in her injured mind a disproportionate significance of evil. This, she said to herself, is the sort of thing I am liable to in this house. And in her thoughts was Markhams where she had enjoyed the liberties and consideration of a guest, and Julian's company.

She nursed both her hand and her grievance secretly. Maurice, who was waiting for her, was not permitted to see either ; but he could hardly have chosen a more inauspicious moment for the revelation he had to make. When old Bright had left the room, Maurice lit a cigarette for Rachel, rejoicing that he could now stand to perform such small services.

" My dear," he said, " now that we are at home again I want to tell you something that I think will please you."

She looked up sharply, and he gained the impression that she was not at all certain that she wanted to be pleased.

"The woman I married in New York is dead. She has been dead a long time. I was a widower when I married you. The law can do nothing to us. We are legally man and wife."

Rachel blew smoke towards the ceiling, considering the grey wreaths carefully, as though they were the matter that Maurice had laid before her. "That's all right then," she said, not looking at him. "That's a load off your mind."

"It is. I should have hated anything disagreeable to touch you, darling."

"You took the chance."

Maurice blenched at the coolness of her tone. "Yes," he said. "Perhaps I should have waited. But I loved you so much, Rachel. You are glad too, to know that—that there is no danger to our happiness?"

My God, thought Rachel. Happiness! What words he chooses! "It makes things altogether more comfortable," she said. "It is not agreeable to have a thing like that hanging over your head."

Her voice was so tired, so bored and casual, that Maurice slumped into his chair. His chin sank into his chest. He pushed his black oiled forelock back from his eye. "I do not think you are happy, Rachel," he said.

At that direct challenge, Rachel looked up sharply. "And what makes you think that?"

"Just this, my dear: that since I have been laid on my back you have not done for me any of the things

I should have loved to do for you, if you had met with an accident and not I."

Gripping the arms of his chair with both hands, he awaited her reply. None came. In a moment he went on as quietly as a judge assessing an impersonal cause "At the nursing home, you visited me as little as you could, and you went away as soon as you could. When I came home, you left all the care of me to Mike Hartigan. There was a great deal you could not do for me, but there were many things you could have done. At Upavon's house there was, I know, every excuse for you. You had discovered a wonderful talent and you had a wonderful opportunity to display it. You were right to use much time on that. I should have done the same. But even there, there were many occasions when you might have sat with me, talked with me ; but you allowed every one to see that I was not deeply in your thoughts."

Again he paused, then asked : " Am I being unfair ? "

" No," said Rachel.

" What are we to do ? "

She had no answer to that.

" We have both been unfortunate," said Maurice. " If it had not been for that accident, I think we should have been happy. I could have done so much for you."

" You might have prevented me from discovering that I can stand on my own feet."

" Does that mean so much to you ? "

" Yes," said Rachel, and he could not overlook the passionate conviction in the word. " It means more than you can ever understand. You don't know what it is to be a woman like me—to want so much and to have everybody who can help you to just a little making you feel that you can only have it if you pay for it in bed. Isn't that what it comes to? Yes, it is. Don't I know it! And if you have lived, as I have, from the time you are fifteen till the time you are twenty-five with that fact staring you in the face, and then you discover that there's another way after all, that you can get what you want and at the same time keep your own respect and the respect of other people—oh, then, you don't ask whether it means much. You know! And that's what's happened, Maurice."

"I see."

"Did I ever tell you I loved you? No, I never did. We married with our eyes open. You knew I was giving you my beauty. I knew you were giving me luxury. And then I found I could have luxury on my own terms."

He had never seen her so passionate, or, he thought, so beautiful. He sat gripping the arms of the chair, very white, recognising the justice of all that she said. But he felt that though it was the truth, it was not the whole truth.

"I am glad, Rachel," he said, "that we have said what is in our hearts. But there is something more to be said. I love you. I loved you from the first time I saw you. I love you now more than ever. You say you did not love me when you married me. But you knew that I loved you. Didn't you?"

"Yes, I did."

"And does that make no difference? Suppose our marriage was just the bargain you have described. Do

316

you go back on a bargain because of something that happens after the bargain is concluded ? "

She did not answer. " You can please yourself," he said, " but I make the point. Oh, Rachel, it is terrible to be sitting here, talking about something that means so much to me—talking about it as though it were some silly point that we could settled like adding up a sum. Who will rejoice more than I shall because you are famous, because you stand on your own feet ? It only makes me love you the more. It is something that could never arise if you loved me too."

" That is true," said Rachel. " In that case it would never arise." She put up her hand wearily to her head, and Maurice saw for the first time the red lines that Omar had scored there.

" What is that, my darling ? " he cried, instantly solicitous. " What has happened to you ? "

" Oh, it's nothing," said Rachel ; " nothing at all. Please let me go now." She hurried to her room, burnt up and exhausted.

II

She had not intended, when she sat down to lunch, to let Maurice know what she was feeling about him. That he guessed a good deal of it she was aware, but she would have been content to go on as they were till it suited her to go some other way. Now she had placed the next move in Maurice's hands. It would be for him to say whether he was content for things to remain as they were.

She turned over in her mind what Maurice had said.

317

They were married. The chance shot she had made to gain Julian Heath's sympathy and interest had misfired. But there was no reason, she told herself, why Julian should know that—at anyrate, for the present. She fidgeted restlessly about the room. If only Julian were in town they could go somewhere, do something. There was a letter on her desk which she had not noticed when she arrived from Markhams. It was from a photographer's in Bond Street. They would like to have the pleasure of taking her photograph, free of charge. One finished copy would be presented to her without payment. Her vanity was enormously tickled. Photographers didn't take free photographs of people who were not famous. She rang them up, found that the pictures could be taken at half-past three, and set off at once for the studio. It was something to do, and, she felt, something very pleasing indeed. The cases outside the studio were full of photographs. She recognised the faces of several famous actresses and scrutinised them intently. They did not worry her after a moment's inspection. She took out her mirror and searchingly examined her own face. The results satisfied her. Smiling secretly, she climbed the stairs to the studio.

The smile left her face when she was in the photographer's presence. She was cold and regal. The photographer knew his job and did not try to bring back the smile. He had seen many famous faces in his time and knew what to do about them. He saw that that cold regal look was what made the face of this famous actress-to-be. The high Muscovite cheek-bones with the taut ivory skin upon them, the dark eyes marvellously shaded and secret under the damson lids and the thin paring of eyebrow, the tight hair, blue-black like a crow's wing, the red line of the lips, not full yet sensuous : all this was best set off by the aloof and haughty dignity that became the whole face better than a coronet.

A beauty, by God ! he thought to himself. It was a long time since he had had a face like this to deal with. There was only one regret. One little ornament, he felt, would help the picture he wanted. He permitted himself to sigh : " If only you had a high comb in your hair, Miss Rosing."

" I have one in my bag," said Rachel. " I always look best like that."

He rubbed his hands. " I see you understand these things."

" Yes," she said simply. " I do."

And though she had never before been photographed by any one who mattered, she was quite right. She did understand these things perfectly.

" Have you ever heard of a man named Augustus John ? " the photographer asked.

" No."

" Well, I hope that some day he hears about you. Then we'll see a picture worth looking at."

Rachel took tea alone at a shop in Bond Street, and when she had come out and was sauntering homewards she passed a window which displayed a couple of portraits in oils. She paused to look at them and saw from a notice that they were by Augustus John. " Good gracious," she thought, " what extraordinary things." She was sure that her photographs would look much better than that.

While Rachel was occupied with her photographer, Maurice was busy with his bone-setter. The result was altogether satisfactory.

"I don't want to see you again, Mr. Bannerman, and I don't suppose you want to see me."

"I do not," said Maurice fervently.

"Very well, then. Reasonable care, and you'll be as good as ever before the summer's over. Look after him, Mr. Hartigan. You can do everything now that I could do myself."

Maurice, left alone, cogitated for a while in his study, then summoned Mike Hartigan, Bright and Oxtoby.

"Oxtoby," he said, "have you ever been to Chichester?"

"No, sir."

"Well, you'll be going in an hour's time. Have the Rolls round here then, and pack anything you'll want. You'll be staying there for the summer. You will take Mr. Bright and Mr. Hartigan with you to-night. To-morrow you will come back for me. Bright, be ready to go in an hour's time. You too, Mike. First of all, ring through to Chichester and tell them you're coming. You and Bright see that everything is in order by the time I get there."

Mike Hartigan, rumpling his black curly head, rushed from the room. Bright followed with more dignity. "Glory be to God!" Mike shouted when they were outside. "Napoleon is himself again. Ordering the troops about. Old times, Bright! Old times!"

"Is Mrs. Bannerman coming, d'you think, Mr. Hartigan?"

"Ach, don't spoil it all," said Mike. He swooped upon Omar the cat, bore him off to the kitchen, and popped him into a large travelling basket that was kept there. "There you are, me darlin'," he said. "Wait there for your Uncle Mike. You'll find something better to chase in Chichester than those damned skinny sparrows."

By the time Rachel returned, they were all gone: Oxtoby and Bright, Mike and Omar. At dinner Maurice told her that he himself would be going on the morrow. He did not refer to the conversation they had had at lunch. He asked: "Have you found something amusing to do this afternoon, my dear?"

"Yes; I have been photographed. It amused me very much, especially as it was done for nothing."

"Ah! That means you are famous."

"The man told me I ought to be painted by some one called Augustus John. Have you ever heard of him?"

Maurice smiled and nodded his head. "It would cost a lot of money," he said, "but it is an idea." He considered her face carefully. "Yes. John would make something good of you."

"I saw some of his portraits in a window this afternoon. I thought they were terrible things."

"Nevertheless, I will think about that," said Maurice. Then he waved the subject aside. "All that—photographs—portraits—all that can wait. When *Thin Ice* goes on in September, believe me, Rachel, you will be bothered enough with that sort of thing. You will be busy, I know. Till then you must rest. I would like you not to stay in London during the summer. It is not good. Too hot. Too stuffy. You have not yet seen my house in Chichester. You can breathe there. You can get air. You will come back in fine form for the play."

Rachel's heart gave a leap in her breast. So, that was it. She had wondered at lunch time that he did not mention Julian Heath. She had wondered how much he knew—how much he guessed. She had dreaded it. She would not have known what to say. And all the time he was quietly working at his scheme —a summer away from London, a summer under his own eye, in some place where she would not see Julian at all.

"It is a nice house," said Maurice. "You will like it. Small but very charming. The gardens are lovely. I have a good gardener there."

He tried to catch her eye, but she kept her head bent over her plate, resolved to master the agitation into which he had thrown her.

"It would be a good chance, Rachel, for you to learn to ride a horse. I have a stable there. Nothing in it now, but we could get you a horse and a good riding-master. Would you like that?"

Then she raised her eyes to his. "But, Maurice, I *can't* leave London now——"

He had expected it. He said nothing, and she began rapidly to improvise her excuses. "It's all very well you and the Heaths and other people saying I am a natural actress, bound to succeed, and so on. I *am* a good actress, I know, but you want any amount of practice and polish. You want to work hard in all

322

sorts of parts before you chance an appearance before the public."

" I see."

" I told Cecil Hansford so, and I told Julian Heath, too, and they agreed that the best thing I could do would be to get a lot of work—Sunday night shows and that kind of thing—between now and September. They're going to help me to engagements of that sort, and then I thought that perhaps I could get a good private teacher too. I want to work hard all the summer. You see how much depends on it, don't you ? "

" I see," said Maurice again. " Well, I shall be going to-morrow. Bright and Hartigan are already gone. You will not find it—distressing—to be alone here ? "

" Oh, no. I shall have so much to do."

" Mrs. Bright will stay and look after things here. You have your car. Perhaps you will be able to come down and see me sometimes."

" Oh, yes, Maurice," she agreed eagerly. " I shall do that."

" And come and stay if you find work too hard."

" Yes. Oh, yes."

" I feel, my dear, that you might like me more if you saw more of me."

" Oh, but my dear, my dear. I do like you ! Oh, Maurice, if it were only a matter of liking, how easy everything would be ! "

She felt tremendously drawn to him, sitting there so calm and pale and collected, so utterly patient and undemanding. It was an attitude that she could not understand, that she could never adopt. She could feel how it abased and demeaned her, while yet she was resolved to exploit it to the utmost. She got up to go, a little frightened by a composure which equalled her own ; but she knew that Maurice's composure went deep and was real, and that hers was a cloak. It was her most successful trick, that wearing of a perfect mask of imperturbability.

Chapter Twenty-seven

RACHEL remained at home the next day in order to bid Maurice a dutiful good-bye. She saw him comfortably tucked up in the car ; she ran eagerly to his study to bring a book which he had forgotten ; she ordered him not to presume upon the strength which was returning to him. And then, when the car had slid out of the square she went quickly past the wise old Jewess whom Rembrandt painted so long ago, up the stairs to her own room, and rang up Julian Heath.

It was Mina who answered the telephone. She said impatiently that Julian was not in. " I've no doubt he would have been if he had known you were going to call."

" Never mind," said Rachel. " It was nothing that mattered."

" So glad of that," said Mina sweetly. " Then I needn't bother to tell him you rang up."

" Oh, but——" Rachel began ; and then realised that Mina had put on the receiver.

" Little cat," she said ; and dismissed Mina from her mind. Mina had not got seriously across her path. Till she did that, Rachel would not bother with her. She did not bother, ever, with troubles that had not arisen.

She told herself, with a nice approving conscience, that her call to Julian was praiseworthy. The lies she had improvised to Maurice about her desire for a summer's hard work seemed to her, as she lay in bed afterwards, to indicate what might be a useful line to follow. She was confident of her ability, fully aware of the unusual opportunity which *Thin Ice* gave for that ability to be made manifest ; but, all the same, she was by now so fired with ambition and pride that anything she could do to furnish her genius with its necessary implements she was anxious to do.

That was what she had wanted to discuss with Julian. It would at once serve her artistic ends and justify the line she had taken with Maurice. Well, she could wait. No doubt Julian would be available soon enough.

It was late afternoon when Maurice left. She must make her own amusements. She read little, and that little was rubbish. She knew nothing of music. She could dance like an angel and skate with unimaginable grace and beauty ; but she did not know whither to go either to dance or skate.

She decided that she would do something which Mina Heath had never consented to do with her. She would dress up to the nines, go to a fashionable restaurant, and afterwards see a play from the orchestra stalls. What play ? She remembered that Cecil Hansford had said he would put *Thin Ice* on at the Crown Theatre. She would go to the Crown Theatre. She would see the stage that herself soon would tread. She would listen to the applause rolling through the very ether that soon would record the accents of her own ovation. It was a grand idea. She wished Maurice had not taken Oxtoby and the Rolls.

She rang up a hire company and ordered a Daimler for seven o'clock, feeling sure that Maurice would not wish her on such an occasion to use a taxi. She was white from head to foot as she walked out to the car drawn up in the loveliness of the early summer evening: a short white fur coat with a collar that stood up and away stiffly from the sides and back of her head, a frock of white satin flowing down from it to the white satin shoes on her feet. In her hair over her left ear was a white camellia. And over all that whiteness was the keen sparkle of her eyes, like black ice.

She knew nothing of restaurants, and on a chance told the chauffeur to drive her to the Ivy, which she had heard Julian and Charlie Roebuck speak of. She sat back in the car and gave herself to the moment's luxury. This was it. This was how Rachel Rosing should move to her ceremonial occasions. All nonsense, those ideas of Mina Heath's—dowdy clothes and a seat in the pit. Roll on, chariot.

The street into which the Daimler rolled at last rather surprised her. The Ivy, she had imagined, must be in a broad thoroughfare gay with city lights. But here she was in this unprepossessing street, not at all well lighted, with the name of the famous restaurant indubitably written between its lamps. A page opened the car door. That was better. She told the chauffeur she would want him at eight, and she entered what seemed to her a disappointingly small vestibule. But beyond the swing door all was gay enough, cheerfully up to expectation. Stately in her white as a tall ship, she followed a conductor, and was pleased to find appraising eyes upon her. She was not, like many in a new environment, muddled by the novelty. Moving as easily and self-consciously as a mannequin, she was able to see and assess what was around her. There was nothing to be afraid of. There was no woman so well-dressed as she, none with more self-possession, none more beautiful. Her face was carved into its expression of almost insolent aloofness.

She could have carried it all through successfully, but nevertheless she was glad when Cecil Hansford rose from a table and came to greet her.

" Are you alone, Mrs. Bannerman ? "

" Yes, my husband's gone to his place in Chichester."

The phrase delighted her, though she had no desire to see the place at Chichester herself.

" Do join us," Hansford urged. " I'm here with Joyce Willows. Have you met her ? "

Rachel's long ivory hand came out from the whiteness. She shook Joyce Willows's hand. " Yes," she said. " Perhaps you don't remember, Miss Willows ? Mina Heath brought me to see you in your dressing-room at the Hogarth Theatre. You asked me if I was stage-struck."

" It is fortunate that you turned up at this moment," said Hansford. " You and Joyce must know one another. She has just consented to understudy your part in *Thin Ice*. You see, I'm losing no time."

Rachel thought that Joyce was only moderately cordial. She was under no illusion about the reason. Joyce was a synthetic creation of paint and enamel beside her own cool beauty. It was to her and not to Joyce that glances were directed from other tables, and it was to her that Hansford was markedly attentive. Joyce ate a scrappy meal and said she must scamper away. " Excuse me, won't you, Cecil ? Good-bye, Rachel."

"Good-bye, Miss Willows," said Rachel.

"Poor Joyce," said Hansford when she was gone. "I thought she was going to spit at me when I offered her an understudy part. But there it is. Her show at the Hogarth has flopped, and there's a general idea that she has caused the flop as much as anybody. She's an extravagant little hussy. She hasn't a penny and no one is offering her work. So she had to calm down. Iris Mearns is a better part for her than the one she's been trying to play. She could do it well."

"She will *not* play Iris Mearns," said Rachel, lighting a cigarette at the match Hansford proffered. "*I* shall play Iris Mearns."

"For God's sake!" said Hansford superstitiously. "Don't tempt the Fates."

He looked at her sitting there, white and imperturbable, the acme and incarnation of *hubris*. A shiver went over him, as though a breath from a cold purposeful iceberg had stirred through the room.

"Be humble," he said.

Rachel, who laughed rarely, laughed. He did not like the sound of it. It was like thin ice tinkling to pieces.

When she told him that she was going on to the Crown Theatre, he asked if she had booked a seat. She had not. "You should have done," said Hansford. "It is always necessary to book for my shows. Didn't you know that? Well, come along. I'll see that you're not disappointed."

He found her a seat in the orchestra stalls and left her. She passed just such an evening as she had promised herself. She surveyed the theatre: the well-dressed stalls and circle, the pit and the high dim gallery.

329

This was her audience. She listened to the applause. This was her applause. She went out in the intervals and drank coffee in the lounge. She listened to talk of the play, of the actors. So, soon, would they be discussing her. She knew no one. That did not worry her. She stood, white and aloof, among the chattering crowds, holding her coffee-cup, sipping delicately. Soon enough, she said to herself, she would not stand like that, alone. A passionate exaltation was burning in her, but no one knew anything about that as, when the bell rang, the tall beautiful woman in white went back impassively to her seat.

Chapter Twenty-eight

I

IN high June Julian Heath took possession of his new flat and Rachel Rosing took possession of Julian Heath. There was no discussion of what this should mean or whither it should lead. She had burned for him, and she took him. He surrendered to her passion with no question or qualification. For the first time in her life she could take a man because she wanted him, not because she wanted something from him. Every accessory of luxury was hers, and now she had, too, her heart's and body's wish. She bloomed to a startling beauty. The rapacity of her desire awed Julian, but it also overwhelmed him. He could not swim against the current into which she drove their lives. He was borne along, a willing, rejoicing victim.

Never before had Julian lived at such high pressure. Vivid voluptuary as Rachel was, she nevertheless carried through her plan to work and work and work. Wherever there was a bit of acting to be done, Julian or Cecil Hansford had to get it for her to do. Nothing, so long as it could conceivably suit her style, was too small. Hansford and Julian watched with fascination the unfolding of a talent which seemed because of its long denial to leap with the surer instinct to perfect expression.

When she was not at work she spent her days and most of her nights with Julian. She told Mrs. Bright that she found the house lonely and that there was no need to worry when she did not come home. She would be at Mina Heath's flat in Panton Street.

Julian's new flat was small and luxurious. Now that, as he felt sure, his days of scraping and " making do " were done with, he abandoned the humble standards of Duck Yard where Charlie Roebuck had found another man to keep him company. Julian discovered a tall house in Park Lane where a range of attic rooms had been startlingly diverted from their old purpose of harbouring boxes and housing the most negligible members of a household staff. Walls had been knocked down to make one long, low beautiful room which was study and lounge combined. There was a tiny all-electric kitchen, a bath-room and two bedrooms. One of these bedrooms it was Julian's intention to turn into a bed sittingroom for a man-servant, but there was no man-servant that summer. A servant of any sort would not have suited Rachel's book. Julian took the place furnished, and calculated with a shudder that the rent he was paying would be enough in five years to buy him a small country mansion with a few acres of ground.

But calculation could not long hold a place in his mind that summer. He gave himself over to the madness of his moments with no thought of the morrow. To wake out of a sleep into which he had sunk exhausted and to see Rachel coming into the room with the breakfast she had just prepared ; to hear her shout from the bathroom " The door's not locked, and there's plenty of room in this bath for two " ; to find her desire for him demanding assuagement in improbable places—out under the windy sky in the loneliness of the Downs, or at night in some warm hay-scented barn upon which they had chanced—these were the entrancing links of the chain that held him.

She seemed to have twice his vitality. She never tired. She was always able to carry out scrupulously all the duties that arose because she would have no servant about the place. He would protest when he saw her, with her hands carefully gloved, bringing his shoes to an exquisite polish ; but she would laugh and tell him of her slavey years and that this was all in the day's work for her. She could make a good breakfast ; but all other meals they took out.

Occasionally she would spend a night in Portman Square, and then, back among the service she had forsworn, she would be tyrannical. Rose Chamberlain would have to put every stitch upon her back, and in the morning she would have her breakfast in bed. Then from that safe and comfortable base she would sally forth again to sink into Julian her talons unassuaged.

June passed ; July was half-way through ; when out of the clear sky a bolt was hurled. There was a tiny bit of roof to which the flat gave access, and there, with little on, and sometimes with nothing at all, they could lie on mattresses in the sunshine. So they lay one morning, Rachel flat on her back, taking the warmth as sensuously as a cat, Julian sitting up so that his eyes were above the level of the parapet and able to wander over the treetops and down into the green coolness of the park. He lazily picked up and opened the newspaper which he had brought with him, and suddenly exclaimed : " My God ! "

Rachel jerked herself up, startled by the cold consternation of his tone. "Bad news?" she asked. "What is it, darling?"

She rested her chin on his bare shoulder. He drew away restively. "Look—there—Hansford," he said.

She took up the paper and read the paragraph into which a photograph of Hansford was inserted. Hansford had dined at a restaurant the night before, had left apparently in good health, had called a taxi, and was found dead in it when Paddington was reached. Heart failure.

Rachel put the paper down thoughfully.

"What price *Thin Ice* now?" Julian asked bitterly.

Rachel pondered for a moment, then said: "I'd better go to Chichester." She got up and went swiftly into the flat. Julian followed and saw her standing there nude and lovely as an ivory statue. He put his arms around her. "This is dreadful," he said.

"It will be all right," she answered. She drew away and slipped on a dressing-gown. "Maurice is enormously interested in the theatre. He won't let us down."

Julian looked at her with amazement. "But, my God! Rachel!" he said. "You can't ask Maurice for money—now."

"I am going to Chichester," she said dispassionately. "You will see."

II

Mina Heath had been in London for a fortnight. She had avoided Rachel and felt annoyed because Julian was avoiding her. He had not asked her to see his new flat, and when she complained about that to Charlie Roebuck, Charlie shrugged his shoulders, smiled significantly, and said nothing.

When Mina read that morning of Hansford's death, she rang up Rachel. Here was something that concerned them all. Her personal likes and dislikes must be set aside. Hansford had engaged the whole cast. Mina felt that they had better all get together and discuss their position. When she got through to Portman Square, she was told : "Mrs. Bannerman is not in. Perhaps you will be able to get her at Miss Heath's flat. She stays there now most nights."

Mina replaced the receiver carefully. "Well, I'm damned," she said. "So that's the alibi."

She got on to a 'bus and went to Park Lane. "Invitation or no invitation," she said grimly, "here goes. At least, they will hardly still be in bed at this time of day."

Julian opened the door. "Hallo, Mina ! Come in, come in ! " he cried, so heartily that Mina knew Rachel must be out. However, she said : "Rachel isn't here by any chance, is she ? "

"Rachel ? No. Why should Rachel be here ? "

" I just rang her up and they told me she had probably spent the night with Miss Heath. I knew she hadn't done that, so I wondered whether they'd got it mixed—whether they meant Mr. Heath."

"Would it surprise you," asked Julian, "if she had ? "

Mina's nostrils dilated. She sniffed the atmosphere of the room. "It would surprise me very much if she hadn't. I smell woman."

335

"Well," said Julian suavely, "shall we leave it at that?"

He thanked goodness that Rachel had had time to get out of the house and he to dress. He looked Mina up and down with exasperating coolness. He pointed to the paper on the table. "That's a bad thing. What are we going to do about it?"

"That's just what I came to discuss. Do you know where Rachel is? We must talk it over—the whole crowd of us."

"I don't know where she is," he lied. Shame would not allow him to say that she had gone to Maurice for money. "I don't think," he added "you need call the clan together just yet. Let's wait a day or two. I know that Hansford had a lease of the Crown Theatre, or a sub-lease, or whatever it is these fellows do. I don't understand it. But there'll be executors or something. They may take on Cecil's commitments and let the show go forward. I don't know. I'm just talking in the air. We must wait and see."

"You sound distressingly vague. However, I know no more about it than you do. We'd better wait. Are your views more concrete about morning coffee? If so, I'd like some. And while you're making it, do you mind if I wander about and sniff the atmosphere of your flat a bit more?"

"Sniff away," said Julian, disappearing into the kitchen.

When he came back with the coffee on a tray they went out on to the little square of roof and sat up looking over the park.

"Well," said Mina, "I've been sniffing. The whole place stinks of scarlet woman."

" You do take sugar, don't you ? "

" What is there about the woman ? "

" Mina, whatever else you may be, you are not a fool. Don't ask a fool's questions."

" You're right. Yes ; I can see she's very attractive —in that way."

" You don't think, otherwise, that a millionaire like Bannerman would have taken her almost out of the gutter ? "

Mina, hatless, stood suddenly upright, her face taut and quivering, her flame of hair appearing, had any one cared to look from below, like a blown banner broken above the parapet. " Do you *have* to drag Mr. Bannerman's name into it ? " she said fiercely. " I gather from novels that it's the honourable convention not to mention the wronged husband."

" Thank you. I shall have to remember that."

Mina sat down, and her cup clicked against her teeth as she drank to still her jangling nerves. " I don't know what you expect my attitude to be over this affair, Julian," she said. " I suppose I ought to be just tolerant and amused and aloof and say ' Bless you, my children.' Well, I can't. I happen to have a pretty high opinion of Maurice Bannerman, and so I can't view your adventure in the calm light which falls in films and novels. I think Rachel's a rapacious slut——"

She had risen, shaken with agitation, and Julian rose, too.

" That will do, Mina," he said sternly. " Cut that out. This isn't your affair."

" I shall find a way of making it my affair pretty effectively," she retorted defiantly. " That's a warning.

Don't disregard it." She strode into the flat and made for the door, leaving Julian standing in the middle of the room. With her hand on the door-knob, she said : " If you want to discuss the play, you know where to find me. I shan't come here. It smells dubious. And I detest the junk on your walls. If you wanted pictures, why didn't you consult some one who knows something about them ? "

The door clicked behind her. Julian sank into a couch and sat looking at the carpet between his upthrust knees. " God save me from women," he said. " Vicious or virtuous, God save me."

III

Rachel had lunch at a roadside hotel. It was three o'clock when her red car crunched over the wide gravel sweep in front of Maurice's house. She had a moment to look about her—at the flat Georgian front of brick, the portico of Portland stone, the lawn which ran out from the gravel, smooth and green, to the shade of the tall graceful beeches that fringed it. A long way off through the trees she could see an old brick wall and marching triumphantly along its sheltering length the varied beauty of a herbaceous border. A cane chair was at the edge of the lawn in the trees' coolness. Maurice was sitting in it, dressed in a light grey suit. His horn-rimmed spectacles were on his nose. He had been reading, but the book, face downwards, was on his knees and his chin was on his chest. He was sleeping.

Bright came to the door. Rachel slid a long silk-

sheathed leg out of the car. "Good-afternoon, Bright,"
she said, the very pattern of affability. "Take in my
bag, will you? I shall be staying to-night."

Then she went quietly across the lawn, through the
drowsy, quiet afternoon, and stood behind Maurice's
chair. She placed her hands lightly over his eyes
and bent down to whisper in his ear : "Who is it?"

Maurice woke with a start, pulled down over his
shoulders those unmistakable long hands with their
blood-red tips.

"Rachel!" he exclaimed, staggering to his feet.
"Rachel."

He turned towards her, put his arms about her,
and without evasion she kissed him full on the mouth.
He drew her closer and she rubbed her cheek against
his. "I *had* to come down to see how you are, darling,"
she said.

Maurice regarded her with a puzzled happiness.
He was remembering the night before he went away,
her frank confession that she did not love him. She
seemed acute enough to see the working of his mind.
"Do you remember, my dear," she asked, "what
you said to me—that I should like you more if I saw
more of you? Now see how wrong you were! What
you really needed was to go away altogether to make
me miss you." She pressed him back into his chair.
"Sit down, Maurice. You mustn't tire yourself."

"Oh, but I am getting strong, strong," he cried.
"And I am learning about women! So you missed
me—eh?"

"The house was terribly lonely," she said.

"And now you will stay here?"

Her heart gave a quick flutter of alarm. "For to-

339

night," she said. "I am working very hard, my dear, but I just had to come and see for myself how you were."

"Well, well," said Maurice, "as long a visit or as short a visit as you please. It is lovely to have you. Come in, now, and let us see that they are making everything ready for you."

"I should like to change," said Rachel. "I brought a light frock in my bag."

He led her to a bedroom looking out on to the lawn. "See," he said, "we keep this ready in case you should come."

She smiled at him archly. "You old bachelor! Do you insist on treating me as a haughty lady visitor?" She picked up her bag. "Ah, they haven't unpacked this yet. Come along. We'll unpack it in your room."

Maurice's dark pale face suddenly suffused with colour. He looked at her speechlessly for a moment. Then he said: "My room is here—through this door."

"Wait for me a moment while I change," she said.

Maurice stood at the window looking out sightlessly upon the grass and the beech trees. He had never seen Rachel look lovelier than she looked that afternoon. He knew that she was at the peak of all that her body could ever do for her, and intuitively he knew why. The bloom on her was the bloom of fulfilment. His heart was riven with anguish. He knew that Rachel was about to offer to him all that loveliness which some one else had called to perfection. Now, when that which for so long he had most dearly wished to possess was his for the taking, he could not take it with a glad heart. A question turned the moment to ashes. Why? Why had she come? What did she want of him?

Presently he heard her whisper : " Maurice," and he went in to his bedroom. She had drawn the curtains together and was standing there in her shoes and stockings and silken underclothes. He had never seen her like that before. She held out her arms to him. " Darling," she said, " lock that door and come and undress me." The ghost of a voice that fluttered to him across the room.

Maurice turned the key and stood leaning against the door. His knees almost doubled under his trembling weight. He felt that he must look repulsive, the veins in his temples crawling like purple worms, his eyes misty with the agony of his humiliation. His arms spread themselves out from his body, the palms of his hands pressed backwards against the panels of the door. Even then he might have taken her, crushing back the dark loathing of the way she had come to him, so beautiful she was, her pale ivory skin taking warmth and richness from the soft fragments of crimson silk that fluttered with the rise and fall of her breasts. He shook his head like a tormented bull at bay, passed a hand across his eyes, and then, seeing her more clearly, saw that suddenly she trembled. A movement of fear shook her. She stepped backwards a pace towards the bed.

Then he came to himself. " Are you afraid of me, Rachel ? " he said.

His words snapped the frightening tension. " You looked at me as if I were a ghost," she smiled.

" No," he said. " I saw you as if you were a body."

He unlocked the door and went with his heavy padding tread out of the room.

As soon as he was gone, Rachel leapt to the door and locked it. Then she flung herself upon the bed and buried her face in the pillow. She did not weep, but lay dead to every sensation save anger and humiliation—anger at her humiliation. Her blood burned through her in wave after hot wave. Her self-esteem lay in shreds about her. She had been so sure. No one, it seemed to her, could reject the offer of a loveliness so unique. She could not analyse it, but it was a professional pride, too, that Maurice had torn to pieces. She had staged the scene so carefully, acted it so well, and now the curtain was down and she could hear nothing but a hoot of derision.

She lay for a long time, motionless, then rose and dressed and packed her bag. For once she did not ring for a maid. Bright, amazed, saw her come down into the hall, obviously ready to go away. She put her bag into the car which was still standing at the door. "Will you please ring up Portman Square," she said to Bright, " and say I shall be there to dinner to-night."

The engine roared and the car sped across the gravel as though anxious to hurry her from the scene of her defeat. To Portman Square. She could not bear to face Julian Heath to-night.

IV

Maurice went heavily back to his seat under the beeches. His knees were like water as he walked, but his heart was glad. He had been delivered. Rachel and Julian Heath. He had known all about that. Had he not confessed his knowledge to Mina Heath that moonlit night at Markhams ? And he had said that in an affair of that sort one did nothing. That was true enough, but at least one did not creep in on the first invitation to snatch a crumb from another man's feast. He had been saved from that. Now, at any rate, Rachel knew that, though there were two roads before her, she could walk on only one. He was patient. He would wait for her to choose. Now she knew that the choice must be made.

He saw the red car leave the house. He was sorry. He would have liked Rachel to stay, to eat dinner with him, to talk with him. Something might have come out of that. He loved her. He was ready for her when she was ready for him. One loved or one did not love. Julian Heath, a clever, handsome boy, who had written a clever, well-groomed play that would make a lot of money : he would not love Rachel as Rachel would some day need to be loved. Maurice sighed with a profound unhappiness, but under his unhappiness was a peace that could not be shaken, the unmoving centre of a great resolve that could abide its time for fruition.

He wondered what strange, powerful motive had brought her to him. It must be something overwhelming to tear her from the embrace of a first passion such as he knew to be gripping her. It was after dinner that he divined the truth. It was then, following his custom here at Chichester, that he had the day's papers brought to him. He saw that Hansford was dead, and it did not take him long to see the significance of that. He sent a message to Oxtoby that he would be going up to town first thing in the morning.

343

Chapter Twenty-nine

1

MINA HEATH rang up Charlie Roebuck as July was coming to its end.

"The cloud has lifted," she said. "A letter came this morning. I must celebrate or bust."

"You couldn't choose a better day," said Charlie. "Goodwood Cup. What about it?"

"I should love to. I've never been there. What d'you think of that for a society dame?"

"Disgraceful. I'll pick you up in half an hour. I think the old 'bus will stand it. Though this is positively its last appearance. It may lie down and die before we reach Chichester."

"Chichester?"

"Yes. Didn't you know you got to Goodwood through Chichester. See you in half an hour."

Mina thoughtfully put on what she hoped would pass as a suitable frock for Goodwood. Thank God one didn't have to dress for Goodwood quite so absurdly as for Ascot. Anyway, what did it matter? She would be blown to bits in Charlie's open boneshaker.

She began to whistle. The letter that had come had put her in good spirits. There had been long moments of horrible doubt after Cecil Hansford had died. The man who boasted that he had never lost money in the theatre must have lost a lot somewhere else. He was found to have hardly a penny to his name. Julian had been going about like a child who has lost an apple ; Rachel was all on edge ; the poor devils who had been promised the other parts, and needed the money, held funereal conclaves. Thank goodness, thought Mina, they'll all be happy to-day. No doubt every member of the cast had received a letter like hers, saying that Hansford's executors now felt justified in backing the play, convinced that it would bring income to the estate, and that rehearsals would begin immediately.

And then Mina thought of Chichester. That was where Maurice Bannerman was staying for the summer. She hoped she would not meet him. She would feel horrible if she did. His patience and gentleness made her go hot with shame when she thought of Julian and Rachel. No ; she would much rather not meet Maurice at the moment. Not that Julian and Rachel were quite so offensive as they had been. They were together a good deal, but Mina was aware of a greater regard for the proprieties. Rachel was living in Portman Square again. Mina no longer had the gruesome feeling that she might find silk stockings or a chemise draped over a chair when she called on Julian. " Let's hope it's blowing over," she prayed fervently as she ran down the stairs to meet Charlie.

II

She had not expected so lovely a day. Charlie's old car droned through the Sussex countryside dreaming in the fullness of July. Wheatfields taking the first touch of russet from the sun ; green domes of elms ; honeysuckle : all this led on to the enchantment of entering a racecourse through the private gateway of a nobleman's house. Round the house acres of parkland, undulating gently and broken here and there by clumps of noble trees, led on to a drive through the tall grey columns of a beechwood. And when they were through the beechwood and Charlie had disposed of the car, Mina felt that, racing or no racing, this loveliness was worth their journey.

They looked from their height down upon the flat and misty plain running southward, with Chichester at its midmost point, the cathedral spire reaching into the sky like the mast of a great ship frozen to stone. Miles beyond that the grey smudge of the Solent closed the view.

They turned about to look northward upon the downs : bald majestic lines to which the forest clung here and there like the mane to a lion. And between them and the downs was the broad highway of the racecourse. The stands nestled under a cliff of beech-trees, which sheltered the pavilions of the clubs and the canvas kitchens of the servants' quarters, some so craftily adjusted that the tall beech trunks grew up through their white roofs. There was a great scurry of chefs in white hats and of waiters bearing trays of meringues and jellies and silver dishes whereon salmon lay couched in cucumber. A grand, bustling day, great clouds bowling across the blue, the downs rolling like the sea and the distant sea smoothed out like a plain.

"You know, Charlie," said Mina, "I'm not sure you were wise to bring me here. A few gulps of this and the Crown Theatre will seem a bit too dusty. I'll become just a society woman and do the whole damned silly treadmill : Epsom and Ascot and Good-wood, on to Cowes, and so to Scotland for the dear old shootin'. What a gorgeous life I could have if I were rather more of a fool. I'm sure father would be happier about me too."

"Oh, he's pleased enough with you, don't you worry," said Charlie. "He wouldn't have put his money behind *Thin Ice* if he didn't like to think of you and Julian as two nice famous children."

Mina looked at him in surprise. "Well, I'm only guessing," said Charlie. "I look at it this way. Hansford's executors, with very little money to play with, couldn't take the risk of backing the thing on their own. They'd have to be darned sure, wouldn't they ? And can any one be so sure as that of a play by a new man, starring a new actress ? I'd say not. Well, puzzle find the fairy god-father. It's some one who wants the thing to go forward, who doesn't want to appear, and who has said to the executors : ' Go on, lads. If you lose money I'll pay the bill.' Answer, Lord Upavon."

"You're wrong, Charlie," said Mina. "That's an interesting theory, and it's probably correct, but it's not my father who's jingling the money-bags. I've heard him and Hansford talk theatre many and many a time, and I know it's a thing he'd never put a penny into. You see, Daddy's a careful man. He hates a speculation and loves an investment."

"Well, if it's not your father, who is it ?"

" I can't think. Perhaps you're wrong about the whole thing."

But she felt that he was not wrong, and she had a pretty good idea who was the benefactor.

They had enjoyed their run out to Goodwood ; they enjoyed watching a race or two ; and then they decided to go home. Neither was so keen as all that on racing. " Dodge the crowds," said Charlie, starting up his old collection of motor parts ; and they rattled along towards Chichester. They were on the outskirts of the town when the car at last put into operation a threat it had held for months over its driver's head : it just stopped like a heart that has missed a beat too many and refused to go on again.

Everything was done that in such circumstances is done, and all was done in vain. Several passing motorists, swollen with a belief that no car was beyond the magic of their ministry, alighted, offered their services, rendered them, expressed their sorrow, and went their way. Several Levites drove by on the other side ; and finally a sumptuous good Samaritan of a car purred up, stopped with soundless precision, and permitted Oxtoby to alight.

Charlie and Mina welcomed him with glad cries. " You couldn't have broken down in a handier place, sir," Oxtoby smiled. " You're right on Mr. Bannerman's doorstep. That's his gate in front of you there. If you'll let me tow her into the garage, I can give her a run over."

So the Rolls took the wreckage in tow—the wreckage which not so very long ago had hurled Julian Heath, on a Lake District road, into Rachel's life.

Maurice was sitting under the trees just where

Rachel had found him not long before. He was glad of distraction. He made much of his visitors, and soon the three of them were sitting down to tea in the green shade, with the sunny lawn stretching away before them to the warm red front of the house.

But Charlie did not sit long. He could not keep away while something was being done to an engine. " Will you excuse me, sir ? I'd like to see what Oxtoby's up to. Then I'll know next time."

When they were alone Mina poured another cup of tea for Maurice. " This is very pleasant," she said.

" Yes," Maurice agreed. " One can be tranquil. That is what I want now. I have been a robber chief long enough. Now I can enjoy the spoils."

He smiled, and Mina thought it a very sad, weary smile. " But you," he went on, " you, I suppose, are finding no rest at all. Working hard, like Rachel."

" We are lucky to have anything to work on," said Mina. " It was an awful shock to all of us when Cecil Hansford died, and an even worse one when we found the poor dear had no money. We all thought the play was finished. Some one's been kind to us."

" Oh, no," said Maurice, " not kind. Some cute business man, I suppose, has seen the chance to make a little more money."

" Well, good luck to him. I hope he does. We all think him kind enough, believe me."

" He will do very well. That play is all right. Not great—no—but clever. There is so much rubbish everywhere—in books, on the stage—a clever thing like that will cut its way like a knife. It is keen."

" You sound so confident," Mina said with an uneasy

349

laugh, "that one would imagine you to be the cute business man concerned."

Maurice handed her a cigarette and lit himself a cigar. "Well," he said judicially, "it is the sort of thing I have always fancied doing. It is not a bad way to spend money, helping something good or something clever to get a show."

"Then you *are* backing the show," Mina plunged.

Maurice smiled at her pale, eager face, shining under its red crown. "You are impulsive," he said. "Keep it to yourself. I trust you."

Chapter Thirty

I

IT was a devilish Rachel who drove the red car back to Portman Square after her call on Maurice. Merely the fact that there was no Oxtoby to take the car to the garage, that she had to put it away herself and walk back to the house, seemed an affront deliberately contrived. She bathed, dressed with as much care as if she were about to entertain an exacting dinner-party, dined alone, and went to her room. She was in a mood to lash out, to hurt and tear ; but she was in complete control of the mood because she knew that there was no one to be hurt or torn. The need for a greater circumspection than even she had ever exercised was clear. She sat down to think the matter out.

She had been counting on success in *Thin Ice* to make her independent of Maurice. That alone had given her the hardihood to flout his wishes so recklessly. She was cynical enough to feel no shame at having attempted to use Maurice in order that she might go on flouting his wishes. All her shame was for having failed. How deep did the failure go ? How far now could she continue to count on Maurice ? That was something beyond discovery at the moment. She was a realist and put it out of her head. She must wait and see.

But one thing she could do : she could be cautious while waiting. She might need Maurice for a long time yet. Therefore, she must be more discreet where Julian was concerned. Julian didn't mean safety—not yet, not while his play was once more only so much typescript—and Maurice did. Rachel was herself a little surprised at the ease with which she came to this conclusion. For the first time she wondered whether her flaring passion for Julian might already have burned at its brightest ; and side by side with that thought there edged into her mind the thought of Maurice—calm, impassive, monumental—the man of her own race. There was about Maurice something rock-like that Julian would not achieve if he lived to be a hundred. Rachel walked restlessly about her room, pausing at the window now and then to look out on the parched midsummer aridity of the square. She tried to be honest with herself.

She asked herself whether there was more to her feeling for Maurice than she had supposed, or whether she was inventing feelings in order to justify her retreat upon Maurice now that her advance elsewhere was checked. She could not be sure, but she went to bed interested that the matter had caused her some speculation.

II

In the morning she rang up Julian Heath.

" Hallo, darling ! " he cried. " I was expecting you last night."

" There was nothing to tell you," she said formally.

" Damn ! That's rotten, isn't it ? "

" Yes, I suppose it is."

" Still," Julian conceded, " it was rather a lot to expect."

" Yes, I suppose it was."

" What's the matter, darling ? You sound huffy. Are you coming round to-day to cheer me up ? "

" I don't think I'd better. I've been neglecting so many things here. There's an awful lot to do. And you know I'm in a show on Sunday, don't you ? There's that to think about."

" Oh, very well."

" I thought we ought to take Mina out to dinner some night."

" My God ! "

" Think it over and let me know. Good-bye."

Rachel hung up the receiver, glowing virtuously. It had been easier than she expected.

She did not see Julian for three days. Then he called at Portman Square. She cunningly invited him to stay to lunch, talked innocuously, and bade him a hostess's polite good-day. She had accompanied him to the door, and, turning back upon the cool marble chequer of the hall, she glanced up at the face of the old Jewess over the fireplace—the wise old Jewess who looked as though she had seen so much with those eyes that were hawed with red. Rachel thought that the old woman looked approving. Remember the ghetto, my child. Remember Cheetham Hill, and weigh well the value of what you see about you here.

Rachel walked from room to room, pondering upon the significance of Maurice Bannerman's house. It represented the conquests of a great personality who had begun as penniless as she herself had been a few months ago. It represented the conquest of material things, conquests of taste and knowledge. It was a superb background for any life. She opened the doors of the ballroom and walked thoughtfully down its splendid length. Supposing she did become famous, could she ever command the like of that? But with this added to her fame! And Rachel permitted herself a rosy vision of the flutter of dresses in the ballroom as it then would be, of famous men and women come to the house because she herself was famous, of all this as her magnificent domestic stage.

She told herself finally and frankly that she did not love Maurice Bannerman, but she could accept these things from him because now she would make a grand return : she would put upon this house the imprint of the fame which she felt as near as a cloak that she was about to put on. There in the ballroom she made with herself a bargain of the head but not of the heart.

It was easier to do because her heart was no longer in question. The bright flame that had lit her life so fiercely had been the affirmation of her woman's right to take a man without the shame of a bargain. It had been a swift revolt from the bondage that poverty had laid upon her beauty. And now she found that when prudence uttered an unmistakably sharp command she could leave the man aside as easily as she had taken him up.

Still pacing the room, she wondered whether a more devouring fire might even yet come upon her. But she need not consider that. That was for the future to show. For the moment there was the vow of her head.

She went back to her room feeling very tranquil. Not for all the summer had she felt so calmly happy. Her life had been such that it was necessary, if she was to have peace of mind, that her affairs should have a solid economic basis. She congratulated herself that she had now done the best in the circumstances to make that possible.

III

Julian Heath was not sorry that Rachel had risen from him, sated, at last. It had been a grand experience. He had learned a lot. But he had never allowed himself to think of the affair as permanent. Beneath his lackadaisical charm, Julian was fiercely ambitious. Less absorbing passions than Rachel's were necessary if he was to get anything done. Nor was he anxious for social complications. He was realist enough to know the value of a life running smoothly. The divorce court did not attract him, nor did a marriage with a Jewess. There were some queer blots in the Heath record : there was the gorgeous Georgiana for one ; but the blots were all of English blood and Julian had no wish that it should be otherwise.

And so, after a few formal calls and a few formal groans such as he thought appearances demanded, he edged away, and he and Rachel did not meet except when the prospects of *Thin Ice* called them together with the others who were interested. They were both so excited by the news that the play was to go forward, and soon so busy with rehearsals that their midsummer madness was shaded to a memory in their minds and they could meet and work un-selfconsciously.

Throughout August the whole company threw themselves into the work with a passionate determination to make it succeed. They had all been under sentence of death ; they had been reprieved, and that gave them zest. So much was at stake for all of them : for Julian the prize he had slaved after so long ; for Rachel the fame for which she lusted fiercely below the icy composure of her bearing ; for others the bread that had almost been snatched from their mouths. Mina alone seemed not to have some deep personal urge behind her efforts, yet Mina alone knew that this was Maurice Bannerman's venture, Mina alone was working in order that Maurice Bannerman might be justified.

Maurice kept out of it. He remained at Chichester. When a letter from him reached Rachel in Portman Square she hardly dared to open it. So much now depended on the attitude Maurice chose to take. She read the letter at last with profound thankfulness. Maurice made no reference to her visit. He said he was sure she would be glad to know that he was improving daily, taking gradually longer walks, and he hoped that when he came home he would be as well as ever. He had heard that the play was to go on and congratulated Rachel on that. "You know," he said, " how highly I esteem the work I saw you do at Markhams. It would be a tremendous satisfaction to me if that success were repeated in London, and if this play should be the first of many to give your genius its opportunity. I don't want to get in your way, to hinder you while rehearsals are on, and so I shall stay here till the last moment. I shall be up for the first night. All my love."

It was a quiet, unemotional letter—just what she would have expected from Maurice ; but it sent her spirits soaring. It removed the last cloud from her sky. Now all her mind could go to the task before her. From that moment she was so sure of glory that she felt she could lift it from her head like a palpable crown.

Chapter Thirty-one

I

MIKE Hartigan came back from Chichester the day before that which was to see the first performance of *Thin Ice*. He brought his cat Omar with him. He had a good deal to do, and one thing was the arranging of a supper party at the Savoy to which Maurice had invited every member of the cast, and Cecil Hansford's executors, and one or two other people.

It was a lovely day, that twelfth of September. When Rachel woke she could see the milky blue of the sky stretched like silk above the red and yellow heads of the plane trees. She had the morning papers brought to her, and read the theatre advertisements. There it was, with her name and the name of the play in equally large type. More than that : the *Daily Telegraph* had a third of a column, with a photograph of herself —one of the photographs that had been taken that day in Bond Street when so opportunely she produced the high comb from her bag—recalling the play's success at Markhams and speaking of her own remarkable performance in it.

It was all very comforting. She did not feel excited, only deeply expectant. She had got over the wonder of it ; the wonder of seeing her name on a dressing-room door, the wonder of watching the electricians at work on the theatre's façade as the light was fading an

358

evening or two ago and seeing suddenly RACHEL ROSING flash out and hang suspended magically isolate over the roar of traffic and the rush of feet. Now she felt nothing but a confidence that went down to the very core of her heart and mind, and a little impatience for this blue and silver day to wane and the night to come.

She knew how much her beauty contributed to her effect upon a stage and when she went to her bathroom and dropped her clothes upon the floor she scrutinised herself like a duellist testing the temper and texture of his blade. She was satisfied. There was no flaw in her. No other woman on the stage had that superb easy insolence of bearing, that preternatural perfection of feature that does not appear twice in any generation. In a sudden access of thankfulness, she leaned upon the mirror, arms outstretched, hand pressed to pictured hand and brow to brow, and with eyes closed she seemed to commune with herself, to draw sustenance and support from that impalpable contact with a ghost embalmed in ice. She pressed herself away from the mirror, and then, gazing upon the hand still resting there, she saw her only blemish—the thin white scars that the cat Omar had imprinted. She scowled at them, as though they were a preface and premonition of all time's scourges that soon or late must obliterate the legend of her loveliness.

II

The day drowsed by into the opalescent languor of afternoon. Julian Heath stood at the window of his flat, looking down into the park, where a faint milky mist was exhaled from the ground, blurring outlines, conferring upon everything the pardoning grace of a beauty that was not intrinsic. But Julian had no eye for the scene before him. He hoped to God he would be all right when the time came, but all day long he had suffered from nerves and fidgets.

He was sick to death of cleaning his own shoes, washing his own breakfast things, making his own bed. It was high time his servant got to work, and it was just like his own bungling methods, he said in righteous self-condemnation, to have arranged for the man to begin to-morrow. There couldn't be a time when he felt less like clearing up than he did that day. Yet clear up he would have to. The flat was full of Rachel Rosing's things, and he didn't want a man to begin by diving into drawers that contained silk knickers and Lord knows what. He'd have to clear up the mess, put all her stuff into a suit-case, and have it ready to take to her in the morning.

He strode into his bedroom and looked upon its frightful disorder. His bed was unmade, his pyjamas were flung upon it anyhow. Rachel had not once been in the place since that day she had dashed away to Chichester. Pots and tubes and bottles belonging to her stood on his dressing-table. Her brushes were there too, and by a chair was a pair of dark-red silk mules with feathered pom-poms.

The drawers, he knew, were full of her things. He pulled them open and began to throw the stuff out. A nightdress of transparent silk landed on the unmade bed beside his pyjamas. A pair of silk stockings trailed from the bed to the floor. He stood up, cursing, and looked at himself in the mirror. He thought himself a disgusting sight ; he hadn't even shaved ; he looked as though he'd just got out of bed himself. The place reeked of perfumes.

Well, a shave and a bath, he said to himself, and then I'll finish this loathsome job. He picked up some wisps of silk between thumb and forefinger as though they soiled him, and dropped them on to a chair. He took off his coat and waistcoat, his collar and tie, and put on a dressing-gown. Then he heard a knock at the door. " Any one in ? "

It was to Julian the last straw. His face went livid with anger. Of all the times to call on a man ! " Come in ! " he shouted savagely, like a butcher inviting an ox to the pole-axe.

Mina came in, and stopped, rigid. Her eye ranged from the pots upon the dressing-table to the tumbled bed, the pyjamas, the night-dress, the stockings and the underclothes. Her face flamed from its customary white to crimson, and slowly paled again. They looked at one another for a moment without speaking ; then Mina said : " Sorry, Julian. I didn't know you were only just up."

Julian raged in his own mind : " Why should I explain to her ? What have my affairs to do with her ? Damned if I explain ! I won't ! I won't ! "

He said nothing. He stood there, red and furious, holding his dressing-gown about him with a trembling hand.

Suddenly Mina cried in a hoarse, cracked voice : " That bitch ! That bitch ! Oh, I thought it was all done with ! I thought it was finished, and it's all going on still in this dirty underground way."

She confronted him, panting, looking as though she she would strike him. Instead, she strode to the dressing-table, seized a cut-glass powder-bowl, and holding it aloft in both hands, crashed it to the ground. The powder flew up in a perfumed cloud and hung in the air between them.

" How can you ! " she stormed. " How dare you ! And she the wife of a man whose money is giving you your chance to-night. You didn't know that, did you ? Well, know it now, and blush if you've got a blush in you."

But Julian was beyond reason. All she said was fuel to the dark anger that flamed in him. He wanted to hurt her, to bring her down in humiliation. He spoke calmly, with a sneer. " We all know, Mina, of your profound admiration for Mr. Bannerman. It is certainly news to me that he's put money behind the play. You may be right, but I think you're guessing. Anyway, he won't lose. And here's a bit of news for you now. Your mighty Bannerman is not Rachel's husband. I'm not seducing a virtuous wife. He deceived her himself. He married her bigamously."

Again the colour drained from Mina's face, leaving her pathetically white and shrunken-looking. " Is that true ? " she whispered.

" You'd better ask Rachel."

" I shall." Again it was only a whisper. Julian did not hear in it any note of warning, any hint to act— now or never. He thought that he had won the bout ; and turned back into the room with satisfaction when she had crept out as though she were wounded.

When Mina reached Portman Square she was told that Mrs. Bannerman had gone to bed but would be up at any moment. She said she would wait, and was taken up to Rachel's sitting-room. The cat Omar ran up the stairs silently at her heels and entered the room with her. Left alone, Mina walked to the window and looked out stonily at the square. The cat arched his back against her leg and rubbed. Carrying his great furry tail aloft, he walked round her, purring like a little dynamo. A handsome, friendly beast. He caused Mina's mind to revert to the day not long ago when Rachel had rated Mike Hartigan in her presence because the cat was in this room. How she had seemed to delight in torturing the man !

The swish of silk across the carpet caused Mina to turn sharply. Rachel was advancing towards her. She wore little jade-green slippers and a dressing-gown of jade-green silk. It fell open below the girdle, and Mina saw pyjamas of a rich gold colour. The gold and the green and the black lacquer of Rachel's hair made a marvellous picture as she came across the room.

" I have been resting," she said. " Now I feel ready for anything."

Mina's strength turned to water. The woman was so poised, so lovely, that one could almost wish for a world where beauty made all the rules. But she stuffed her hands in the pockets of her old tweed jacket, set her jaw, and looked Rachel fiercely in the eye.

" I have just come from Julian," she said.

" I expect he's terribly nervous. Thank God, I have no nerves."

" Have you anything that a normal woman has ? "
Mina shot at her suddenly in a harsh accusing voice.

Rachel raised her eyebrows in mild astonishment at
the swift uprush of hostility. " The usual things," she
answered softly, with a smile so dark and secret that
all the lures of Aphrodite seemed to live in it for one
lustful second. It set Mina raging.

" You're not usual," she shouted. " You're not usual
in any sense of the word."

Rachel looked down at her from her greater height
and inclined her head slightly in ironical acknow-
ledgment.

" There's something all wrong about you," Mina
cried desperately ; " something wicked, something that
does no good to any one you have dealings with."

Rachel did not raise her voice or lose her balance.
" This is surprising," she said. " I really don't think
I shall go on with this conversation. I have to play
to-night. So have you. You are being unwise."

She turned to leave the room, and Mina, stung by
her composure, suddenly seized her arm. She felt it
twist, supple as an eel under her fingers. " You shall
not go till I have said what I came to say."

Rachel swung round, freeing her arm, and Mina
recoiled, frightened by the swift magnificent indignation that flamed in Rachel's eyes. " You ! " she said
in a voice low and intense with passion. " You, to dare
to lay a hand upon me—upon my body ! "

She towered, dark and quivering, above the girl who
continued to shrink as before some lithe beast of prey.
Mina understood. *Upon my body*. That was Rachel's
holy of holies. That was all she had. It was her
armament, her lure, her reward. Who touched her

body, unasked, committed the deadly sin. A terrible desire to strike at that temple, to destroy it, entered Mina's heart and trembled along her fingers. It steadied her nerves and brought her upright, the green eyes in her thin white face taking fire and giving back an equal intensity to Rachel's dark regard.

"You are destroying my brother," she said quietly.

Rachel's tension relaxed. She laughed, snapped her fingers in contemptuous dismissal. "There is a balance in these matters," she said. "Your brother will owe me much."

"You deceived him. You lied to him about your husband. You told him you were not married to Mr. Bannerman."

"So he is that sort of fool. He cannot keep his mouth shut."

"Neither could you, it seems."

Rachel had no answer to that. She paced between the fireplace and the window, swinging the tassel of her girdle. Suddenly she turned again to Mina. "Here is Maurice," she said. "You can ask him for yourself."

Mina heard the sound of a car stopping at the door. "Oh, God!" she thought. "I cannot go on with this. I cannot see him mixed up in this." She turned to Rachel. "I am going," she said. Her face was as white as a clown's under the flame of her hair.

"Well," said Rachel, "that is satisfactory, then." In the insolence of triumph she held out her hand. Mina looked at the long beautiful ivory fingers, then up at the dark eyes that danced with mockery. She struck the hand aside, and the blow loosed all the torrent of hatred that was in her heart. She struck again, flat-handed, full upon Rachel's cheek. It was a heavy blow, but not so much the weight and power of it as its complete surprise made Rachel reel. Her foot caught under the carpet's edge and she crashed to the floor. The cat Omar had been lying there, full of philosophy and sleep, as they wrangled above him. He leapt as Rachel fell, but leapt too late. Her elbow hit him heavily in the ribs before he sprang aside with a spitting hiss and came up with back arched and bristling, tail swaying to a slow murderous rhythm, mouth redly open upon the white menace of his teeth. Mina shouted : " Christ ! The cat ! " and lost a second while her hands flew to her eyes. In that second Omar sprang, smarting from his present hurts and remembered injuries. He landed, with his feet splayed out and hooked with tearing claws, full on Rachel's face. One awful shriek rang through the house, and the sound of running feet answered it. Mike Hartigan was the first to arrive. He tore the cat away from the bleeding mask upon the floor and ran with it from the room like a mother who hides from punishment a child that has sinned.

Then Maurice came, his face beaded with sweat, his knees trembling. He found Mina kneeling upon the floor beside the ruins of the temple that she had destroyed.

He lifted her up gently and put her in a chair. She sat there, incapable of speech, as he knelt and raised Rachel till she sat leaning against his knee. For a long time she did not speak. Her hands moved blindly upon her face, tremblingly feeling her cheeks, her forehead, her chin. Suddenly she shrieked : " Oh, my face, my face ! My beauty ! " She bent over, collapsed in his arms, and her hair which had loosened in her struggle sprayed out in a dark fountain over his knees and feet. Sitting white-faced in her chair, Mina could see nothing of the loveliness that had been Rachel's. She could see only the golden nape of her bowed neck and the hair that streamed upon the floor and covered Maurice's feet. There were tears in Maurice's eyes. They fell slowly upon the dark hair. He moved his hands upon it.

"Rachel," he said. "My Rachel."

THE END